SAVAGE PURSUIT

A GRIFF SAVAGE ADVENTURE #1

CHRIS MARES

WAYZGOOSE PRESS

CONTENTS

1

RAIN

IT's early morning and the streets of Key West are deserted. Tropical rain pounds the warm asphalt, but Savage walks slowly, shoulders hunched, his head down. There's a stiffness in his right shoulder. He is thinking about the last time he saw his brother alive. His thoughts weigh on his heart. After a pause outside a diner, he pulls the door open and walks in.

Inside, four officers from the Key West Police Department eat breakfast at the only occupied table. Savage sits at the bar and takes a menu, his back to the officers. The last thing he wants is to deal with cops at this time of day, or any time of day—not any more. His short black hair is wet, his unusually ice-blue eyes razor sharp, catching everything. He stretches his strong hands on the bar and feels the rain water trickling between his shoulder blades. He's six foot two, strong, but lean and athletic.

"Coffee, hon?" the server asks. Savage nods and turns, a hint of a smile on his face. He likes her raspy voice. It's the voice of a woman who has lived, a woman who's seen it all.

She looks directly into his eyes, gauging him, her face impassive. "Take your time," she adds, putting her hand on his shoulder in the way an older woman can, a touch maternal yet sensual.

"Life can be tough sometimes." She taps his shoulder twice. He's not sure if she's joking or not. She looks back at him and winks.

Savage rubs his right shoulder, and then runs his hands back over his head. "No kidding," he says, quietly. Sometimes, he thinks, people know about life and about humanity, about all the paradoxes and complexities. The server could be one. He could see it on her face and hear it in her voice. He was one, too. He thinks she has seen it in him, in just those quick seconds when she seemed to see into his soul.

Savage draws in a slow breath and exhales as she disappears into the kitchen. He wonders what her story is. He knows she has one—everybody does, eventually—especially in a place like Key West.

Savage looks at a coffee ring on the counter, the thoughts of his brother returning. He rubs his shoulder again and winces, and then wipes his forehead with the back of his hand. Outside, lightning flashes and thunder rumbles across the charcoal sky.

The police officers get up from their table and head for the door. Savage senses one of them looking at him—it seems like a professional interest. Savage pivots just enough to show his smile, but not enough to show his eyes.

"Have a good day, gentlemen," he says, his voice deep and slow. He's tired. It was supposed to be a vacation, but it's not.

"Day like this... it seems unlikely," a chubby officer says.

"You, too," another cop adds. He looks like he's fifteen.

Then they're gone, and Savage is the only customer. He closes his eyes and shakes his head. The strange circumstances of his brother's death and their recent phone conversations invade his thoughts. He finds it hard to reconcile one with the other.

She returns carrying a plate heaping with hash browns and eggs. The warm smell rising from the plate makes him realize how hungry he is.

"Not a vacation, huh?" she says, sliding the plate in front of him.

"No," Savage says, "not a vacation. It was going to be. Should have been. But no. Not a vacation."

"Are you Australian?" she asks.

"Nope. English. At least that's where I was born. It's a long story." Savage pokes the hash browns with his fork. He cocks his head. He hadn't ordered—she'd just brought the food. She winks.

"That's what you would have ordered, right?" Her eyes twinkle. Her intonation is musical.

Savage chuckles. It is what he would have ordered. "You've made my day," Savage says. "I'm not kidding." He begins to eat. You just never know, he thinks. You walk into a diner and suddenly you're talking to a clairvoyant server.

"It's still early. Somebody else might make it even better." She's wearing a perfume that Savage recognizes. Someone he knew, but can't remember.

"They might," Savage begins, "but then again, this could be it. The highlight. That wouldn't be bad." The server's eyes linger on his tanned, chiseled profile. She leans forward again.

"You know, I've done this so long, I can tell about people. Believe me, I've seen them all--the winners, the losers, the runners, the liars. You, hon," she pauses, "I can't tell about you, though. You're different. There's something I can't quite put my finger on, but I know it's there. You're not on vacation, I know that much. And, that was smooth--with the cops? Being polite, not trying to hide. But I tell you hon, I know. You're not your typical, run-of-the-mill kind of guy."

"Have to respect the law," Savage says, with a hint of irony, shaking some Tabasco sauce onto his hash browns.

She laughs and shakes her head. "I don't know what that means, and I bet you don't either. I don't get a sense that you respect the law if you don't want to." Savage ignores the bait. He continues to eat, though he is amused.

If he had been on vacation, he would have asked her out for dinner, older woman or not. He likes her matter-of-fact confidence, the way she notices things, and the way she saw him. But this isn't a vacation--he has work to do.

He eats steadily and then pushes his empty plate across the counter. Part of him wants to remain within himself, unavailable to others. Another part wants to talk, to tell his story. He's been alone too long.

The server hovers, expectant. Savage is about to say something, his mouth half open. But he worries that if he starts, he might not be able to stop. It's been months since he's spoken to anyone about anything of significance. He closes his mouth and retreats into himself. The moment has passed like ships in the night.

"Thanks," Savage says, sensing her frustration. She still lingers nearby. Savage still can't place the perfume. He points at his empty coffee cup, his thick index finger bent at the end. She doesn't move. Savage wonders why she cares about what he has to say, but he can tell she does.

Savage turns to look at her, feeling the holstered Glock 9mm under his arm as he moves. He hears voices from the kitchen—the sound of a faucet, two men bantering.

"I'll get you more coffee, hon," she says. He listens to her walk away, then return. The coffee smells good. He takes a sip and puts his mug down.

"My brother owned the boatyard on Stock Island," he says, getting to the heart of the matter, staring at his empty plate again. He swallows then presses his fingers against his forehead.

She clears her throat. "Oh, God," she says. "I'm so sorry. That fire," she looks away. "Terrible, terrible. I'm really sorry. I'm sorry about your brother. So that's why you're here..."

There is a flash of lightning outside followed by thunder roiling the purple clouds. The rain is relentless, the world gray and dark outside.

Savage clenches his fists and draws in a breath, his heart empty. He feels powerless. His brother is dead. They'd spoken just two days ago, and now, they would never speak again. A tear slips out and creeps across his cheek. Anger is close behind. He feels lost and seething at the same time. He rubs his shoulder and focuses his energy, clearing his mind. Now is the time. There are things that need to be done. He pushes his emotions away and places his hands on the counter, spreading his fingers and flexing them. A new energy infuses him.

"You didn't see me, by the way. I wasn't here," he says. "I know I probably don't need to say that, but, you know. I don't want to complicate things. I just got here. Still new in town. I'm here to clear things up. I'm sure you understand. Legal stuff. Paperwork."

"You look like you want to do more than clear things up, hon. Be careful. This is a peculiar place."

"I don't know," he says, taking out his wallet. "I still can't believe it. I was going to come down next month so we could spend some time together. A couple of months. Do some fishing. Catch up. We hadn't seen each other for years. Finally, we could. Then this." Savage pulls out a twenty.

"It's on me," she says.

Savage is both surprised and touched. "No. I appreciate that, but no. I'm down, but I'm not broke."

"No, really," she says. "Put your money away. I want to." Savage can tell it's her way of saying sorry.

"I appreciate that." He wonders if he will see her again. He touches her shoulder. "Really, I appreciate it." He gets to his feet, and as she turns away he discretely slips the folded twenty under his plate.

"Be careful, hon," she says. "And I'm real sorry about Jake. I knew him. You know, in the way you know people around here. You know bits of them, not all of them."

"You did?" Savage pictures his brother joking with the server. He takes a sip of water. He can imagine they liked each other.

"Everybody knew Jake," she says. Savage waits to hear more,

but she doesn't add anything else. She swallows and touches her hair.

"You know, I wish this was a vacation," Savage says. He knows he doesn't need to explain. She remains silent and gives him a sad smile, her eyes wide and vulnerable. Savage walks to the door, heading back out into the pounding rain as the thunder rolls overhead.

———

A couple of blocks from the diner, on the corner of Eaton and Caroline, opposite the laundromat, Savage sits on the bed in his brother's second floor apartment. He'd come up the outside steps to the deck and jimmied the lock on the door as the rain pounded on his back.

He cracks his knuckles, then his neck, and stands. He takes the Glock from its holster, puts it on the desk then removes the magazine. He examines the weapon, checking all the moving parts. A professional habit, done quickly and efficiently. He's killing time, thinking. Somehow, he's still hungry, the taste of coffee lingering in his mouth.

He is focused on his task, the rain in the background, when he hears someone coming up the outside steps to the deck. Savage deftly reassembles the Glock, inserts the magazine, and slips the weapon back in the holster. He crosses the room on tiptoe and goes into the bathroom.

Savage doesn't move, his breath quiet, his body tensed, ready to react. A key turns in the lock. The door opens slowly, and a slim, blonde woman, somewhere in her late twenties, steps in. She closes the door, looks around nervously, walks to the bed and sits down. Her head drops. She cradles it in her hands, her elbows on her knees, and starts to cry. Savage steps out of the bathroom, eyeing her as he approaches. He moves easily, but a floorboard creaks under his weight, and she turns and starts. She tries to scramble to her feet.

"It's okay," Savage says, his voice soft but insistent. He's used to dealing with people under duress. He stands still, raising his open hands to show he has no weapon. "I'm Jake's brother. Savage. Griff Savage."

The woman looks unconvinced, angry, her eyes flitting from side to side. She pushes herself to her feet, and reaches for her purse. Savage grabs her wrist, and says, "No, really. I am Jake's brother. Stay calm. You don't need this," pulling a small pistol from her open purse and putting it in his pocket.

"You scared me," the woman says, her body losing its tension. "I don't know what's going on. I just had to come here, to his place, before someone else did." She speaks in a clipped voice.

"Someone else? Like who?" Savage's pulls his thoughts together, trying to be clear and procedural.

"I don't know. The freaking people who ... I don't know. I wanted to check on his place. Protect his stuff." She clears her throat.

"Stuff?"

"His stuff. This is his place. I have a lot of good memories here." She pauses, her eyes teary. "You're really Jake's brother?" Savage knows she wants to believe him. "I hope you are. I'm sick of this crap." Her voice has a southern lilt. She draws the words out. She wears a silver ring on her left index finger.

Savage waits for her talk again, the emptiness returns inside him. The void, a hollow sadness. Then he imagines Jake's laugh, his bonhomie, his voice.

"Well, you both have the English accent thing. Cute, yes, and annoying. And you're tall. But he's darker, much darker. And not as," she eyes Savage up and down. "Let's just say you're in shape." She pulls at the ring again.

"Well, yes," he says, rubbing the back of his neck. "We can't help the accent thing, as you put it. And yes, I'm his brother. Got here yesterday morning. I got a call. From Nikki. My brother mentioned her a few times over the years."

Thunder shakes the windows, and the wind blows the cover off the barbecue. It hits the deck with a clang.

"I gather they were pretty close. Nikki sounded pretty cut up. Said he was dead. The fire. I didn't know what she was talking about. Dead. I couldn't process it. I'd only spoken to him a couple of days before. Then she lost it and hung up."

Savage looks out of the window onto the deck. He sees the barbecue and imagines sitting with his brother, talking about what they'd been up to over the years and about what they would do next.

"I know Nikki," the woman says. Savage notes the precision in her pronunciation. There's a history. Savage waits for more. He notes her tone, remembering everything. He lets it go. He's not sure who this woman is, but he has an idea.

"He lived on the edge. I don't think he meant to. He just did. This could have happened any time," she says, more to herself than him.

"Why do you say that?" Savage asks.

"This is a weird town, with some weird freaking people. They want things, they don't get them, and then this happens." She avoids his gaze. She fumbles in her bag, pulls out a pack of cigarettes, and then puts them back.

Addict, Savage notes. Jakes's friends were always marginals.

"Bastards," she says under her breath.

"You know what happened? Who killed him?"

"I don't know. There was the fire—it was an accident, or so they say. You know, the cops. That's what they said. it's what the paper said. But that's not what I heard on the street."

"Who told you?" asks Savage.

"Hey, it's a nightmare of a small town. People talk because there's nothing else to do." She snorts derisively, pulls at her ring, and closes her eyes. Her shorts and t-shirt are soaked.

Savage can't decide if she's telling the truth, but he thinks she is.

"You need to go dry off," Savage says.

She ignores him, runs her hand through her hair, reaches for her purse, and then stops herself. "The bastards killed him! I know they did." She spits the words out, her face contorted with a rage that came from nowhere.

"Who are *they*?"

Savage sees her shoulders shaking, her eyes darting toward the window. There are more footsteps on the stairs outside. He holds up a hand to silence her.

"Quick," he whispers. He hands her pistol back to her, grabs her wrist, and then steers her towards the kitchen. They pass through a second bedroom, then out a door leading onto the landing. He hears the door leading to the deck open, and two men entering, speaking Spanish in short, agitated bursts. Savage and the woman are separated from the men by the kitchen.

"Ella no está aquí."

"Mirar alrededor."

"Nadie."

Savage closes the door to the landing. The men are moving through the kitchen, getting closer. Savage leads the woman down the stairs, leaving through the door onto Eaton Street. He puts his arm around her shoulder, and they walk towards Duval Street. The storm has passed. The clouds are breaking up. The light and heat returns, bringing color back into the day. Savage pulls the woman close.

"Put your arm round me. Nice and natural," Savage says. "Like a couple. Walk slow. No rush. They'll be here soon." A black Mercedes with tinted windows crawls behind them, and Savage pulls her close to him, shielding her.

"Could be them, don't look," Savage whispers.

The car slows, pulls up even with them, and then speeds away. They watch it accelerate down the street.

"Now what?" the woman asks. She sounds exhausted.

"What's your name?" Savage asks.

"Angie."

"Angie. Jake told me about you. He liked you, too." He immediately knows he shouldn't have said that, noting the change in Angie's expression.

"*Too?* You mean like he liked Nikki?" she asks.

"I guess he liked you both." Savage shrugs.

"I hope he didn't tell you too much," Angie says. Her voice is calmer, her composure returning.

He starts to laugh, remembering some of the things his brother had told him. "Not much. Something about stripping." Savage waits for Angie's reaction. A smile crosses his face. She shows a flash of surprise and anger.

"You're freaking kidding, right? He told you that?" Angie begins to cry.

"In a good way," Savage says.

Angie squeezes Savage, but he feels her strength ebb as she leans on him, sobbing.

"Look, I just got here," Savage says, "Yesterday. Seems like there's a lot going on that I don't know about. Am I right?" She's beautiful, Savage notes, but frazzled.

"Why bother? He's dead. What difference does it make?" Her voice is flat and empty, as if she's given up.

"Because Jake is... was ... my brother. I'm going to find out what happened to him, and why. If someone killed him, then I need to settle the score." Savage's voice has an edge to it. His own anger surprises him. Angie pulls at her ring, looking even more worried, and Savage calms himself.

"Fine. I'll help," Angie says. She grabs Savage's arm and leads him down a side street.

She pauses by a Pepto-Bismol pink scooter parked near a light pole. A Vespa, Savage notes, with double wing mirrors. She opens her bag, takes out a key, and puts it in the ignition. Then she wheels the scooter from the side street to the road. "Get on," she says, nodding at the seat behind her.

"What? On this?"

"Not manly enough for you? Jake didn't mind." She revs the engine.

Savage lets out a sigh of disbelief and gets on the back, towering over Angie.

"You'd better hold on," she says. She opens up the throttle, and the scooter merges into the traffic.

"Where are we going?" he asks.

"Well, hell, you obviously can't stay at Jake's. You have to stay some place, right?"

"But...," Savage begins, his words drowned out by the engine. Angie's blonde hair blows into his face as they make their way east over the bridge and onto Stock Island.

————

"Nice picture," Savage says, looking at a photograph of Jake standing next to a sailfish suspended on a scale.

"I think it was a record," Angie says. "For these parts at least."

They both fall silent. Water splashes against the side of the houseboat, soothing Savage's nerves.

"I've always liked houseboats," he says.

"Me, too," Angie says.

More silence.

"I don't know where to start," Savage says.

"Start what?"

"Figuring all this out. Jake. The fire."

"Talk to that idiot Nikki. She knew Jake as well as I did."

"You don't like her, I gather."

The waves slap against the hull of the houseboat.

"I did like her," Angie says, "I did. But things change, you know."

"Was it about Jake?" Savage asks.

"Maybe. It doesn't matter." Angie says nothing more, and goes into the kitchen, returning with a couple of beers.

"So, what about you?" Angie asks. "What's your story, Griff Savage?

"Just Savage. You really want to know?"

"If it's anything like Jake's story, bring it on."

"You won't believe me," Savage says.

Angie hands him a beer. "Try me," she says.

"I was a monk."

"A what? Like a priest?" Angie laughs. "You don't look like a monk."

"A Buddhist monk."

Angie looks Savage up and down. "You definitely don't look like a Buddhist monk."

"So, what do Buddhist monks look like?"

"Not like you, that's for sure. Is that it?"

"Is what it?"

"Your whole story," she says.

"Before that, I was in the Legion."

"Are we talking French Foreign, or American?"

"Very funny," Savage says.

"But you are kidding me, right? A monk, and then a legionnaire. Right?"

"It's true. I wasn't a particularly good monk, but I was a damned good soldier."

Angie closes her eyes. "Jesus, what a pair. And I thought Jake had been around. You his younger brother?"

"Older."

Angie looks skeptical. "You look younger. You're what, thirty-five?"

"Ish."

"Thirty-five-ish?" Angie says. "Jake's gone and suddenly you turn up. I can tell you're trouble, too. And the monk thing? A Legionnaire. I don't know. People around here are full of bull."

"I'm not from around here."

"Nobody is at first. But you seem to fit right in."

Angie takes a swig of beer, grabs her purse, takes out the pack of cigarettes, puts them back, and pulls on her ring.

Savage watches. Full of bull, he thinks.

"Give me some time and I'll tell you more about it. Right now, I need to get my stuff from the airport, then talk to Nikki.

Angie takes a long pull on her beer then puts it on the counter.

"Savage," she says, her voice softer, more vulnerable. "I said I'd help you. I will. This is one big mess. I don't think what happened to Jake was an accident either. I think someone killed him, and I'm pretty sure I know who and why."

2

BIG UGLY

THE STORM PASSES, and the sky is a cobalt blue again. The air is hot, heavy, and humid after the rain. Rivulets of sweat run down Savage's back as he walks up the steps to the Whistle, his brother's favorite pub on Duval. He'd heard about it for years. And here he was, without his brother—alone and not on vacation.

Grief crushes Savage, robbing him of his breath. He finds himself incongruously surrounded by revelry. Happy hour is in full swing in Key West, the night stretching out ahead--the sound of laughter, everyone from somewhere else, here to party. The drinks are flowing. The air is tinged with sex and intoxication.

This is not a place to mourn.

Savage stands at the bar, glancing at the bartender, an Asian woman with long black hair, dressed in black. She's pretty, just as Jake had described her. She's busy, efficient, elegant, and in control. Savage waits. He wonders how she's coping with it all, and what she'll say when she learns who he is.

He thinks about Jake, then looks back at the woman. No rush--he can speak to her later. There are groups of tourists, a few young couples and a smattering of other marginals found in any tourist town. A loud group of men occupy the other end of the bar--Columbians, Savage thinks.

They grow even louder. Men, Savage thinks, to himself. He looks at the woman behind the bar. Men are checking her out. One of the Columbians licks his lips.

"Jesus," Savage mutters. If Jake were here, he thinks, things would be different.

He drums his fingers on the mahogany bar, noticing that he really doesn't want a drink. He'll order one for his brother and make a toast anyway.

Maybe the drinking's done, he thinks.

One of the Columbians looks over at him. Savage clenches his fists.

He has spent the day gathering information, reading reports, and talking to people. The fire was so hot that a body was never really found—just a few charred bones and some blood outside the office building. DNA testing proved it was Jake's. The police called it an accident--a spark, a gas leak, maybe flammable chemicals. That was the story.

He hadn't seen Jake for three years. They'd been embroiled in their own lives.

A young man walks over to the jukebox, glances back at his girlfriend, and selects Van Morrison's "Brown Eyed Girl."

Savage almost smiles. It wasn't an accident. The story was in the news, then it disappeared. The day after the fire, Nikki left a message on his phone.

"Hey, this is Nikki, umm," she paused, her accent Japanese or Korean, he couldn't tell. Her voice was surprisingly deep. "I'm a friend of Jake's. Something's happened, I think you should get down here now, umm." The pause again. That was the entire message. He listened to it three times. His body chemistry changed as he envisioned scenarios of what might have happened.

His mind began to whir. He'd heard of Nikki from Jake, like

he'd heard of Angie. They were people who mattered to him. Jake's close friends were usually women.

He'd been looking forward to meeting Nikki and Angie, but not like this—not at their worst, or at his worst.

And here he is, waiting for the right moment. The bar is still filling, the acoustics changing, sex in the air. "China Girl" plays next on the jukebox. Nikki is busy.

Savage catches himself in the mirror behind the bar, his eyes meeting his own. He looks at himself and into himself, feeling his anger change into determination.

Figures move in the reflection. He is stationary, solid. The loud men are laughing, cracking crude jokes in Spanish.

He can tell someone is looking at him. It's a sense he has practiced and honed. He doesn't turn his head. It's one of the men at the end of the bar, one of the Columbians. Savage focuses on his breathing, drops his head, and continues to stare at the bar, listening and not moving.

He looks up into the mirror again, into the reflected world. In his peripheral vision, he sees a large Latino standing apart from the group, gazing down the bar at him, like an animal spotting his prey.

But Savage is not prey.

The Asian bartender walks by, and Savage finally says, "I'll have a vodka tonic, whenever you can. And a tonic with ice and lemon." His voice is soft, deep, and clear, but not demanding.

She walks past him to the Columbians. Savage finally turns to look at them. His movements are smooth and measured—nothing is rushed. He sees everything, his eyes are unblinking. One of the men leers at the bartender as she approaches. Savage swallows, loosens his shoulders, and spreads his feet. He has no respect for men who harass women.

She takes their orders without speaking and then returns. She mixes a vodka and tonic and a tonic with ice and lemon, her hands moving fast.

He's been in a lot of bars and known a lot of bartenders. He feels for them.

She brings the drinks, placing them on two coasters.

"Assholes," she says, without looking at Savage.

"Thanks, Nikki," Savage says, letting her name slide out, testing her.

There's no reaction beyond a twitch of her mouth.

"Two drinks, one man?" she asks.

"One's for my brother."

"Your brother," Nikki repeats, slowly. There's no eye contact.

Savage waits. *Soon*, he thinks.

Big Man is still watching him, but more intensely now. Savage's face is impassive. He scratches his ear. He can smell Nikki's perfume. It smells expensive.

"Do I know you?"

"You called. Here I am."

"Jesus!" Nikki whispers, looking away. "Amazing. I thought I saw something. You move just like him, you know? When you came in—there was something familiar. I mean, there's the different hair, different eyes, but ... Loose, you're both loose. He's ...," she pauses and tears up. "Bigger," she adds, almost a whisper.

"Brothers. The same, but different."

"I guess," Nikki says. "Look," she continues, "I can't talk now, but we need to talk."

————

She wipes the bar, moves away from him, nods at a waiting customer, pops two Coronas, slides thin wedges of lime in the necks of the bottles, and delivers them to a couple of jocks at the other end of the bar. She finally comes back.

"Start Me Up" is blasting out of the jukebox.

Savage picks up his glass and chinks it against the other one—Jake's drink.

"To you, my brother, wherever you are." Savage lifts his glass. "Well, here I am," Savage says after a moment, "being stared at by a big Columbian who's got the hots for you and hates me. Funny old world."

Savage notices Nikki's nails. They're long and expensively manicured, painted emerald green with pointed tips.

"I'm sorry," she says. "Just so sorry."

She moves down the bar again. Two women, both blondes, are checking out the guys, and checking out Savage.

Nikki gets their drinks and comes back again. The air is getting hotter, bodies press together, voices shout over voices, and a fan turns overheard.

"The guy staring at you ...," Nikki starts.

"Go on."

"He's got a thing for me—particularly when he's drunk. And he's drunk. And ..."

"And?"

"There's more. Not here, though."

"Weird," he says. "I feel as if I know you. He talked about you. He notices everything."

"Really? Like what?"

"Called you 'Brains'. Said you were one of the smartest people he'd ever met. You know. The *New York Times* crossword, the sudoku."

Nikki drops her eyes, tears welling. Her guard is down. "It's sweet that he'd say that about me, you know?"

"He cared about people. A lot. The ones he liked."

"I know," she says.

"I better get out of here," Savage says. "I'm getting that trouble-in-a-bar feeling."

Nikki nods and moves away, her perfume lingering in a wake of air behind her.

Big Man is staring at Nikki. Then he turns and looks at Savage, then Nikki again. These are primitive male signals—territorial, macho, and wrong. The signs of alcohol-driven male turmoil, Savage thinks.

"He bothering you? The big one with a thing for you. Looks like a Colombian thug."

"That's just what Jake would say, you know?" she says.

"That's Big Ugly, be careful--don't do anything," Nikki says under her breath. "Please."

"Don't worry. I could, but I won't. I'll finish my drink, and then I'll leave."

"*Qué tengo que hacer para conseguir una ronda de copa aquí?*" the big man barks impatiently, pointing at his empty glass.

"I could tell him what he has to do to get a drink around here, but he wouldn't like it," Savage mutters.

"Go, now. Please," Nikki says, barely moving her lips.

One of Big Ugly's friends puts his hand on his shoulder. "*Compadre*," he says, steadying the big man.

Savage keeps his anger in check, and doesn't look up. He's seen men like this all over the world.

"God," she begins, "he was nice, but then he wasn't. Now he's drunk. He's jealous, angry. He thinks I'm his. He hated Jake, and couldn't believe we were just friends. Then he started harassing Jake. There was something about the boatyard. Jake wouldn't tell me."

Savage listens, looks in the mirror, and thinks. Jake wouldn't stand for this.

"The boatyard and the Columbian?" he asks.

Nikki wipes the bar.

Big Ugly's friend is talking to him, holding his face with both hands, turning him away from Nikki and Savage.

"Look Savage," Nikki says. "Be careful, okay? It's complicated. There was something going on with the boatyard. Jake was under a lot of pressure."

"Okay," Savage says. "I'd better get out of here. I need some air."

"You hear me?" Big Ugly says, this time in heavily accented English, stepping out of his group and towards Nikki. "What the hell do I have to do to get a drink around here?"

Nikki puts a coaster in front of Savage, upside down. Savage looks the neat cursive handwriting, and sees an address.

"Be there at three, tomorrow morning," Nikki says quietly, her head down. Savage reads the address written around the edge. He memorizes it, then casually rips the coaster into four pieces.

Big Ugly is staring at him now, swaying. He is jowly, with full lips and thick eyebrows. He's broad and strong looking, but with the beginnings of a belly.

Savage stares back, unblinking, and sees fury spread across Big Ugly's face. The bar is filling up with noisy customers. Jimmy Buffet starts up on the jukebox—"Margaritaville," of course, the local anthem of Key West.

He leaves his drink, barely touched, looks at Jake's full glass, and makes a silent promise to himself. He slips a twenty-dollar bill under the coaster and makes his way towards the door.

Savage walks slowly, listening, and taking in the energies around him. A tonic water with ice and lemon, he thinks. How often has that happened? His drinking days are done. He goes down the outside stairs to the street, hesitates at the bottom, and then walks down the side street, away from the hubbub of Duval.

Savage immediately hears footsteps behind him. He takes a sharp left down a dark, narrow side street. The footsteps speed up. Savage slips behind a brightly blooming tabebuia tree and waits. The lumbering footsteps come towards him.

Big Ugly appears, breathing heavily, his shirt sweat-stained. Savage stills his own breathing, and all his senses are focused on the big man, who is now walking towards him but unable to see him in the crescendo of yellow blossoms.

As Big Ugly passes, Savage steps swiftly from behind the tree. He falls in behind him, making no sound.

"Looking for me?" Savage asks.

Big Ugly turns, surprised. "Don't ever look at her again!" he hisses, his chest heaving.

This is all I need, Savage thinks, *a primitive drunk*.

"I don't forget a face, asswipe. I'm going to remember you," Big Ugly growls in heavily accented English. He clenches and unclenches his fists--his breathing growing heavier. "Wait, don't I know you?" he asks, swallowing. He squints and sways.

Savage assumes a fighter's stance, with his weight on his back foot, and his shoulders loose. It's just a matter of time. He wishes he'd just kept walking, lost himself in the crowd, and gone back to the hotel.

"You look ... like someone...". Big Ugly searches Savage's face.

"Someone?" Savage says. "I look like someone?"

"The guy at the boatyard. The jackass. You look just like him. But not as fat."

"Jackass. That's what you call him?" Savage whispers. "Fat. You called him fat."

"What's it to you?" The big man steps back as Savage inches forward.

"What's it to me? He was my brother, *jackass*."

"What do you mean, your brother? You're his brother?" The man stops moving.

Savage says nothing. The street is eerily quiet.

"Yeah, well, so what?" Big Ugly says. "I don't care. I don't like you talking with Nikki."

This guy's a jealous drunk, Savage thinks. But there's something else.

"Your brother's dead," he says.

"You know anything about it?" Savage asks.

"An accident," he says.

Savage steps forward again. The big man wobbles.

"I know that whatever happened out at the boatyard, whatever happened to Jake out there, wasn't an accident. Now, are you going to tell me what happened?"

Big Ugly laughs nervously. "Me? Why? And no, I'm not. I don't know. Except he should have known better. And I don't like you either. Maybe you got it coming, too. *Comprende?*"

He's confused, Savage thinks, wondering what's going on in the big man's addled mind. "I've got it coming, too? You mean like Jake had it coming? You *do* know something."

"Your brother's dead. That's all you need to know."

"I need to know what happened." Savage hisses, "And I'm going to find out."

Big Ugly wipes his brow, moves his feet, and sizes Savage up. "You need to get out of here. You don't know what you're getting into. This is way bigger than you or your jackass brother."

"My what?"

"You heard me."

"You scared?" Savage asks.

"Scared? Of you? Hell, no."

Savage is ready. He waits for Big Ugly to reach for whatever is in his jacket. However quick the man is, he won't be quick enough.

"You don't have to do this," Savage says. "We can both walk away. Forget about it."

Big Ugly turns away, but Savage recognizes the feint. He steps to one side as the man turns back, a knife in his hand. Savage blocks the thrust, spins, and elbows the man hard in the throat, feeling his Adam's apple give a little. Savage spins again and brings his knee up into Big Ugly's face as he falls forward, crushing his nose. He hits the ground hard—out cold, but not dead.

The man would be more of a problem dead than alive, so Savage leaves him on the quiet street and walks through the thick tropical air, back towards buzz of Duval, and the madness of a drunk town that was going to get madder, and drunker.

3

THE CONTENDER

THEY SIT on the back deck of Angie's houseboat, surrounded by potted spider plants, watching a pelican fly low over the mangroves. A small plane lines up for its final approach to the airport.

"*Pretty Woman?* Your houseboat is called *Pretty Woman?*" Savage chuckles.

"Cute, right?" Angie says.

Savage rubs the back of his neck. It's not a time for small talk. Images of the night before come to him—the big man going down after Savage's knee crunched his face.

"What?" Angie says.

"Last night. The big man. That didn't have to happen."

"But it did."

"I know. I kind of made it happen, though. I should have just ignored him. Left. I can see that Nikki can take care of herself."

"You didn't know. How could you?"

"I mean, of all the guys in Key West, the one hitting on Nikki probably killed my brother."

"It's a small town."

"That small? Really?"

"Really," Angie says. "Believe me."

Savage rubs the back of his neck, then runs his hand over his short hair, pressing down hard, trying to relieve the tension.

"So, this guy, the one hitting on Nikki, the Columbian, who is he?"

"Raul Ramirez. There are two of them, the Ramirez brothers. Raul and Stefano." Angie pauses, and Savage waits for more.

"Go on," Savage says. "You don't have to tell me everything."

"What do you mean?"

"You know." He watches another pelican glide by, admiring its effortless grace.

"What are you? A mind reader?"

"Kind of. Just sensitive. Go on."

"Let's just say I know them. Nikki does, too. If you live here, you know, work here, you end up knowing everyone here. That's just how it is."

Savage cracks his knuckles and looks down at his scarred hands. "I don't need to know all the details. I just need to know what I need to know to find out what happened to Jake."

"Raul's the younger brother. Stefano's the smart one. They're into all sorts of stuff. Not all of it legal. The one you jumped was Raul." Angie speaks in staccato bursts, clearing her throat at the end of every sentence.

"I didn't jump anyone. He pulled a knife on me."

"And you defended yourself, right? And half killed him."

"I should have walked. I could have." Savage scratches the light stubble on his chin. *Must shave*, he thinks.

"You can't undo what's done. Whatever. Just stay away from the Whistle and don't call Nikki. Lie low and stay here."

Savage hears something else embedded in Angie's words. Her voice is clear and her thoughts ordered. She's pragmatic. She looks off into the distance above the mangroves towards the vast blue Caribbean sky.

Another pelican circles the lagoon.

The bow of a boat slowly makes its way past the tip of the dock, and turns towards the houseboat.

"Get down," Angie spits. "Now, get down."

Savage drops onto the deck, and then crawls military-style down the starboard deck of the houseboat. The twin powerboat engines rumble across the channel. It's 32-foot Contender ST, with Mercury 240 outboards. Angie stays in her seat and picks up a book.

"It's Raul—Big Ugly. Stay down."

The boat slows, drifting towards them. Two men stand on board—Raul and a sidekick—a short, stocky man, sporting tattooed arms, a broken nose, a pock-marked face and a pair of mirrored Ray-Bans.

"Beautiful day, huh?" Angie says as the boat approaches, her voice lilting.

"Shut up. Where is he?" Raul growls, his jowls loose. He's dressed in a white t-shirt, loose white pants, and a thick gold chain around his neck.

"Who?" Angie puts down her book. Ramirez leaps onto the deck, and Angie takes in his black eye and bruised cheek.

"You know who. The one on your scooter. Jackass's brother."

Angie sees Savage low in the water, out of view of Ramirez and the other guy at the wheel of the boat.

"I don't know what you're talking about, but you're welcome to take a look around, Raul."

"I will. You stay here." Raul pushes past her, opens the glass sliding door to the houseboat and walks in. The Contender's engines idle. The short man looks at Angie, a lecherous grin flickers across his face. He runs his tongue over along his top lip.

Angie flips him off. He says something that can't be heard over the engines.

Raul emerges from the deckhouse, a look of fury on his face. He peers over the side into the water, scratching his head.

Savage slips quietly over the stern of the powerboat.

Raul kicks a potted plant.

"What's your name, handsome?" she asks the man on the boat.

"My name?"

"No, that pelican over there," Angie says, pointing at a bird circling overhead.

"Funny."

"Your name is funny?" Angie stares at the man. Savage's half-empty glass sits next to hers on the deck.

Savage lifts the lid of a fish storage bin, climbs in, and lowers the lid.

Raul is muttering and cursing in Spanish. He climbs the ladder leading to the roof of the deck house. His feet are heavy on the rungs.

Angie pushes Savage's glass between the two flower pots, inching it over the side. The splash is masked by Raul cursing from the roof. He looks around and comes back down to the deck.

"*Nada.*"

"*Vamos a salir de aquí,*" the short man says.

"Good idea," Angie says. "Get out of here."

"You speak Spanish?"

"No," Angie says. "*No hablo español,*" she mouths, looking directly at the stocky man.

"We'll be back," Raul says. He points at Angie. "You'd better start remembering where he is."

Raul jumps into the Contender. The short man swings the bow away from the houseboat. Raul looks back at Angie and spits into the warm waters of the lagoon. "Start remembering."

The boat moves around the corner. Angie watches, staying where she is, drumming her fingers on her thigh.

Twenty minutes later, the Contender returns. It passes close to *Pretty Woman*. Raul is holding onto the console.

"We'll be back tonight. Then you're going to tell me where he is. And if you can't remember, I'll help you. Got it?" he yells. "And when I find him, I'm going to kill him. Understand?"

"Whatever. What do I care?" Angie stares at Raul until he looks away. The Contender edges its was along the wharf to gas up next to the Hogfish Bar and Grill.

———

Inside the fish bin, Savage is sweating. The men talk as they gas up the boat. He hears Raul talking to Angie, and then silence. The boat moves slowly through the channel. It's a wake-free zone, and the Contender is doing just five knots. Savage waits. There's no point doing anything until they pick up speed.

Five minutes later, the engines roar to life, and Savage is thrown to the back of the fish locker. The bow of the boat rises then settles as it begins to plane, scudding along the tops of the waves. Savage cracks the lid just enough to see out. Raul and the short man are standing together in the open wheelhouse, looking straight ahead as the boat heads east. They're about five hundred yards off shore.

One chance, Savage thinks. Two men, one chance.

Savage lifts the lid and crawls out, crouching low. He grabs a gaff from the bottom of the boat, lifting it slowly, getting its measure. It's big—designed for offshore fishing. The hook is sharp. *It'll do*, he decides.

The boat is rising and falling in the swell. The engines are roaring. Raul and his sidekick stare at the horizon ahead. Savage steadies himself with one hand, creeping forward until he's within reach of them. One chance; two men.

"When I find him, I'm going to kill him," Raul says.

The stocky man grunts, adjusting his Ray-Bans.

Savage readies himself.

He springs up and whips the gaff through the air, hooking it into short man's windpipe, and pulls him backwards, slamming him into the deck. The man lies there, immobile, clutching his torn windpipe, his eyes wide with fear, a desperate gurgling sound coming from his throat. *A very big fish*, Savage thinks.

Raul grabs the wheel and reaches for the gun in his waistband, but he's slow. Savage is on him immediately. He grabs Raul's hand, twists it, and forces it up behind his shoulders while he slams his head into the wheel before throwing him to the deck. The pistol, a Glock, clatters to the floor. Raul gets to his knees, clutching his broken wrist. He reaches for the Glock, but Savage kicks him twice in the groin and he collapses, retching and gasping. He begins to whimper.

The Contender skims the waves, keeping a straight course. Savage grabs the wheel, throttles back, and then eyes the shore, looking for a secluded spot, one with no other boats.

Short Stocky is unconscious. Raul groans, lying in the bottom of the boat, his eyes wide with fear, blinking like a flounder.

"You shouldn't have come looking for me. Now I have a serious problem. And that problem is you and that little runt."

"What do you want?" Raul gasps.

"I want to know what happened to my brother. I told you, and you should have listened."

Savage turns to face Raul. He sees the stubborn hatred on his face and feels a surge of anger. He lets go of the wheel, and moves towards his adversary.

He grabs the injured wrist and twists it. He feels bone scrape on bone. Raul screeches.

"Tell me! Tell me who killed him."

"No!"

"Why not?"

"He'll kill me."

"Who?"

"My brother, Stefano. He'll kill me if I tell you."

Savage drops Raul's arm. "You just did."

———

Angie is ready when the powerboat returns. She has a Smith and Wesson .38 in her waistband and a knife in her purse, just in case.

The sun is huge and orange, setting over the Atlantic. Tourists gather in Mallory Square, waiting for another perfect day in paradise to come to an end. Fireworks explode in the sky, twinkling as the dusk covers the beach. Night is ready to make its entrance.

Angie squints and fingers the gun.

"It's me," Savage says. He brings the Contender alongside, cuts the engines, jumps on *Pretty Woman*'s deck and ties the boat off.

"Are you okay?" Angie asks.

"I'm alive. Raul and the short guy didn't make out too well, though. You got a boat?"

"No, but I can get one." Angie bites at her cuticles.

"We've got to lose this one for good."

"Jesus. I don't need to be wrapped up in your freaking revenge killing spree."

Savage closes his eyes. He doesn't either. But some things just have to be done.

"After this, we're done. Okay?"

"You think I'm going to say okay? Not okay. No."

"No choice, really. Not now. You with me? This is a big mess but we're in it now."

Their eyes meet. Savage sees the sadness and fear, and behind it, the reluctant acceptance.

4

PRETTY WOMAN

RAUL'S EYES register fear as Savage stares down at him.

"You know about family, right? He was my brother. Bad choice."

Raul tries to speak through the duct tape covering his mouth, but only the sound of desperation escapes.

"Look out for boat traffic," Savage says to Angie, who is in a Zodiac alongside the Contender. The lights of Key West glimmer in the distance. The night is still, and there is no moon. The running lights are off on both boats. The Contender's engines are idling—a slow, steady rumble.

Raul kicks at Savage, but with a broken leg, he only winces in pain. Savage delivers two powerful jabs to his gut, and Raul's eyes bulge as he retches, twists, and thrashes on the deck.

"You'll be conscious, Raul, all the way, right up until the point when the boat hits that concrete wharf, then there won't be much left."

Raul's eyes are wide and teary.

"Angie, I'm going to fire up the engines. Get her planing and lined up, then I'm going over the side. Pick me up. Then it's back to the houseboat, okay?"

Angie gives him a thumbs up. Raul brings his broken wrists up in a position of prayer, but Savage ignores him.

"Try anything, Raul, and you'll get hurt."

Savage moves the throttle forward and turns the boat. The bow is heading towards the concrete wharf, a half a mile away.

"Okay, on three. I'm going to hit the gas. She'll rise and level, and I'll be over the stern. Ready?"

Angie releases the Contender and lets her Zodiac drift away.

"One... two... three." Savage pushes the throttle, and the twin Mercury engines roar. The bow lifts and the boat gains speed. It's on target. Savage steps over Ramirez and Short Stocky, and in two strides he's at the stern of the boat. Then, in a single leap, he's over the outboards, hand springing into a somersault and landing in the water. Angie's Zodiac pulls alongside. Savage hoists himself in.

"Back to the houseboat. Quick. We don't need to be around when she blows."

Savage is gasping for air, adrenaline coursing through his body.

Angie spins the Zodiac around and lays a heading for the mangroves by Sock Island.

They can hear the Contender's engines gunning at full speed as it heads straight towards the wharf. It jumps across the surface, whining.

"Holy...!" Angie gasps as the boat hits. There's a loud crash, a brief stillness, and then the gas tank explodes in a fiery ball, and a plume of flame rises into the sky.

"There won't be much left after that," Angie says.

"Better not be. Throttle back, then come in slow. Nice and easy. Don't draw any attention."

They're in the channel, passing the wooden wharfs and the neatly moored boats. The sea is inky black. There are no lights on the water.

Angie brings the Zodiac alongside the houseboat, cuts the

engine, and ties it off. Savage springs onto the deck. He goes inside, and Angie follows close behind.

Sirens howl up Roosevelt, and a helicopter flies low along the shore towards Stock Island.

"Jesus!" Angie says. "This is too much for a Sunday night."

"It's Sunday?"

"It was this morning."

"I'm losing track of time," Savage says.

Angie turns on the light.

"No lights," Savage says, and switches them off.

"I don't like this, Savage. Count me out. It's out of control. You're dealing with the wrong people."

"You're already in, Angie. We both are."

"I don't want to be."

"But you came round to Jake's place. What were you looking for?" Savage asks.

"I don't know. Something."

"You had a gun. Hardly squeaky clean."

"Plenty of people have guns—this is America. That doesn't mean anything. Look, Jake was my best friend. No one is doing anything to find out what happened. I can't get anything from the police. They won't tell me anything. The story died just like that." Angie snaps her fingers.

"What are you saying?"

"I'm saying there's something weird going on, Savage. There was nothing about a body. Just 'presumed dead', 'signs of a struggle,' that sort of stuff, you know? I read it."

Angie is on the floor, pulling her knees up to her chest, rocking back and forth.

"Presumed dead? Based on what?"

Savage thinks about Raul and Short Stocky. The desperation in Raul's eyes; the explosion. His shoulder stiffens.

"Some blood stains, a shoe," Angie continues.

"Jesus, Angie. Jesus. I missed that."

"Missed what, Savage?"

"There should have been more. The blood was outside. Not inside." He pauses, lost in thought.

"No more killing," Savage says almost to himself. "No more." He draws in a breath and feels a tremendous wave of tiredness come over him, a wave of regret and remorse.

"I don't get it, Savage. What are you saying? You think he's still alive?"

Savage flexes his fingers. His eyes burn.

"I've got to sleep, Angie. I've made a big mistake." Savage walks over to the couch, lies down, and feels the strength ebb from his body. He has nothing left.

He drifts off into a deep, dark sleep.

———

"You were speaking French in your sleep," Angie says, looking at the front page of the *Key West Citizen*. The headline reads:

No Survivors in Boating Accident

"What?" Savage says, stretching and yawning. He shakes his head.

"You must have been dreaming--you were speaking French. It sounded like you were giving orders."

"I probably was. It's stress. It happens sometimes."

"Not to me, I hope." Angie picks up the paper, and shows the front page to Savage.

"No, not to you, no," Savage says, trying to remember his dream. It's lost in the night.

Morning light floods through the windows. The sky is a perfect cerulean blue.

"I have nightmares sometimes."

"I'm not surprised, given this is how you live. So what's your story, Frenchie? I need to know who I'm dealing with."

"I was a Legionnaire. For just a few years." Savage stands up. He's still tired. He rolls his shoulders and shakes out his arms.

Angie watches the way he moves. "A Legionnaire? Really? I thought they were all done a long time ago."

"No. Still at it. Four years."

"Jake didn't tell me that."

"No. He wouldn't. I don't usually talk about it."

"Unless you're asleep," she says.

"Apparently," he agrees. He looks out of the window at the morning light dancing on the water. A pelican sits on a piling on the wharf. Savage squints, his ice blue eyes scanning the shore, just in case.

Angie reads from the paper: "The force of impact and the explosion left very little evidence. The number of people on board is currently unknown."

She frowns, the anxiety clear on her face. "I hate this, Savage. I want a normal life. Not on the edge like this, knowing what happened. I'll think about this for the rest of my life."

Savage grunts.

"Doesn't that bother you? You did that. I'm part of it. I don't want to be. You know, I've been involved in a few sketchy situations, but this one is something else."

"Listen, Raul was going to come for me. He'd have kept coming until he got me. I stopped him. He's gone. It's done. We've got to move on. We're here now. That's all there is to it."

Angie lets out a sigh and puts her head in her hands.

"I was supposed to be coming here for a vacation. Then a new life," Savage says.

"Well, this is no vacation. It's a mess."

"I'm not like this."

"Like what?" Angie asks, incredulous.

"Violent," Savage adds, his voice trailing off.

Angie laughs a hard, coarse laugh. "You have got to be kidding me."

"No, I'm not. I just got caught up in the heat of the moment. I'll make things right." Savage can't bring himself to look at her.

Savage strokes the stubble on his chin, then rubs his hand over his short black hair. His arms are thick and muscled, covered with scars. Angie looks at his piercing blue eyes as he stares out the window. Savage knows she sees a troubled man.

Savage starts to think about the phrase 'presumed dead'. He'd just assumed, from talking to Nikki, that Jake was dead.

"What's the tattoo?" Angie says. She touches Savage's arm. Only half the tattoo is visible—the rest under his black t-shirt. "It looks kind of like a coat of arms. Sort of Italian Renaissance, you know?"

"Good eye. It is."

"I studied art history in a former life," Angie says. "N.M.? Hmmm."

"Niccolò Machiavelli. It was a long time ago."

"Of course. *The Prince*," Angie says. "I remember him. Anyway, about your dream. The French."

"Memories of something. I'm not sure." But he remembers—the helicopter, the flames, the screaming, the jungle, his men. Savage's jaw tightens. He wants to tell Angie, but stops himself. He doesn't want to talk about his nightmares, about what had happened in the past. He needs to focus on Jake.

"Machiavelli," he says instead. "I had a thing about him. The best political thinker and observer of the human condition, ever. He knew about power and how to keep it. I wanted to serve a prince like that, someone who believed in the greater good. I was very young."

"So, you ran away and joined the Foreign Legion?"

"Basically. That's part of it. Nothing's black and white."

"No kidding," Angie mumbles.

She picks up her purse, opens it, takes out a pack of cigarettes, and then puts the purse down. She rubs her hands up and down her thighs.

"He kills, he talks French in his sleep. He was a Legionnaire, and he's got a thing for Machiavelli."

"He was the only thinker to articulate that we are not moral creatures, though we pretend to be. I carried a copy of *The Prince* around with me for years. Back when I was a soldier. It put things in perspective for me."

"But not now?"

"Not now, no. I still believe a lot of what he said. About power. About expediency. About doing what needs to be done to keep what you have. But..."

"There's a 'but'?"

"There's not a 'but'. Those Ramirez brothers are bastards, cold-blooded bastards."

"And you? I'm not saying... you know... that you're a ..."

"Cold-blooded bastard?"

Angie pulls at her ring. She picks up the newspaper and looks at the headline, then drops it on the table. She stands, paces, and sits down.

"Look," Savage continues, "you have to believe in the greater good. What is good for the people, not just yourself. Not just the Prince. Anything is acceptable provided it's for the greater good. You know? I mean lying, stealing, cheating, taking the Lord's name in vain, murder. For the greater good. Getting rid of people like Ramirez."

"I don't know what you're talking about. You sound like a vigilante."

"Something happened to Jake. Whatever it was, it was the Ramirez brothers. Bad people. You told me. Maybe I shouldn't have done what I did, but I did. And I'm going to get Stefano Ramirez—for the greater good. Then I'm going to take all his ill-gotten gains and put them to work for the greater good." Savage pauses. "Although I might take a slice for retirement and compensation."

"Are you crazy?"

Savage's eyes are bright, a searing blue. The light brings out their translucent quality. He doesn't blink, just stares ahead. "No. Not crazy. This is just how it has to be."

His voice is soft, almost a whisper. Angie shivers, despite the heat of the day. Her face is expressionless.

The light streams into the houseboat. Angie picks up the paper again and puts it down.

"It sounds like you're going on a crusade. And I'm in it with you, too, whether I like it or not. Right?" There are tears in her eyes. She wipes them away and twists her long blonde hair.

"I can't see a good alternative."

"We could turn ourselves in," Angie says.

Savage grunts. "We're not going to do that. You're going to have to help me. This is your town."

"Help you with what?"

"Finishing this up."

"How so?"

"Finding out about the fire. About Jake. Putting Stefano out of business."

"You really mean that, don't you?"

A boat passes by, and they both turn frantically. It's a charter fishing boat heading out to sea, a group of overweight men standing in the stern.

"I do mean it. Not revenge; just put them out of business. Clean things up." Savage's biceps twitch.

"And how are you going to do that?" Angie says, her voice tired, resigned, and sad.

"I don't know," Savage says. "But I will. One step at a time. One step at a time."

Angie stands up, straightens herself, and draws in a breath.

"Okay, I don't know how we're going to do this, but I'm in. I don't want to be, but I don't have a choice. No more killing. I don't want any part of that, not ever. But I'm in—for Jake. Just for Jake."

"Listen," he says. "You need to go the boatyard. There's a kayak by the main building, next to the restroom. There's a kitbag in it. I need it."

"Hey, I don't *need* to go to the boatyard. You can ask me if I *would* go to the boatyard. Then I might."

"Could you? Please?"

"Don't order me around like you were ordering people around in your little French dream."

"Angie, I said please. I'm sorry."

"A bit late," she says.

"But really, would you mind? Get the kitbag?"

"I'll get it. What's in it?"

"Don't look. It's heavy."

"Okay. I've got some other stuff to do, too."

Angie turns and walks towards the door.

"Where are you going?" Savage asks.

"Into town. I'll be back in a couple of hours. What size is your waist?"

"I'm a 36 waist and 36 leg. Everything else is extra-large."

"I bet it is."

"So, you and Jake? Were you lovers?"

"No, just good friends. I could ask why you ask, but I guess I won't."

"Go ahead."

"It's more fun if I don't. It's against the rules to spell everything out, right?"

Savage laughs. "And the lesbian thing? Jake mentioned that."

"He did? What did he say, exactly?"

"Well, he didn't give too many details... just enough to whet the appetite, really."

Savage stretches his fingers, places his hands on his knees, and draws himself up to his full height.

"It was ... she was a friend at first. And it was more me than her. She was off men at the time. It happens," Angie says coyly.

"It does? So, now? Lesbian?" Savage raises his eyebrows and feels a stirring.

Angie giggles.

"More bi than lesbian, though then I was more lesbian than bi. And now, really, more straight than bi... I don't even know why I'm telling you all this. I mean, I can't believe we're having this conversation, as if nothing happened."

"Nothing's simple," Savage says. "Life goes on. And on. One thing after another." He feels a slight flutter in his belly. "Interesting. Is this a Key West thing? This back and forth."

"Maybe. I don't know. Stop asking."

"Okay."

"And don't look at me like that," Angie says. "You know what I mean." She puts on her pink baseball hat and sunglasses. "What about you, Savage?"

"Me? So far, strictly ladies."

"So far?"

"You never know." He looks at Angie's long blonde hair and sea-green eyes. He could reach out and touch her, but he does nothing. The moment has gone.

"Don't you be going through my underwear drawer when I'm gone, okay?" She slides the door closed as she walks out onto the deck of *Pretty Woman*, then climbs up onto the wharf.

A pretty woman in a tourist town.

Savage picks up the paper, and wonders what Raul Ramirez thought about as he hurtled towards the wharf towards his fiery end.

No more killing, he thinks.

Done with that.

5
———

THE FLUTTER

"CAN'T CHANGE ANYTHING NOW," Savage says, looking out across the water. "I need to be more strategic about what I do next, and when I do it. That was a mess."

The stiffness in his shoulder nags at Savage. A memory of fire creeps in. He represses it.

"Yes. You were a drunk-ass man, doing stupid man stuff, and all because of a woman. Right?"

"Pretty much," Savage shrugs. "But hey, shit happens. That was a mistake. I was worked up. Emotional. Too many thoughts. I lost it. Sorry."

Savage picks up a bottle of Tabasco sauce from the table and throws it from hand to hand. His mind begins to wander again, first to Jake, then to the anger he felt when he pointed the boat at the wharf. He puts the Tabasco sauce down, the explosion vivid in his mind. He'd killed in anger. But anger is not enough. *I'm going to have to live with it*, Savage thinks. He knows he can do better.

The fan turns overhead. There is tension in the air, tension that only time will dissipate.

Angie clears her throat. "Do you want a drink?"

He replies with a blank expression. "Thanks. Cranberry and soda. Hold the vodka."

Angie moves towards the fridge with a dancer's grace. "I've never heard that before."

Savage feels the flutter again. It's associated with tension, he decides.

"I've done all the drinking I need to. Believe me," Savage says. He could tell her, but not now.

"What is it with you guys? It's always all or nothing. Jake was the same way."

"Excess, you mean?"

"Yeah. Haven't you noticed? Excessive trouble, excessive fighting, excessive women."

"Women?"

Savage watches and wonders. Does she mean him or Jake?

"You know what I mean," Angie says, as if he does. But he doesn't.

Savage steps towards Angie, reaches out, and strokes her hair. She drops her eyes after looking into the searing blue of his.

His face relaxes, and she touches the stubble on his chin.

Savage's thoughts and emotions jump from one to another.

"I like that," Angie says. "You're hot, too," she continues, keeping her gaze on Savage.

He feels his breathing getting heavier with desire.

"Hot?" Savage returns her stare and then laughs. "I didn't expect you to say that. I like it though. You're pretty"—he pauses, and then adds—"gorgeous, I mean."

"Thanks," Angie says.

"Is this awkward?"

"No," Angie says. "Not awkward. Yet."

"I was going to say 'you're pretty hot', but I shouldn't really. It doesn't sound right, somehow."

Angie shakes her hair.

"What about you and Jake?"

"Like I said, friends—good friends. I lived at his place for a while. He helped me out, I helped him out." Angie smiles, and the tension dissipates. She runs a hand through her hair, each strand catching the radiance of the sun.

A pelican glides by outside as waves lap the houseboat.

"Jake liked to cook, and when he cooked, we'd talk. We just liked being around each other. He was so special. I loved him."

Savage imagines Angie and Jake, laughing, sharing stories. It was easy to see. "And the lesbian thing? Just an 'I've had it with men' thing?"

"Back to that again?"

"Just curious."

"That was a phase. I was having a rough time. A lot of people who come here are running away from something. I guess I was, too. Women felt safer. I liked them, and I liked the sex. I felt good about it; while it lasted, anyway."

Their eyes lock and linger. A man and a woman. A simple moment.

"Am I making sense?"

"Honesty always makes sense. I don't mean to interrogate you or spoil anything."

"Don't spoil anything." She reaches out and strokes his cheek, moving towards him.

The flutter again.

"I'll try not to," Savage says, stroking Angie's arm. His hand slips down to her wrist. He brings her hand up to his mouth and kisses it.

"What are you doing?" she says, putting on a Southern accent. "I do declare!"

"Probably not a good idea."

"Probably not, but that's never stopped me before."

"I like you," Savage says. "You're all right."

"All right?"

"It's an English thing. A compliment. Means I think you're something. Something special."

Angie steps closer to Savage. She strokes his head, then kisses his cheek, her hand running across his firm muscular shoulders.

Savage feels the cold in his belly, the hollowness in his chest—a stirring.

"You're all right, too, but right now we need to get you some surf shorts and sunglasses. And maybe a hat. Or you could dye your hair, get some colored contacts."

Smart woman, Savage thinks. "No. I'll take my chances. I'll just stay low."

"I'll tell people you're my cousin who's visiting from the old country."

"Okay. But let's go back a bit. The Ramirez thing. And Jake. Know anything?"

"I don't know much. After Hurricane Katrina, a lot of people moved up here from New Orleans. Lot of sketchy types. There were some real lowlifes. Ramirez and his brother were part of that, but they were further up the food chain. I don't know what they were into exactly. There was talk of drugs, but I think what they really wanted was Jake's boatyard, for some reason."

Savage squints, gazing out of the window, watching a tourist on a paddle board. He notices the cautious wobble of the guy's pasty white legs.

Angie shrugs and leans against the counter, her hair catching the sun's rays again. "I know they were putting pressure on Jake," she says. "He wouldn't talk about it. He said it would be better if I didn't know. I was scared."

"So Jake wouldn't sell?"

"No, he wouldn't." Her bottom lip quivers as a tear runs down her cheek. Savage remembers the explosion. He wants to hold her, but doesn't move.

Angie makes two drinks and passes a glass to Savage. He takes a sip.

"This one's yours," Savage says. "It's got vodka." He passes the drink back and takes the other.

"You weren't kidding?"

"About not drinking? Not kidding. I've been down before, and I'm not going back down. And right now, I need to think straight. I just killed two guys, and I shouldn't have. Connected guys, right? This thing isn't going to go away, Angie. It's got to be finished."

"Finished? How?"

Savage shrugs. "Right now, I don't know. But I will." He stretches his fingers and makes two fists.

"I miss him," Angie says.

Savage steps forward, but Angie turns. A small jet passes overhead, climbing slowly over the gulf. She turns back with an anger in her eyes.

"Who are you, Savage?" Angie asks, staring squarely into his eyes. "I know you're Jake's brother, but who are you? Jake mentioned you, but not about what you did, or where you lived, nothing like that."

"He didn't know. I don't talk about it."

"So why don't you tell me?"

"Okay. Jake told me a little about you, so I'll tell you a little about me. I told you I was in the Foreign Legion for a while, and then Asia."

"The Foreign Legion. I still find that hard to believe. And Asia?"

"I was young, rebellious. I ran away. I didn't know what I was doing."

"Like running away to sea?"

"I didn't fit in. A loner. Couldn't see myself doing a regular job."

Angie laughs. "You're kidding!"

"I wish I was, believe me."

"The French Foreign Legion," Angie enunciates each word clearly and slowly, shaking her head.

"I was a romantic. There was something about it. Sounds odd now. I ran away. Marseilles. Corsica. Freezing my ass off in France the first winter. Then South America. Then Africa. I was a different man, four years later. And when I got out, well..."

"Well what?"

"I didn't have any structure. No more orders, no more training, no more missions, no more adrenaline. I spiraled, almost lost it, but I couldn't let that happen. I just made it. Just...it happens a lot to guys in the service. Then not. Coming undone, falling apart."

"So now it's a life of cranberry and tonic?"

"Has to be."

"Then Asia? Were you just *being* in Asia? You know, finding yourself?"

"Met a guy. Funny story, really. I was walking along this road in France, near Cahors. Southwest. Rural place. Middle of summer. I see this guy down by the river. He has an easel, and he's sketching. English guy. Wearing a beret, you know, in the way English guys do, in France. Artist type. I talk to him and he tells me he'd been in Japan a long time. Very into Zen, Eastern philosophy, Buddhism, but a bit like me. He'd fallen apart somewhere along the line and gotten himself back together. I was already beginning to fall apart, regularly drinking and fighting. But there was something about this guy, like he really had found something."

"So off you went?"

"Basically. He gave me the names of a few contacts. I went to Kyoto and found this poet friend of his. He helped me out. Then I began studying."

"Studying what?"

"To be a monk. Like I said, I was a monk. Three years in Japan, then Thailand. A robe, hat, begging bowl. I'm not kidding. I know it sounds ...."

Savage purses his lips, picks up the Tabasco Sauce, and puts it down again. Her eyes are sparkling. She touches his arm and looks out of the window.

The tourist falls off his paddle board.

"It does. It sounds like a crock ... but that's what Jake was like. He had all these stories about kick boxing, and it was all true."

"Runs in the family."

"You were in the Foreign Legion and then you were a monk?" Angie laughs, "Lord save me. What a pair."

"It's true. That's the short version, anyway."

"You mean there's a longer version?"

"There is. But, that's it for now. The long version would need a book. Or maybe a movie. I'll tell you sometime. I became a better person. At least I thought so. Now, I'm not sure. I've let something back in. That anger. I thought that was gone."

Angie sips her drink as Savage thinks about his anger. "You're just like your brother. He played a close hand."

"We're usually not big talkers. Then sometimes... out it comes."

Angie's smile comes slowly, her eyes fill with tears. Her shoulders begin to shake but she catches herself. "God, I wish Jake was here. It would be amazing to see you two together."

Savage looks at the tears in Angie's eyes. He rests his hand on her shoulder. Angie puts her drink down.

"I hear revenge is a dish best served cold," Savage says.

"Meaning what? Don't involve me in some revenge scheme."

"I won't. We'll do this slowly and carefully. And we'll do it right. Enough of this. For now."

"Meaning?"

"Meaning right now I don't feel like a monk."

"Meaning?"

"Bed. It wouldn't be a good idea," Savage says. "But it wouldn't be a bad idea."

"Will you elaborate, please?"

"I'm being serious. I'm going to put all this Ramirez business to rest. We can't make any mistakes. And I'm trying not to think about bed. And you."

"And that means we can't have sex? Or that we can?"

Savage looks at Angie's sarong and loose cotton top, her blonde waves spilling over her shoulders.

"Well, aren't you just the romantic?" Savage laughs again.

"Me?" Angie says, running her hands through her hair, pulling it back into a ponytail, and letting it fall over her shoulders again.

"We may have to have sex just so I can think straight."

"Who's the romantic now?"

"Okay. Get in there," Savage says, pointing to the bedroom door. "Let's make this quick."

"No, let's make this good. And remember, you started this."

"I did?"

"You did. I'm not complaining; but you did."

Savage watches Angie as she moves light and easy, straight back and smooth calves.

"Okay. Maybe not that quick," he says.

———

"How's the thinking?" Angie says, gazing at the ceiling. Savage is lying naked next to her.

"Clear as a bell! That really worked."

Angie gets out of bed as he stretches. "Stay there, Savage. I'm going to pick up some more things for you."

Savage watches Angie dress. "Okay," Savage says. "Thanks. I'm going to start using this clarity to get some serious thinking done."

"I'm scared," Angie says.

"You can be a little scared. That's a good thing. Keeps you on your toes. Don't let it eat you up, though."

Angie looks distant.

"I can't just say it's going to be okay."

"I know."

"Be quick. I need to get to know this town and figure out what's next," Savage says. "Oh, and Angie?"

"Yes?"

"This is just us. Not a word."

"You didn't have to say that."

"I did," Savage says. "I did have to say that."

6

LYING LOW

"I KNOW you said you liked the stubble, but you know what? I feel better clean shaven." Savage passes his hand over his smooth face. He sees Angie in the mirror, behind him—close enough to smell.

"You look all right," she says, elongating the words *all right*. "You know, for a weird English guy with a strange history."

Her eyes blue eyes gleam in the sunlight, and Savage feels a flutter in his belly. His face changes. A cloud scuds across the sun, plunging the houseboat into shadow.

"I should have left you out of this, Angie. Gone rogue."

They move into the living room.

Angie pulls at her ring finger and clears her throat. She leans to one side and runs her hand through her hair.

"No, I'm in. Someone has to keep an eye on you." Her voice is soft.

The cloud passes and light floods back into the room. A pelican sits on a piling by the dock, perfectly still, beak down.

Savage rotates his shoulder, spreads the fingers of his hands, and begins to pace.

"We should lie low. For a month or so. Not do anything rash. I need to get a better feel for how things work down here. Where things are. And I need to get back in shape. Get my head clear."

"You look pretty good to me, mister," Angie says.

"Not gym rat in shape. I mean hardcore. Military." Savage cracks his neck and watches the pelican ease itself into the air.

"Not just crunches and curls, huh?" Angie steps towards Savage and runs a fingernail down his back. Savage closes his eyes.

"Funny. No. Strong. Loose. Agile. Clear mind. Senses alert."

Angie sighs. "Does the training involve ... you know"—she runs her finger down his back again—"sex?"

Savage lets out a chuckle, turns, and runs his hand through Angie's hair. "I can't tell you that. Confidential. But I can tell you that if it does you will know about it."

"Well, okay then," Angie says. "Just asking."

"Good attitude. Now listen. Can I borrow the jeep for a few days? There's a chap I know, up the Keys. I need to pick up some stuff."

"Stuff? A chap? Where?"

"Better not to know. Let's just say I'm going fishing."

"Let's," Angie says. "And yes, you can take the jeep."

———

Four days later, Savage parks the jeep behind the Hogfish Bar and Grill, gets out, and stretches. It's been a two-hour drive, and it's now dark. The smooth water by the gas pump reflects the light at the end of the wharf.

He walks down the wharf with a kit bag slung over his shoulder. In the other hand, he carries a cooler and fishing rod. He whistles the theme to *The Third Man*, a song he's whistled before.

There's a light on in the houseboat. A figure emerges. It's Angie.

"You're back," she says, her eyes sparkling in the moonlight, her voice excited.

"Catch anything?"

"Sure did," Savage says. He puts down the kitbag and cooler. He lays the fishing rod down, steps towards Angie, and kisses her forehead.

She looks at the kit bag.

"I need to put this stuff somewhere," Savage says. "Out of sight."

"I won't ask," Angie says. She pulls the braided rug aside in the living room, gets on her hands and knees and lifts a panel in the floor, revealing a cubbyhole.

"Jolly good," Savage says.

"I'll leave you to it. Fix something to eat."

Savage touches her cheek then squeezes her shoulder. "You're a good girl, Angie."

"And you're a bad man, Savage. I know." She goes into the kitchen.

Savage opens the kit bag and takes out the Pelican gun case. There's a Glock 17 and some ammunition.

"I don't even want to know what you've got in there," Angie says from the kitchen.

"No," Savage says. He puts the last of the supplies into the stowage area. "Better to be prepared. Hope for the best, prepare for the worst."

He puts the panel back in the floor and moves the rug into place.

Savage can smell tortillas and cheese. He walks into the kitchen and gets the broom and the dustpan. He goes into the living room, and sweeps up.

"You'd make a good wife," Angie says, from the kitchen.

"It's a military thing. Always make your bed. Make it right. Whatever else happens, at least you've done that. Same with sweeping. Order helps."

"What else did they teach you, soldier?" Angie gets out two plates and puts them on the counter.

"Oh, the usual. How to survive on roots and bugs. How to kill people."

"Ask a silly question," she says, serving the tortillas.

After they eat, and Savage has done the dishes, they sit and listen to the water lapping the hull of the houseboat.

"Wouldn't it be nice," Angie says, "to just, you know, get to know each other? Chat. Have fun."

Savage raises his eyebrows, and a slow smile spreads across his face. "Good heavens, yes," he says. His expression changes—eyes sharp, ears pricked.

"What's that noise?" he says, standing up.

Angie doesn't look concerned. "Probably some drunk up at the Hogfish."

Savage moves towards the door.

"Where are you going?"

"Stay here. I'm going to see what's going on. Didn't sound good."

"Don't. Savage! You don't need to get involved."

"I know. Story of my life," he says. He jumps onto the dock and then runs, taking long strides.

At the end of the wharf, behind the Hogfish, a woman is shouting in Spanish. A man yells back, his voice gruff and hard. Savage hears glass breaking and then a scream.

It's late. The wharf is deserted except for the man and the woman. Savage pauses. The man is big, his arms thick and strong. He has a bull neck and neatly trimmed hair, with a scar etched on his face. The woman is slight, but drawn up, proud and defiant.

Savage is in the shadows. The man and woman are staring at each other, locked in the heat of battle.

"Pagar ahora!" the man hisses.

"Nunca voy a pagar!" the woman spits, not backing down.

Savage watches.

Angie appears beside him, and Savage pushes her behind him, deeper into the shadows.

"It's all Greek to me," Savage whispers.

"He says to pay now. She won't pay."

"Isn't that guy..." Savage begins.

"He looks like one of Stefano's guys," Angie whispers. "I know he is. Savage. Don't do anything ...".

"I can't leave her to that thug," Savage says. "Look at him."

"No. Please," Angie implores.

"Stay right here!" Savage pushes Angie back into the shadows and steps forward. The light from the end of the wharf casts a soft glow over him.

"You guys hear anything?" Savage asks, looking from the man to the woman.

The man starts. "What the hell! Yeah, I heard something. I heard me screaming at this bitch and this bitch screaming at me." He's breathing heavily.

"That's not a nice way to talk to a lady, friend. Don't use that word."

"Who the hell are you? And she's not a lady." The man gestures to the woman with his arm. "She's a bitch, *pendejo!*"

Savage steps closer, getting his measure. He's in the man's space.

The woman looks back and forth between them. "You'd better go," she says to Savage. "I can take care of this."

Savage doesn't take his eyes of the man. He flexes his fingers, adjusts his feet, and bounces on the balls of his feet.

"You heard her!" The man spits on the ground. "Get out of here!"

Savage steps to one side, where he is more brightly illuminated.

"You heard me, *pendejo*. Get out of here! *Entiende?*"

Savage's breathing is slow and steady. The adrenaline begins to flow. He watches the man's stance, his clenched fists, the fury, the lack of any plan. Then he sees the animal fear.

"What's your name? José? You work for Ramirez? Do you?"

A look of confusion and concern flashes across the man's face. His lips move. "Who?" he says weakly.

"You heard me, José. Or is it Hector? Raul is gone, you know. The one with the navigation problems."

There's sweat on the big man's brow. "What the hell are you talking about?"

Savage swallows keeping his eyes on the man, seeing everything. "I heard it was an accident. Too bad."

"Who are you?"

"I'm my brother's brother, José. Or is it Hector?"

"*Tu madre,*" the man mutters. His mouth is contorted in anger and frustration. He moves his hands, preparing.

"Don't," Savage says.

"Don't what?"

The woman watches Savage. Angie is deep in the shadows. The light is soft. Water laps against the wharf.

The big man adjusts his weight, and his eyes begin to flit from side to side. His breathing gets heavier.

"Go now, Juan. Get out of here and make it easy on yourself. Apologize to this young lady and leave."

The man spits on the ground. He mutters again in Spanish, moving his hand towards his jacket pocket.

"No," Savage says. "Leave it. I don't want to hurt you."

"You're the one who is going to get hurt, asshole!"

The man reaches into his jacket. He's quick for a big man, but not quick enough. Savage springs forward, grabs the man's wrist, sweeps his feet from under him, and brings his elbow down on the top of the man's head as he falls to the ground. He struggles to get to his knees, groaning. Savage has him in a wrist lock at the breaking point. The woman has her hands up by her mouth, talking rapidly in Spanish.

"Don't try to fight. Stop it," Savage says as the man groans and tries to get a purchase on the ground.

He kicks out at Savage's shin, but Savage moves effortlessly to avoid it and pushes the man to the ground with his foot. His falling body weight breaks his wrist and the man shrieks in pain, a high-pitched, desperate sound.

"Savage, stop it," Angie pleads. The woman looks at Angie in the shadows, then back to the man, fear in her eyes.

Savage pulls the man's gun from his jacket pocket. "Get up!"

He looks at the woman. "You work here?"

The woman nods.

"You closed up?"

"*Sí.*"

"Go and get me a bottle of tequila. Now."

"Savage," Angie says. "Let it go. Let it go."

Savage is staring at the big man who is clutching his broken wrist, his face twisted, unsteady on his feet.

"Don't shoot," he says. "I'll go. I'll go. Then I'll come back. Then you'll know who I am."

Savage points the pistol at the man's chest, levels it, and steadies his breathing.

"No, Savage! He's gone. You can't bring him back."

The woman's heels click on the concrete as she returns with the tequila.

"Open it and give it to me," Savage says.

She opens the bottle and passes it.

"Now leave. Go. Go home."

She does as he says, walking off into the shadows. Her scooter comes to life and pulls away into the night.

Savage holds the bottle up to the man's lips. "Drink! Now!"

The man opens his mouth and the tequila pours in. He swallows, chokes, and coughs.

"More!" Savage says. "Drink."

Savage tosses the Glock into the water and pulls a butterfly knife from his pocket. He opens it in a single, swift motion and presses the blade against the man's throat. He sees the pulse.

"Drink!"

The man gulps. Savage pours. The man staggers. He's whimpering, clutching his wrist. Drunk, he coughs and slurs something in Spanish. Letting go of his wrist, his face contorts in agony.

"More!"

Savage pours the tequila in. The man can't take much more. He can barely stand.

"Angie, go back to the houseboat." Savage doesn't look at her, but he hears her feet moving from the concrete to the wooden wharf, her footfall fading as she walks away.

The man sways. Savage takes the knife away from his throat and steps back.

"Who are you?" the man says.

"The boatyard," Savage says slowly, his eyes piercing the man. "Stock Island. Mean anything to you?"

The man's face changes. He swallows and closes his eyes, sweat on his brow.

"That was my brother."

"It wasn't me. I didn't do it," the man slurs, tears running down his cheeks.

"Do what?"

"Cut him up."

"Cut him up? They cut him up? Who cut him up?"

"The ones who will kill me if I tell you."

"They won't have to, Juan." Savage puts the knife against his throat again. He presses the blade against the sweaty flesh. "Who?"

"Raul and Stefano."

Savage removes the blade away from the man's throat. The night is still. They're standing in the soft, eerie light.

"We're going for a little walk," Savage says.

The man is swaying. The bottle is almost empty. Savage walks over to the only vehicle in the lot, a black Mercedes, and lays the bottle on the ground next to the driver's door.

"You were too drunk to open the door," Savage says.

"What? I was?"

"Yes," Savage walks back to the man, stabilizes him by putting his palm in the small of his back. "Now walk."

"Where are we going?"

"You were drunk. Very drunk. You went for a walk."

"What are you saying?"

"You were very, very drunk."

"I was? I am. Drunk. What? Where?" The man stumbles again.

Savage pushes him forward towards the old wooden wharf where fishing boats are moored, towards the dark, still water.

Savage stops. He's holding the man's jacket to keep him upright. It's a six-foot drop to the water.

The man can barely keep his head up. He's muttering an *Ave Maria* in Spanish. "Drunk," he splutters.

"When I let go, you're either going to fall forwards or backwards. That's the way this goes, friend."

The man's feet are right at the edge of the wharf. Savage straightens him up and begins to let go of the jacket.

He teeters. His right foot moves forward. He leans. His good arm begins to windmill backwards, slowly at first, and then faster. He grunts.

His other arm hangs, useless, at his side. He twists around as gravity begins to take hold of him. His eyes are wide, whites showing all around. Time stops. Then he falls forward and plummets into the water with barely a splash. He is swallowed and then bobs up, gasping, a single hand reaching desperately for something, anything, but there's nothing. He gasps, chokes, and slips under.

———

"What happened, Savage?" Angie asks.

Savage looks at the floor. "Nothing. We settled things."

"I don't want to know how," Angie says.

Savage steps towards her. She gets up from the couch, and he reaches out.

She pushes him away, but he pulls her close.

"Angie," Savage says.

"Don't say anything, Savage."

He pauses, feels her body against his, and smells her hair and warmth. "I wish it wasn't like this," he says.

"But it is, Savage," she says, taking his hand and leading him to the bedroom. "It is like this."

7

THE CYCLIST

TWO DAYS LATER, the body is recovered by the police and the Mercedes is towed away. The Hog Fish Bar and Grill has come back to life. There was a small story in the local newspaper, but nothing on the news. A drunk was dead, and life went on.

Savage and Angie are staying on the houseboat, unwilling and afraid to leave its security. Tension had arisen between them. They are a couple on the rocks.

Savage wakes up, clears his throat, and rubs his clean-shaven head. He wishes he could go back to sleep. His head feels tight inside. His shoulder aches. He sits up in bed. The early morning light spills in through the window—another beautiful day in paradise.

"What?" Angie says, opening her eyes, her blonde hair draping across the pillow. She looks tired and worried.

A light breeze wafts through the open window. Savage scratches his head. "I'm sorry, Angie."

"I said I'd help, Savage, but I didn't mean I'd help you kill anyone. You understand that, right?" She gets up, picks up her shorts and t-shirt from the chair by the dresser, and puts them on.

"I know, Angie. It's about Jake."

"No, it's about you. It's about revenge. And you. I don't like it. You're like two different people. It can't go on."

Savage hears a boat in the channel outside, the engine throbbing. "You're right. It's me. My problem. My demons. It's not fair. Not right."

He looks up. Angie is watching him, and her face is sad, her blue eyes soft.

"No," Angie says. "It's not. But I know you're not a bad man, Savage. I can feel it. I can feel a lot. Really." She steps towards the bed and then stops herself.

Savage gets up and dresses. "I'm going to slow down," he says. "Think. Take my time. I'm here to figure out what happened to Jake. That's what matters. You're right. It's not about me. It's about him. My brother."

There are tears in Angie's eyes. She leaves the bedroom, goes into the kitchen, and puts the kettle on.

"We had this plan," Savage says. "He was in a good place. Ready to kick back. I was, too. We were going to spend time together. Brothers."

A boat passes, a bigger one with a more powerful engine. It's moving slowly, making its way to the fueling dock.

Savage walks over the window and watches it pass. A Contender. It's sleek and expensive. He sees it turn towards the dock as it glides in.

"Savage," Angie says. She holds out a mug of coffee for him. He takes it, noticing her face has come back to life.

"Yes?" Savage says. He brings the coffee to his lips, smelling the dark Cuban aroma.

"I don't want anything to happen to you. Jake was my best friend. I loved him." She holds her hand up to her breast. "He was always there for me. Always. He wouldn't want anything to happen to you, either."

"I know, Angie. I know."

"There was something on his mind, I know," Angie says.

"Something he wasn't talking about. He kept a lot to himself. He never complained, ever."

Angie shakes her head, walks into the living room, and opens the doors onto the deck overlooking the smooth water. "I keep expecting him to walk in," she continues, "to call, to drop by. I wish I could see that smile again—his curly hair, that laugh. I can't get used to him not being around."

Savage is behind her. He strokes her head and runs his hand down her hair. "I'm not crazy," he says.

Angie turns. "I hope not, Savage. But you have to stop it, okay? You have to."

"Let's go for a run," Savage says. "A long one, around the island. Nice and slow."

"A run?" she says.

"Yes. I need to clear my head."

Angie reaches out and strokes his face. "Okay, crazy man. Give me five minutes."

———

They jog up North Roosevelt, along the bike path. It's hot, and Savage is sweating. Angie is running a few yards ahead of him. They pass an old man walking his Maltese and an elderly couple in matching Polo shirts and shorts.

"Pink doesn't work for me," Savage says.

"I don't know," Angie says. "It could work."

"I'm not a runner," Savage pants. "I'm in shape and I've got stamina, but I'm not a runner. You're a runner. Slow down."

"Was a runner," Angie says. "I was a runner. Not anymore."

Savage grits his teeth and digs in.

"Tell me something. All this monk stuff, and the military story. Did you make it all up?"

"No, I didn't. And I can't tell you anymore."

"You can't?"

"I can hardly breathe," Savage gasps.

A bicycle passes, moving fast, the rider bent low over the frame. He looks like a triathlete in training.

Angie slows down as they approach the intersection by the yacht basin. There's a sudden squeal of tires and the sound of the bicycle bouncing off a car.

"Shit!" Savage shouts, sprinting ahead to the downed cyclist. His bike is half under the car, the back wheel still spinning.

Savage crouches down next to the cyclist, who is lying on his back groaning, his chest rising and falling.

"Don't move," Savage says. He checks for cuts, breaks, or other injuries, then takes off the cyclist's sunglasses and looks at his pupils.

"You feel okay?" Savage says. "Flex your fingers and toes."

The man flexes his fingers then moves his head. He raises one grazed knee.

"I think so. Yeah. Yeah. I'm okay. The light was green, man. I had that light. That guy ran it, man."

The driver is out of the car, moving towards Savage.

"*Que demonios!*" he shouts. He gets back in the car and reverses over the back wheel, buckling it completely before pulling forward and then reversing again over the bike, cursing in Spanish and banging the steering wheel.

The bicyclist gets to his feet. He's a little unsteady but unharmed. Savage stabilizes him and watches as the driver reverses over the bike again.

He looks at Angie and she shakes her head.

"No, Savage," she says. "No."

"I can't believe it, man! Hey, what the hell are you doing? You ran the light. Stop!"

A small crowd has gathered.

"*Idiota!*" the driver shouts through the open window, shaking his fist at the cyclist.

The cyclist shakes his head in disbelief and moves towards the car, heading straight for the driver's window. The car stops. A hand shoots out and grabs the cyclist by his shirt and pulls him into the open window.

"No, Savage!" Angie shouts.

Savage is there in two bounds. He jabs the driver's eyes with a spear hand strike, then grabs the thumbs holding the cyclist's shirt and twists them until the driver lets out a bleating yelp and lets go.

Savage's hand shoots into the man's jacket and grabs his wallet. He looks at the license. "Ramirez."

Savage pushes the cyclist back with an open palm, then takes out the stack of hundred-dollar bills that are in the wallet and throws the empty wallet back into the car.

"Your fault. You pay. There were witnesses. You ran the light."

The furious driver harangues Savage in Spanish, foaming at the mouth.

Angie is at Savage's side, six feet from the car. "Let's get out of here, now. This won't end well. Please." Her voice is pleading.

Savage steps into the road and picks up the battered bicycle and pulls it to the curb.

"He's crazy," the cyclist says. "Crazy. You saw what happened, right?"

"You had the right of way, yes, I saw that," Savage says.

The driver spits at Savage, still shouting. He peels out, leaving two slicks of rubber on the road. The crowd begins to disperse. The old man with the Maltese walks past.

"What's your name?" Savage asks.

"Brandon."

"You sure you're okay?"

"Yeah," Brandon says, picking up his bike. "Destroyed. He destroyed it. Carbon fiber. Man."

"Savage!" Angie pulls at Savage's arm.

The Mercedes has gone. Only Brandon, Angie, and Savage are standing at the intersection. The traffic is flowing again.

Brandon takes of his yellow helmet.

"Here," Savage says. He hands Brandon the stack of hundreds.

"What's this?"

"He wanted you to have it. Said he has anger issues. Take it. He didn't want to deal with the police and the insurance company."

Brandon looks at the stack and counts it carefully. "Wow. He said that?"

Savage nods, but Brandon is still counting.

"I guess it's time for an upgrade," Brandon says.

"Let's just pretend it never happened," Savage says.

"Okay," Brandon says. "It never happened. What's your name?"

Savage gives a brief salute, turns and jogs off.

"Guess it never happened," Brandon shouts after him.

———

They jog on. Angie is silent. She has picked up the pace.

"Did you see the license plate?" Savage asks.

"RAM2. Florida plate."

"What strange webs we weave," Savage says.

"No shit. I told you not to do anything."

"And I didn't!"

"You stole his wallet! You poked him in the eyes and twisted his thumbs half off."

"I held back," Savage says, "on purpose. I listened."

"Well, that will just piss him off."

"That guy Brandon could have been killed."

"Could have been. But he wasn't."

"Sorry," Savage says.

"Stop saying sorry. What is it about English people and saying sorry? You're not sorry. You're just trying to shut me up, Savage. All I'm saying is that ... oh, never mind."

Angie pulls ahead, passing a couple pulling a double wide stroller with twins in it.

"Slow down," Savage says.

They fall into silence.

Angie stops by a small park.

"We're stopping?" Savage asks.

"I'm stopping," Angie says.

"Look..."

"Don't, Savage. Don't say you're sorry, okay?" Angie walks off a few paces, sits on the ground, and starts to do some crunches. Savage turns away, instead watching a skateboarder pass on the sidewalk.

A biplane is flying overhead. It's towing a banner saying, *"Maria, will you marry me?"*

Then he notices a black Mercedes parked ahead, behind a juice vendor next to the seawall. He walks towards it.

"Where are you going, Savage?"

"To look at the sea," Savage says.

RAM2, Savage reads. The vehicle is empty.

Savage hears a man's voice talking loudly from the beach. He turns.

Stefano Ramirez is sitting next to two sunbathing women. He is gesticulating. Both the women are looking at him, propped on their elbows. They are dark, gleaming with oil.

Savage walks back to the Mercedes, pulls a key from his shorts pocket, and scratches two fish on the driver's door, just below the handle.

"Something for you to think about, amigo. Two fishes. Two brothers."

He can hear the women talking now. He doesn't look back. He walks to the park. Angie is doing push-ups.

"You're impressive," Savage says.

"Yeah," Angie says. "I've nearly got rid of it."

"Of what?"

"My anger!"

"Anger?" Savage sounds surprised, "I didn't do anything, did I?"

Angie gets up, shakes her legs out, and begins to jog again. "You're going to have to keep up. And not a word. Not one word."

Savage tries to keep up, in total silence.

8

VICTORY

"I WAS WAITING for you to call," Nikki says, standing behind the bar as Savage walks in. The fans turn slowly overhead, pushing the heavy, thick air.

"Sorry, there's a lot going on. But on the bright side, here I am." Savage slaps his large palms on the bar.

It's early evening, and the Whistle is virtually empty. The windows are open and the sound of traffic from Duval Street drifts in.

"Yes," Nikki says, eyeing him closely. "Here you are."

Nikki sweeps her long black hair back over her shoulder. Savage takes a step to get a stool and pulls a stool over.

"You know, you move just like Jake."

Savage takes off his baseball cap and sunglasses, sits on the stool and puts his elbows on the bar. He rests his chin on his knuckles.

"I can't change the way I move. I move how I move."

"You don't have to change it. I kinda like it."

"Kinda?"

Nikki winks and sweeps her long black hair back over her shoulder. She looks down and methodically wipes the bar.

"He had a boat," she says quietly. "He moved most of his stuff out there."

Savage frowns and grunts. "Well, he built them. I guess it's not a surprise he had one."

"He didn't build this one. It was some kind of deal. A guy owed him a lot of money and he couldn't pay. Jake got the boat instead. I don't think he wanted it, really. It's off Stock Island. *Victory*."

Savage chuckles. "Typical."

"What?"

"I bet it wasn't called that when he got her."

"No. It was called *Mirabelle*, something like that."

An older man in shorts and a white shirt walks in to the bar. He looks around, then walks out.

"*Victory* was Nelson's flagship. You know, Admiral Nelson," Savage says. "Trafalgar. 'Kiss me Hardy', and all that."

Nikki gives a small laugh, remembering. "He told me. I thought he said, 'Kiss me harder'. We laughed about that."

"Very Jake. Dry but funny. Runs in the family," Savage says. "That's how he was. A private joke. He would like it if people knew, though not many people would."

"Yes," Nikki says, drawing the word out. "He was his own guy, that's for sure. Runs in the family, too, I imagine."

She smiles, and their eyes meet. Savage feels the flutter.

"He has his stuff on the boat." Savage leans forward. "I need to check it out. See what's there. Who knows? Something might turn up."

"Like what?"

"I don't know. It doesn't matter. A note, a letter, a computer file, a phone. Something."

"Okay," Nikki says. "But be careful. No one knew. He hardly went out there. Like I said—no one knew."

"Not even Angie?"

"Angie? Definitely not Angie." Nikki looks away. "What is it about you and Angie? Is there something between you?" She turns back to him, her black eyes fixed on his.

"I like her," Savage says, not looking away. Expressionless. Ice-blue eyes.

"She's cute," Nikki says. "Guys like her. Blonde. Obvious." Nikki shakes her head, looks up, closes her eyes. Her neck is long and slender. "Be careful with Angie."

"Why?"

"She was a mess when she first got to Key West. That was before Jake knew her. She did a lot of stuff." Nikki pauses and adjusts some bottles behind the bar. "She got into some trouble."

"What kind of trouble?"

"Doesn't matter. Just be careful."

"Stay away from her? Not be with her, you mean?"

"You're with Angie?" Nikki says, unable to disguise her surprise.

"I'm staying with her. You know. Things happen."

Nikki turns away, picks up a towel, and puts it down. "Figures," she mutters. "Jesus. Sometimes."

"Is this a girl thing?"

"Maybe. Don't ask. I'm pissed."

"Want to tell me more?"

"No. Not really. Definitely not now."

The air is fraught between them. Savage clears his throat.

"Listen," he says, "I like her, okay? I like you too. You're both Jake's friends. That's important to me."

"Savage," Nikki says, her voice clipped, "I'm only going to say this once. So, listen. When you first walked in here, there was something about you. Believe me, I've seen a lot of guys. But you... I noticed you. You know? I don't have to explain."

Nikki walks to the end of the bar, picks up two glasses, and brings them to the sink.

"Angie worked at a place the Ramirez brothers ran. She was

close with them for a while. Very close. You hear what I'm saying?"

"I hear you. I'm not sure if I know what you're saying, though."

"I'm just saying be careful."

Savage watches Nikki's face, trying to catch her eye. He rubs his chin, contemplating what he's just been told.

"Are you looking out for me?"

Kind of... bastard." She looks away.

"If you weren't working tonight, I'd take you out for dinner," Savage says.

"How do you know I'd go?"

"You would," Savage says. "And by the way—I like you."

Two young men in Lost Reef Adventure t-shirts walk in. Nikki moves down the bar to serve them. The men are sunburnt, excited, and laughing. Savage looks in the mirror behind the bar and sees his own blue eyes, staring at him.

Things to do, he thinks.

Nikki comes back. Savage puts a twenty on the counter.

"I like you, too," she says.

"I've got to go," Savage says, placing his hand over hers.

She doesn't pull it away.

————

Savage rides his bike down South Roosevelt, crosses to Stock Island, and padlocks it to a tree. He goes to the rental shop next to the Hogfish Bar and Grill and gets a paddleboard for a couple of hours. He keeps his t-shirt on, along with his black baseball cap and Native sunglasses.

"You done this before?" the young man asks, not really caring, his voice laconic.

"Oh, yeah," Savage says, "I'll be fine."

He steps onto the board with an easy confidence, and the

young man walks off. Savage eases himself away from the dock with strong, steady strokes of the long paddle. He passes a pelican sitting on a piling. A fishing boat comes in to fuel at the dock, a fat middle-aged man at the wheel, two teenage girls in bikinis behind him, laughing and chatting. One looks at Savage. Then the other.

Savage paddles east, around the mangroves and into the channel where the smattering of pleasure boats lie at anchor. There's is a light breeze rippling the water, and the sun glints on the tiny waves. Savage digs his paddle in, moving it with short, measured strokes, turning his shoulders with each pull. He paddles from boat to boat. He checks the names on the stern as he passes by. There's is no sign of *Victory*.

Then, at the end of the row, near where the channel opens into the gulf, he sees her—a beautiful two-masted trimaran. *Victory* is written in beautiful italics in black on the pristine white hull. Savage paddles alongside, climbs up onto the port outrigger, leans back down, and pulls the paddleboard onto the webbing that covers the space between the main hull and the outrigger. He flips the board, puts it on the webbing, and makes his way to the central hull and the cockpit.

The hatch to the cabin is locked. Savages removes the keys he took from Jake's apartment from his pocket and tries them one after the other. The fourth key slides in, and he turns it and feels the click as the padlock is released. He opens the hatch and climbs down the steps into the spacious cabin.

It's neat, well laid out for blue water sailing. A serious, professional vessel. Savage looks around. GPS. Radar. Chart table. Everything is clean; nothing out of place. The air is surprisingly fresh, as if it has recently been aired out. Savage raises his eyebrows.

On the table at the far end of the cabin is a copy of the *Key West Citizen*. Savage picks it up. November 22nd. The headline reads, *One Dead in Mystery Boatyard Fire*. Savage looks closer, skimming the article. There are no real details. He re-reads it more thoroughly and stops at the last sentence: *Remains, presumed to be of the boatyard owner, Jake Savage, were discovered at the site. The cause of the fire is unknown.* He had read the paper before, but not in the same dispassionate way. His heartbeat picks up, 'presumed to be', he mutters. He puts the paper down and looks around the cabin. 'Presumed to be,' he repeats. He looks at the dateline again. Two days after the fire.

"So, what are you saying?" Angie asks, leaning forward in her chair on the back deck of the houseboat.

Savage is standing, looking down at her, still in his surf shorts, black t-shirt, black baseball hat and sunglasses.

"The copy of the *Key West Citizen* that was on the table was datelined two days after the fire. Two days. See what I'm saying?" Savage's eyes are sharp, excited. "He's alive!"

"Jake's dead, Savage. I don't see what you're saying." Angie pulls at her index finger and clears her throat.

"Look," Savage continues, "you said it was all very quick. No real investigation. Circumstantial evidence. They said, 'presumed to be' and that's it. Case over. Back to business as usual in paradise. All good. No family. No relatives. No uproar."

Angie takes off her sunglasses. "Two days after," she says in disbelief. "Two days after, so ... We don't know though," she continues, "for sure."

"No. Not for sure. But..." Savage looks out towards the mangrove swamps. They're green, but reflecting the perfect blue of the sky above.

"Oh, God," Angie says, putting her sunglasses back on. "I don't know if I can dare to hope. Oh, Jake," she shakes her head. "Please be alive."

Then she starts. "I didn't even know he had a boat. Apart from his little fishing boat. How did you know?"

"Nikki," Savage says.

"Oh. Well, that figures," she snaps.

Savage adjusts his baseball hat and looks down at Angie. Her face is concealed behind her straw hat.

"Savage. I have to tell you something. A while back, years ago, when I first got here, after Hurricane Katrina, I was working at a bar the Ramirez brothers had just bought. I didn't know anything about them. We were all new in town. Fun times, you know. I had this, this thing with Stefano, the younger brother. It wasn't a big deal. It was just a bit of fun for me, until it wasn't. He started to act like he owned me."

Savage looks thunderstruck. He thinks of Nikki. *Be careful.* He feels his body change, becoming alert and ready. His mind focuses.

"It's in the past. This is a long time ago. I've let it all go. But Nikki won't let it go. She's never trusted me."

Savage replays Nikki's words in his mind while he watches Angie's face.

"I'm just telling you, Savage. Now, maybe Jake…"

"The boat was locked when I got there. I unlocked it. The paper was right there. I thought it was just left there—you know, in the way papers are left. But now…"

"Now what?"

"Part of me thinks Jake left it there for me to find. He knew I would."

"I don't get it," Angie says, putting her head in her hands and letting out a sigh.

Savage steps over and strokes her hair. "It was good to tell me," he says. "About Ramirez. Stefano."

"It was a long time ago. I hate him. I hate them." Angie is crying.

Savage takes his hand from Angie's hair and wipes the tear from her cheek. She looks up.

"Listen," she says, "this is a small town. You're going to run into Stefano again, sooner or later. Raul is dead. One of his other heavies is dead. He knows. You've been seen."

"I'm just a guy in surf shorts and sunglasses. There are a lot of guys in shorts and sunglasses."

"Not like you, Savage. Believe me. You shouldn't go to the Whistle or to see Nikki."

"Is this about me or you? Sounds a bit like it's about you, Angie."

"No, it's not about me. It's about Jake. You're his brother. He was my best friend. The rest doesn't matter." Angie makes a dismissive gesture with her hand and stands up. She steps into Savage's arms, and he comforts her.

"I've got an idea," Savage says.

"That's all we need."

"No, really."

"Tell me then, mystery man."

"Want to go away for a few days?"

"How about a few months? A couple of years? Sure. I'm tired. I'm tired of making jewelry for tourists. Tired of two-bit jobs. My heart is aching for Jake."

She looks up into Savage's face and takes off her sunglasses. He sees her exhaustion.

"I've had enough," she says.

"So let's go. It'll take your mind off things. Our minds off things."

"Jesus. If it's not one thing, it's another. What is it with you Savages? Always on the go, never still, always up to something, always having ideas. Your brother's the same. I should have learned by now."

"I'm going to make you a list, Angie. You need to go to the store. Provisions."

"I need to go?"

"You. I'm lying low. Remember?"

Angie goes into the houseboat. Savage watches her in her yellow bikini. Not too much later, she comes back out in shorts and a halter top.

"Make the list. Then let's go on vacation. Savage, I don't know what's happening. One minute, Jake's dead and now..."

"I know," Savage says, "but that's what we're going to do. It's the right thing to do."

"How do you know? And what would you know about *right* things to do?

"Trust me. When I know, I know. Right now, I know."

"What about those other times?"

Savage ignores the question. He goes into the houseboat and writes a list on a pink post-it note, and then goes back out.

"Hope for the best. Prepare for the worst. Right?" he says, a lightness to his voice.

"I guess."

Savage gives Angie the list and some cash.

"Where are we going to go?"

"Trust me," Savage says.

"Do you trust *me*?" she asks.

"Almost. Not quite. There's something I haven't quite figured out," Savage says. He wants to ask Angie more about Ramirez.

"I'll be about an hour. Then I'll have to pack. Okay?"

Savage knows there is something important she isn't telling him.

"Yes," he says as she walks away. He watches the way she moves and feels the stirring.

————

The breeze comes in from the southwest and *Victory* is heading due east on a broad reach, doing fourteen knots. The sails are trimmed perfectly and the main hull and port outrigger effort-lessly slice the creamy turquoise waters.

Angie is at the wheel, looking at the compass.

"Keep her on this heading, Angie. I need to check a few things."

"Don't be too long. I don't know what I'm doing." Her voice is tense.

"Do what you're doing. Let me know if you see any other vessels."

"You're a sailor too? A monk and a soldier and a sailor?"

"I've done a bit," he says, jumping out of the cockpit and walking past the first mast. He ties off a loose line, comes back, and goes below.

"What haven't you done?"

"A lot."

A gust of wind ruffles the water, and *Victory* heels and accelerates.

"Savage!"

"You're fine." He comes up the companionway.

"Where are we going?" she asks.

"We'll put in at Sugarloaf Key, get organized, spend the night there. Then..."

"Then?"

Victory rights herself and slows. Savage then takes the wheel. "Then I'll let you know."

Angie stays by his side, looking off towards the horizon. She sighs. "One day I'll tell you everything, but not today."

"Remember the day we met?" Savage says. He checks the compass and adjusts the wheel.

"How could I forget? It was in Jake's apartment on a rainy day. You were hiding like some burglar, and then those guys..."

"Right. Did you notice anything unusual in the apartment?" Savage looks up at the sails.

"Just this big guy who bore an uncanny likeness to Jake, except he was in shape."

"Did Jake have a computer, or did he just use his phone?"

"He hardly used his phone at all. He did have a computer. A laptop. A MacBook. He kept it on his desk. Wait a minute."

Savage remains silent.

"Wait a minute. It wasn't there. His desk was clear. I noticed that."

"It's all below deck, neatly stashed. Some notebooks. And a MacBook."

"So..." Angie begins, drawing out the word, thinking.

"Precisely," Savage says.

————

"Hold her into wind, like that. Yes. Perfect." Savage starts the engine. "I'll drop the sails."

Victory lies still in the water. The sails flap in the breeze. Savage drops the first main, reels it to the boom, does the same to the second, and then furls the genoa. He works quickly, efficiently, comfortable on his feet. It's easy on the boat.

"There," Savage says engaging the engine. "Follow the channel markers in. Keep the green cans to the left."

Victory begins to move. Angie steers.

"You trust me?" Angie says.

"At the helm? Yes." He puts his arm around her and squeezes.

"Jake trusted me. I'm not just a pretty face, you know."

They pass the first green buoy, moving at a steady three knots.

"I know," Savage says. "He told me." He doesn't tell her what else Jake had told him.

The sun is sinking to the west. The sky takes on a golden orange hue. The wind drops and the sea is still and flat.

Victory is lying at anchor in a lagoon a quarter mile off shore, far from any boat. Savage has dropped a second anchor for safety, checked the weather, and listened in on the shipping channel. He scans the sky for signs of wind but sees nothing.

Angie is sitting on the webbing between the main hull and the outrigger.

"You think he's alive. Right, Savage?"

Savage steps onto the webbing and then over to Angie. She's

in her yellow bikini, her golden hair hanging down over her shoulders.

Savage rotates his shoulders. He sits and rubs Angie's thigh, and she leans towards him.

"I know he's alive."

"Let's go below," she says, taking Savage's hand as he gets to his feet.

9

COAST GUARD

THE US COAST GUARD ZODIAC skims through the chop, a machine gun mounted in the bow, four Coast Guardsmen onboard. The cutter it came from is also bearing down on *Victory*. She is on a heading due south, fifteen miles north of the Cuban coast, three miles outside Cuban territorial waters—a fact of interest to the Coast Guard.

As the Zodiac draws closer, Savage hears the crackle of the onboard speaker system.

"This is the US Coast Guard; heave to and prepare for boarding. Repeat. This is the US Coast Guard; heave to and prepare for boarding."

Savage can see the Guardsman who is making the announcement. Sunglasses, peaked cap, dark blue uniform, lifejacket. All business.

Savage has been sailing for three days, having cleared the Keys unseen at night. He has combed the boat from stem to stern. He knows exactly what's onboard and what isn't. He furls the jib and lowers the mainsails. He starts the engine and engages it just enough to hold her into wind, facing due west. His movements are unhurried, purposeful, and professional.

He feels the warm breeze on his face. Sunlight dances on the water. Savage squints.

The Zodiac appears at the stern. Three Guardsmen come up the stern ladder and into the cockpit. They're all wearing sunglasses and dark uniforms. They're armed, fit-looking men. They know what they're doing. This isn't a social visit. They're used to boarding boats, and they do it often. A lot happens in these waters; much of it illegal. Savage isn't surprised. He isn't worried. Uniforms and protocols are familiar to him. He stands straight, arms by his side.

"U.S. Coastguard, sir. Standard procedure for these waters. Stay at the helm. Keep her into wind."

"Not a problem." Savage doesn't question the claim of 'standard procedure'. He says nothing. He keeps *Victory* headed due west as the officers below look around. He can hear their voices but not what they're saying. He looks at the Zodiac to the stern. The officer onboard is staring at him, expressionless. Savage can't see his eyes behind the sunglasses. He knows they're looking for something. Or someone.

"You're three miles north of Cuban waters, sir. Are you aware of that?"

"I am. We're heading east. Turks and Caicos."

"Vacation?"

"Cruising," Savage says. "No particular plan."

No one has asked to see Savage's ID or *Victory*'s registration. That, Savage knows, is standard procedure.

The officer looks at Savage. Savage takes off his sunglasses, and lets the officer see his eyes. He smiles. The officer's face is blank.

"Nice breeze, though," Savage says. The officer nods. He doesn't take his eyes off Savage.

Savage hears the other men talking below. They're opening cupboards and drawers. Their search is systematic, practiced and careful. He doesn't feel they think he's a suspect in anything, but he senses it could circle the drain quickly.

"Your accent... Australia?"

"English. But I've been around. It's worn off a little."

"Out of Key West?" the officer says.

"Uh huh," Savage says. "Today. She's registered in London." He knows the officer is trying to keep him talking, to get him to say something that won't add up. The officer looks at Savage, then hears a noise and turns.

Angie is coming up the companionway, stretching. She's in a bikini with a white cotton top, and Savage winks at her as she comes onto the deck. *Smart girl*, he thinks.

"Oh, hi. I didn't know we had company." Angie moves her hips, smiling brightly. "Ooh, the Coast Guard. I love men in uniform."

The officer looks at Angie and then looks away. Then he looks back at Savage. Savage shrugs his shoulders. "I know," he says. "What can I say?"

The officer laughs.

There's a clattering of footsteps on the companionway, and the two other officers emerge.

"All clear, sir," the officer says. His voice doesn't have the conviction of a man who truly feels that things are 'all clear'.

The officers look at each other, then back at Savage. Savage stares into the westerly wind. There's a fleeting moment of tension when something could be said. Something could happen, but it doesn't.

"Very good. Thank you, sir. Have a safe trip. Perhaps we'll see you again." The officer is chisel-faced and expressionless.

"Three miles, sir, remember that," one officer says, pointing south, in the direction of Cuba.

"Yes, sir," Savage says. The officers prepare to climb into the Zodiac.

"You take care, officers. It's been a pleasure having you on board," Angie says.

Savage keeps *Victory* on her heading, the engine ticking over, holding her in position against the oncoming breeze. The officers board the Zodiac, push off, and then the twin outboards engage. Savage doesn't watch them leave, but just listens without moving. He stays at the wheel, thinking.

As the Zodiac turns to the north to head back to the cutter, Savage unfurls the jib. He hoists both mainsails, taking his time, working methodically. When the sails are up, he returns to the wheel, disengages the autopilot, bears off, and waits for the sails to fill. As they do, the boat begins to heel and then slowly pick up speed, in the breeze. To the north, the Coast Guard cutter recedes into the distance, heading for the Keys.

Victory bears off, until she's on an easterly heading. The sails are trimmed and the trimaran picks up speed, listing in the breeze.

"What was that about?" Angie asks, her hair blowing behind her. She's holding onto the railing around the cockpit.

"They said it was standard procedure. We're close to Cuban waters."

"Is that a problem?"

"Well, yeah, potentially. For an American vessel. American vessels can't sail to Cuba. But this isn't an American vessel. She's registered in London. But they were looking for something. Or someone."

"Weird," Angie says.

"Guess we'll never know," Savage says.

"Never say never," Angie says.

She stretches, and Savage looks at her. He feels a stirring and reaches out to her. Taking her wrist, he pulls her towards him.

"Jake's alive, Angie."

Angie's eyes open wide, and her lips part.

Savage enjoys her pleasure, the light in her eyes, the relief. She clenches both hands and bounces on the spot.

"What? How do you know?"

"It's on his laptop. He's left a short story. He knew I'd read it. He's in Trinidad, Cuba. The southern coast. That's where we're going."

"Oh, my God! You're sure? Oh, God." Angie lifts her hands to her mouth. She has tears in her eyes. "I can't believe it. I can't believe it."

"He's alive, Angie. Dead certain."

Angie wraps her arms around Savage.

Savage bears away, the boat heading off the wind, then jibing, as he sets a new course, west south west, to clear the western tip of Cuba in order to harden up and head east to Trinidad.

"Clever, that's what you are. Both of you. Jake's alive."

"I'm prepared to bet on it," Savage says. "But, there's something going on that I don't understand."

"Like what?"

Savage monitors Angie's face, looking for something, a glimmer of knowledge, a hint of fear, something to tell him that she knows something she's not telling him. He's not sure, but his gut tells him. He wonders whether to push, but decides not to.

"I don't know yet," Savage says. "Get some sleep. I need to check the charts and make sure everything's in order for a night passage. We'll be there tomorrow. We'll take four-hour watches. I'll wake you when it's your turn."

After Angie goes to her berth in the stern, Savage returns to the computer. He finds the story he'd skimmed through earlier, *Cuba Libra*—it's in a folder labeled "JSFiction."

The story is loosely based on the boatyard and life in Key West. The protagonist is clearly Jake. He—in the story—is under pressure to sell the yard, but there's nothing explicit in terms of a reason, just a tone of tension and foreboding. People are watching the yard; there are break-ins. The story reads smoothly, but interjected in the story, in italics, are non sequiturs.

I know you'll get it. Not what it seems. Complicated but better (and worse). (21°48'06" N 79°59'03 W). Old Sugar Mill. Delete this.

The coordinates were for Trinidad, Cuba. Jake had to know that Savage would find the boat, find the computer, and read the story. Savage commits the coordinates to memory and deletes the paragraph.

On Angie's second watch, just before dawn, Savage opens the safe with one of the keys from Jake's apartment. There's nothing of interest—no cash, no weapons, no files. Just a flash drive and a silver coin.

The coin is old. Savage recognizes the two pillars of Hercules on one side and the Spanish coat of arms on the other. It was most likely minted in the New World and then shipped back to Spain in the sixteenth century. There's just one coin, which seems odd. Savage scratches his head, then rubs his shoulder. Jake left it there for him to tell him something. There's no reason to leave just one coin in the safe unless it's meant to be a sign. One coin could mean more coins—a fortune. Savage can't be sure, but he's willing to bet that Jake somehow came across a trove, and he wanted his brother to know this.

Savage takes the flash drive back to the computer, downloads all the files, and emails them to himself. He then deletes all the downloaded files, and on his next watch, throws the flash drive overboard.

———

As the sun rises, Savage is sitting on the cabin roof, cross-legged, his breathing slow and regular, his mind settled. When he uncrosses his legs and stands up, he feels clear. He has untangled his thoughts, separated observations from feelings, and has come to a certain clarity. Angie is not telling him something, and it is something important. He'll watch her. He can't tell if she is a threat somehow, but she may be. He'll only tell her what she needs to know. Perhaps he'll tell her things to see what she does. She will be tested.

"Beautiful," Angie said, as the sun slowly inches above the distant horizon.

The sails are furled, and *Victory* is making five knots as she makes her way north to the marina of Sancti Spiritus.

"Have you been here before?" Angie asks.

"A long time ago. It's an old colonial town. Very nice. Sixteenth century architecture. Different from Havana. I like it. It really comes alive at about midnight. Good jazz."

"Where do you think he is?" Angie asks.

"Somewhere," Savage says. "I don't know." Though he does. Savage stares at Angie. His blue gray eyes are intense.

"Stop it!" Angie says.

"What?"

"Looking at me like that, Savage!"

Savage consults the compass. "Angie?" He turns again and looks at her, his eyes piercing.

"What? You're making me uncomfortable." Angie edges away from him.

"Is there something you want to tell me? Something you should tell me?"

She doesn't respond. It seems at first she's going to speak, but she doesn't. There is something. He sees the tension in her body.

"What is it, Angie?" Savage's voice is soft but insistent. He will find out.

She looks away. A gull circles overhead and squawks. A fishing boat is coming towards them.

"This is serious, Angie. We're going to get Jake. I don't know what you know, but if you know something, you'd better tell me."

Angie swallows and looks out to sea.

Victory is approaching the marina.

"You're not telling me something, Angie. I sense these things. And I know you know that. Look at you. I can read you like a book. This is serious."

"It's nothing. It doesn't matter. Just drop it, will you? We're nearly there. Let's just get Jake and get out of here."

Savage wants to grab her. His anger is rising. But anger doesn't help. Anger gets people hurt. He wants to leave anger out of this.

"Okay," Savage says, steadying his breathing. "Okay. I'm sorry."

Angie puts her hands on her cheeks, then runs her fingers through her hair. "You scared me, Savage. Don't do that again, please. Get angry like that."

Savage stays silent, thinking, watching the channel markers.

The entrance to the marina is dead ahead, and Savage eases back on the throttle. The breeze has dropped, and the water is glassy smooth. Savage smells land and makes out the buildings along the shore.

"Hey, Angie," Savage says, and she turns. "I want this to all be okay." He continues: "I want to get Jake and get out of here. I need you to help me. I wasn't angry with you."

He was.

"It's just... you know..." Savage shrugs. "All that's happened. You know?"

Angie nods, but something about her demeanor and the expression in her eyes leaves Savage unsettled.

I'm going to watch you, he thinks. Carefully—very carefully.

10

CUBA

"BETTER TO STAY ON BOARD, Angie. Always have someone onboard, that's what they say. Basic rule of seamanship in a foreign port. You never know." Savage secures the mooring lines. He needs to keep her close, but not too close—just close enough to make her think she knows everything.

"Will you be long?" Angie's tone is apprehensive.

"As long as it takes. I'm going to try to find Jake and bring him back here. But you never know."

Angie rubs her hands together, then scratches her forearm. "What if something happens? Give me a time. Something to focus on."

"It's 7:00 pm right now. I'll be back by midnight. If not, then you can assume something's happened."

"Something's happened? What does that mean? Savage, I'm getting scared."

Savage runs through a checklist in his mind. The boat is secure. The safe locked. He has the ignition key. It's nearly time.

He looks up to see a sliver of a moon and stars sparkling against a black sky. He hears voices from the dock as the smell of food wafts through the thick air, and the water rhythmically laps against the hull of the boat.

"It means I can't get back. And if I don't get back, you're on your own. You'll have to figure a way out."

"Jesus, Savage. This is serious."

He rotates his shoulder and winces. "It is, Angie. But we're in it now and can't turn back. We've got to find Jake, and this is our best shot. Okay?"

Angie clasps her hands again. Savage steps over, gives her a hug, holds her close, and then lets go, turns, jumps onto the dock, and walks towards town. He looks back once. Angie is watching him. She waves.

Something doesn't feel right.

Savage flags down a cab, a 1956 Chevy Bel Air. The driver is sleepy but friendly. He patiently listens to Savage's Spanish, repeats the address, then drives off. The radio is on, and the driver hums along with the lyrics. Savage looks out of the window as they wind their way out of town. He's surprised by how few lights there are. He thinks of Jake and wonders what Angie's secret is.

Twenty minutes later, Savage watches the cab turn, gears grinding, and head back to the main road, leaving him by the abandoned sugar mill. There are no street lights. The air is sultry. It's dark; clouds have moved in. The sliver of a moon is not visible, and there are no stars. Not a good time to be looking for someone in an abandoned sugar mill. But then he didn't have to look. Part of the deleted message in the story had read, "You find the mill, I'll find you."

The clamor of cicadas fills the heavy air. He stays still, waiting for his eyes to adjust and his ears to begin to filter the new sounds that fill the thick darkness. There is a light in a house a few hundred yards up the road.

A vehicle turns off the main road, its headlights sweeping through the darkness, until they light up the road where Savage is.

The car comes towards him, but is still two hundred yards away. Savage is alert. In the moment. He makes no sound as he walks slowly towards the sugar mill. His arms are loose, by his side. His eyes sweep the darkness. At the mill, he finds a passage between two buildings which he follows until he is out of sight from the road.

The acoustics change. The air is different, stagnant. There's a smell he can't put his finger on; something rank.

Savage opens a door and discovers steps leading up into the darkness. He can hear his own breathing. He goes up, looking for a vantage point. At the second floor, he comes to a glassless window. He stops.

There is nothing to do but wait. The car continues slowly down the road, passes the mill then turns into the driveway of the house Savage saw earlier. It stops. A door opens, then another. Savage squints, but darkness is thick and oppressive. He listens. One door closes, then the other.

Savage hears the voices of two men. He watches, not taking his eyes off the car. One man goes into the house, but the other doesn't. Savage's eyes adjust to the darkness. The man by the car is tall and well built. He turns and walks away from the house, down the road towards the mill. A shadowy figure, moving slowly.

Savage is kneeling on the hard floor, waiting and watching. He has no weapon. Jake is here somewhere. Angie is on the boat. Angie. Savage wonders what it is that isn't right. There's something. The man has stopped. Something she can't bring herself to tell him. He trusts his instincts. They've saved him often enough before.

A noise comes from downstairs, followed by silence, and then he hears footsteps. The boards creak with every step. Savage quietly gets to his feet and stands behind the door. He stills his breathing and waits. The footsteps are coming from the staircase now, in slow, measured steps.

Savage's legs are bent. He is loose and ready. He flexes his fingers, swallows, and listens.

The message had said, "I'll find you." It could be Jake, but it might not be. Prepare for the worst; hope for the best. Strike quickly and make it count. Savage doesn't have to think about this. He is trained. The adrenaline comes, but Savage is in control. There is no tension in his body. He is balanced and ready to move with speed. He can disarm and kill as soon as anyone enters the room.

There is a soft howl that is barely audible. Savage swallows and breathes in deeply, exhales, then steps out from behind the door. He walks out of the room to the hallway and hears the howl again. It's coming from the bottom of the stairs.

Savage turns away from the window and looks down the stairway. He's sure, yet not sure.

"Jake? Is that you?"

The figure moves. "Griff? It's me. Yes, Jesus, it's me."

"Quiet," Savage whispers. "There's a guy on the street."

"I know," Jake says. His voice is deeper than Savage remembers.

Savage comes down the stairs quickly and silently. At the bottom, without thinking, he pulls Jake towards him, hugging him hard. He feels the tears coming.

"I thought you were dead, Jesus."

"I nearly was, Griff. I nearly was."

Savage holds his finger up to his lips. He steps past Jake, out into the alley, and makes his way towards the street. Jake follows.

At the corner of the building, Savage stops. He peers around the corner and notices the man has stopped walking. He's smoking a cigarette. Back to the mill, facing the house. Then he starts to walk back to the house.

"Who's that guy?" Savage whispers.

"It's okay. People I know. Relax."

"Not easy to do these days. I saw this car. Two guys. I was

watching. Waiting. I didn't know if they were something to do with you."

"They're all right. We've done some business. Bit of this. Bit of that."

Savage waits for him to explain, but he doesn't. He takes a step back and eyes his brother up and down. A slight frown.

"I knew you'd find me, Griff. I had no doubt. But still. A close shave."

"I bet. I've had a bit of trouble, too. More than a bit." Savage steps back and looks at his brother.

"You look, different," Savage says.

"80 pounds different. I would look different, right?"

"280?"

"300." Jake feints a punch and a knee job.

"Hasn't slowed you down much, though."

Jake chuckles, a soft laugh Savage remembers. But now isn't the time to remember. Savage peers around the corner again. He sees the light from the house, the man standing in the street.

"It's okay, Griff. I know them."

"Jake, I'm jacked on adrenaline. Waiting like that."

"Well, I'm here now and in one piece."

"Let's keep it that way."

"Follow me, bro." Jake moves in a similar way to Savage. A big man, but moving surprisingly lightly. Easily.

"Glad I didn't have to arrange your funeral."

"You may still have to."

Savage's mind is spinning. He chuckles. "And when I ask you what's been going on, don't tell me it's a long story."

"It's a very long story. How's that?" Jake says.

Jake stops on the dusty road. The noise of cicadas fills the darkness. Savage is sweating.

"Angie's with me."

Jake's eyes move from side to side. "Angie? She's here?" He scratches his head and looks around.

"On the boat. I told her to stay there. Someone had to keep an eye on it."

Jake puts a large hand on the back of his neck. Savage notices the tattoos—a sleeve, intricate and detailed.

"Angie, Angie, Angie," Jake mutters, shaking his head. "I don't suppose she told you anything."

"No, she didn't."

Jake rubs his chin and stares off into the darkness. His shoulders are broad, his chest deep. He's considerably bigger than Savage. His hair is black and curly, flecked with a little gray.

"I think we may have a problem, Jake."

"I've already got a problem, Griff. You've got more?"

"I killed Raul Ramirez and one of his henchmen."

Jake turns to face Savage. His face has weathered, eyes wide and surprised. "You killed Raul Ramirez?"

He rubs his forehead and closes his eyes. "Not good," Jake mumbles, "not good. They are seriously bad people. Seriously bad. The world won't miss Raul Ramirez, but somebody is going to come after you, you can count on that."

A gust of wind blows down the street and the clouds part. The air changes. Savage looks up at the moon.

"I lost it, Jake. I thought they'd killed you. I was bent on revenge."

"Well, they haven't got me yet, but they would have killed me. That was the plan. That's why I had to get out of town. I don't know what to say, Savage. Think of it as revenge in advance. You know, pre-emptive revenge."

"Why come to Cuba, though, Jake?"

"Great cigars," Jake says. He shrugs, amused at himself.

The sky begins to clear.

"Tell me about the Ramirez brothers."

Jake is watching the sky. He glances at the house, scratches his back, and turns to Savage.

"They're into a lot of things. They wanted the yard. They'd

heard we'd stopped building boats and had this storage and main-tenance thing with Homeland Security. We'd store and maintain boats they weren't using. There's a lot of space at the yard."

Jake's voice is deep and slow, measured. "They figured that if they ran the yard, it would be a great place for their own storage."

Savage raises his eyebrows. "What were they going to store?"

"Drugs, weapons, who knows? But they really wanted it and didn't care if anyone got in their way. They figured if Homeland Security had boats there, no one would ever suspect it of being used for other ends. Smart, really."

"And you were in the way?"

"That's part of it. There's more. I'd been doing some salvage work with a guy I know, and we'd recovered some coins."

"Go on."

"A lot of coins."

"Jake. It's me, your brother. Don't be a cagey bastard."

"This was money for the Spanish crown. A ship's worth." Jake pauses.

Savage draws in a breath and lets out a slow sigh. Jake turns to look at the house. Then back.

"Must have been taking silver coin from one of the New World mints to Spain and she'd gone down, probably in a storm."

Savage looks at Jake. "So that's a problem?"

"I'd got a visit from a couple of the Ramirez brothers. They'd come to talk about the boatyard while I was cataloging the first load of coins. They were interested. They wanted the yard first, and then they wanted the coins and any more I had. I told them I wasn't selling the yard and they couldn't have the coins."

Jake walks over to the side of the road and relieves himself. Savage shakes his head.

"I started getting threats. I was being followed. I'd get calls. It was hard to go diving. Boats would follow me, so I'd have to go to other sites, to keep them away from the wreck. Then they sent a guy out to the yard—not a Ramirez, but some heavy. He'd come with a deal, a settlement for the yard and the coins and the location of the wreck. I asked him what the alternative was, and he told me there was no alternative. Period. The Ramirez brothers were just testing my threshold. He was expendable."

Jake closes his eyes and scratches his back. There is another gust of wind, and clouds scoot beneath the moon.

"The guy starts talking tough. He has a knife and says he knows how to use it. He doesn't see the harpoon gun next to me, behind some paint cans. I figure I don't want to fight the guy, but if he comes at me, I'll have to kill him or be killed. He starts to move towards me. I just stand there. I tell him to leave, but he just laughs. He wants to use his knife. I pick up the harpoon gun and he reaches into his jacket. I don't want to find out what he's got in there, so I shoot. The harpoon goes straight through his leg, and it hits an artery. He drops, bleeds out... right there. Not what I had in mind, but there we are. So, I get the harpoon, his knife, and the Glock from his pocket. I take his wallet, remove his rings and watch."

He pauses, remembering. "I took all that shit and got rid of it. We were in one of the trailers. They're made of wood, and there are a lot of highly flammable resins in there. I left my wallet by my bicycle, which was padlocked to the fence, away from the trailer."

Another pause.

"Place goes up in flames. A roaring inferno. Burns all night. Next morning, they find a body, unrecognizable and my wallet by my bicycle, and they figure the body's mine, not that they know. It's a tourist town, after all. Accidents are okay, but murder's not good. End of investigation."

Savage looks up the street. The man has gone into the house. The lights are on; the car's in the driveway.

"I got my diving buddy to run me over here. Unfortunately, we were followed."

"And now we're in Cuba. You're dead, apparently. You've found a wreck full of coins. And I gather there's something about Angie. Not to mention the fact I've killed two Ramirez brothers for something they didn't do."

"Doesn't sound too good when you put it like that."

"We're in deep shit. The other Ramirez brothers are going to be looking for me. Who knows what'll happen to the yard, but we know the Ramirez brothers want it, right?"

"Right. Though I don't think they'll get it. Someone's going to have to find my will."

"You have a will? Impressive."

"You don't?"

"I don't have anything or anyone, Jake. Just me. But let me get this straight. You're saying that sooner or later, someone is going to find the will? Wouldn't it be easier if you weren't dead?"

"But if I'm alive, there's a greater risk of me actually becoming dead. They'd be looking for me. Since they think I already am dead, there's not much point looking, right?"

"So what are we going to do?"

"I have a plan."

"Does it involve me?"

"It'll have to. I'm dead, remember?"

"Let's go to the house."

They start walking up the street when a vehicle drives by exceptionally fast.

"That's odd. It's usually pretty quiet round here," Jake says. "Just Eduardo and his brother."

The car screeches to a stop outside the house. It's more like a shack—small, single story white with a corrugated iron roof. A short, stocky man walks up to the front door, opens it, and walks in.

"This doesn't look right," Jake says, a hint of urgency in his voice.

Jake and Savage begin to jog up the road when two sharp cracks come from the house. Then two more. Jake picks up the pace as the stocky man runs out of the house, jumps into the car, and peels off down the road.

"What the hell?" Jakes shouts as he sprints towards the driveway.

Savage is running hard just behind him. They reach the house, and Jake runs inside, rushing to the kitchen. Savage looks behind him, checking for anyone else. The street is deserted.

"Eduardo!" Jake calls as he enters through a side door.

Savage comes in after him. They're in the kitchen. It smells of cooked beans. There are plates on the table, unfinished food, and some car keys. A chair has been knocked over. One man is lying on the floor, and the other is slumped over the table. Both dead.

Jake is kneeling on the floor.

"Eduardo?" he mutters in disbelief.

Savage snatches the car keys from the table. "Jake. Back to the boat, now!" he hisses, hoping the keys are the ones to the car in the driveway.

Jake looks stunned. He gets to his feet.

"We have to get out of here, Jake. Back to the boat. This is getting out of control."

Savage leads the way, pulling Jake with him.

———

At the dock, all looks in order. *Victory* is moored as she was, the cabin lights are on, and the dock lines and fenders are all as they were.

"Angie?" Savage calls. She's nowhere in sight. He jumps on board and goes down the companionway to the main cabin. It's empty. He moves from cabin to cabin. He checks the head.

"She's not here," Savage says. His heart races, adrenaline flooding his system.

Jake goes below, his feet clattering on the companion way.

Savage can hear him going from cabin to cabin before coming up, shaking his head.

"I told her to stay on board," Savage says. "Either she ran or someone took her. Either way, we're not going to find her. We'd better get out of here."

Jake hesitates. He looks over to the town. It's late. The breeze is picking up.

"Jake, she's not here. There was something about the way she was acting. I don't know. Something was off. I think she ran."

"She can look after herself," Jake says. "Believe me. There may not be much of her, but she's tough."

Jake starts the engine as Savage unties the mooring lines and pulls the fenders on board.

Jake eases *Victory* away from the dock and sweeps her around and brings her into the channel leading out beyond the breakwaters to the open sea. The night lights are on, and the engine rumbles slowly.

Jake is at the wheel, checking the GPS. Savage looks back as they move away from the lights of Trinidad.

"Going to have to put some heavy weather gear on," Jake says. "There's a front coming in."

Savage is thinking about Angie.

"She'll be okay," Jake says, as if he can tell. "You don't have to worry about her. Right now, we just need to get out to sea."

Savage gets the heavy weather gear out and they put it on.

"Bit of a mess," Savage says.

"A bit," Jake says.

They pass the channel markers and clear the breakwater. The breeze is still picking up.

Savage hoists the genoa and one of the mainsails. Jake cuts the engine and looks at the GPS, then the course plotter.

Victory heals, then surges forward as the sails catch the breeze.

"We'll head due south, get out of Cuban waters, then lay a course west to clear Cuba. Then northwest, then tack and head southeast back to Key West. Just have to hope we don't run into the Coast Guard. Get the binoculars, Griff. Keep watch. I'll plot a course."

Savage finds the binoculars and turns north to scan the receding Cuban shore. He sees nothing, just the lights on the coast, fading as *Victory* begins to ride the swell.

Then, in the distance, on the horizon, Savage sees something. He steadies himself on the rail.

"Jake. I can see a boat."

"Can you make it out?"

"Not yet."

"Keep an eye on it. I'll run up the other main. Let's see what we can do under full sail."

Jake sets the automatic pilot and goes to raise the second mainsail. Savage is leaning against the aft cabin, his binoculars trained on the boat just leaving the harbor.

Victory begins to accelerate, the bow cleaving the growing swell and the lee hull cutting into the waves.

Jake returns to the wheel. "We're doing sixteen knots. We'll know if that boat's coming after us soon enough."

The wind has picked up again, and Jake has exchanged the genoa for a smaller jib and put a reef in each mainsail.

"Still doing sixteen knots. There's some weather coming. Wind's picking up and swinging round. I'm going to bear off and head due west. Keep an eye on that boat, Griff. If she changes course, she's coming after us."

Savage leans on the stern rail and focuses the binoculars as best he can. As *Victory* bears off the wind, he concentrates on the boat's trajectory.

"She's holding her course, Jake.

"That's good."

"No, wait—she's turning. She's coming after us, Jake. She's dead astern. And she's gaining on us."

11

THE WHALER

THE WIND IS STILL INTENSIFYING, and Jake has put a second reef in each mainsail. *Victory* is built for blue water sailing, and she's riding the swell comfortably, the lee hull keeping its trim. The seas are rolling hills of green, flecked with white windblown spume. Jake returns to the wheel. He's an enormous man, broad and thick, and his curly black hair is unruly in the wind. He looks at the console by the wheel.

"Steady eighteen knots. What's going on astern?"

"There are three of them... and Angie. They're bouncing all over the place. Looks like they're struggling to keep up," Savage says.

He feels betrayed by Angie, and yet he doesn't believe she would betray them. He grips the binoculars to try and steady them, but it's difficult in the swell.

The bow rises and falls, the water rushing past.

"Good." Jake squints into the wind, and sees the Boston whaler *Outrage* bearing down on them, gaining slowly but operating at its limit.

"The sea's too big for that boat at that speed. They don't know what they're doing," Jake adds.

"What are you doing, Jake?" Savage shouts as *Victory* slows, letting the whaler catch up a little.

"Spilling some wind, slowing down, and then we're going to speed up. Keep a close eye on them."

Jake adjusts the mainsails and furls the jib. He works quickly, his strong arms firmly gripping the ropes. He is methodical and careful. *Victory* loses some hull speed. The sea is an angry, heaving green, the rollers long and steady.

Savage grips the binoculars. The whaler is creeping closer, smacking hard into the waves, struggling to keep a line, buffeted by the cresting waves.

Angie sits in the stern of the whaler. One man is at the wheel, and the three others are holding onto the steering console.

The sea is wild. The wind picks up, and then there are angry gusts. *Victory* is pressing on, riding the swells. Jake spills some more wind, and the trimaran slows again.

The whaler draws closer to the stern, and one man grabs a boat hook and comes to the bow to try to reach *Victory's* transom. The man is unsteady. The whaler skews and tips. Angie screams.

"They're going to try to board us," Savage shouts.

"I know. Let's see how they deal with this."

Jake tightens both mainsails, glancing at the luff, knowing exactly how to trim the sails to get *Victory* to do what he wants.

A gust of wind howls through the rigging.

Victory rises then heels and picks up speed. The whaler falls behind, then starts to catch up again. Jake looks up at the sails, then back at the whaler. He bears off, the sails fill, and then he tightens up and *Victory* accelerates into the waves, and the whaler falls behind again. *Victory* is a powerful, fast boat, built for ocean crossings. She's is in her element. The whaler is struggling like a desperate swimmer swept out to sea.

The whaler's helmsman guns the engine, but too quickly, throwing the bowman back against the console and Angie against the stern. One of the men falls against the helmsman, who lets go of the wheel and stumbles backwards. The whaler lurches to one side as it rises on a huge wave. It lists further as the whaler rises to the crest of the green, wind-frothed wave.

Two of the men fall overboard. Angie springs to her feet, leaps to the unmanned steering console, and navigates the whaler up and over the wave, leaving the two men behind in the water, their shouts swallowed by the wind. Savage watches, impressed by Angie's boat handling skills. His eyes are fixed. He sees what she's trying to do.

Angie steers wildly, keeping the remaining man off balance. He can't get to the console.

"Jake, we need to be quick here. That guy's about to make a run at Angie." Savage prepares himself to climb onto the trampoline to crawl to the lee hull so he can reach the whaler when it comes alongside.

Savage stops as he sees Angie swing the wheel again as the whaler rises over another looming wave. The boat lists hard, almost capsizing, and throws the man off balance.

"Savage, get further out. It's going to come alongside. Now!"

Jake checks the sails, then the whaler, then Savage, who is on the trampoline, the water racing past beneath the webbing. He has no safety line. *Victory* climbs a wave, heels, gains speed, and then settles again between two house-sized rollers.

Savage reaches the lee hull. He can go no further. He grips the edge of the trampoline and flattens himself, waiting and watching.

Angie is steering the boat towards *Victory* as best she can. The whaler pounds the surface, pitching and yawing. The remaining man is holding on, shouting something at Angie.

"We're going to have to get her onboard without damaging the hull. Bring it closer, Savage, but tell her to keep just astern until we're ready."

Savage shouts to Angie, gesticulating with the open palm of his free hand. His words are lost in the wind, but she drops back, dead astern of the hull. *Smart woman*, Savage thinks. Angie turns and looks at the man behind her. He's crouching, as if to spring forward. Angie slows and then speeds up. She steers hard right then hard left until the man is forced back to the stern where he fumbles for a grip.

"I'm going to tighten up. Tell her to catch up, and then I'll bear off, and come alongside. She'll have to jump. You need to pull her onto the trampoline, Savage. We have just one good shot. Got that?"

Savage gives Jake a thumbs-up and beckons to Angie with quick, urgent arm motions. He kneels on the trampoline at the point where it is secured to the outer hull of the trimaran and inches closer to the edge. He has one foot on the slippery hull while kneeling on the trampoline, one arm outstretched to grab Angie. The whaler starts to gain on *Victory* again. Jake spills some wind to slow down.

The two boats are running parallel, riding over the heaving white crested swells. This is an angry and untamed sea. The wind whips the tops of the waves as the storm grows. Angie moves the whaler closer. The outboard is roaring, and the flat hull buffets the surface hard. She sets the throttle and waits for *Victory* to sink into the next trough before she runs forward into the bow and climbs onto the coaming. In one leap, she hurls herself towards Savage. She seems suspended over the water at the apex of her jump. Jake adjusts the helm, his large hands gipping the wheel firmly. Savage is poised.

The force of the jump moves the whaler's bow away from *Victory*.

Jake makes a quick adjustment, and Savage stretches out just as Angie is about to fall into the water. He grabs her. He's stretched as far as he can, gripping with one hand. Angie is soaked, grimacing as she clings to Savage's arm.

Victory is doing sixteen knots, and Savage is holding onto Angie in a forearm-to-forearm grip. He pulls her closer to him as

Jake tightens up and *Victory* begins to accelerate away from the whaler.

"Hold on, Angie, hold on."

Angie's left leg is in the water, and she's being dragged back. Savage can barely keep his grip. Jake spills some wind, *Victory* slows again, and in the instant that the drag decreases, Savage yanks her onto the trampoline next to him.

Jake tightens up and *Victory* leaps ahead, the force enabling Savage to pluck her from the water and drag her onto the hull and then the trampoline. His muscles ache with the effort, but the adrenaline is there. He won't let go. He will get her to safety. Savage and Angie crawl across the trampoline to the cockpit where they climb over the coaming and drop into the cockpit, both gasping.

Savage grabs Angie, holds her close, and squeezes her hard. "Thank God you're okay." Savage presses his face into Angie's wet hair and kisses her neck. Jake adjusts the wheel.

They watch as the whaler turns broadside on to a huge, barn-sized wave with no one at the helm. The lone man scrambles forward to regain control of the boat, and his arms flail as he balances himself. The whaler is pounded by another wave.

Angie leans on Savage and steps towards Jake at the wheel. "Jake! Oh, God, Jake. You're alive," she gasps, clenching her fists, her brow furrowed and her face contorted with emotion.

She flings her arms around Jake's massive frame, and he drapes one enormous arm around her.

"I'm alive. You're alive. Now get below. Dry off and get some heavy weather gear on, and bring up two life lines."

Jake is a master mariner. He eyes the sails and sea, listens to the wind, checks the boat, watches the whaler, and grips the wheel.

The whaler is falling behind, making its way back through the swell. The man left on board is at the helm, beginning to circle, appearing to search for his crew.

"Jesus," Savage says. "That was pretty hairy. They won't be coming after us. It'll be search and rescue for them."

"Good luck with that. With these swells, he might find them, he might not."

Jake watches as the whaler slips into the distance. He tightens up and sets a course northwest, to the Gulf of Mexico. He sets the autopilot and takes the binoculars and scans the horizon for other vessels.

The storm passes and the gusts ease. The wind blows strong and steady, but the sea is losing its fury. *Victory* sails on, fast and steady, heeling, one hull flying, the other gripping the water as she leaves Cuba behind.

They sail hard for the rest of the day. Gradually, as the afternoon wears on, the wind begins to lose more of its bite, and the swells temper.

As night comes on, Jake switches on the navigation lights. He won't leave the helm. Savage and Angie are asleep below, Angie in the stern, Savage on the couch in the main cabin.

By the time dawn comes the wind has finally eased to a much gentler breeze and *Victory* is a hundred miles west of Tampa, in the shallower turquoise waters of the Gulf.

Savage comes on deck. Jake smiles, his face dark and weathered, but his eyes are clear.

"I'll bring her about and put her on a course for Key West," he says.

Savage sheets in the jib as *Victory* comes about. A school of fish makes the smooth waters boil and ripple. Ahead, two dolphins break the surface in parallel, their backs arching as they slide effortlessly through the turquoise sea.

"Beautiful," Angie says emerging from below. "I wish it was just another day in paradise."

Savage looks at her and asks, "It's not?"

"Okay," Jake says. "We're going to have to clear a few things up here."

A tension comes over the cockpit.

Savage looks at Angie. "What happened after I left the boat? Did you run?"

Angie's eyes flash. "I did *not* run. I stayed on board, watching and waiting. I was scared. I didn't know when or if you'd come back. Then these guys came."

"Friends of yours?" Savage asks.

Jake's eyes move from Savage to Angie and back.

"I've never seen them before! Never. I'm on your side, okay? Yes, I had a thing with the Ramirez family. That was a long time ago. Let it go. You're treating me like some kind of traitor." Angie spits her words, her eyes dancing with fury.

"Angie, listen! You too, Griff," Jake says. "This is serious stuff. We need to be on the same page. We have to work through this very carefully. What did they want?"

"They were looking for you, Jake. They followed you across from Key West, apparently, and said you'd given them the slip when you came ashore. But they knew you'd head for Trinidad. They're not dumb. People talk—someone saw *Victory* putting into port and figured you'd be connected somehow."

"Well, they found me. And lost me. And here we are. A day's sail out of Key West."

"Jake, she's with us," Savage says. "You know she wouldn't rat on you. Right?"

"Let's hope not," Jake says.

"Enough," Angie says. "Give me some respect. Both of you. What a pair. I don't know sometimes. One was bad enough. Now there's two of you."

Angie puts her hands in her hair, spreads her fingers and leans back to feel the morning sun.

"All right. Key West it is," Jake says. He slowly sets the course. "I'm not going to be intimidated by anyone, or give up the boat-yard." He grips the wheel hard, his face set, squinting towards the distant horizon. Savage puts a hand on his brother's enormous shoulder, feeling his rock strength.

"What if we just let it go?" Savage says. "Move on. Sail off into the sunset."

Angie lets her hair fall and looks out over the sea.

Jake drops his hands from the wheel. "No. That yard is my place. Key West is my town. I'm staying. No one's going to push me out. No Ramirez can do that. I get to choose. No one makes choices for me."

Angie's lips part, as if to say something. But then she goes silent.

Savage frowns. He rotates his shoulder and winces. His face catches the sun, and he rubs the stubble on his face. His eyes are ice blue, piercing anything he looks at.

"You think that's going to work—coming back to Key West? They're still going to want the yard. One Ramirez is dead, and I kicked the shit out of another."

"Maybe they should worry," Jake says.

Savage and Jake both survey the horizon. A fishing charter is making its way across the Gulf.

"Strange how they reported the fire and your death. Police didn't do much of anything. What's that about?" Savage says, turning to Jake.

"Beats me. Ramirez may have the police in his pocket, or he could have paid someone off at the newspaper. Money talks in this town."

Jake sets the automatic pilot. He checks the GPS and navigation console. His fingers move quickly for a big man. His eyes are focused.

Savage looks out across the waters of the Gulf. "We don't want a war with Ramirez, but we have to bring you back to life. You could go to the police, tell them you were out of town, didn't see the news, perhaps. Maybe you heard about the fire when you got back. No one's going to call you on it."

"And then what?"

"See what Ramirez does next."

"Jake, Ramirez wants you out of town, right?" Angie says. Her anger has gone. She leans on the cockpit coaming.

"He wants me out of the boatyard. I don't think he cares if I'm in Key West or not."

"Put it on the market. If he wants it, let him buy it at your price. Why not?" Angie looks down, waiting for Jake to reply.

"He doesn't want to buy it. Not at any market price. He wants to muscle in on the cheap. I'm just in the way."

"What if you put it on the market, and I buy it?" Savage says.

Jake frowns and straightens up in surprise.

"You have that type of money, Savage? I mean we're talking a lot of money here."

Savage rubs his shoulder and looks out to sea. He clears his throat as ideas spin in his mind. He turns back, then looks from Angie to Jake. Angie leans in to listen. *Victory* is easing her way southeast towards Key West.

"You put the yard on the market. Private sale. By owner. I, you know, 'buy' it."

Jake raises his eyebrows.

"Then you have the problem. They'll be after you and not me. You would be taking my problem and making it your problem."

Savage says, "I can handle it."

"Meantime I can go quiet. Not be around. Do something else? Is that what you're saying?"

A silence falls, both men thinking as *Victory* slips easily through the water.

Savage looks at Jake. No smile. He knows.

"I don't get it," Angie says.

"Better that way," Jake says.

"I'm going to make some coffee," Angie says. She walks towards the companionway and then climbs into the cabin.

Savage waits until Angie is out of earshot. "I saw the coin in the safe," he says. "Figured you were trying to tell me something."

"There are a lot more. A fortune, like I said. No one else knows how much, and I want to keep it that way. I still need to..."

A noise comes from below deck. Angie comes up the companionway holding two mugs of coffee.

"Here. Coffee." Angie passes the mugs to the brothers. "Are you keeping something from me? I think you are. Jake is like that. Close with the information. Lets you know when he wants you to know. Right, big man?"

Jake puts an arm around her. "Would we do a thing like that?" he asks.

"Yes," Angie says. "You probably would, and he"—Angie points at Savage—"he definitely would."

Savage chuckles, wondering how Angie can know him so quickly.

"You know what?" Jake says, his face lighting up. "Let's give Key West a miss. Moor up at Sugarloaf Key again and give Nikki a call. She can pick us up."

"Nikki?" Angie snorts.

"Is that a problem?" Jake asks, feigning surprise.

"It's a trust thing," Savage says.

"As in, Nikki doesn't trust me," Angie says.

"Why not?"

"You know—the Ramirez thing. It was years ago, a fling. I'd just got here and didn't know what I was doing. Nikki never really let go of that."

Jake falls silent, thinking about Nikki and Angie, his two good friends. He was close with both, but they weren't close with each other. And this was it.

"I know," Jake says. "I see that. But that was a long time ago."

"Yes," Angie says, "it was. It's not as if I'm the only one who makes mistakes." She looks at Savage, her eyes firm and defiant.

"And I was jealous. I've always been jealous of Nikki," Angie continues, looking away from Savage and staring across to the horizon. "She's so smart and hot, and she's got this Asian thing. All the guys like her, and you like her, Jake. She makes you laugh. I was just jealous."

Jake sips his coffee and looks from Angie to Griff. He's glad his brother is here, even though the circumstances are both perilous and complicated.

"Just being honest. Better to say it. I can go to Sugarloaf Key and try to make it work with Nikki. I'll get over it."

The Keys come into view, low in the distance. Savage contemplates the return, wondering about the Ramirez family and the boatyard, about what is going to happen.

"Angie," Jake says, stretching out to touch her shoulder. "Listen. I'm sorry. You've been a great friend. Always. You've always been there for me. I trust you, you know I do."

"Me too, Angie," Savage says. "I trust you too. I just need to be careful."

"Aw, the brothers trust me, that's cute." A flash of anger suddenly passes across Angie's face, then it's gone as quickly as it came.

"Go ahead and call Nikki. I'll get over it. I had a bit of a thing for her—she's hot, you know. But that was a long time ago."

"You're not too bad yourself."

Jake stares at the horizon ahead. "What's that coming towards us?" He points as the tip of Key West emerges on the horizon. Savage picks up the binoculars and trains them on a distant boat.

"Zodiac. Orange wheelhouse. Could be the Coast Guard?"

"And that?" Jake says, pointing above the Zodiac.

"Helicopter. Definitely Coast Guard."

"Think they're coming for us?"

Savage scans the water. "No. Look." Savage points to their stern. A powerboat is going flat out, about a mile to the south, making its way towards the Keys. The Zodiac and helicopter change course, as if to intercept them.

"Not us. Looks like they're going to cut that boat off before it gets to the Keys."

"Makes me nervous," Angie says.

Savage and Jake watch the helicopter and Zodiac giving chase to the powerboat.

"What do you think, Jake?" Savage asks.

"Could be anything...or nothing. Don't know, Savage. Drugs, guns, people?"

The sky is a deep rich blue, the water smooth and creamy as *Victory* continues at a steady nine knots.

The powerboat approaches the Keys, engine roaring, the helicopter and Zodiac in pursuit.

"Glad it wasn't us. I've had enough for one day," Jake says.

"Me, too," Angie says, her voice tired. She strokes her hair and leans against Jake.

The sound of the helicopter unsettles Savage. He feels a tension in his shoulders and back. A memory has been triggered. He forces it out of his mind, but not before a bead of sweat appears on his brow. He closes his eyes and rubs the back of his neck. It's gone.

Victory makes her way around the western tip of Key West, heading east for Sugarloaf Key. She's a mile off shore. The breeze picks up. A few charter boats are heading out to sea. A catamaran full of tourists makes its way towards the Dry Tortugas.

"Be a great place for a vacation," Savage says.

"Oh, yeah," Jake says. "Spot of fishing. Lie on the beach."

"You never lie on the beach," Angie says.

"I wouldn't now," Jake says. "Greenpeace would probably drag me back into the ocean. Beached whale."

Savage laughs, looking at Jake, three hundred pounds of solid man. Then his smile disappears, his face suddenly blank, his eyes flat.

"What is it?" Angie asks.

Savage snaps back to the present. "I've really messed up," he says, shaking his head. "I've caused this chaos. I need to do better. Much better."

"It was already chaos," Jake says. "You just made it a lot worse."

A gust of wind causes *Victory* to heel.

"I'll do better," Savage says to himself. "I will."

12

THE THREAT

SHORTLY BEFORE SUNSET, Savage and Jake are on the beach at Fort Zachary, drying off from their swim. The evening breeze quiets as the sun begins its journey past the horizon. The sunset cruise schooners wend their way back into port. Key West is stirring, preparing for another night. Mallory Square filling with an endless rotation of revelers, bidding farewell to the sun as they await the joys and despairs of another night on the town.

"I live again," Jake says, looking out to sea, as the sun dips its last ray, the horizon ablaze with orange.

"I can see you, so I guess you do," Savage says. He rubs his shoulder, attempting to relieve the pain.

"I went to the *Key West Citizen*'s offices this morning and spoke with the reporter who wrote the boatyard fire story. She said she'd just used the police report. Her editor hadn't wanted a big thing made of it. Said it surprised her, but she's new and didn't really think it was important. So she just wrote it and moved on. She did say that upon reflection, it seemed a bit odd. Don't think she really wanted to talk about it," Jake says.

Savage pulls on his dry surf shorts and t-shirt. He winces, the simple movement sending pain up his arm.

"What's she going to do now?"

"Said she'd tell her editor and see if he wanted her to write anything about it. You know a correction or a follow-up. She seemed a little off; uneasy. I didn't want to push anything. She wouldn't look me in the eye. You know? That always means something."

"What about the police?" Savage asks.

Jake looks out at the sea before turning and leading the way back up the beach, past the lifeguard tower and the barbecue area.

"I went down to the station and asked to speak to the detective who was working on the boatyard case. I was taken into a back room and told there wasn't any investigation, since they'd determined it was an accident. So, no case. Then I explained that it had been reported that I was assumed to have died in the fire, but obviously I hadn't, as I was talking to him at the moment. He was tense. You know? Didn't want to talk about it. Didn't want me there. It was... odd."

"What did he say?"

A fisherman ambles up the beach and waves at Jake, who raises a hand in friendly response.

"Not much. He just repeated himself, and then said he was glad I was alive. Then I told him the story about being out of town, like we talked about. He told me that they'd decided it was an accident, something electrical or a gas leak. Then he said it was time to move on. I didn't push it."

"Probably a good idea," Savage says. He wonders why it seems so important to everyone that the fire be an accident.

Jake stops and turns to Savage, noticing two big men coming back from a swim.

"You know, it seems odd that the newspaper and the police were not interested. More than that—they didn't want to do anything. Now I have to file an insurance claim."

Jake shakes his head. The air is warm, and a light gust of wind blows an empty can across the asphalt of the parking lot.

"Should be straightforward. Right?"

"Well, you know, in my experience in this town, not much is straightforward. At least not anymore."

"You were out of town. Now you're back. That's not a problem, is it? Any evidence you set the fire?"

Savage notices that despite Jake's years in Key West, his English accent hasn't faded. He's tanned and weathered from the sea, but he's still an Englishman to the core. America simply hasn't rubbed off on him.

A gull swoops low overhead and lands by a trash can. Fireworks explode in greens and blues over Mallory Square.

"Hope not. Oh, and I got a call this morning," Jake says, "about the boatyard. You know I was going to put an ad in the paper, see what I could get for it if I sold."

"Someone you know?" Savage says, his interest piqued. He rubs a hand over his head.

"Someone we both know, in fact. Pretty sure it was Ramirez. The thing is, the ad hasn't even run yet. I put it in this morning, after I'd spoken with the reporter. I was told they'd run it tomorrow."

"Someone at the paper told Ramirez."

A gull is working on a scrap of bread from a Subway wrapper.

"Looks like it. I mean, he didn't say he'd seen the ad, but he did say he'd heard I wanted to sell. How would anyone know? There's only us... and Angie." Jake sighs. "Jesus."

He turns and looks back down the beach, observing with envy the simplicity of the sand. Small waves lap the shore as a fishing boat motors in from the expansive sea.

"You think Angie told him?" Savage asks.

Jake's shoulders are slumped and tired. He watches the fishing boat. Savage wonders how his life has been at the boatyard, beneath the relentless sun.

"I hope not. I trust her. I think."

"Unless he has something on her," Savage says. He puts it out there, thinking on his feet, an idea developing, merely flirting with the possibility.

"Like what?"

"Who knows? Information. Pictures. She has a bit of a past, I hear." Savage watches his brother intently, thinking. He waits.

Jake takes in a breath, his shoulders straighten. "Seems unlikely. But, anyway, he offered two million. Cash."

Jake turns, and the gull flies off. The last of the cars leave the parking lot.

"What did you say?"

"That I'd had a previous offer of 2.5 million."

"And?"

"He wanted to know who from."

"Did you tell him?"

"Nope," Jake says. "Why would I? I told him that's not the way it works. You make an offer. Someone else makes an offer. You make a better offer or you don't. It's business. Doesn't matter who makes the offer. He didn't really like that." Jake scratches his stubble.

"Who was it from?" Savage asks.

"You." Jake says. "Remember?" There is a glint of humor in Jake's eye.

"Right," Savage says.

"I told him I'd decide by Friday."

Jake shakes his head again, takes a tin out of his pocket, and rolls himself a cigarette. Savage watches the careful ritual, the big hands deftly handling the paper and tobacco.

"Three days," Savage says, almost to himself. "He didn't make a counter offer?"

"Said he'd think about it."

Jakes lights the cigarette, inhales, and leans back, letting the smoke out in a steady stream. He smiles at the brief pleasure.

Jake's phone rings, and he takes it from his pocket, checks the screen, and swallows.

"Hello ... Yes, it is." Jake mouths the word *Ramirez* to Savage. "I see. But like I told you, I can't tell you who the offer is from."

Jake takes another drag as he listens, tilting his head from side to side as Ramirez talks.

"If I could say something, Mr. Ramirez," Jake says, his voice firmer, pushing back, "I think you're threatening me. I'd advise against that." He hangs up, puts the phone back in his pocket, and takes a long drag on the cigarette.

Savage looks out to sea and notices a fishing boat is heading out, running lights on.

"He could have waited until the ad ran to call. Unless he just wants to show you he knows things others don't," Savage says.

"Maybe. He's used to getting what he wants; likes to have the edge. Probably just wanted me to realize that he has the paper and the police in his pocket."

Jake takes a last draw, squeezes the last of the cigarette, puts it in his tin, and looks at Savage.

"I don't litter," Jake explains.

"Might as well sell the yard to me, then. At least get the paperwork done. Then you can take off for a while, right? Get some fishing done, do some sailing."

"And leave you alone with Ramirez?" Jake says. "You really think that would be a good idea? It's his town. You're a stranger here."

"Sometimes it helps to be a stranger," Savage replies. His brother watches him carefully.

"I guess that depends," Jake says, putting the tin in his pocket.

"I'll be fine," Savage says. "Really."

More fireworks climb into the sky before forming stars and rings over Mallory Square as the sun finally dips below the horizon. Savage hears the *pop-pop-pop* of the explosions. His face is blank. Beads of sweat collect on his brow. His heart quickens. He swallows. A memory begins to surface, but Savage forces it down. He doesn't want to remember. Not now.

Jake is walking ahead. Savage follows. The sky transforms from postcard orange to a dark magenta, and then the night arrives.

Soon the streets and bars will swell with people, the scooters tearing up the streets. The booze will flow as bored house musicians take the stage and strippers ready themselves.

Another night in paradise.

Beneath the streetlight, they unlock their bicycles and begin the ride back to town. Noisy scooters shoot by, the tourist train passes, and sidewalk amblers make their way towards Duval.

"Here we go," Jake says, over his shoulder. "This is why I never go out after six. It's like this every night. Except when it's worse."

"Jake," Savage yells. "Go home. I want to pedal around a bit. Check things out."

"You sure?"

"Yes. I'll peel off here."

Jake raises his hand and doesn't look back.

Time to become less of a stranger, Savage thinks. He grips the handlebars and pedals a little harder.

He cycles up Roosevelt. Wearing a black baseball cap, Native sunglasses, orange surf shorts, and a black tank top with no logo, he looks almost like a tourist, but he's still recognizable to anyone who has run into him before. A big man on a small bike. It's a small town. He'll have to avoid the Whistle.

Soon, Jake will be out of town. Savage will let the dust settle, then start getting down to work. Ramirez is going to go down. It will be a carefully orchestrated collapse, not a massacre.

Savage crosses the bridge over to Stock Island and hangs a hard right to the Hogfish Bar and Grill. He gets off his bicycle and locks it to the bike rack by the palm trees in the corner of the lot. He walks casually past the restaurant to the docks, checking his peripheral vision and focusing on any noises he hears. He's reminded of being on patrol. He remembers the *pop-pop-pop* of the fireworks. It's the beginning of the flashback—the jungle, the sound of helicopter blades churning the hot thick air, his uniform soaked, the fear.

Savage's heart begins to race; sweat forms on his brow. He suppresses the memory, instead turning his mind to Angie—her blonde hair, the sass, her eyes. The story they told.

He wants Angie to be on her houseboat. He wants her to be pleased to see him, but she isn't there. He takes the key from under the flowerpot and opens the glass sliding door. No one. The interior is clean. Savage looks around. Nothing seems to have been disturbed. Angie's phone is on the kitchen table.

He walks into the bedroom. The bed is made, and there's a journal on the bedside table. Savage picks it up and opens to a random page. The handwriting is small and meticulous, page after page of dense prose punctuated by some sketches, mostly of jewelry, but also a heron, a manatee, some boats, a face. And then, his face.

The sound of footsteps comes from the wharf. Savage puts the journal down and moves to the living room. He opens the sliding door to the deck to see Angie in blue jogging shorts and a form-fitting yellow running vest, still breathing hard from her run.

"Savage. God, I'm glad you're here," she gasps. She looks scared.

Savage turns. He puts an arm around her and pulls her close. She leans against him for a moment and then steps back.

"What happened?"

"Some guy. Following me." She's still trying to catch her breath.

Savage straightens up and walks across the deck to the wharf.

Angie points towards the Hogfish, but there's no sign of anyone—just the sound of waves lapping against the dock.

"He took off on a scooter. You won't find him now. I hate this."

Her phone rings, and she grabs it from the table.

"Hi. Nikki? What's up?" There's a pause as Angie listens. "Jesus. Does Jake know? Okay, are you at work? Give me half an hour. I'll text you."

She turns to Savage, her eyes wide and scared. She's trembling. Her breath steadying, she leans forward, puts her hands on her knees, and then draws herself up.

"Someone slashed Nikki's tires. She tried to call Jake, but he didn't pick up. Then, when she was opening the car door, she found three dead fish on the seat."

"Where is she now?" Savage asks, his eyes moving around, checking the dock, the shadows, the darkness, anywhere someone could be hiding. Waiting. He takes Angie's arm, leads her inside the houseboat, and turns out the light. They're standing in the darkness.

"She's at the Whistle."

"Wait here. I'll be back."

"Where are you going?"

"To make sure she's okay."

"Don't go. What about Ramirez?"

Savage can hear the fear in Angie's voice. The lights on the dock are bright enough for him to see the tension in her eyes, the fear.

Angie takes his wrist and pulls it. She feels his strength, his presence, his resistance. There's nothing she can do, though. She knows he will go.

"Angie, listen, I don't want to go either. I don't want any more trouble. But I have to look after Nikki."

"Don't go. Please. I don't want anything to happen to you."

There are tears in Angie's eyes. Savage feels the restless urge to do something, to not be on the houseboat.

"Is this about Nikki or about you? She's scared, right? I can protect her."

"It's about me, but it's about Nikki, too. And you and Nikki. I'm jealous. There, I've said it."

This is all I need, Savage thinks, wondering about the way things work, the layers, even in moments of crisis.

"Hey, Angie, come here." Savage pulls her towards him. He squeezes her and smells the sweat and her hair. He feels a churning inside, an unsettled flutter.

"This isn't about me and Nikki; this is about watching out for her."

Savage knows this isn't completely true, that it's something else, too. Playing two hands is never a good idea.

"Bullshit," Angie says. "But go ahead and go."

"Angie. Listen. I like you, okay?"

Not the right word, Savage knows. Silence would have been better.

"*Like?*" Angie asks, her voice dripping with sarcasm.

"A lot. You know that." Savage knows Angie is falling in love with him.

"I hate you, Savage."

He steps back from Angie and holds her by the shoulders, looking her in the eye.

"No, you don't, Angie. You don't hate me. And I am coming back."

13

FLASH DRIVE

SAVAGE CHANGES HIS CLOTHES, his movements slow and smooth. He puts on a pair of loose off-white linen pants, a light green short-sleeved shirt, and straw hat. He's clean-shaven. In the mirror, Savage sees someone else.

"Lock the door. I'll call when I get back," Savage says, his voice soft but insistent and business-like. His mind is already elsewhere.

Angie tugs at her hair. Her eyes are flat, her expression resigned. "Be careful," she says.

Savage cycles into town, past the airport, down South Roosevelt, pedaling easily. He passes the early evening joggers, a leather-skinned local walking a pair of ancient dogs, a young couple sitting on the sea wall. It's a comfortable evening, for some. Savage pulls his straw hat down and pedals on. The crank-shaft squeaks rhythmically. There are more people coming out into the night.

The Whistle is noisy and crowded, the jukebox playing Jimmy Buffet. The night is coming alive. Savage finds a place at the bar and waits. Nikki is busy. It seems she doesn't notice him, but between serving customers, she pours him a vodka and tonic—

Jake's drink—and places it on a coaster in front of him. She says nothing and doesn't look at him, moving from customer to customer. She gives a comment here, a laugh there—smooth and professional. She's wearing a white blouse and expensive black jeans, with understated make up. She is perfect.

"Give me your car keys," Savage says under his breath, his face down, as Nikki passes. Next time she walks by, she drops a set of keys and leaves them there.

Savage raises his eyebrows, leaves his drink untouched, and puts twenty dollars under the glass. He moves his stool away from the bar, stands, and leaves.

It's shortly before midnight when Savage returns to the Whistle. He sits at the bar again. The place is full. The drinks are taking hold and the night has truly set in, with the sounds of loud laughter and voices.

"When do you get off?" Savage asks Nikki.

"Three," Nikki says, drying a glass, then pouring another drink.

"Long night."

Nikki nods without smiling. "Drink?" she asks, pausing and looking at Savage questioningly as if she expects him to tell her something.

Savage feels a slight release in his body. He looks at the nape of her neck, the olive color of her skin, the blackness of her hair. "I'm good, thanks. Some water, though, when you have a moment."

A flash of a smile passes across Nikki's face. "When you have a moment," she mimics in a perfect English accent.

Nikki leaves him a glass of water.

"Car's fixed," Savage says.

"It is?" Nikki raises her eyebrows. "I'm impressed."

"Amazing what money will do." Savage's head is down. He rubs the smooth wooden counter and marvels at the finish.

Nikki stops between customers. She leans close to Savage and puts her elbows on the bar. "That was scary. Bastards."

She's close enough for Savage to feel her breath on his face. She moves away, but a hint of perfume lingers. He feels light inside, and wishes he were on vacation.

"I know. You want me to wait until you get off work?" Savage asks.

"I'll be okay. I'll get one of the bouncers to see me to the car."

"Get one to see you home," Savage says. "A big one," he adds, wondering who is out there in the night.

"I might do just that."

"Jake's out of town for a bit. I'm at the boatyard."

"Are you living up there?" Nikki asks. She takes two empty beer bottles from the counter and eyes the customers. It's not a good time for talking.

"For now. Sorting some things out. I need to clear up the mess. Get things working again."

"And Jake?"

"Raising some capital," Savage says.

Nikki looks at him and says nothing, but her eyes are processing him. Angie would have asked what the capital was for. Nikki doesn't.

He slides the keys towards Nikki and leaves them. She covers them with her hand and they're gone.

"Thanks. I still don't really know how you got the car taken care of."

"Doesn't matter. It's done. Can't even smell the fish," Savage says.

"What was that about, anyway?" Nikki asks.

"Who knows?" Savage says nonchalantly, though he does know. A threat is a threat. "Just have to see if it happens again," he adds.

"Do you think it could happen again?" Nikki speaks quickly,

glancing up and down the bar. A man laughs. A young couple arrives at the bar, dressed up for a night out on the town.

"Well, yeah. If it happens again, we've got a problem."

Nikki serves the couple. Savage hears her joking, complimenting the woman. Savage rubs his shoulder, closes his eyes briefly, and winces.

The bar is busy again. Groups come and go. Savage decides to stay awhile. When Nikki turns to pour drinks, he notices her face in the mirror is not the same one she shows the customers. She can deal with the looks and the comments. Savage wonders what she's really like, as a lover or even as a friend. He thinks about Jake and Nikki, Jake and Angie, he and Nikki, he and Angie. He feels the lightness again, the desire. He puts another twenty on the counter, and then walks down the outside stairs and into the night.

As soon as he's on the street, he senses something. He stops and takes two steps, then turns and looks at the Whistle's outside staircase. A man is staring down at him from the top of the stairs. So he *is* being watched. Perhaps he'll be followed, too.

He gets on his bicycle, and instead of heading up South Roosevelt, he cuts north and takes North Roosevelt. On the way, he passes Jake's apartment. There are no lights on. Then he sees a figure on the balcony, crouching, in the shadows. Savage gets off his bike, padlocks it to the window bars of the laundromat, and runs across the road, around the side of the building, and approaches from the back garden.

As Savage stealthily climbs the stairs, he hears someone in the apartment. His mind is buzzing, his senses sharp. Someone is looking for something. The lights are on now, and the front door is ajar. Savage stills his breathing and listens. In the spare bedroom, drawers are being rifled through. Savage enters the master bedroom. He moves through to the kitchen, then catches a glimpse of the intruder pawing through the cabinet against the wall. He puts something in his pocket. The man is young, moving nervously, making too much noise—an amateur, unaware of Savage's presence, of what is going to happen.

Savage waits, wondering what the burglar is looking for. His eyes never leave the young man. He glides silently into the room.

It's clear that the man senses something. He pauses and turns, his eyes instantly wide with fear. He stumbles, lifting his hands to defend himself, but it's too late. He doesn't know what's hit him. All the air leaves his body as Savage strikes a tremendous blow to his neck. He goes limp. Savage catches him and eases him, unconscious, to the ground. The man is incapacitated but alive.

Savage takes the man's wallet from his back pocket, removing cash and credit cards but leaving the driver's license. The man has a Saturday night special in his waistband. Savage finds some duct tape in the kitchen and tapes his mouth and eyes, then binds his wrists to his ankles. He lifts him over his shoulder and carries him outside to the balcony. He leaves him slumped against the railing.

The man begins to gain consciousness.

"Find what you were looking for?" Savage asks, kneeling next to him, his mouth close to the man's ear.

The man groans. Savage notices a scar across his cheek, from a knife, no doubt; probably from fighting.

"Yes or no? Did you find it?" Savage asks again.

The man shrugs.

"I'll take that as a yes. In your pocket?"

The man nods.

Savage reaches inside the light linen jacket and takes a flash drive out of the inner pocket.

"Somebody pay you to do this?"

The man is shaking. He's young, no more than twenty.

"Don't do it again. Got it? And if you do, you need to make less noise and be more aware of your surroundings. You're lucky I've turned over a new leaf. Last week you would have been in trouble. Got it?"

The man's head bobs again.

"I don't forget a face and you don't know mine."

He mumbles something through the tape.

Savage leaves him slumped against the balcony, crosses the road to the sidewalk, jogs back to his bike, and then cycles back to Stock Island.

Halfway there, he calls Angie to tell her he's on his way back. It's late and the night is quiet. Most of the revelers have gone to bed. Key West is getting its brief few hours of rest. Lights flicker out at sea. Savage crosses the bridge, reaches the Hogfish Bar and Grill, and walks the bicycle down the wharf, past the other boats to the houseboats. He feels like he's coming home.

Angie opens the sliding door, steps out, and throws her arms around him, giving him a big kiss. He kisses her back. She takes his hand, pulls him inside the houseboat, locks the door, and takes him to bed. They don't talk. They don't need to.

"I've been thinking about this for a while, Savage. Even though I hate you. Sort of." She laughs, then smiles, her face a mixture of emotions. She strokes him.

Savage doesn't resist. He caresses her hair, then pulls her towards him. They breathe heavily as they kiss, becoming lost in each other. There's a closeness and a naturalness to their passion —an easy hunger, a forgetting and release of all the recent tensions.

They lie close. Angie's head rests on Savage's shoulder, and he holds her hand. They both drift in and out of sleep.

"Go to sleep, Savage. Don't fight it. We can talk tomorrow. That felt good. So good."

Savage is tired, but he's thinking about the flash drive and Jake. He kisses Angie, but he's still thinking about Nikki, and the intruder in Jake's apartment. He kisses Angie again. It's been a long time since he's been with a woman. It does feel good, but there are other things on his mind.

14

THE BOATYARD

SAVAGE LOOKS at the computer screen. He clicks on the flash drive icon, and a series of folders scrolls across the screen. He opens the first one, clicks on the first file, and a chart appears. It shows the ocean floor. There are three coordinates marked, each of them on different points of a single submerged marine ledge.

Over the next ten minutes, Savage opens all the files, one by one. There's a series of photographs and a detailed inventory of the findings, plus a prose speculation of what happened. Savage's eyes skim over the words. Three wrecks, each carrying mostly silver coins—hundreds upon thousands of them, all minted in Peru and on their way to Spain. The ships must have been lost in a storm, all hands lost without a trace. Five hundred years later, Jake came across them. Savage pauses, draws in a breath, then slowly exhales. He leans back in the chair. *Millions of dollars of coins*, he thinks. *That explains that.*

It's been a long day. He thinks of Angie first, though. Her body—flesh on flesh, the scent of a woman. He had forgotten how powerful intimacy could be. In his life, there have been long periods of abstinence. Not by choice, but because that was just how his life has been.

Not that he couldn't have had sex in the Foreign Legion. In Africa, there were plenty of whores, but that wasn't Savage's style. And later, as a monk, he'd learned to control his desires as best he could, which was not well. He'd clumsily suppressed his desires, but they lingered and would resurface, leaving him frustrated and ill at ease. Prayer didn't help, though he tried. He did have self-discipline, and he restrained himself from pleasure, but it ate away at him. He began to doubt the value of abstinence.

These days, he lets things just happen, for better or for worse, and he's had a fling here, a fling there, without thought of the consequences. This is why he has Angie on his mind. He likes it, but it unsettles him that desire can have such a hold over him, to the point that passion can overcome reason. He doesn't like that. And yet he does. He finds the tension between the two to be exciting.

"Focus," Savage spits, feeling the urgency of discovery. He stands and looks around the office. He's straightened out the paperwork, seen Jake's lawyer and the realtor, and now he has the deeds to the property in his name. Jake is no longer the owner. For now, Jake is gone. It's better that way. At least Jake is safe, Savage reflects, and now he, Griff, was in control.

He'll take care of the yard until it is time to give it back. He thinks about Jake and his years in Key West, the slow building of the boatyard. Savage isn't about to let anyone take it away. And now this—a fortune scattered on the ocean floor. That only complicates matters. A find like this doesn't remain a secret for long.

Savage's breath quickens—one step at a time. He needs to slow down, clean things up. Plus, after killing Raul, he wants to be a better man, to put all this behind him and live a simpler life. But that will have to wait. Now there are things to be done.

A contractor has cleared and removed the burnt-out trailer. Savage had all the locks changed and installed a new fire-proof safe and a gun cabinet, and he locks the flash drive inside.

Jake has a contract with Homeland Security to store and maintain boats that are currently not being used or are being repaired. It's a good contract; the Feds are reliable. They pay on time and don't ask questions.

The yard consists of outside storage space for up to twenty boats, waterfront with a slip and a single shed, 150' by 150'. The boats are neatly moored along the dock. The shed is state of the art, made of metal, like an aircraft hangar with a tilting door.

For Savage, ramping up security came easily. He was trained in the military to looks at things systematically and spot vulnerabilities.

Within three days, the perimeter fence is repaired and razor-wire has been installed. There are new motion-sensor lights every twenty feet and an alarm system, linked to a local security provider. To the locals, it appears that the boatyard is being upgraded by a new owner. Businesses come and go all the time in Key West.

Savage spends the day on the phone, walking around the yard dealing with contractors. He's wearing aviator sunglasses, a black baseball cap, and a black t-shirt. He looks tough and in control, ex-military—not a guy anyone would want to mess with. But there's always someone.

Outside the air is hot, intensified by the stones and concrete which radiate heat back towards the sun. A Mercedes slows down at the gate and stops, and a large Hispanic man with a scar on his cheek gets out. He's broad and strong looking, but out of shape.

Savage comes out of the office when he hears the slow-moving wheels crunching the stones outside the gate.

He's been waiting for this—the first visit from Ramirez.

"Hey, is Jake around?" the man says. He sizes Savage up as he walks towards him.

Savage keeps his eyes on the man, watching for any sudden movements. He doesn't like the loose jacket. No doubt there's a gun.

"Mr. Savage?" Savage asks, beginning to spar, asking for the respect the man isn't giving.

"Yeah, whatever. Mr. Savage. I need to talk to him." Ramirez is disdainful. He spits on the ground, scowling.

Savage is unmoved. He stares, his breathing slow and measured, and the man becomes unsettled.

"Mr. Savage isn't here. He no longer owns the yard."

"You know where he is?"

"No idea. Think he said he was going to retire."

Savage moves towards the vehicle. Ramirez looks uneasy. He steps back, and then tries to regain his composure.

"Looks like you've done some security work already. Very professional."

"Yes, things needed tightening up after the fire," Savage says. He takes a step towards Ramirez.

Savage feels an anger rising inside him, a desire to hurl himself at Ramirez. He suppresses it and breathes in deeply, then out. He stretches his fingers and shakes his arms to loosen his muscles.

Ramirez steps back.

"Nice to meet you, Mr. ..."

Savage thinks of using an alias, since he'd told Jake he would, but he pauses. The situation is personal. He wants Ramirez to know who he is.

"Savage," Savage says.

"Savage? Like in Savage?" Ramirez says. "Like Jake Savage?"

"Like Jake Savage. Yes. The man who owned the yard."

"And you don't know where he is?" Ramirez says, the intonation rising in disbelief.

"No idea," Savage says. He stares at Ramirez, expressionless, but his anger is building.

"We'll talk," Ramirez says.

Savage continues to stare at Ramirez. When he takes off his sunglasses, his blue eyes are unblinking. Ramirez holds his stare for a beat and then looks away.

"Nice to meet you Mr. Ramirez," Savage says. He wants to disarm Ramirez, to give him mixed signals with both polite formality and an icy glare.

Ramirez opens his mouth to speak but stays silent. He seems unable to think of anything to say. Then he turns on his heel, walks to the Mercedes, gets in, and drives off.

Savage watches the vehicle drive down Shrimp Lane, wondering how long it will take for matters to come to a head, and what he'll do when they do.

Savage walks back to the office and takes a seat at the desk. The phone on the desk rings. After the fourth ring, Savage answers.

"It's Jake."

"What's up?"

"Just checking in. See what's happening."

"A lot. Someone tried to rob your apartment. They went through everything—drawers, cupboards, all of it."

"Bastards," Jake spat. "How did you find out?"

"I was there. I caught the guy. I left him taped to the fence on Elizabeth Street," Savage says.

Jake laughs. "Serves him right. Ramirez won't like that—assuming he sent him," he says.

"He took a flash drive, but I got it back. I also bought a new safe."

"Did you check out what's on the drive?"

"Yeah. That's quite a fortune you found. Word's going to get out eventually."

"I know," Jake says.

Through the office window, Savage can see a small Cessna overhead. It banks and begins to circle Stock Island. The engine drones, and Savage feels edgy, as if the Cessna were circling his yard, watching him.

"Ramirez came by looking for you," Savage says.

"Predictable," Jake says.

"We had a little chat."

"Try to limit it to that," Jake says. "How about Angie and Nikki? How are they doing?"

"Good," Savage says, watching the Cessna banking again, before leveling off and flying south. "As far as I can tell."

Savage doesn't want to say anymore.

"Do what you have to do, Griff. I'm going to be gone and incommunicado for a while. I'll let you know when we come in. We need to get on it while we can."

Savage hears the phrase 'come in'. *So he's going out*, Savage thinks.

"Got it. You take care, brother."

"You too."

The phone clicks as Jake hangs up. Savage organizes the paperwork on the desk, locks the filing cabinet, leaves the office, and then heads out into the heat of the afternoon.

————

He goes down to the old port and buys an iced tea at Alonzo's. He sits under an awning, listening to a house guitarist playing *Country Roads*. The guitarist has a sad look on his face, but a sweet voice, and he picks well. Savage watches as he sips his tea and surveys the crowd.

It's almost happy hour. Another evening is coming alive. He wants to go see Nikki, but then he thinks about Angie. From around the corner, Savage hears the unmistakable throaty roar of a Harley starting up. Savage saw one earlier in the day, on a trailer with an Oklahoma license plate. It had struck him as odd— driving from Oklahoma to Key West with your Harley on a trailer.

Two tourists at the next table are talking about a manatee that comes to the dock to drink fresh water from a hose. "Big, he was. Like a compact car."

Savage turns to look at the couple. The woman catches his eye, and Savage smiles at their conversation.

"With that cute little doggy face. Those whiskers," the woman says, looking at Savage. He raises his glass. This would be a good place for a vacation, he thinks.

Savage wonders if he could live in Key West, with people always coming and going. There are so many tourists and service workers. There's also the seamy underside, the marginality.

He sees two men talking, dressed more for business than a vacation. They're having an intense conversation in a corner, away from the bar. Savage isn't sure if one of them is watching him. He should have seen them earlier. He refocuses. His cell phone vibrates—it's a text from Angie that says just "Massage?" Savage feels a wave of desire, but he doesn't reply. He decides to surprise her.

Savage pays his check and walks out of the bar. He goes around the corner ten paces, but then turns and walks back. The two men are coming out of the bar, walking purposefully, facing Savage. He walks straight past them, past the bar, turns left, then takes a quick right down a side street where street artists are vending their wares. Three more strides, another left, straight, then left again and then he's back by the bar.

He unlocks his bike and pedals up North Roosevelt to Stock Island. They might be following him, Savage thinks. He should have noticed. This isn't a time to be careless. He wishes he were more like Jake, whose friendships with women have always been close and strong but, as far as Savage can tell, not sexual. Seeing Jake with women, Savage realizes that his own relationships with women—at least the ones he finds attractive—always have a sexual tension. Savage pedals harder. He thinks about Angie and Nikki.

———

Angie's shoulders are tight, and Savage's fingers and thumbs work against the knots of tension.

"I thought you were going to give me a massage," Savage says, looking down at Angie's smooth, muscled back.

"I was. I will. Don't stop. Mmmm... harder."

Savage continues. He's trying to stay focused, but his mind is wandering.

"What are you doing?" Angie says. "Don't stop."

"Sorry," Savage says, trying to stay in the present.

"That's better," she says.

The fan turns slowly overhead. A boat passes by outside the houseboat. Savage finds another knot.

"Hey, not so hard. Focus," Angie says. "Stop thinking. This is about me."

Savage laughs. He looks at Angie's back, at her blonde hair on the pillow. The stirring begins.

"Mmmm, that's just right. Like that. Perfect."

"Good," he says.

"Where are you?" Angie turns her head to one side, looking at him.

"Here. Just thinking. A lot going on. Sorry. I'm worried about Jake. And you."

Savage moves his hands onto Angie's arms. He squeezes them and slides his hands down from her shoulders to her elbows.

"That's better. Much better."

Savage repeats the action then starts on her back, pressing hard with his thumbs. He finds her knots and kinks and works them out, feeling her tension leaving.

"Yes. Keep doing that. I like that. Think about me. More oil."

Savage takes in a breath and lets it out. He needs the release of sex. He pauses to get more oil from the bedside table and then works her until they both want each other, and then he takes off his clothes and her panties and they make love, easily and languidly at first, then with passion, until their sweat mingles and Savage's mind finally empties and he finds himself at peace.

Angie holds him tight and afterwards they kiss for a long time.

"Scary," Angie says. "Letting go completely like that." She runs a nail down Savage's back.

"I know," Savage says. "But I needed that."

"To have sex?"

"No. To let go like that." Savage is on his back, breathing slowly, his muscles loose.

Angie snuggles close to his side. "Stop it," she says.

"What?"

"Thinking. I can tell when it starts. You stiffen up."

"Who's a sensitive girl, then?" Savage says, laughing.

They fall silent.

"Maybe in a month," Savage says.

"In a month what?"

"We can have some fun," Savage continues, stroking Angie's hair.

"This wasn't fun?"

"That's not what I meant. This was wonderful. I mean, when this is over, we could go on vacation."

"To Key West?"

They both laugh.

"Yes, that would be nice," Savage says.

He continues to stroke Angie's hair.

"What are you thinking?"

"I was thinking I wish I could stop thinking," he says.

"You're just like Jake. Joking, joking, joking,"

"No, really. I just want it to stop. I just want to be here, like this, and all of this other stuff to go away."

Angie wiggles closer. "Awww," she says, "so you do like me."

Savage flexes his toes, smiles, and pulls Angie towards him. "We'll go to the Tortola. Then work our way down the windward islands."

Angie's breathing is steady, her body relaxed. She falls asleep.

That's what we'll do, Savage thinks, *when this has all been cleaned up.*

Savage works through his thoughts systematically. He hears the water lapping on the hull of the houseboat. He lies still, breathing in Angie's perfume. He feels a hollowness in his belly. The stirring again. For now, Ramirez can wait.

Angie stirs in her sleep, opens her eyes, and smiles; all her worries seem gone.

She turns towards Savage, pulls him towards her, and kisses him.

He closes his eyes, lets himself go... lets everything go.

15

THE OFFER

A HURRICANE IS BREWING in the southeast on the satellite image. Savage checks the coordinates for the wrecks, and sees that the eye of the hurricane will pass directly over the area where Jake will be diving. The eye isn't the problem, but the winds ahead of the eye will be gusting up to 120 miles per hour—more than a small vessel can comfortably handle.

Savage sits back from the desk. Jake knows his way around, but he's still worried. He's protective of his younger brother, even though he feels Jake is the more competent of the two of them, both on the sea and underneath it.

A passenger jet flies low over the yard on approach to the airport, bringing in more tourists. Ominous clouds are gathering on the horizon.

A Coast Guard advisory has gone out for small vessels. The tourists who would have been fishing, diving, or parasailing are filling the bars even earlier than usual as the town prepares for a few days of wind and rain.

Savage closes the doors to the storage shed and surveys the six Defender 250s neatly lined up inside and secured in their bays.

Outside the wind is freshening, though the sky is still blue. There's nothing to do but wait and see what the storm brings.

As the days passed, Savage has felt that Key West could be his place. After years of roaming and years of deployments, this could be the place, he thinks, to finally settle down, to build a life once things have calmed down. Assuming they ever do calm down.

Somewhere to the south, Jake will hopefully be making passage north, ahead of the storm, heading for a sheltered anchorage. Savage realizes, though, that Jake could have chosen to head out into the Atlantic if the seas weren't too big. Sometimes, it's worse to come ashore when the winds are howling and the Atlantic swells are pounding the coast. He wonders what the storm was like that founded the very Spanish galleons Jake has been diving on. They all start in the same way.

The wind masks the sound of tires on stones as they approach the gate. Savage doesn't hear or see Ramirez and the other man get out of the black Mercedes and walk towards the office. But he senses them. Turning, he moves behind the keel of a sailboat that is standing on chocks, twenty-five yards from the office. The two men are talking, facing each other, and don't seem to notice him.

A few clouds scud across the sky, and the wind increases. The men lean into it as they walk towards the office, and Ramirez knocks on the door. They wait, then Ramirez nods at the second man. He opens the door, and they walk in and close the door behind them.

Savage doesn't want any trouble. He wonders if the men have come to talk—or something else. He jogs towards the office. Through the window, he can see that the men are standing by the desk. A gust of wind blows a box across the concrete, tumbling and scraping along. The men look up at the noise, and Savage opens the door.

"Gentlemen?" He smiles, not aggressively.

"Mr. Savage," Ramirez says. He looks less nervous. The other man is large, full-chested—he's the muscle.

"I've come to talk," Ramirez says. "Just talk."

Savage takes in a breath and squares himself. He assesses the big man. He puts himself closer, in physical range. Ramirez swallows, glances at the big man, and then looks at Savage.

"Just to talk, understand? I'm not looking for trouble. I'm a businessman."

Savage doesn't reply. In Asia he learned the value and power of silence both as a means of communication and a way of unsettling an adversary.

"I made an offer on the yard, Mr. Savage, but apparently your brother preferred your offer. Correct?" Ramirez clears his throat, and a bead of sweat appears on his brow. The big man frowns and adjusts his feet.

Savage's eyes are ice-blue, his look unwavering. He spreads his fingers and settles his body weight.

The big man looks at Ramirez, who shakes his head *"Está bien."*

The big man turns his head towards Savage, then lowers his eyes.

"I'm not selling the yard, Mr. Ramirez. Not at this point in time."

"So, you might someday?"

"Not now."

"What if I matched your bid and paid you for the improvements?"

"Not now, Mr. Ramirez."

Ramirez scratches his neck. He presses his lips together, then they part.

"There's something else," Ramirez begins. "Maybe you heard. My family had some troubles recently. Bad troubles."

Savage raises his eyebrows, waiting for the accusations to come.

"My brother. He was badly beaten, and then he died."

Ramirez waits. Savage swallows. The big man straightens himself up as the tension rises.

"What are you saying, Mr. Ramirez?"

Ramirez feels his confidence return. He edges forward and drops his voice.

"I know a lot of people, Mr. Savage. I have a lot of interests in this town. That's what I'm saying."

Savage can see the anger rising in Ramirez, but he can tell that Ramirez won't let it out. Not today.

"My brother died when his boat hit the wharf, just over there," Ramirez points. "Did you know that, Mr. Savage?"

Savage says nothing, but maintains his poise. There's no point to doing otherwise.

"*Él sabe,*" the big man says, spitting the words, impatient for a command from Ramirez.

"No hable."

"No one knows what happened," Ramirez continues, waiting for Savage to react. "No witnesses. Nothing left. Bang. Gone." He makes a sweeping gesture with his hand.

The big man clenches his fists. Savage judges the distance and assesses his options.

Ramirez lets out a sigh. "How long have you been in Key West, Mr. Savage?"

"Not long."

Ramirez turns his head to the window. "The hurricane's coming."

"You know what they say?" Savage waits. "The winds, when they come, they bring trouble, but when they leave, they clear the air."

Ramirez clears his throat, steps back, and turns to the big man, "*Vamos!*" There's frustration in his voice.

The big man fixes his eyes on Savage and mutters something Savage doesn't catch, but it's clearly a threat. Savage raises his hands slowly, palms open, and shakes his head. He doesn't say anything, though part of him wants the confrontation, just to end it all.

"We'll speak again, Mr. Savage. And if you hear from your brother, I still need to talk with him."

Ramirez blinks, then opens the door, and the big man follows him out, turning one more time to glare at Savage. Savage walks over to the door and follows the men to their Mercedes. He watches them get in, as they talk rapidly in Spanish. Ramirez slaps the wheel and holds both his hands up. He's yelling. Then he grips the wheel and beats it.

Savage expects the Mercedes to peel out, leaving stones spraying behind it, but it doesn't. Instead the Mercedes reverses, the driver's window opens, and Ramirez turns his head back, a strange smile on his face.

"You don't have to like a man to do business with him. We could do business, Mr. Savage."

Savage pauses. Ramirez's eyes are dark and deep-set, bordered by thick black eyebrows, like those of his brother.

"Perhaps we will, Mr. Ramirez," Savage says. "Perhaps we will."

Ramirez smiles. It seems as if he is going to say something, but he doesn't. The window closes and the Mercedes drives off.

The sky is beginning to darken and the first warm drops of rain begin to fall. Then the deluge comes, and the wind begins to howl.

————

It rains for three days. Then, as quickly as it came, the hurricane is gone. The air clears and the sky turns a rich blue. The streets bustle again and a new energy fills the town. But Savage is not thinking about the sun or the pelicans circling the filleting table on the dock. He's looking at the body being pulled from the water next to the dock.

He recognizes the man as the intruder. His head lolls as he's pulled from the water, and there's no mistaking the scar on the man's cheek. Savage watches the body being loaded onto the waiting gurney, and then he turns and walks towards Caroline Street to pick up some coffee and buy a paper. A few tourists are standing in bemused amazement as a pelican circles overhead. The ambulance doors close, and it pulls away.

"Did you see that?" an elderly man with ghost-white legs and knee-length socks says to his wife.

"I did," she says, sipping her coffee.

Savage thinks about the fear in the man's eyes when he was taping him to the fence. It wasn't about what he thought Savage would do; it was because of what he knew Ramirez would do when they found him taped to the fence, having been caught and having failed to get the flash drive.

Savage walks by Lost Reef Adventures down to the dock, where he sits on a bench and nurses his coffee. The police have gone now. A captain starts the engine of his boat. Tourists are beginning to gather on the dock. Coolers of bait and supplies are being loaded. A young, muscled man jumps from the dock onto the stern of one of the boats. A couple of fishing charters make their way out of the harbor, and a dive boat follows.

Another day in paradise.

"Hey, stranger," a voice says.

Savage turns and sees Nikki.

"First time I've seen you outside the Whistle," Savage says.

"You too," Nikki says.

Their eyes linger in that easy place, and Savage feels a flutter in his belly.

"Well, yeah," Savage says. They both laugh.

Savage steps forward, puts his arm around Nikki, and kisses her on the cheek. He catches a hint of her perfume. His hand brushes her long, thick, dark hair. It reminds him of Japan. "*Nihongo ga hanashimasu ka?*" Savage asks.

"*Sukoshi.*" Nikki smiles and laughs. "My grandparents only spoke to me in Japanese, but they've been gone awhile. I haven't spoken in Japanese in years."

"I was there a while."

"I know."

"What are you doing here?"

"Sailing. Waiting for my boyfriend. He's got a boat. We were going to sail down the Keys. Do you want to come along?"

"Love to. Stuff to do, though." Savage recognizes the look in her eye. It's an invitation—and a challenge. Savage lets go, and the flow takes him.

"Come and see the boat. Come on!" Nikki grabs his hand and leads him down the dock.

They make their way between the tourists and crews. Savage can smell the bait and the diesel engines idling.

Nikki stops, turns, and gestures. "Ta-da!"

"Nice. A Beneteau 43-footer. Very nice. You like to sail?" Savage asks.

"When it's not too windy. I don't like all that leaning over splashy stuff."

They step on board. The boat is new, top of the line, and hardly used.

"He's not here yet," Nikki says. "I'm early."

They stand in the cockpit, Nikki close to Savage. He can smell her perfume again. She looks up at him and touches his shoulder.

"Want to go below?"

Savage feels a flutter in his heart.

"Sure," he says. He follows Nikki down the steps. "Nice layout," he adds, not sure what's happening, but feeling on the brink.

Nikki turns and touches his chest, lightly running her fingers down his shirt.

"How's Angie?" she asks.

"How's your boyfriend?"

They both laugh. Their eyes meet. Nikki steps forward, and Savage catches another waft of her perfume. He can hear her breathe. He reaches out to pull her close, but he stops, hearing feet on the dock outside.

"Nikki, honey?" A man's voice calls from on deck.

"Down here! I'm showing Savage around."

"Savage?" They hear footsteps in the cockpit, and then coming down into the cabin.

"You got off lucky this time," Nikki says. "I'm going to get you, and when I do..." Her eyes are wild.

Savage thinks about Angie and feels a wave of relief, and then guilt at what he would have done.

And then his phone rings—it's Jake.

16

MONKEY BUSINESS

SAVAGE ENDS THE CALL. A biplane buzzes overhead, towing a banner that says, "Carrie, will you marry me?" Savage puts the phone in his pocket. He wonders who Carrie is. The plane banks and turns, coming around for another run.

"Well, will you, Carrie?" Savage says out loud. He stares across the harbor.

Nothing ever had been simple, he muses, so why expect it to be?

The question was what to do about Ramirez. Savage would play him like a fly fisherman and keep him on the line. He needed him to think there was a possibility of doing business. He could tell that Ramirez was cautious; he had seen a glimmer of wariness in his eyes when they talked. He would wait until the right time.

The biplane sweeps by again, out to sea. It passes over the Beneteau as it heels in the warm breeze. He can see Nikki in the stern. *That is a woman who gets what she needs.* Angie, on the other hand, is different—a woman who needs something else. Savage just isn't sure exactly what it is.

Savage thinks about Nikki's finger on his chest—the gentle touch of her nail, the look in her eyes, and the flutter in his heart.

Nothing happened, but at the same time it did. Another ten minutes and who knows what chaos would have followed? But Savage does know, and he wonders how he would have felt, how he would feel now.

He sits at a restaurant table outside, near the schooner wharf, watching the day go by, listening in on snippets of conversation. Everything is moving slowly beneath the blue.

"Do you want a drink, honey?" an overweight man in voluminous shorts asks his wife.

"A drink? I just finished breakfast!" There's exasperation in her voice.

"But we're on vacation."

"You might be. I have to spend every waking minute with you. That's work."

Savage chuckles. The couple walks by, and soon they are swallowed among the other tourists.

He orders an iced tea and drums his fingers slowly on the wooden table. He listens to the snippets of conversations and begins to feel hungry. His phone vibrates—the screen reads *Angie*.

"Hey!" Angie's voice is sprightly, oddly cheery, as if her chipper disposition is forced. Savage straightens his back.

"What's up?" Savage says, his voice low. He's never gotten used to the way Americans boom into their phones.

"I don't know. All this stuff. Where are you, Savage?" She stresses the *you*.

"At the Schooner Wharf," Savage says. He knows that isn't what she's asking.

"I mean in your head, Savage. I'm not sure where you are. I'm not sure if we're too close or not close enough. Savage?"

Savage sips his tea, not sure what to say. She's played her hand.

"We're where we are," he says. He's frustrated by how meaningless his statement sounds.

"Well, that helps," Angie sighs.

"Lunch, then?"

"I don't know. I should say no, but I don't want to. I want to say yes, but I think *you* don't want to."

"I want to," Savage says.

A musician walks by carrying a guitar case. Time to set up for the lunch crowd.

"Bring the jeep," he continues, "and pick me up at Lost Reef. We can drive out of town."

"Okay," Angie says, before hanging up. "Give me a few minutes." Some life has returned to her voice.

Savage watches the Beneteau tack again and heel into the wind, the white sail contrasting with sky and sea. *So simple*, he thinks.

The musician is tuning up, plugging in his amp.

Savage hears the rough sound of Angie's jeep as it comes around the corner. She waves, and he gets to his feet and stretches.

They drive with the top down, listening to Bob Marley and not talking much. Angie's face is set, focused on the road.

"You're beautiful, Angie," Savage says, without thinking. He wishes things were easy.

"He talks!"

"Really, you are. Even when you're angry. Look, I'm sorry. I didn't mean to sound dismissive or distant. I've got a lot on my mind, with Jake and the boatyard. And Ramirez. I hadn't seen this coming."

"What? Hadn't seen *what* coming?"

"You. Us," Savage says.

"So... there's an us?"

"I like sleeping in your bed, watching you when you sleep, caressing your hair in the morning."

Angie smiles and strokes her hair with one hand. She takes her sunglasses off and looks over at Savage.

"Beautiful eyes, too," he adds.

"Stop it, Mr. Smooth. Enough already. Let's have some fun."

"That would be good," Savage says. The warm wind soothes his face.

A Harley passes, heading towards Key West.

They cross a bridge linking two keys. A fishing boat passes underneath, and Savage watches it as it heads down the channel, two rods mounted in the stern. Angie puts a hand on Savage's thigh. Savage puts his hand on Angie's and squeezes it. Savage feels the frisson. It's what he wants.

"We'll keep it simple," Angie says.

"Nothing's ever simple," he replies. He wishes he had kept that sentiment to himself.

"We can try." Angie's eyes are on the road.

"The last time I was in love it ended badly," Savage says. "Very badly. That was a while back. Made me very cautious. I find it difficult to be close. I mean emotionally. Don't know why. Not sure why I even said that."

"You like me," Angie says. "That's why you said it. Now go on."

"A long time ago, maybe five years, I was in Thailand. I was still a monk, still living as one, or at least trying. I never found it easy—the simple life. I really worked hard on myself. I was following the Middle Path, trying to eliminate cravings and practice the four noble truths." Savage pauses.

"Savage—keep talking. I want to know. Please," Angie says, drawing out the *please*.

"After the military, I was wild. It was fall apart or reassemble myself. I'd seen enough people fall apart. So, yes, Japan, then Thailand. It's not about being a good monk or a bad monk. I was living as a monk. It all made sense. The Eightfold Path to the Cessation of Suffering." Savage mocks himself as he says this, putting the words in quotation marks. Then he pauses again and shakes his head.

"I don't like talking about myself," he says. "I don't know why. I had a complicated childhood. Weird family. No one ever said what they meant. Everything was always fine, even when it wasn't. Particularly when it wasn't, in fact."

The jeep crosses another bridge, rising slowly above the light blue of the shallows.

"But *I* want to know, Savage. And I've never heard of the eightfold whatever. What is it?"

The light turns red, and they sit in silence. Savage puts his hand on Angie's thigh, leans over, and kisses her.

"Go on, Savage. The path. Tell me."

"The path. To the cessation of all suffering. It makes complete sense. Right view, right intention, right speech, right action, right livelihood, right effort, right mindfulness, and right concentration. I was on that path."

"That sounds good. It sounds right," Angie says, changing gears. The jeep shudders.

"A lot of things sound good and right. It's harder than you think. But I tried. Believe me, I tried."

"Then what? You stepped off the path? Took a wrong turn?"

The light changes. Angie works her way through the gears.

Savage swallows. His mind drifts back to Thailand, to Chiang Mai. He'd been standing in the shade of a tree near the zoo on a hot, quiet afternoon. He was standing still, bowl in hand, head tilted down. The picture is clear in his mind, as vivid as if he were there. He closes his eyes.

"Hello, Savage? Come back."

He opens his eyes and returns to the moment. "A woman comes up to me and puts some money in my bowl and walks off. I know it's a woman because of the sound of her feet. My eyes were closed. I was meditating. But the sound of her feet had an effect on me."

Angie turns on the indicator and slows to turn into the restaurant parking lot. She waits for a break in the oncoming traffic, crosses the road and parks in a corner of the lot. She turns off the engine and sits back in her seat.

"There," she says. "We're here."

Savage is still staring ahead, his memory clear.

"It was right then at that moment that everything changed. I opened my eyes and there, on the other side of the road, was this Thai woman, watching me. She was leaning against a stone wall. It was the woman who'd given me the money, and for some reason, I got to my feet, walked across the road, and when I got to her, I took the money she'd given to me and gave it back to her."

"Why?"

"I told her I couldn't take it as I'd just stopped being a monk." Savage shakes his head and smiles. "Without thinking, that's what happened. She put the money in the bowl, and it all came to an end. Just like that. Funny, really."

"And she took the money back?"

"Yes. From this crazy blue-eyed foreign monk she was trying to help. She said she was sorry, as though it was her fault. I said no, and I thanked her. And that was that. Beautiful, in a way."

Savage opens the door to the jeep and gets out. They walk together towards the restaurant.

"But what was it?" Angie asks, "And why her? Was there something about her?"

"I don't know, to be honest. It was just a realization. You know, like I said, I tried to be a monk. I lived like one. But, really, I hadn't truly let go of anything. I had just suppressed desires and rechanneled some of my energies. I thought I was being authentic, but I wasn't. I was kidding myself. That probably sounds odd. But I can tell you I really felt it, right at the moment she put the money in my bowl."

They find a seat near the water, under an awning. There's a light breeze rustling the palm leaves above them. Savage takes off his sunglasses and rubs his eyes. Angie squeezes his hand and smiles at him.

"Well, there I am in my robes, giving money back to a woman I don't know, telling her I'm not a monk anymore. And she listens. She takes me to her house. She's living with her father. Her mother's dead and she's looking after her dad who's a raging alcoholic, but he's got a lot of land and some businesses, and she's trying to help him out. And there we are. I tell her my story."

Savage picks up an ashtray from the table and hefts it in his hand. He puts it back down and picks up a bottle of hot sauce.

"Some of my story," he continues, "and I still can't believe that I did what I did or said what I said."

"What happened?"

"I stayed. I had Jake wire me some money. I didn't have anything; at least, not in Thailand. Jake helped me out. I had to get some clothes. Basics. I had nothing, having been a monk."

"How long did you stay?"

"Long enough to fall in love, to want to stay with her. Long enough for her to realize that it wasn't going to work."

Savage remembers the biplane. *Carrie, will you marry me?* She would have had to say yes. He rolls his shoulder.

His thoughts return to Thailand, the day he left Chiang Mai, taking the train to Bangkok. They'd hugged at the station, and then the girl had turned and walked off into her future, leaving Savage to wallow in his past, his heart broken.

Angie lets Savage be.

There's a long silence. The server comes over, but Savage isn't ready to order. She looks at Angie questioningly, knowing something might be up.

"I'll have whatever you have," Savage says.

Angie orders conch sandwiches and iced tea. The server smiles at Angie and walks back to the kitchen.

"It's 'conk', not 'conch', by the way. Just letting you know," Angie says.

"Thanks," Savage says.

"You had your heart broken, Savage. I'm sorry. We all have, I guess."

"My fault, though. Not hers."

"It wasn't anyone's fault, was it? Which doesn't make it any less painful."

"No. No, it doesn't. But I wanted you to know. That was a while back."

"So, you're not an asshole? Is that what you're saying?"

Savage gives a big laugh that lights up his face. "I'm just saying I may be a different kind of asshole than the one you think I am."

"That's great! What kind are you? I've seen most."

"Listen. I spoke to Jake today. He's going to be gone a while."

"A while? You mean a week? A month? What kind of 'while'?"

"He's got some business to take care of."

"Business to take care of. Monkey business. You and your brother. I don't know. And something tells me you're not going to tell me what it is, right?"

The conch sandwiches arrive. The server puts the glasses and bottles on the table and smiles at them. "Enjoy," she says.

Savage watches her leave—sees her tight haunches and tanned legs.

"Stop it!" Angie says, slapping his hand.

"Sorry. Old habit. Weakness of the flesh."

He leans towards his sandwich.

"Right," Savage continues, "as you were saying, better not to know. I'm not sure what Ramirez has in mind, but the less people know, the better. Right now, it's me and Jake. For your own safety, Angie. Doesn't mean I don't want to stroke your back and watch you when you sleep. You know that."

"Annoying," Angie says.

"I know," Savage says, lifting his sandwich, "but it's what we've got to do. For now." He takes a big bite.

"He's okay, though? You can tell me that, right?"

Savage nods, his mouth full. He swallows and wipes some mayonnaise from his lip. "He's good. Better than okay. I can tell you that."

Angie lifts her glass and sips her tea. She has something on her mind. Savage watches her carefully. He won't ask. He wants to mention Nikki, but he doesn't.

"Savage?" Angie says.

"What?" Savage asks.

"I haven't been entirely honest with you."

Savage coughs and leans forward. "And I thought it was me! Go on."

17

AN ISSUE OF TRUST

IT'S LATE ON A STILL, moonless night, the air is thick and heavy. Savage walks west along Petronia Street as two men follow him. They've been trailing him for half an hour, stopping when Savage stops, walking when he walks. Savage takes his time. He can tell they're not professionals. He thinks about looping around to the cemetery, vaulting the gates, and luring them into following him through the maze of mausoleums. But that wouldn't do him any good—it's better to lose them. His breathing is steady, ears alert, eyes accustomed to the dark.

He pauses by the cemetery gates, waits for the men to stop, then walks on. It's time. Savage sees an alley on the other side of the street. He could be there in seconds, then gone until the next time. A sound. Savage turns. A car drives up behind him, slows and the driver's window opens.

"Get in. Quick," Nikki says. Savage jogs around to the passenger side of the black Porsche Boxster, opens the door, and gets in. Nikki puts it into gear and takes off. She takes a left, then another left onto Olivia. She's quick with the gears. Confident.

"They were in the Whistle, at the bar," Nikki says. "One of

them got a call, he was speaking Spanish. One said, you sure it's him? And off they went."

Savage is crammed into the passenger seat. Low. He can't stretch his legs. He winces and rotates his shoulders. He looks over at Nikki.

"Thanks for turning up. Things were just about to get complicated. Or ugly. Probably both." Savage straightens himself up a bit.

"I know what Ramirez is doing," he continues, "by keeping the pressure up. Just letting me know he knows where I am and what I'm doing. Letting me know that if he wanted he could start squeezing me a little. Right?" Savage winces again.

"I guess," she says. She keeps her eyes on the road.

"Where we going?" Savage asks, beginning to relax. A drunk tourist wobbles down the sidewalk. A scooter speeds by in the opposite direction.

"You better come to my place," Nikki says, sounding very matter-of-fact, eyes straight ahead. He could ask her to stop the car right now. He could get out, go back to the boatyard or go to Angie's. He could, but he doesn't.

He raises his eyebrows, stares straight ahead, and feels the power of the engine as Nikki changes gear. Savage feels a stirring inside.

Nikki changes down. The car slows, she turns, and the Porsche grips the road.

"You certainly know how to drive this thing," Savage says.

"I know how to do a lot of things, Savage. Driving is just one of them."

The Porsche surges ahead. Nikki works through the gears then eases off the accelerator.

Nikki turns and smiles, her eyes sparkling under the streetlights.

"Are you messing with me?" Savage asks.

"Maybe." There is a lilting playfulness in Nikki's intonation.

"Why your place?"

"It's safe. There's good security. They won't try anything there."

"They might not try anything anywhere."

"True. But they might. You can't be too careful, Savage," Angie takes her hand off the gearshift and squeezes his thigh, then runs a fingernail towards his crotch.

"Okay," Savage says, pressing his feet against the floor of the car, feeling his muscles tighten, a tingle in his belly. He closes his eyes, then opens them. Nikki takes her nail from his thigh.

"Actually, it's not my place. It's his place. Brent's."

"Great!" Savage says. "He didn't like me from the very first moment he saw me on his boat. No guy's going to like a man called 'Savage' being shown around his own boat by his woman when he's not there. He thought I was hot for you. Sniffing around. You know that. I don't think he's going to like it. Especially me turning up at his place in the middle of the night."

Savage shakes his head, then laughs at the ridiculousness of the situation.

"Nikki? Come on. I mean, really."

"He's not going to know. He's out of town on business in Chicago. Won't be back until next week."

Nikki checks her rearview mirror and the side mirrors, her look serious.

"Being followed?" Savage says. His voice is low and urgent, his mind flitting from Nikki to the men following him earlier.

Savage wiggles in his seat and puts his hand in his pocket, stretching his legs so he can work his fingers in.

"No. Nada. What're you doing?" Nikki asks.

"Texting Angie. Saying something's come up."

Savage texts slowly with his large index finger.

"I hate these things," he says.

"She was expecting you?"

"I don't know. Don't want her to worry."

Savage finishes the text, hits send, and watches the message change color.

"You got something going on there?" Nikki asks

Savage leans back in his seat.

"Not sure. Kind of. I'm not used to all this."

He raises his open palms, unsure how to finish.

"She thinks you do."

"She does?"

"Don't sound all surprised. I'm not an idiot, and neither are you. Angie definitely isn't."

Nikki's eyes are on the road ahead. She drives on, turns down a narrow side street and parks, and turns off the engine. The car is still. The energy changes.

Nikki leans over and touches his face. Savage reaches out and strokes her long, black hair. The night is still and languid. Savage opens the passenger door and smells the fuchsia. He smiles and laughs, the serenading sounds of cicadas fill the air.

"What? What's so funny?"

"Fuchsia. Smell it. Love it."

"Why's that funny?"

"Did you know it was named after a German scientist?"

"It was?"

They get out of the car. Savage stretches and looks up into the stillness of the night, feeling the warm air on his face.

"Yeah. Leonhart Fuchs. Fuchs. I always thought that was funny."

"That's the type of thing Jake would say."

"He told me, that's why."

Savage chuckles and shakes his head.

"Fuchs," Savage says in a German accent.

"You two. Where is Jake, anyway?"

"Out of town. He'll be back."

Savage follows Nikki to the house. She unlocks the door, lets

Savage in, and then locks the door behind them. He counts three locks. She turns on the alarm system.

"Make yourself at home," Nikki says. She walks upstairs.

He walks into the kitchen—it's expensive—very stylish and tasteful, all cherry wood and stainless steel, with Sub-Zero appliances. Savage runs his hand along the smooth granite countertop. He opens the fridge and sees nothing but a bottle of Chardonnay and a six-pack of IPA. He frowns, closes the door, and hums to himself a Jimmy Buffet song.

"One thing after another," Savage mutters, running his hand along the counter top, looking up at the soft recessed lighting.

Savage hears a shower turn on. He walks into the living room, wondering about the men following him, glad there had been no show down. His muscles become tense at the thought. The shower stops. He takes his phone out of his pocket and puts it back. He can hear Nikki moving around in the bathroom. A hairdryer purrs.

Five minutes later she comes down the stairs wearing a white terrycloth robe.

"Drink?" she asks. "I can't offer you anything to eat. There isn't anything."

"White wine or beer?" Savage asks. "I looked."

"Snooping around, huh?"

"Not really. I like looking in fridges. They tell you a lot."

"Like what?"

"Like you need to go shopping."

Nikki laughs, opens the fridge, and takes out the bottle of Chardonnay.

"What are you thinking, Savage?"

"About you, Angie, Jake, my vacation in Key West, me, everything." Savage pauses. Nikki pours two glasses of Chardonnay.

"You and Jake never had anything going on, and Jake and Angie never had anything going on. But you and Angie had something going on. And now," Savage takes a step towards Nikki. He can smell her perfume and feel her closeness.

"And now? What?" Nikki says. "You and Angie have something going on? I'm okay with that. I have something going on, too. I know what I'm doing, Savage. Don't worry about me. I like you. You're hot, and smart, and funny. Savage. I don't mind about Angie. It's not about that, Savage. I just want you. Sometimes it's that simple. Don't make it complicated. I've done that. Been there."

Savage draws in a breath. He's close enough to reach out and touch Nikki. He wants to. Nikki steps towards him and runs her finger down his chest, and then puts her arms around his neck and kisses him.

"Forget that drink. Let's go to bed."

Nikki turns off the lights and they go upstairs.

"Spare room," Nikki says. There's a skylight, and the stars are out. "It would be too weird in his bed."

Savage rubs his hair, smiles, and sighs. He follows Nikki, watching the way she moves in her robe.

The room is spacious, the bed low. Nikki stops and turns as Savage's heart begins to race.

He pulls Nikki towards him. He doesn't feel tender. They kiss. They are both breathing heavily. He undoes her robe and she begins to pull his t-shirt off.

"Wait," Savage says. He breaks from Nikki, and takes off his pants.

"Commando, huh?"

"It's a habit."

Nikki strokes Savage, then bites his chest and nipples. She rakes her nails down his back. Savage's breathing quickens.

"You're strong. I like that. Scars, too. A lot of them."

"They've all got their stories," Savage says, running his hands through Nikki's hair, stroking her back and pulling her towards him.

"You going to tell me any of them?"

"Not tonight."

"I don't think it's tonight any longer."

Savage peers through the skylight and sees the black has acquired a hint of dawn blue.

They kiss, and then make love. Nikki's passion is stronger than Angie's. More urgent. Nikki knows how to enjoy herself, and how to get her pleasure. She pushes him on his back and holds him down.

Nikki gasps, her chest heaving as Savage eases himself in to her, nuzzling her neck.

Afterwards, they lie, looking up through the skylight as the dawn comes. Their heads are close. Savage is holding Nikki's hand.

"That worked," Nikki says.

"Sure did," Savage takes her hand and places it on him.

"Jesus!"

"Why not?" Savage asks.

The second time there is more passion, more closeness. They both feel it.

"Your boyfriend. Not love, then?"

"No. He's a boy and a friend. And I like him. He's easy to be with. Doesn't make any demands. He's rich, convenient. How about you and Angie?"

"I think she's falling in love with me."

"Is that a problem?"

Savage thinks about this.

"I don't know. Probably. Usually is."

"Love? Or falling in love with you?"

"Both. I think."

"What about you? You and Angie? Are you falling in love?"

"You know, I don't know. The other day something happened. I felt something, or let myself feel something I hadn't felt for a long time. But I don't know."

"Then you're not. If you were, you'd know. Right?"

They are both on their backs, watching the clouds through the skylight.

"Don't know," Savage says.

"Life," Nikki says. "What're you going to do? You've got to take it as it comes."

She sighs.

"I don't know. I think we can shape it a bit more than that. I'd like to think we can. But, hey, while we're at it, you and Jake? Nothing? And what about Jake and Angie?"

"Jake's different. There aren't many men like him. He listens. He's not on the prowl. He's not a manipulator. He's a really, really good friend, and he takes care of his people. And there comes this point, when that's how it's been set up, you just can't cross the line. You can have dinner, talk, help each other out, but that's how it stays."

"What about me?"

"You. You're different. You're an animal."

"That doesn't sound good."

"Maybe it doesn't. But that's how it is. You have this quality about you. There's something unsafe about you. Something edgy and definitely different. Can't say I've met many people like you, anyone who's been where you've been, or done what you've done. And you have something else."

"What's that supposed to mean... 'Something else'?"

"You know--that indescribable thing that makes some people irresistible. I don't know what it is. It doesn't matter what it is. You have it, whether you like it or not. It's going to get you in all sorts of trouble. I presume it probably already has."

Nikki props herself up on one elbow. Savage turns his head.

"Just doesn't sound good. Very superficial. I don't feel superficial."

"Still waters run deep?"

"I think so. I think I run deep."

"Shall I take your word for it?"

Nikki strokes his head.

"No. Don't do that. You have to know that. You have to find out--give it time."

"What do you want, Savage? I mean here, in Key West?"

"I want Jake to feel he has his boatyard back. I want to put an end to any bad blood that exists with Ramirez. I want Jake to do what he wants, and I want to figure out what I want because right now, I don't know. Except I could really do with a vacation, and this seems like it would be a good place in an odd sort of way."

"You're going to try a bit of everything, and see what you like? A bit of me, a bit of Angie, a bit of something else?" Nikki asks.

"I didn't mean that. Look, I'm here. I'm trying to do right for Jake. Everything else is just happening to me. I had a long time on my own."

"You're making up for lost time?"

"That's not what I meant. I mean the closeness is all new. I'm not sure how to handle it, what to do with it."

"Savage, I need to tell you something about Angie. Not in a bitchy way--you just need to know."

Savage turns and looks at Nikki. "Go on," he says.

"She has a kid."

Savage waits.

"Ramirez's kid."

So that is Angie's secret. She hadn't been completely honest, she'd said. But she was trying to be honest. She had been about to tell him, but she hadn't—and now Nikki had.

"The thing is, they have a little boy, but she isn't raising him, the Ramirez family is. I'm not judging her. These things happen. But. She didn't want to have a kid, and she wasn't capable of raising one. Ramirez wanted to have the kid. He wanted to have Angie, too, but that's not what she wanted."

"Complicated. Poor Angie. She tried to tell me," Savage says. "She started to tell me. You're saying Ramirez has leverage?"

"I trust Angie."

"So do I."

"But before you said you didn't."

"It was too hard to explain then. I didn't know you. What I mean is that Angie would do anything to keep her son from harm. She's a mother, of course; no one can blame her for that," Nikki says.

"I get it," Savage says. "Ramirez isn't going to harm Angie. He's just going to threaten to harm her son, and she'll do anything he asks." He closes his eyes. "Angie. But you know what?"

"What?"

"We just have to be careful. Perhaps this might be useful. Just can't tell her anything that might put us in any kind of danger. She'll tell Ramirez anything we tell her, if he asks, right? If he really wants to know, she's not going to refuse."

"I think that's right."

"So, we act accordingly. If something's happening on a Tuesday, we say Wednesday. We know white, but we say black." He lets out a long breath, stares through the skylight. "We should sleep," Savage says.

"We should," Nikki says. "But not quite yet."

18

THE BOY

SAVAGE IS sure it's her, but he doesn't want her to see him. He keeps cycling by the playground. The black Mercedes is parked near the water fountains, its tinted windows up, the vehicle idling. Ramirez, Savage thinks, must be in the car watching.

Savage pedals slowly around the park. He dismounts and wheels his bike to a bench, next to a bush where he can't be seen from the car. Savage stretches out his legs, slumps back, pulls his baseball cap down low, and watches.

The boy is five or six years old and dark, but not as dark as Ramirez. Angie kicks a soccer ball to him, and the boy picks it up and runs off with it. Angie laughs as she chases her son. He turns to look for her, stumbles and falls, lands on the ball, rolls off it, and finally comes to a stop on his back. A young Hispanic woman has been sitting on a bench near Angie and the boy, and she walks over to say something. Angie looks up, says something in return, shakes her head, and waves the woman away.

The door of the Mercedes opens, Ramirez gets out, stands by the door, and watches as Angie scoops the boy up in her arms and cuddles him. The boy throws his arms around Angie's neck and hugs her closely. Ramirez gets back in the car.

Angie slowly puts the boy down. They hold hands and walk back to the ball. The boy kicks it and Angie runs after it, takes a swing at it, misses, and falls over. The boy laughs, runs over to Angie, and jumps on her. They roll on the ground, laughing and hugging each other, mother and son. Savage smiles at Angie's naturalness with her child.

The door of the Mercedes opens again—Ramirez gets out once more. He walks over to the bench where the young woman is and says something to her. She gets up and walks over to the Mercedes, opens the passenger door, and gets in.

"*Tiempo para ir,*" Ramirez shouts. Not too loud, but loud enough for the boy to turn and look. "Let's go."

"*No papá. Quiero quedarme,*" the boy says. "Stay."

"*Su abuela está esperando,*" Ramirez says. "Your grandmother wants to see you."

The boy turns to his mother and she talks to him, kneeling as she speaks, stroking his hair and kissing his cheek, comforting him. She picks up the ball, takes his hand, and leads him over to his father. Ramirez opens the rear door to the car. The boy, resigned, hugs his mother, kisses her, and gets in. Ramirez closes the door.

He stands stiffly, talking to Angie for a while. She looks completely dejected. Savage can't hear what Ramirez is saying, but his face is intense, angry. Angie's arms hang by her sides as she listens to Ramirez. Savage wonders how often this happens. Ramirez raises a finger and begins to shake it at Angie, who says something back. Savage sits more upright. He can see the growing tension.

The rear door of the Mercedes opens, and the boy starts to get out. Ramirez turns and talks to the boy. The boy gets back into the car, and Ramirez closes the door. He turns back to Angie, says something, makes a dismissive gesture, and then gets into the car and drives off.

Angie waves, watching the car as it turns from the side street into the traffic. She stands briefly until the car is gone and then walks over to a bench, sits, and clutches her head in her hands. She's sobbing. Savage can see her shaking. He straightens up, stands up, takes his bicycle, and wheels it over to Angie. He wants to be near her and make her feel better.

"Hey, Angie."

Angie looks up, surprised, "Savage? What are you doing here?" She wipes her eyes with the back of her hand. "God, I bet I look like shit."

"No," Savage says. "You just look sad."

"I was going to tell you," Angie says, looking up at Savage, trying to smile.

"I know. It's okay. I was watching you with him. He was so happy. You look like a great mother." Savage gives a small smile. Angie's eyes tear up again, and she starts to cry.

"It's so hard. I only see him once a week. But at least I get to see him." Angie wipes her eyes and shakes her head. Her lips are tight, shaking. Savage reaches out and strokes her hair.

"What's his name?"

"Juan." Angie smiles through her tears. "He's such a great little boy. God, what a mess."

"A mess?"

"His life. Me being his mother. Ramirez."

"Did you love him? When you were with him, I mean. What was Ramirez to you?"

Angie rubs her eyes, reaches out, and pulls Savage down to sit on the bench next to her. She leans against him, and Savage puts his arm around her. He wants to look after her and take care of her.

"I don't know. I'd just arrived in Key West. It was all new. I was a barmaid, running away like everyone else here. I'd never been to a place like this. I'd never had any money. Suddenly I was getting big tips. Guys liked me. It was fun. I was young, and I'd never seen rich people. I was such a small-town girl, and then suddenly I began to feel like somebody. Ramirez started to make me feel like someone special. He'd stop by the bar, take me home, drop me off." Angie looks up and turns towards Savage.

"It happens," Savage says. "We find ourselves *in* things, right. One minute you're not, the next minute you are. You don't really know how you got there, right?"

"Uh huh. I never loved him. I just got used to him. I liked doing things with him. He was fun with his cars, boats, and cash. He'd buy me things. I was young and stupid. It was better than where I had been. At least I thought it was. And then…"

"You got pregnant?"

"Yes. I didn't know what to do. He was clear. He wanted to marry me, but I wouldn't marry him. I actually didn't want to have the baby. But I couldn't do anything else… I just couldn't. Who wants a pregnant barmaid? In Key West, I mean. So I lost my job. I didn't have any money. He showed me how tough things were going to be for me."

Two young mothers come into the park, both pushing strollers. They sit on a bench on the other side of the park.

"That's tough," Savage says. "Really. I mean it, Angie." Savage hugs her. "So you never married him?"

"No. We made a deal. He still wanted to get married, but I couldn't. We fought, but I think he knew it would be a disaster. What would the point have been? I wouldn't have been happy. He's not an idiot. So, we made a deal. I would have the baby, and he would raise him. Raise Juan." Angie tears up again and puts her head in her hands, her shoulders shaking.

"Hey, Angie. It must be hard. I was watching you and Juan. He looks so happy with you. You look happy with him. Don't be too hard on yourself."

"I came here to get away from all the shit that was going on in my life."

"You can't get away from it. You can run as far as you like. And when you get there… there you are." Savage shakes his head,

"Believe me, I know. I ran and kept running. In the end, you just have to take it all on. All of it. It makes you who you are."

One of the young mothers gets her daughter out of the stroller and bounces her on her knee. Angie watches.

"Back then—at the beginning—it all seemed such fun. I didn't even think about what I'd been through, why I'd wanted to run."

A scooter drives by, and then the tourist train. Couples sit together as the driver explains that they are about to come to the highest point of land in Key West. "It's eighteen feet above sea level," the driver announces through the sound system. "You'd want more than that in a hurricane." And the train rumbles on.

"I could give that tour," Angie says. "I've heard it so many times."

"It's complicated," Savage says, almost whispering, thinking about his own life and how much time he's spent running and doing. Perhaps now, he thought, now might be a time to slow down, work on himself.

"Life?" Angie says, smiling sadly as she watches the two young mothers laughing and chatting.

"That, too. No, I meant this. You. Juan. Ramirez. He has something over you. You know what I mean? With Juan."

"What do you mean?" Angie straightens. "Savage? What are you saying?" She removes his arm from her shoulder and slides across the bench, creating a space between them.

Savage clears his throat, rotates his shoulder, and scans the park. "He's got leverage."

"He'd never do anything to his own son. Ramirez may be a bastard, but he'd never do that, Savage."

"He could make you think he would. Or stop letting you see him."

"Why would he do that?" Angie turns to face Savage. She's thinking.

"He could say something happened to you, that you were sick, that you'd moved. That happens. Kids believe what they're told. Then they adjust; they get through. That's how it works."

"I still don't see what you're saying." Angie's voice breaks with emotion.

The little girl gets off her mother's knee and walks over to the other stroller, wobbling.

"If he felt it would help him, he might need to know things, things you could help him know." Savage speaks slowly, his voice soft and deep—a thinking voice.

"Like what? What exactly are you trying to say?"

"About the boatyard. About Jake. About me. This is serious, Angie. I care about you, you know, and you're Jake's friend. He wouldn't want you in a position where you had no choice, because you have a son. That makes you vulnerable. Do you see what I'm getting at? I know you do."

The little girl is stroking the boy in the other stroller as he sleeps. His mother leans forward, and the boy wakes up.

"What's going to happen? What are you going to do?"

"It's what I'm not going to do," Savage says.

Her eyes are wide, soft with tears, but there's strength in them too. "What do you mean?"

"I'm not going to tell you things. About me, Jake, or the boatyard. I can't, Angie. You're a weak link here. Nothing personal; just how it is for now."

Savage stops talking. They both stare ahead. The mother of the boy gets him out of his stroller and puts him on his feet. A homeless man walks slowly by with a shopping cart containing clothing and a blue tarp. The wheels squeak. The man stops by a trash can, peers in, then moves on.

"Wonder what he's running from," Savage muses.

Angie looks at the man. He's in his fifties, with shaggy white hair and a life-ravaged face.

"Who knows? Himself, probably. What a place. Most people

escape here. Others run here. And when you're here... it's not how you thought it would be."

"Nothing ever is," Savage says.

"Come on," Angie says, "can't you just say things clearly? Jake's the same way until you pin him down."

"I'm saying that things are going to get tricky. If Ramirez starts to pressure you, I don't want you in a position where you know anything valuable."

"I wouldn't tell him."

"Angie. Everyone has their limits, believe me. If he wanted to get you to talk, he could. And he'd know if you were lying. He'd know if you knew something. Like you said, he's not an idiot."

"So what does this mean?" Angie puts her hands together, linking her fingers. She begins to rock back and forth.

"About us, you mean?"

"About everything. I don't know if I can carry on like this."

They fall silent, following their own thoughts. The two mothers put their children back in their strollers and move off, slowly, still chatting.

"I just want life to be like that," Angie says, pointing her chin towards the mothers.

"Well, it's not," Savage says, rotating his shoulder. "Not for people like us."

"People like us? What do you mean?"

"I'm starting to like you, Angie. You know what I mean?"

"Don't say that, Savage. Not like that. It sounds so, 'I like you but ...'. I've had enough of that shit, too. I've heard it before. I thought you... us... It felt... different."

Savage thinks about the houseboat, the lapping of the water on the hull.

He takes Angie's hand and pulls her towards him. She starts to pull away, but then she gives in. He strokes the back of her hand with his thick strong fingers.

The park is empty now. Two scooters shoot down the street. A small jet begins its descent to the airport.

They sit in the park long enough for the light to change. The sky becomes a richer blue, and Savage stares at the grass, thinking about his meeting with Jake later that evening. He lets go of Angie's hand.

"Have you seen Jake?" Angie asks, like she's reading his mind.

"No," Savage says, matter-of-factly, head down, watching some ants scurry around his feet. They're carrying a small piece of bread.

"Wouldn't tell me if you had, huh?" Angie's voice has come back to life, the sadness evaporated.

"No." Savage purses his lips and shakes his head.

"Why is it that I really think I could fall in love with you?" Angie says. She leans against him, and he can smell her hair. He puts a hand on her thigh and squeezes it.

"Because I'm the strong, silent type?"

Angie chuckles and pulls away from him. "I don't know what it is, but I sure do feel something. And I was really liking it. Then life came along again, right?"

"Life. Just one thing after another," he says.

"What's that supposed to mean?"

"It means it doesn't matter how you want things to be, or how they might be, or how they appear. They just are how they are. You just have to let go."

"Me? I have to let go?" Angie sighs and runs her right hand through her hair.

"All of us. There's only so much we can control."

The tourist train rumbles by again with another group of passengers. The sound system crackles into life, and Angie and Savage both listen as the driver makes his announcement about the highest point of land and the hurricane.

"But you know what, Savage? I do feel good when I'm with you. I wanted to help you and Jake. I still do."

"I know. I want to help you, too."

Savage squeezes her thigh again, adjusts his shoulder, and winces. The train rumbles off.

"I don't need any help," Angie says, turning away. She takes Savage's hand off her thigh. "What did you think you wanted to help me with anyway?" she asks, turning back towards Savage.

"Life."

"You think you could help me with my life?"

"Yeah. Actually, I could."

Angie laughs. "No one's ever said that to me before."

They fall silent for a while.

"I like sleeping with you," Savage says.

"Bastard."

"Bastard?"

"Yes," Angie says, "because I like sleeping with you, too."

"Juan's a beautiful little boy," Savage says.

"He is," Angie says. "I wish ..."

"Want to get something to drink?"

"Maybe," she says, tilting her head.

"You had something else in mind?"

"Maybe," she says again. She reaches up to run a finger across Savage's belly. He feels goosebumps and a wave of desire. She runs her hand down his thigh.

Savage thinks about his meeting with Jake. He thinks about Nikki and Angie, about desire, and how complicated life can be.

He also thinks about how he's just about to make it even more complicated.

19

THE WRECK

SAVAGE SITS on the sandy beach at Fort Zachary, watching the huge orange orb of the sun slip past the horizon. He's tired—his mind is full of tumbling thoughts and images. There's so much to make sense of, to order and organize into what will become how it will all be remembered. He feels a wave of desire for Angie. Could he love her? Could he settle down with her?

His shoulder is stiff, and he's been gritting his teeth. A fleet of jet skis roars by, and a Boston whaler heads slowly out to sea through the channel.

"I should go for a run," Savage mumbles. "Work out. Train. This is pathetic." He shakes his head and rotates his shoulder.

A grinding, squeaking noise grows closer to him, and he turns. The homeless guy is pushing a shopping cart towards the beach. A police officer watches from his cruiser, and then opens the door and gets out. He approaches the homeless guy. They talk a bit, and then the homeless guy turns his cart around and slowly walks away from the beach. The officer gets back in his cruiser, makes a sweeping U-turn, and then drives back toward town.

Savage continues to watch the sun, his thoughts idling, losing their focus for a moment. He senses someone else behind him.

He turns his head and sees Jake standing under a palm tree. He walks towards Savage.

"Jake," Savage says, automatically, with surprise, getting to his feet. He strides over to his brother and clasps his shoulders.

"Good to see you," Jake says. His face is dark, weathered, and fuller than Savage's.

"You too, Jake."

"Best place to see the sunset. Right here," Jake says. "A weird little beach where the bums sleep."

"Life's odd," Savage says.

"Even odder than that," Jake says. "Let's walk for a while."

Jake scratches his chin and watches the Boston whaler. The jet skis disappear around the point.

"You look tired, Griff. You okay?"

"A lot going on. A lot of thinking... too much thinking." He grinds his teeth and feels the tension in his jaw.

Savage nearly mentions Angie, Nikki, and Juan. He wants to talk about his fear about Angie, but he decides against it. Savage realizes then that this is not the type of thing that Jake and he ever talked about—matters of the heart. They only really spoke about problems that needed to be solved—practical problems like work, money, and bad people.

"Ramirez came around. He still wants the yard. Badly," Savage says, as they pass the bum pushing the shopping cart.

"He's not going to get it," Jake says, tersely. "I know it's in your name. That makes sense. But he's not going to get it."

A couple walks in to the water, holding hands, their skin white, untouched by the sun. A boy, about ten, is snorkeling. His mother watches from the beach. His back is straight as he scans the water.

Savage wonders why his brother is so set on keeping the yard. He could sell it and set up another business. It might be good to be done with it.

"Guess you're clear on that?"

"Uh huh. I've been here a long time, Griff. I built that yard, built a life around it. Sure, I could let you sell it, but I don't want to. And not just because it's Ramirez who wants it."

Savage sees the anger in his brother's eyes. It flashes quickly, then leaves. They walk to the parking lot, where Jake has leant his bike against Savage's. He undoes the lock.

Jake leads, cycling slowly. He turns onto a side street, then another, then a very narrow street, just wide enough for a single vehicle to pass. He stops outside a gate to a guesthouse. He punches in the entry code and the gate opens to reveal a small walled garden with a kidney-shaped pool, beyond which stand a main house and three cottages.

"Belongs to a friend," Jake says. "Gays only... except me, of course."

Savage smiles, wondering.

"Nice," he says, his eyes sweeping across the walled compound of tidy guest cottages, the pool, and the neatly tended garden.

Jake unlocks the front door to the second small cottage. Inside, an air conditioner is humming, and a slow-turning fan overhead stirs the air. The lighting is soft. Jake closes the door.

"You staying here?" Savage asks.

"When I'm in town," Jake says. He walks over to the refrigerator and takes out a large bottle of Perrier, pours two glasses, and hands one to Savage.

"Not drinking?" Savage asks.

"You can't live in Key West and drink," Jake says. "You'll lose. I quit a long time ago. You?"

"I went from excess, to excess in moderation, to moderation, to clean." Savage takes a gulp of water and savors the cold bubbles in his throat.

"Cheaper, too," Savage adds. "I don't even want to think of how much I've spent on booze."

Jake sits on the couch. Savage stands by the sliding glass doors, looking at the pool.

A gay couple is lounging on recliners, chatting and holding hands.

"A few years ago, I met this guy, a diver. Used to do work salvage," Jake begins. "He'd worked with this guy back in the 80s, looking for the *Nuestra Señora de Atocha*, one ship in this fleet of about thirty Spanish vessels. You know, preparing to head back to Spain after gathering treasure and loading it in Panama. Imperialism at its best. Took two months, apparently, just to load the *Atocha*."

Savage is still watching the couple. One of the men is rubbing sunblock into his partner's back. They're laughing and having fun.

"Okay," Savage says. "Go on. I think I read about the *Atocha*. A lot of people have looked for her, right?"

Jake scratches his chin. Savage notices he's developed a tic in his right eye, a quick blink every minute or so. He looks older to Savage.

"Yeah. It's legendary. A salvage guy found her, but it was complicated. There was a big trial to decide who got what—the salvage operators or the state. Anyway, that's all history. But this diver was working for pretty much nothing for the salvage guys. He just loved to dive. He saw all this treasure being brought to the surface. It sold for millions and millions of dollars at auction, but he hardly got anything, so he was bitter."

"Well," Savage says, "I can see that."

Jake takes a sip of his drink. Savage doesn't say anything. He waits and rotates his shoulder. Jake continues.

"His name's Franky. Used to work with me up at the yard. Very good with boats. A great diver. Taught me a thing or two. So, one day, we're going to go fishing. We're way out to sea, six miles or more. Franky is drinking a lot. Not drunk-drunk, but talking drunk. We've known each other a few years, and Franky likes me. He starts telling me about his days in salvage. The low pay and dangerous conditions. He's doing all the work, but not getting any of the rewards.

"Anyway, during one of these trips, they're doing some exploratory dives, and they find a wreck. Franky's sent down to check it out. He finds a commercial fishing boat—nothing worth salvaging. But he looks around, pokes the sand a bit, and comes up with a ring and some coins. Seems the fishing boat had settled on another wreck. Now, Franky starts thinking. He leaves the ring and the coins, surfaces, and tells the salvage operators that it's just an old fishing boat that had already been cleaned out. He checks the coordinates before they move off, and decides he'll save that one for himself."

"Okay," Savage says. "I think I see where this is going. And this was back in the 90s?"

"Right. Franky keeps working for the salvage operation until they find a motherlode of treasure about thirty-five miles off Key West, near the Dry Tortugas. They figure that's enough anyway. Franky earns his meager portion, his hourly wage, and watching the salvage operation owners get rich and famous, he quits.

"He works fishing boats, biding his time until he can go back and see what he'd found under the fishing boat. But he started drinking, and then sold all his gear. He became just another washed up drunk in Key West. He didn't say anything to anyone. And the years rolled by. He began to think he'd imagined it."

"Then something happened when he ran into you?"

The gay couple is in the pool now. The water is clear and smooth, and a breeze rustles the palm fronds. Savage grinds his teeth.

"We met when I was fishing from the dock at the boatyard, having fun with the tarpon that run there. Franky was watching. He liked to watch. Think and watch. Another Key West character. So, I'm fishing, and Franky tells me I'll never catch a tarpon in the harbor. Too many places to get tangled up. I said I knew that, but it was fun playing with them all the same. We had a good laugh watching this tarpon dart around, and then jump six feet out of the water—beautiful, blue and silver fish glimmering in the sun. Long story short—Franky became my handyman. He could do anything. I let him sleep at the boatyard and got him on a straighter path."

Savage hears the gate open and close. Another couple of guys walk in, holding hands. They stop and kiss, and then they walk into the main guest house.

"Except you, right?" Savage asks, looking at Jake.

Jake chuckles.

"Except me, right. Anyway, like I was saying. A couple of years back, we were out fishing, and Franky goes all quiet, and he asks me if I want to be his partner. I didn't know what he was talking about at first, then he explains that he wants to go back and get what he can of the treasure. Now, Franky's getting up there. He's not in great shape. He's broke, but he knows where this wreck is, and he has a plan."

"You front all the expenses, and he gives you a cut?"

"Fifty-fifty."

"Good deal."

The guys in the pool start to splash each other, laughing and having fun.

"Very good deal. But it takes time. I have to learn to dive. We have to get a boat. No one knows but us, and that's how we planned to keep it."

Jake's face takes on a sadness. His eyes grow distant and flat.

"Jake? You okay?" Savage sees his distress. "Jake?" He's never seen emotion like this on his brother's face.

Jake swallows, "Yeah. Give me a minute."

Savage waits a few minutes before speaking. "Something happened to Franky?" he finally asks, slowly and with compassion.

"We'd done about twenty trips. We'd got a lot of silver and gold, plus jewels. We're talking millions of dollars' worth. Tens of millions. It was crazy. Franky knew he'd found something, but he had no idea it was going to be so much."

"Jesus," Savage says.

"Then things start getting strange. I kept a coin we found—one with the pillars of Hercules on it. It was just for luck. Not really thinking—stupid, really. If it wasn't in my pocket, it was in a little lacquer bowl you gave me from Japan, on a shelf in my apartment. My lucky charm; or rather, my unlucky charm."

"Someone saw it and knew what it was?"

"I think so," Jake says.

"Angie?"

The two brothers lock eyes. Savage swallows and grits his teeth. Jake rubs his chin. His eye twitches.

"I don't know. But then everything changed. Boats began to shadow us, people on the dock, vehicles driving by the boatyard. It had been fun, you know, with Franky. Just me and him, diving and telling stories. Perhaps if we'd just found a few coins, not so much. And then... Franky...".

"Franky?"

Jake's eyes are blank. He swallows. "He's dead."

"What happened?"

"Stabbed and left for dead. He called me before he bled out. Two guys tried to get him to tell them where we'd been diving. He was a tough bastard, though. Wouldn't say a word. Last thing he said was, 'Get that bastard Ramirez'."

"Ramirez?"

"Yeah, Ramirez."

"We could," Savage says. He looks at his brother as his own anger rises.

"Not yet, Griff. I've had enough of this. Nothing crazy. Let's just take our time, figure out how to do it."

"I'm losing my touch, Jake."

"What do you mean?"

"Letting feelings in. Clouds the thinking. I had that all under control. But now ... I'm slipping."

"That's not a bad thing, brother. To feel. Maybe that's something we should both do more of."

Jake chuckles. Savage smiles and sighs.

"You might be right," Savage says.

"I am," Jake says, as he pours the rest of the Perrier into their glasses.

"He was such a great guy. A great guy." Jake lifts his glass and takes a gulp.

"We were going out for what we thought would be our last trip, and this boat followed us. We were ten miles out. Fortunately, we had this heavy fishing tackle on board and there was a fighting chair, so Franky took the helm while I fished. We got a marlin. The boat circled us, at a distance, and then headed back in to Key West. But we were followed, I know that."

Savage sees the pain in his brother's eyes, the distant look of a sad memory, the accompanying vulnerability.

"Franky," Jake continues. "It's his birthday next week. He'd have been seventy-five. We'd got practically all of it. Two years of work. Franky was excited. He was going to set up a little fishing charter business. He'd straightened out, cleaned up as best he could."

"God, Jake, I'm sorry." Savage looks at his brother but can't help but think about Angie. He wonders if Angie told Ramirez about the lucky coin. It must have been Ramirez who followed Jake and Franky out to sea. Angie had to have told him.

"You know, I'd give up all that treasure to have Franky back. The fun was about finding it with Franky. It wasn't about the millions—it was fun seeing Franky's face and listening to him talk about setting up his charter business. He was so chuffed about remembering the coordinates and for keeping his secret for so many years."

Jake clenches and unclenches his fists. Savage wants to help him, but he doesn't know how.

"I see why you want to keep the boatyard, Jake, I do."

"It's not just about pride," Jake says. "It's about Franky, too."

"I know. So what do you want to do?"

"I want to settle things."

"With Ramirez?"

Jake looks at Savage. Savage wonders if he will ever tell Jake about Angie or Nikki. Probably not, he thinks. Maybe he knows. Maybe he doesn't care. Maybe it's something he'll have to figure out himself in time, if there's time.

"What?" Jake asks, his eyes coming back to life. He's in the present again.

"Just thinking," Savage says.

"Probably best if we both do that for a little while," Jake says. "Just think. Sit on it. Don't do anything. I could go find Ramirez right now and finish it, but that would just start something new. Or end something in a bad way. Franky wouldn't want that. I don't want that."

"Well, let's just sit on it, then," Savage says.

"I'm going to stay here tonight," Jake says. "There's a spare bed if you want, Griff."

"I think I'll go back," Savage says.

"To the boatyard?" Jake asks.

"Yes," Savage says, but he's thinking about Angie. He has a question for her.

20

KNOW THYSELF

IT'S STILL and warm on the houseboat. Savage watches Angie sleeping. She looks so young. Savage pictures Angie and Juan. He thinks of Angie in his arms, her warm, lithe body, the passion. He wonders what it would be like to live with Angie, if he'd love her, if he'd love her son, if they could be a family. He lets himself feel all this, something he hasn't let himself do before.

Angie sighs and turns from her back to her side, and Savage decides to leave before she wakes, as quietly as he'd arrived just five minutes before. She'll never know. Better that way. Particularly when he doubted himself. And the question he had for her can wait.

"Savage?" Angie doesn't open her eyes. Her voice is soft. No anxiety. "How was it?"

"What?" Savage says. He comes over and strokes Angie's hand, squeezes it.

"Watching me sleep." Angie smiles, keeping her eyes closed. Her face looks soft and smooth. Savage feels his body tingle.

"Good."

The questions surface again in Savage's mind. He wants to ask her about Franky, if she saw the lucky coin in Jake's apartment, and whether she told Ramirez about it. He doesn't. He wants to ask her about Ramirez and what she feels for him now. He doesn't. He's not sure why. His feelings are layered, complicated. He's feeling desire as well, and he doesn't try to stop himself from feeling it.

"Savage?"

"Yes?" Savage knows Angie wants him to talk about himself. This makes him uncomfortable. He's just not sure how to do it.

"What do you want? You have to talk sometimes. I'm not a mind reader, Savage. I can't just look at you and know what you're thinking or what you want."

Savage wants to say he wants to sleep with her. He wants to say that he wants to ask her questions that need answering, but he doesn't. He thinks, swallows, and reaches his hand out and strokes Angie's hair. She opens her eyes. He realizes that he just doesn't know what he feels. It's not clear to him. He wants and doesn't want.

"I'm serious. Really."

"I know," Savage says, "it's just the wrong question."

"For you. Because you can't answer it. Or maybe you just don't want to. But it's the right question for me. Savage, I told you... I'm feeling something here... slipping and falling. I don't want to get hurt. You know? I could get out now, while I can, while I'm not too far in."

Savage slowly takes his hand away from Angie and leans back in the chair. He doesn't want to talk about love. Or whether he's falling in love. Or whether Angie is. He wants her. He wants things to be simple. But nothing is simple. Savage knows that, yet he still wants things to be simple. He wonders what Jake would think if he knew that he was by Angie's bed about to make love with her.

"Angie. There's a lot going on, right now. You know? Jake. Stuff. Things happening. Things I can't talk about." Savage's desire is beginning to leave him.

"You mean things you don't want to talk about, or things you can't talk about? Come on, Savage. You know I'm ... you know. I know you know. I can't just keep doing this. I don't think you can actually do it either. You don't know what's going to happen, do you? Something hurt you, Savage. I know that."

Savage swallows. He looks at Angie, and he begins to picture a life with her. He thinks it could be possible.

"I told you, Angie. I can't tell you anything. We talked about this. But you know what?"

"What? Savage, what?" Savage hears the tension and frustration in her voice.

"If I could, I would. Believe me. As a friend. I'd really like to get this all sorted out. But you know what? Maybe you're right."

"About what?"

"Us. Maybe we should both stop it here. Now. While we can. Except ... I like you too, Angie. And I want you too."

"Like? I'm not talking about 'like'. You know that."

"You know what I mean, Angie."

"No, actually, I don't know what you mean. I know you don't tell me what you think. I don't even know if you know what you think. Do you? Savage?"

Savage stands up. He looks down at Angie. She's staring up at him now, eyes focused with intent, the sleepiness gone. There is tension.

"Listen. I'm going to go back to the boatyard," Savage says. This is not what he'd wanted. He's wondering what he does think. He's wondering where his deep affect is. He doesn't want to feel flat inside. But he does, as if something that should be there just isn't. He wants to explain that somewhere in the past, something happened that left him flat. He knew he had feelings, but there was something blocking them. He couldn't feel them, and worse, he felt afraid of what might happen if he began to feel. There might be too much pain. He doesn't know how to say this to Angie, as he's only just let himself know this.

"Savage?" Angie takes his hand, looks into his eyes. She sits up and gets out of bed. She's wearing shorts and a running top. Savage looks at her, his desire returning. He could leave right now. Or not. She puts her arms around his neck. He doesn't leave. He kisses her forehead and pulls her close.

"You can trust me, Savage. I know you'll say you can't. That's okay. We're just where we are, right? We've done what we've done, said what we've said. And yes, I share Juan with Ramirez. And maybe you're right. Maybe he will put the pressure on. Why are things always so complicated?"

"They're not. They're just not as simple as we'd like to think they are. We think too simply and explain too simply. That's why we misunderstand."

Angie doesn't say anything. She looks up at him, waiting.

"I hear you, Angie. About trust. I do."

"Something must have happened to you, Savage. You're not very good at this. Are you?"

"At what?"

"Being honest."

"Being honest?"

"With yourself. That's the only way to get anywhere. The starting point for everything."

"Know thyself."

"Know thyself?"

"Socrates. He meant that. That it's our first mission. You can't do anything until you know yourself."

"So how are you doing with that?"

Savage sits down again. It's a good question. One he's been thinking about. He slumps and lets out a sigh. He feels a relief. He draws in a breath and looks up at Angie. Her eyes are questioning, expectant, and she raises her eyebrows in encouragement.

"You know, when I was a soldier, it was about training—technique, discipline, obeying orders, having orders obeyed. The last thing it was about was knowing yourself. No reflection. I guess I didn't do that well at that time. Then there was Japan, Buddhism, Thailand, being a monk."

"And did that get you anywhere?"

"You know, really, I think it did, but not in the way I had expected. I learnt about letting go, about unknowing, about not being a slave to emotion. It was a different kind of discipline."

"I thought the Zen thing was all superior."

"No, there's humility. I was good at some things, but not others. One of my teachers told me that ultimately Zen really is about coming face to face with yourself. I don't think I ever did. I learned a lot, though. But I never came face to face with myself."

"What are you saying?"

"I guess I'm saying that you're right. I've spent a lot of time avoiding myself—running, soldiering, being a monk. It was the best I could do. Then."

"And now?"

"I can do better now. I will do better now. I am doing better now. Doors have started opening."

"Where?"

"In my heart." Savage wonders if this is what he hopes or what he wants.

"Your heart? Doors to where?"

"To me."

"You sure?"

Savage wants to believe this. He thinks it's true, but he has doubts.

"Come here." Angie reaches out and takes his hand and pulls him towards her.

"I trained for years to overcome desire," Savage says.

"Well, that's too bad," Angie says. She takes off her top and slips out of her shorts.

Savage takes off his t-shirt.

"And your shorts."

Savage takes off his shorts.

"Gosh."

"What?"

"You said you'd trained for years to overcome desire."

"I did. But that was then. I'm reappraising things."

"I'll say."

Savage steps forward and gets on the bed with Angie. "Enough talking. Okay? Let's have some fun. In the here and now."

"Sounds Zen. The here and now."

"I'm not talking about Zen. I'm talking about here and now. You and me. In this bed."

Angie puts her arms around him, kisses him, and pulls him towards her. The air is warm and thick, sensuous. Savage can hear the water lapping against the houseboat and a motorbike in the distance. He lowers himself onto Angie. Their bodies meld together, and he holds her close.

"Mmmm, that's nice," Angie says.

They kiss and make love in silence, but Savage feels a closeness he hasn't felt before.

Afterwards he lies on his back, watching the ceiling fan swoosh in slow circles overhead, stirring the air, but not enough to dry his sweat. He wonders how close he could be to someone like Angie or Nikki. Or whether he's too damaged. Or whether closeness isn't what he wants or needs.

"You're so loud," Angie says, "when you think. I mean really. And don't say you're not. I know you are."

"I need to get things prioritized."

"What are you saying?"

"Like I said, there's so much going on. I need to decide what to do and in what order. I need to be methodical and rational."

"Are you trying to dump me?"

Savage turns his head to face Angie.

"Bastard," she says, ruffling his hair.

"Like that. I like that."

"Ruffling your hair?"

"No. Well, yes, but I meant the smile. The laugh."

"Simple, you mean?"

"Simple. Yes."

"But nothing's simple, right? That's what you said."

"That is what I said."

They fall quiet.

"Savage?"

"Uh huh."

"I know about you and Nikki."

Savage closes his eyes and swallows. He doesn't hear any anger or recrimination.

"I'm not mad."

Savage doesn't say anything, though he wonders what Angie is going to say. He wants to say that Nikki was different. But he doesn't.

"Weirder things happen, Savage. I kind of thought it might. I didn't expect you to tell me."

"I didn't tell you, no."

"No. You didn't. Nikki did."

"Nikki?"

"Surprised?"

"Nothing really surprises me that much anymore. But yes, really. Got to wonder why, I suppose."

"I guess she didn't tell you, then..."

Savage turns.

"About us." Angie waits for Savage to say something. He furrows his brow. She can tell he's surprised.

"You? You and Nikki?"

"Surprised?"

"I could say nothing much surprises me anymore, but then that wouldn't be true anymore. Is this a Key West thing, or did I miss something?"

"Key West. Definitely."

"I guess I can see why Jake doesn't really get involved. I mean with people."

"Oh, he does. He just doesn't talk about it. He's worse than you."

"I'm not sure I want to know."

"About what?"

"About what you're going to tell me."

"And what am I going to tell you?"

"That although I was under the impression that you and Jake were just friends and that Nikki and Jake were just friends and that you and Nikki were just friends, in fact it's not quite as simple as that. Right?"

"Right," Angie says. "But it's not that big a deal here."

"Is there anything I need to know? Or maybe anything I don't need to know?" Savage shakes his head, looks up at Angie, and smiles.

"Depends," Angie says.

"Does Jake know?"

"Jake doesn't care. Things happen. Then they don't. He's very philosophical."

Savage chuckles to himself. "I was the monk, but he's more Zen than me. Naturally."

Angie takes Savage's hand and squeezes it. He squeezes back.

"You think you know things," Savage says, "but what do we know? Really? I mean really."

"I don't know," Angie says. Savage feels himself respond to Angie's nearness, and he strokes her thigh.

"Let's just keep it simple," he says, rolling Angie towards him, then lifting her on top of him.

"Good luck with that," Angie says, biting Savage's neck as he begins to stroke her back. She moves herself slowly and sensually, and Savage closes his eyes.

"Angie?" he says.

"Shut up," she says, her eyes closed, working herself into a frenzy and beginning to gasp, throwing her head back and groaning.

Savage can feel her grip him in her spasms of pleasure.

"Is this enough for you, Savage?"

"What?"

"I could call Nikki, get her to come over."

The idea excites him, but the reality is clear.

"No. This is enough," Savage says. He feels Angie's fingers tickle him.

"Good," Angie says. "Even if you are lying."

Savage begins to lose himself and his eyes close hard as he groans. He wants this to be enough, for Angie to be enough, but he's not sure. Not yet.

21

AN UNEXPECTED DINNER

THE BLOW MISSES its target and glances off Savage's shoulder. Savage hadn't seen the man, but he'd heard him. He had stepped to one side, caught the man with a knife hand strike to the throat, and followed it with an elbow punch to the solar plexus, then a hammer fist to the side of the neck.

The alley is dark, and the man is on his knees, disoriented, dazed, and swaying back and forth. Seconds before, he had been stalking Savage, and made the first move. Savage stops himself from delivering another blow, grabs the man's wrist, twists it behind him and brings it just to the point where any struggle would break it. The man is breathing hard. Savage walks him deeper into the alley and around the back of a dumpster.

"Make a noise, I break your wrist, and then I'll really hurt you. Understand?"

The man nods, his teeth clenched, his eyes squinting in pain.

"You were following me. Who are you? Why were you following me?"

The man says nothing, and Savage twists the man's wrist.

"Okay, okay. Paulo. Paulo Blanco. Someone paid me."

Savage twists a little harder. Blanco winces, eyes closed, his yellow teeth gritting. Bad breath.

"To follow me?"

"To rough you up. Bad."

Savage pulls back from Blanco's breath.

"Who?"

"A guy. Didn't tell me who he was. I didn't need to know."

The cicadas chatter in the night air.

"Well, I need to know."

The anger is welling.

"I don't know, okay?" Blanco's face contorts in pain. Savage bends his wrist further to its limit.

"Are you going to give the money back?" Savage hisses.

"*Qué?*"

"Give the money back. You didn't do your job."

Blanco is silent. Savage feels the fight leave him, the animal surrender. Savage has him.

"How badly were you going to rough me up, Paulo?"

"Enough to scare you," Blanco whimpers.

"If you were me, what would you do?"

Blanco swallows and frowns. "*Qué?*"

"Nothing? You don't know? How much did they pay you?"

"Five hundred bucks."

"Where is it?"

Blanco moves his free hand towards his jacket pocket. Savage senses the ruse, and before the he can pull out the switchblade, Savage has pulled his hand back out of his pocket, put his own into the pocket, and pulled out the weapon. The man gasps. Savage has him in a choke hold. The blade clicks open.

"I'm not going to kill you," Savage says. He holds the tip of the blade against Blanco's throat. "I could, but I'm not going to. Understand?"

"*Sí,*" Blanco whimpers, gasping.

"You don't know who wanted me beaten up, but I do. Give him his money back."

The man gasps as Savage tightens his grip on his throat.

"I'm going to take you to a restaurant. We'll go in together and sit down. You're going to do what I tell you. *Entiendes?*"

"*Sí,*" Blanco says, wheezing, the strength ebbing from his body, the fight gone.

"Your wallet and your phone. Now."

A rat scurries across the alley and Blanco starts. Savage tightens his chokehold.

"Okay, okay," Blanco says, fumbling for his wallet and cell phone. He drops them on the ground.

In a single, swift move, Savage folds the switchblade, picks up the wallet and phone, and puts them in his pocket.

Blanco's breathing has become heavy.

"Now do what I say. Got it?"

Blanco nods. Savage pulls him to his feet, releases the chokehold, and grabs Blanco's wrist.

He gasps. He doesn't resist.

They're standing side by side, Savage with the man in a wrist lock.

"We're going to walk along. Like friends. We'll go into that seafood restaurant. I'll do the talking. You say nothing. Got it?"

The man kicks at the ground.

"We're going to just stay cool, and you are going to smile. Like you're having a good time. Okay, Paulo?"

Paulo tries to smile.

They walk into the light at the end of the alley. Savage takes a left, then a right. They're on Duval now, amid voices and people. The swaying night. Tourist town. Savage pulls Paulo close and whistles in his ear like a drunken friend.

Savage stops. A scooter backfires, and Blanco starts. Two girls laugh as they pass, a waft of cheap perfume in the air, the click of heels.

"Been here?" Savage whispers.

"Nunca aquí," Blanco says. "Not here."

Savage steers Blanco into the crowded restaurant. There's a buzz of conversation and laughter. Steaks sizzle in the kitchen. A young couple gets up to leave.

"It will just be five minutes, gentlemen," the hostess says. "Sorry."

Her eyes pass quickly over Savage, then between Savage and Blanco.

Savage catches her eye, holds it, and smiles a slow smile, eyes burning. She looks down.

"No rush," he says. The woman looks back up. Savage draws in a breath. Her eyes look from one of Savage's eyes to the other. A woman looking at a man. In that way.

"Nice place, huh?" Savage says. Blanco says nothing.

Urgent Spanish voices come from the kitchen, and the door opens and swings shut as a server carries out a platter of mahi mahi. He strides to a table. A hissing sound comes from the kitchen, and then more voices and the door swinging back and forth.

"Hungry, Paulo?"

Blanco looks at Savage. His eyes are blank. He says nothing, and looks scared.

"Well, I am," Savage says, "and you're having a good time, Paulo. With your friend. Smile, Paulo, like you mean it."

Savage still has Blanco's wrist twisted, his grip solid. Paulo begins to close his eyes and tries to smile. Savage smells Blanco's breath again and shakes his head.

The hostess finally leads them to a table in a corner. Savage points at the seat by the wall, and Paulo sits, looking out at the diners. Savage sits opposite.

The server comes with menus. Savage orders a tonic water with ice and lemon.

"Paulo, what are you drinking?"

"Same," Paulo mutters, rubbing his wrist.

Savage smiles at him. "Put a couple of shots of vodka in his, okay?"

"Sure," she says. "I'll be right back with your drinks."

"What's happening?" Paulo asks. "You take me to a restaurant. After that? I jump you and we're on a date?"

"It's not a date, Paulo, and you're going to do what I tell you to do, or you're going to experience a sudden medical emergency. Got it? Look at me."

Paulo nods and swallows weakly, his eyes flat. Animal surrender.

Savage riffles through Paulo's wallet and finds eight hundred dollars in cash, a couple of credit cards, and a driver's license.

Paulo's breathing is short and shallow. Savage senses him looking for a way out.

"Don't try anything, Paulo. Act natural. Relax, okay?"

The restaurant is buzzing as cutlery clinks and servers come and go, gliding by with orders and trays of drinks.

"Okay," Paulo says.

"Order what you want," Savage says. "Hungry? You never said."

Paulo shrugs and drops his limp shoulders.

"You gotta eat, Paulo. Keep your strength up." Savage smiles.

The server comes over, poised to take the order

"I think we'll both have the mahi mahi," Savage says. "Right, Paulo?"

"Sí. Bueno."

"Good choice," she says, taking Paulo's menu, and then Savage's. "It's my favorite."

She moves her head, revealing the nape of her neck, and Savage's nostrils flare. The server tilts her head, smiles, and begins to turn away.

"Oh, and by the way," Savage says, "is Mr. Ramirez in tonight?"

She pauses, and then says, "Later... he should be in around ten." Her eyes are questioning.

"I see," Savage says, holding her look. He takes her in. There's something about her, something familiar. He nods and tilts his head, his eyes narrowing somewhat. Just enough. She looks away, then back.

"Thanks," he adds.

"Should I tell him you'd like to see him? I'm sorry, I don't think I know.."

"No. That's okay," Savage says. "You don't need to tell him anything."

Paulo watches from his corner. His eyes follow the server.

"Ramirez?" Paulo says, frightened.

The server looks over her shoulder. Savage knows she'll tell Ramirez a man wants to see him. And he will come to the table. Savage looks forward to watching Ramirez's face when he sees Paulo.

"Yes, Paulo, Ramirez."

Savage flexes his fingers under the table.

There are beads of sweat on Paulo's brow. His lips part, trembling.

A bottle of champagne pops at the next table, and a woman laughs. The kitchen door swings open, then closes. More voices.

"Ramirez?" Paulo repeats.

"He's not as bad as he seems," Savage says.

Paulo leans forward, raising his thick black eyebrows. "No?"

"No," Savage says. "He's worse. Much worse."

Paulo mutters in Spanish and looks around the restaurant. Savage sees his fear, his desperation.

"You like Key West, Paulo?"

Blanco shrugs. "It's where I pay my bills."

"I could get used to it," Savage says. "I might just stick around after this is all over. I could get to like it."

Savage draws in a breath and watches the servers and the customers and Paulo. It's nearly time. He can tell.

"Oh, yeah?" Paulo says. His eyes dart nervously around the restaurant.

The server brings their drinks. "Thanks," Savage says. "Wait... haven't I seen you somewhere before?"

He recognizes her face. She shows no recognition in return.

"I'm not sure." She looks at his short black hair and his searing blue eyes.

Savage taps the edge of the table with his thick, strong fingers. "I remember!" he says. "You know Angie. Right? With Juan, at the park."

"The park?" The light in her eyes changes, and she fidgets. Different lives begin to collide in her mind.

Then she knows. But this is not the time.

"Sorry, I'm busy," she says, flustered, her poise gone. She steps back, turns, and glances back at Savage.

Savage sips his tonic. "Another?" he asks, as Paulo finishes his.

"Sure," Blanco says.

"No problem. You're paying."

"I am?" Blanco asks.

"Yes, Paulo. You're paying. It's the least you can do."

The server returns with their orders. Savage studies her. She has regained some of her poise, but she's still tense and unsure.

"It's all right," Savage says. "Don't worry. I don't want to make you uncomfortable." His voice is soft, confident, and unthreatening.

Her tension leaves. Paulo watches. Savage looks at the nape of her neck again. He knows it's the woman from the park. He wonders what her relationship is with Ramirez and how well she knows Angie. Her skin is smooth and dark. There's intelligence in her eyes, and loneliness. He sees history.

"Life," Savage says.

"Excuse me?" she says.

"Just one thing after another," Savage continues.

"What?" she says, laughing. "You're... I don't know." Their eyes meet.

She blinks, and her eyes come alive. But this isn't the place, not now.

Paulo keeps watching.

"It's just...," she continues, and then stops.

"I know," Savage says, hearing something from the kitchen. He pauses.

She's waiting, expectant. He's about to say *continue*, but the kitchen doors swing open, and he sees Ramirez and hears his stern voice.

She hears it too, and fear flickers in her eyes. She's not sure what to do.

The moment's gone.

This is it, Savage thinks. Party time.

"Hmmm," Savage says. The server leaves. *Now it's wait and see.*

They eat in silence. Savage is hungry. Paulo prods his fish, eating a little. He picks up his drink. He's fidgeting and restless. His energy changes.

"Look, I have to go," Paulo says, draining his drink. "Keep the money. I don't want to see Ramirez." There's desperation in his eyes.

"Not yet. We're not done yet." Savage pulls a credit card out of Paulo's wallet and slides it to the corner of the table.

The server comes. "I'll run this for you," she says. She doesn't look at him directly, just takes the card and walks away.

Savage sees Paulo's eyes widen as the kitchen door opens again. He's seen Ramirez. Paulo moves back in his seat so he's against the wall.

Savage watches his eyes. He can tell Ramirez is coming. He counts the seconds—one, two, three.

"How was your meal, gentlemen?" Ramirez finally says.

"Surprisingly good," Savage says, not looking at him.

"Why 'surprisingly'?"

Savage doesn't answer. "Paulo, Mr. Ramirez. Mr. Ramirez, Paulo. Unless you already know each other, of course."

Blanco is silent. Ramirez ignores the comment.

"A friend of yours?" Ramirez asks.

"A friend of yours, no?" Savage says, positioning his legs, moving his hands, finding his balance.

The patrons at the next table begin to stand. The restaurant is still full. Ramirez is on stage.

Savage waits.

The server returns with the check. She hands it to Savage, but he points at Blanco. Blanco signs the check.

Ramirez frowns. He stares at Blanco, clenching and unclenching his fists. Savage can hear his breathing.

Savage takes a hundred-dollar bill from Blanco's wallet and puts it under his glass.

"Excellent service, Mr. Ramirez. Excellent. And great food." Savage brings his index finger and thumb to his lips.

"The mahimahi. Superb. I don't know why Paulo didn't eat his. Paulo?" Savage continues. "You have something for Mr. Ramirez, remember?"

"What?"

Savage tosses Blanco's wallet across the table. Blanco takes it.

Ramirez scratches his belly. Savage listens to his heavy breathing and rolls his shoulders.

"Come on, Paulo," Savage says.

Paulo counts out five hundred dollars. He's sweating. He holds it in front of him and then offers it slowly to Ramirez.

Savage can sense the fury building.

Paulo's palm is open, suspended above the table, with five hundred dollars sitting on it.

"What's this for?" Ramirez spits, staring at Paulo, anger raging across his face.

"For you, Señor Ramirez."

"Why for me?" Ramirez looks from Paulo to Savage.

"Gentlemen, if you'll excuse me," Savage says, getting to his feet in a single smooth motion. He's suddenly standing next to Ramirez.

Ramirez starts. Savage is too close.

Paulo swallows, looks at Ramirez, and then says, "For the job I didn't do."

"A job you didn't do? What are you talking about?" Ramirez drops his voice as diners look at them.

Savage leans towards Ramirez's ear, and speaks softly and clearly. "He didn't do it. And he won't do it. I told him to give the money back."

Ramirez is frozen. Customers are looking at him. The kitchen door opens. A server looks over at them, and the hostess is coming over.

"You want to sell this place, Ramirez?"

"Sell? To you?" Ramirez says in confused disbelief. Paulo's head is down.

The maître d' is talking with the hostess, watching Ramirez.

"Sure," Savage says. "I think I could make something of this."

Ramirez's breathing is getting heavier, and sweat beads on his brow. There is nowhere for his fury to go.

The tension builds, and Paulo looks increasingly desperate. He looks towards the door and measures the distance.

Ramirez draws in a breath and lets it out.

Savage smiles at a couple at the next table. "Wonderful food," he says. They both nod.

Savage looks back at Ramirez.

Ramirez moves around the table and leans down towards Paulo and whispers to him in Spanish before walking back to the kitchen. Blanco looks finished, his eyes blank.

Savage rubs the back of his neck. Ramirez has gone, and Blanco is a spent man.

"Strange night," Savage mutters, making his way through the restaurant to the door.

He passes the server, feels her energy, and pauses. She turns towards him. Deep, dark eyes. Smooth skin. The nape of her neck long, elegant, and vulnerable.

"It was you. In the park with Angie. Right? I know I've seen you."

"Wait," she says. She walks over to the register, takes a slip of paper, writes something on it, and takes it back to Savage. She moves easily, fluidly, like a dancer.

"Help me," she whispers, glancing around the restaurant. She gives the note to Savage, her eyes suddenly frightened. She's put herself on the line. Savage nods and puts the note in his wallet.

Ramirez is in the kitchen, and Paulo is staring at them. The restaurant is alive with conversation and laughter.

Their eyes speak to each other.

"Call me," she says.

Savage nods, touches her arm, and smiles. She closes her eyes briefly. He wants to hold her. But she's gone, gliding between the tables.

Paulo is pressed against the wall again, staring towards the kitchen from which Ramirez has just emerged.

He's striding towards Blanco's table, a big, heavy, and very angry man, trying not to draw attention to himself but failing as customers watch him.

Ramirez arrives at Blanco's table, sits next to him, and leans his head close to Blanco's. It looks like a very intense conversation.

Savage catches the server's attention one last time, her eyes sharp and dark, for a brief, frozen moment across the restaurant.

He nods twice, smiles, opens the door, and slips out into the night.

22

MARIA

SAVAGE PUNCHES the number into the phone and lets it ring. There's no answer—it goes to voicemail.

"Call me," Savage says. He hangs up and rolls his right shoulder.

He puts the note back in his wallet and sets his phone on the desk, drums his fingers slowly, and stares at the phone in frustration before he gets the folded note out of his wallet again, opens it, and just picks up the phone to try one more time when it rings.

"It's me," the woman says.

"I know," Savage says.

"From the restaurant," she continues, her voice tense. But it is her. She did call.

"Where are you?" Savage asks.

"At work still. I can't talk. Meet me later."

"Okay," Savage says. "Name a place."

"Midnight. Do you know the laundromat on Caroline and Eaton?"

"Yes. I'll be there." She hangs up.

The laundromat is opposite Jake's apartment. Seems like a coincidence. Everything these days seems connected. Wherever he goes, whatever he does, the dots always join when you least expect it. Savage wonders where the next dot will be and what he'll see when he looks back.

Rain is pounding on the office trailer's roof, and puddles are forming on the driveway. Thunder crashes out over the flat dark gulf. A black Mercedes passes by the yard, driving fast, its tires hissing in the rain. *Maybe Ramirez*, Savage thinks. Just another dot waiting to be connected.

Savage looks at the clock on the wall. He has plenty of time, he calculates, standing and stretching, feeling the tension in his shoulder. He walks to the door and opens it. The air is warm and the rain heavy, but as quickly as it started, it stops. The clouds lose their grip on the sky, and patches of blue appear, followed by the sun, which hangs low and hot. He can smell the wet concrete beginning to dry.

Time to cycle into Key West. It's a cathartic act—watching and pedaling. Kids playing soccer. The scooter repair shop. A homeless man with his shopping cart, and another standing and swaying. A pick-up with two Cuban fishermen he recognizes. He raises a hand, and they wave.

On the bridge from Stock Island to Key West, he sees a yellow jeep, its top down, waiting at the light, heading in the opposite direction. Angie. He raises his hand, beginning to smile, wanting her to respond. He's pleased to see her. She doesn't see him, however. She's wearing a baseball hat and dark glasses.

"Hey Angie!" Savage shouts. A man outside a scooter repair shop looks around, stares at Savage, and nods, his expression impassive behind his sunglasses.

Angie looks over, her mouth in a tight line. She lifts one hand briefly from the wheel, but doesn't smile. It's hardly an acknowledgment. Savage can't see her eyes behind the sunglasses; she's too far away for him to really read her face. The lights change, and she drives towards him.

As she moves closer, something doesn't look right to Savage.

There's no easy smile. He considers turning around and cycling back to the houseboat to see what's up. Then he catches himself. He wants to sleep with her.

Savage grips his handlebars and lets out a sigh. This isn't about sleeping with Angie, Savage thinks. It's about Jake.

"I can do better," he mutters. "Much better."

He pushes down on the right pedal and the bike moves forward, the wheels turning slowly. He's in no rush—just thinking and pedaling.

The sea is sparkling. A white-hulled yacht is making its way west, heeling in the breeze, sheeted in, flag flying at the stern. Savage takes in a long slow breath.

Great place for a vacation, he thinks.

His phone rings. He stops, pulls his it from his pocket, and sees the call is from Jake.

"Hello, Jake?" The call abruptly ends. Savage waits for the phone to ring again. It does. "Jake?" The line goes dead. Savage waits again. He feels a panic begin to rise inside him.

Stay calm, he thinks. *Wait. He'll call back.*

The yacht is holding its course on the shimmering sea. Savage squints and shields his eyes with his left hand; the phone is still in his right hand, his bike between his legs.

He's by the seawall on South Roosevelt, looking over the water towards the mangroves and Stock Island and the Gulf. The water is a perfect blue. The boats at anchor are facing south, from where the breeze is coming. The water ripples from the wind, darkening briefly with each gust. A bank of billowing cumulus clouds amasses along the horizon, and sand swirls on the concrete of the bike path. *A storm is coming*, Savage thinks, as he begins to pedal purposefully west.

A plane takes off and slowly banks to the north, the twin propellers noisily churning the air. His phone rings again. Savage stops. "Jake? Hey." The line dies once more. Savage returns the call. He waits, and the call dies again.

Savage swallows and ponders the possibilities. A bad connection? It could be something simple., not necessarily a worst-case scenario. And Angie could just have been in a rush and had something on her mind.

We fabricate our worlds, Savage muses. We try to make sense of them, organize them, and we don't always get it right.

But Savage is *usually* right.

He gets back on his bike and continues down South Roosevelt, weaving between the joggers and tourists on the rental bikes, heading towards downtown.

It takes him fifteen minutes. He padlocks his bike to a rack near Duval and goes up the steps to the Whistle.

Nikki is on her phone at the bar. She's talking rapidly, in a soft voice, her face set. She looks over at Savage and waves, then turns her back on him and finishes the call.

Savage walks over to the bar. "Weird day," he says.

"Weird? In what way?"

"Odd little things, all day. You know how that is. First one thing, then another. And before you know it, a weird day. Just like that."

Savage pats the bar with his spread fingers.

"Like?"

"Things. After a while, they take on a shape, gather some cumulative momentum. Do you know what I mean?"

Nikki shakes her head and says, "No, not really. I don't know what you're saying, actually. Things happen. Sometimes there's a shape and sometimes there isn't."

She wipes the bar with a white towel, a slow sweeping action.

"Hmmm," Savage says, "maybe."

He rubs the back of his neck, squeezes the muscles, and feels the knots of tension.

Waiting for Nikki to say something, Savage feels a distance— the normal light banter isn't there.

"Are you all right?" Savage asks.

Nikki shrugs, stops wiping the bar, and looks at Savage. Her hair is shiny, long, and straight. But she looks tired.

"Yeah," she says. "I'm alright."

The bar is deserted. It's that dead time in the afternoon—too late for lunch, too early to start drinking. The tourists would be by their pools or on the beach.

"You got any coffee?" Savage asks.

"I could make some." A light returns to Nikki's eyes.

"Thanks." Savage catches a glimpse of her face in the mirror behind the bar. *All of us*, Savage thinks, *are in our own worlds. Sometimes they intersect, and sometimes they don't.*

"No problem," Nikki says.

"Do you know something I don't know?" Savage asks.

Nikki turns to look at him. "Probably," she says. There's a flicker of a smile on her face. "Like what?"

"I'm picking up on something going on. Jake tried to call several times, but each time, the line died. And some other things..."

"Other things?"

"A guy tried to roll me. He didn't, but he tried."

"You didn't talk to Jake?" Nikki asks.

"No. I told you. We kept getting cut off. He wouldn't pick up. Or couldn't pick up. I don't know. Been a couple of days. Could be nothing. Could be something."

Then there was Angie.

Nikki is standing by the coffee maker. Savage looks at her back and her dark, thick hair.

"Nikki, what's going on?"

"I can't tell you."

Savage doesn't react. He stares at Nikki, trying to read her.

"Stop it, Savage!" she says, adding a nervous laugh.

"What?"

"Looking at me like that. I can feel it." She puts the coffee in front of him and steps back.

"Thanks."

"You're welcome."

Perhaps it's the incoming storm, the change in pressure. *In the end*, Savage thinks, *we're just animals. Smart sometimes, but not always. Right sometimes, but not always.*

"Listen, Nikki. It's been a very odd day, okay? I'm not trying to grill you. I'm just concerned about Jake, and about what people aren't telling me."

He smiles and feels a tiredness infuse his body. "I need a vacation," he says.

"Want to come over tonight?" Nikki asks.

Savage does, despite Angie. "Can't. Got to meet someone," he says. He's wondering if he could see Nikki later, but part of him wants to reject her.

"Oooh... A date?"

"No. Not a date. Business."

"Monkey business?" she laughs, raising an eyebrow.

"No. Business-business." Savage smiles, even though he's annoyed with her for not telling him what she knows. He's also annoyed with himself because he could be seduced by her. As well as by Angie.

"I must be stronger," he says, thinking aloud, thinking about Jake, about the reason he's in Key West.

"What?" Nikki asks, frowning, picking up the towel again. *That hair*, Savage thinks.

"You know what I mean."

"I do?"

"You do. Jake. He's okay? Is he?"

Nikki's face changes again. "I'm not sure," she says.

"But you've heard from him?"

Nikki nods.

"You have, but I haven't? Something's not adding up."

Savage doesn't say anything more. Whether she's heard from Jake or not, she's not telling him something. Savage tells himself to trust his gut, which tells him that he can't trust Nikki and he can't trust Angie. It also tells him that things are complicated. He was going to mention his meeting with the server, but he doesn't. He wants to talk to Angie, and to Jake.

"What? Savage?" Nikki asks.

He's looking at himself in the mirror, ice-blue, piercing eyes.

"Just thinking."

"Looks like pretty serious thinking." She pauses. "Right?"

Savage looks up. "Yeah. And no."

"I can't tell you. I would, but I can't."

"I'm just trying to help Jake," Savage says. "And I hope you are, too."

Savage finishes his coffee and leaves ten dollars under the saucer. Two tourists walk in, older men with white knee socks, white legs, and black sandals.

I need a vacation, Savage thinks, turning and walking towards the door.

"I get off at two if you change your mind," Nikki says.

Savage leaves without responding.

———

He's waiting across from the laundromat. It's nearly midnight. He's standing in the shadow of a tree, the surrounding area dimly lit by the street light. He hears a footfall approaching and steps out from the shadows.

"Hey," Savage says.

She gives him a little wave.

"I'm Savage."

"I'm Maria."

She's slight, smaller than she seemed when he was sitting in the restaurant. She's got high cheekbones and large, deep eyes, more indigenous than Spanish.

They're standing beneath the street lamp on the corner. A scooter roars past, driven by a young, blond, student-looking type.

Then it's gone.

"You okay?"

Maria looks over her shoulder. "I don't know. I'm scared," she says. "You've got to help me. I can't go back. I think someone was following me. I don't want him to find me. I won't go back. I won't." Maria looks up at Savage and he can see her desperation.

"Come with me." Savage takes Maria's arm and leads her across the road.

Savage opens the gate to the overgrown yard below Jake's apartment. There's a barbecue in one corner, two chairs, and a small stagnant pond.

Savage closes the gate behind Maria. "Have you ever been here before?" he asks.

"Yes."

Savage leads Maria up the wooden staircase to the deck, which creaks beneath his weight. He turns around, scans the yard and the deserted street, takes out a key, and opens the door to Jake's apartment.

They walk in, and the acoustics change. Savage switches on the light. The air conditioner is running. The room is neat and clean, the bed made.

"Sit down, Maria."

She sighs, blinks, and sits on the bed.

Waiting.

Savage watches her in her black outfit. She doesn't have the confidence she had in the restaurant. More a frightened girl.

"Is it Ramirez?"

Maria leans forward, shaking as she begins to sob, in little gasping breaths. Savage waits until she finally regains her composure. She wipes her eyes and tries to smile, her teeth strong and white, bordered by full lips.

"I'm okay. I feel better now." She pauses and takes in a deep breath. "I was dating Jake. He was good to me. Fun and kind." She raises her head and looks at Savage. "He's a good man, your brother."

Savage raises his eyebrows.

Dating Jake, Savage thinks. So he *does* date women.

"And I had seen you before," Maria continues, "I just couldn't remember where. But now I do. He showed me pictures of you."

"He showed you pictures?" Savage is surprised.

"You're his brother, his family, so of course. He cares a lot about you."

Savage realizes he doesn't know much about Jake. He feels the bond of brotherhood, but hasn't had the experience of friendship over time—just the fleeting calls, the occasional text, an email or two, an exchanged picture, news of their parents. And now this.

A scooter buzzes past. The air-conditioner hums.

"I got that job at the restaurant. I was going to move in with Jake," Maria says. "I was so happy."

She pauses, looking like she's going to cry again. "I was working at the restaurant. I didn't know Ramirez then. He didn't hire me, the manager did. But Ramirez came in one night. He saw me and, well, he liked me a lot. But I was dating Jake. And I was happy with Jake. I hadn't been happy for a long time. I liked the restaurant, and my job, but Ramirez wanted me. That's when I made a stupid mistake."

"You and Ramirez?"

"No, not that. I told Ramirez that I'm an illegal. I didn't mean to. It just came up. Everything changed then." Savage doesn't interrupt. "He said I had to live with him or he'd turn me in to immigration."

"Did you tell Jake?"

"No, I was too scared. Jake was away a lot. Diving or something. I didn't want to say anything. I'm so sorry. Jake is a good man."

Maria wrings her hands and rocks back and forth on the bed.

Savage feels her sadness. *You just never know,* he thinks. Everyone has their story, their world. We're all connected but fractured at the same time.

"Ramirez forced you to live with him?"

"Yes—in an apartment in his house. He lives with his mother and Juan. He made me look after Juan and work at the restaurant."

"He kidnapped you, essentially. You're his slave. Jesus."

Maria nods and wipes tears from her eyes.

Savage flexes his fists, feeling the anger begin to rise. He focuses on his breathing.

"Then he started to force me to have sex with him. He is not a good man."

Savage's mind reels. "Stay here tonight, okay?"

"It's not safe here. Ramirez knows this is Jakes's place. He made me tell him about Jake. He's jealous and crazy."

"Just for tonight. I'll stay, too. I'll sleep in the other room. You're not going back to Ramirez."

Maria bows her head and begins to sob. "But Juan," she says, "little Juan."

Savage realizes she has a bond with the boy.

"How long were you there with Ramirez?"

"A year." Maria lets out a sigh.

Savage's head is spinning. He stands, watching Maria, thinking about Ramirez.

He turns and locks the door. "Let's get some sleep," he says. "I'm tired. I'll leave the door open."

"Thanks," she says.

"I'll look after you. Don't worry."

A flicker of a smile crosses Maria's face. She wants to believe him.

———

In the middle of the night, the bed in Jake's room creaks, then bare feet on the floor are crossing the room, coming through the small kitchen into his room. He feels the quilt being pulled back. Maria gets in and snuggles close to Savage.

"I'm scared," Maria says.

"That's okay. Try to sleep."

Savage lies on his back for what seems like hours. He hears Maria's steady breathing as she sleeps. He checks the bedside clock—2:30am. Nikki would be home now. Savage tries to sleep.

Then he hears another noise, this time outside on the deck. Slow, heavy steps. Savage pulls back the quilt and sits up. Maria stirs but doesn't wake.

Savage is on his feet, naked and light on his feet.

He makes his way across the room into the small kitchen and then into Jake's room.

The air-conditioner hums.

Someone is trying to jimmy the door open.

Savage is ready.

23

PAULO'S PROBLEM

SAVAGE WAITS in the corner by the door, his eye on the Glock in the man's hand as he creeps into the room. He can hear the man's breathing, rapid and nervous. The pistol shakes. Savage is ready, his breath steady. He decides not to use the knife. He doesn't want to kill.

The man's arm sweeps the room from left to right. The moonlight reveals a previously occupied bed, now empty. The quilt is pulled to one side, just as Maria had left it when she left for Savage's room. The man's body is almost in the room.

Savage is quick and silent, and then there's a crash as the pistol drops to the floor. Savage strikes the man's windpipe, turns him, knees him in the groin, and places his hand firmly over the man's mouth.

The man begins to whimper. He can feel the strength in Savage's grip.

Savage pushes him onto the bed and grabs the Glock. He presses the barrel against the base of the man's skull. "Don't struggle. You'll get hurt."

The man tries to speak, but Savage's hand is covering his

mouth. He tightens his chokehold and feels the man begin to fight.

"Don't," Savage cautions, "don't try to fight me." He moves his head close to the man.

"Jesus!" Savage hisses, "Paulo, don't you ever learn?" Paulo tries to answer again, but Savage clamps his hand down harder. "I guess not," he chuckles.

Savage pulls Paulo to his feet and grabs his throat hard, pulls him off the ground, and squeezes. Paulo's eyes bulge.

Maria is at the door now, her eyes wide, clutching the doorframe. Savage turns. "See if there's any duct tape, rope, anything. Something to tie him up with."

He hasn't released his grip. His fingers are thick and strong.

Maria goes into the kitchen, and Savage can hear drawers opening and Maria rummaging around. Paulo has stopped struggling, but his breathing is labored.

"We're going to have to go out for dinner again, Paulo." Paulo shakes his head vigorously. "I'm assuming Ramirez sent you. Did he?" Paulo nods and mumbles something unintelligible through Savage's hand. "You going to be a good boy, Paulo?" Paulo nods.

Maria returns with a roll of duct tape and a handful of Thule straps.

"Perfect," Savage says.

Ten minutes later Paulo is trussed on the bed, his eyes wide. He blinks, rocks back and forth, and tries to speak through the duct tape.

"You know, Paulo, this is getting old. You hear me?"

Paulo nods.

"What do you think Ramirez will do this time, Paulo? I'm going to take you right back to that restaurant and we're going to sit down again and I'm going to have a word with Mr. Ramirez. You think he'll listen to me?"

Maria watches, still scared. The air conditioner hums. A bead of sweat falls from Savage's brow.

Paulo shakes his head back and forth. He's still trying to say something. Savage looks at him, but starts wondering about Jake, and why things seem to be teetering on the brink of being out of control again. He looks at Maria—pretty but frightened.

"I'll look after you, okay?" Savage says. Maria turns towards him. There is a flicker of a smile and a light in her eyes. The fear returns quickly, though she wants to believe him.

Savage takes a switchblade out of his pocket. It sits in his palm for a beat and then the blade appears, elegant, sharp, and deadly. Paulo watches, and his breath quickens.

"I'm not kidding, Paulo, we're going back to the restaurant, and you're going to be a good boy. You got that?"

Paulo nods.

"If you're not a good boy, I'm not going to be happy, Paulo. You got that?"

Paulo blinks, swallows, and nods again.

Savage walks over to Paulo and loosens the Thule straps. Paulo stretches out on the bed, shakes his wrists, and circles his ankles. He brings his knees to his chest, then rolls forward and sits on the end of the bed. Savage watches as Paulo puts his hands on the corner of the mattress and brings his legs together.

"Don't." Savage watches the poised tension leave Paulo's body.

"Stand up," Savage says. "Now." It's a barking command. Paulo stands and Savage reaches out, takes the duct tape in his fingers, and slowly pulls it off his mouth. His eyes don't leave Paulo's.

"Ready?" Savage asks.

Paulo nods.

"How much did he pay you this time?"

"Nothing," Paulo says.

"Because you fucked up the first time?"

Paulo closes his eyes and drops his head. There's a hint of a nod. He looks up. "Yeah. He said I owed him. Said he was giving me another chance."

"A last chance?"

"Something like that. I need to take a leak, okay?"

Savage points his chin towards the bathroom. "Leave the door open."

Paulo walks to the bathroom. Savage knows he's weighing his options. His head turns towards the closed window.

"I said, don't."

Paulo begins to take a leak. Long. Slow. Heavy.

"Maria, listen," Savage says in a hushed whisper. "Here's some cash. You know how to use one of these?" He pulls the Glock from his waistband. Maria shakes her head.

"Safety on. Safety off. Hold it with two hands," he says, demonstrating. "Aim for the center of the body. Squeeze the trigger. Don't pull it. Take a cab to Stock Island. Go to the boatyard. Here's the code to the main gate." Savage writes it on the back of a business card lying on Jake's desk. "Key to the office. Go and lock yourself in. I'll call when I'm on my way." Savage gives her the Glock. "Safety's off. Put it in your bag."

"I'm scared, Savage. I don't want Ramirez to find me and take me back."

"He won't."

"How do you know?"

"Trust me."

Maria reaches out and touches Savage's forearm. He responds by squeezing her small hand, wishing everything were different.

The toilet flushes, and water runs in the sink. Savage watches the open door. Waiting.

Suddenly, the bathroom door closes, and the door lock turns.

Savage shakes his head. "Damn, Paulo," he says. "Idiot just won't learn." He looks at Maria, and mouths, "Come with me."

He turns off the lights, walks out through the door onto deck, takes Maria's hand, and leads her down the outside staircase to the garden. Savage opens the gate gingerly, steps out, and peers up at the outside of the house. Paulo emerges from the second story window, lowering himself to drop to the sidewalk.

Savage pulls Maria close to him. "Cross the road. Get a cab on the corner. Got it?" She nods, and he hands her a set of keys.

"Keep these. Go," Savage says. "Remember, take a cab to the boatyard on Stock Island. I'll be there when I can."

Maria nods, dashes across the street, and heads for the corner.

Paulo's hanging from his fingertips. His feet have no purchase. There's no way back up the wall to the window, and there's an eight-foot drop to the sidewalk.

"Just let go and drop," Savage says. Paulo turns his head and looks down and then tries to scramble back up the wall without success.

"I said don't try anything, right? Should have listened. Now let go. I said now."

Paulo drops, lands, heavily, and tries to run. But Savage sweeps his right foot from under him, and Paulo falls hard. He struggles to get to his feet, ready to fight, but Savage knees him in the thigh and punches him in the side of the head, and he goes down on all fours.

"Okay, okay, my ankle." Paulo is still doubled over. He doesn't put any weight on his ankle. Savage puts a hold on his wrist, and then twists his arm behind him.

"Act like you're drunk. Like we're taking a cab."

"I don't want to see Ramirez," Paulo says. "Please. He'll kill me."

"But you were going to kill *me*, Paulo. Remember?"

"Oh, Jesus," Paulo says, half sobbing. Savage leads him to the corner. He can see Maria in the eastbound lane, getting into a cab.

Savage flags a westbound cab. The door opens, and he eases Paulo in. "Duval," Savage says, climbing in next to Paulo. They pull away.

The night is coming alive with tourists. Savage looks at the bars and restaurants. He wonders what it would be like to be on vacation.

"You here on vacation?" the cabbie asks.

"I wish. Just business," Savage says. He offers nothing else. At an outdoor café, he sees a pair of college students toast each other with margaritas in plastic glasses. One of the students staggers and catches himself on a table, nearly knocking it over.

The cabbie shakes his head. "Like this every night," he says. "Every night. Been here fifteen years. Every night."

The radio is playing Cuban salsa.

Savage looks at the revelers. He remembers being that young. But at that age, he was in uniform, first in Corsica, then in France, and then in Africa. Another time. Another world.

"Right here's good," Savage says to the cab driver.

Paulo is mumbling something in Spanish. Savage helps him out of the cab, and they cross the road.

"Come on, Paulo," Savage says. "You can do better than that. You need to straighten up."

The restaurant is busy. Laughter floats out as Savage opens the glass door. Guests are being seated and tables cleared. Savage and Paulo are shown to the same table as last time, but this time Paulo faces the wall. Savage can see through the door and into the kitchen. The door swings open and closed.

"I'm not hungry," Paulo says.

"That's not the point. We're not on a date. Order a salad," Savage says. "I don't eat alone."

Savage orders the grouper, Paulo a seafood salad.

Savage watches the patrons and imagines their lives. He wonders about their hotels, their guest cottages. He imagines they are tourists from the Midwest, paying for their fun. His eyes move around the restaurant, then back to Paulo, who is alert, coiled, angry, and ready.

Glasses chink. Cutlery clatters. The kitchen door swings open, then closes.

I have got to talk to Jake, Savage thinks. *Soon. Make a plan. Wrap things up. Move on.*

Take a vacation.

Paulo is muttering again, a prayer in Spanish.

The door to the kitchen swings open and their server arrives. The door opens a second time, and Savage catches a glimpse of Ramirez's profile. He's berating an employee insistently, pointing a finger, his teeth clenched. *Just a matter of time,* Savage thinks.

"Pepper?" the server asks, proffering a pepper mill the size of a small baseball bat.

"Sure," Savage says. He glances up and sees another young and beautiful Latina, like Maria. With a story, no doubt. There's always a story.

"How do you like working here?" he asks, surprising himself.

Her eyes light up. "I don't know yet. I only started yesterday. I think I like it, though."

"Good. That's good. I hope you will."

Paulo is looking over at the kitchen.

The server leaves for another table with a spring in her step. The kitchen door swings open again for another server with a tray full of entrees. Ramirez turns and catches Savage's eye. The door swings shut, but not before Savage sees Ramirez's face redden in anger.

"Paulo?"

"Huh?" Paulo snaps from his morose stupor.

"I've been thinking. You want to make a deal?"

"What kind of deal?"

"Let's put it like this. You know what will happen if I hand you over to Ramirez, right?" Savage takes the index finger of his left hand and draws it across his throat.

"Jesus," Paulo says, pulling at his napkin. "I don't want that."

"Doesn't have to be like that, Paulo. Work with me. Do what I say. I won't hand you over."

Paulo's eyes are wide, frightened and desperate.

"Good evening, gentlemen. Mr. Savage." Ramirez nods deferentially. "I see you like our food."

"Very good. Yes. I brought Paulo back. We ran into each

other, and I thought you might want a word with him." Savage watches Ramirez's eyes carefully for any reaction or hint of what he is thinking.

Ramirez rubs his chin, trying to suppress the welling anger. "Oh, yes. I have something to say to Paulo. There are just a couple of things we need to clear up."

Paulo looks straight ahead, not acknowledging Ramirez, pulling his napkin, tears in his eyes. Waiting. For Savage.

"Your dinner's on me, Mr. Savage. You can leave Paulo here when you go. I'll take care of him."

Ramirez turns and walks back to the kitchen. Paulo is sweating. He hasn't touched his food. Savage watches the door close behind Ramirez.

"So, you want me to leave you here or are you going to come with me?"

"I'm with you," Paulo says. "He'll kill me."

"You don't think I will?"

"You would have already if you'd wanted to. I'll take my chances."

Paulo makes the sign of the cross over his chest. A customer laughs at the next table. The server passes by, her eyes alive.

Savage turns to Paulo, expressionless. He feels a twinge in his shoulder. "I kind of like you, Paulo. Even though you've tried to get me twice. What's that about?"

Paulo shrugs his shoulders. "I'm a nice guy. Just don't give me to Ramirez."

Savage continues to eat. He's hungry. Paulo pokes at his salad. Savage takes his time. There's no rush. Not here. Not in the restaurant.

Savage finishes and lays his knife and fork at an angle on his plate.

Their server stops at the table. "I'll take your plates. Would you gentlemen care for dessert?"

She has a sweet voice. Savage hopes her life is good.

"We're good, thanks," he says.

"Mr. Ramirez is taking care of the check." She collects the plates.

"Tell him the food is excellent." Savage leaves five twenties under his glass after she leaves.

"Okay, Paulo. Time to leave." Savage moves his chair back and is about to stand when Ramirez returns from the kitchen.

"You have a good evening, Mr. Savage. Paulo, sit down. You're staying here."

Savage stands in front of Ramirez and says, "I'll see you by the door, Paulo."

A look of anger flashes across Ramirez's face. Paulo stands, slowly, head down, and pushes the table out. He walks over to the door and waits. He knows better than to run.

"You don't want to leave him with me?" Ramirez asks.

"I have a better idea," Savage says.

"What better idea?" Ramirez juts his chin forward, his voice low, aware of the guests.

"One that's much better... for me."

"I'll pay you what you want for the yard, Mr. Savage. Just give me a number," Ramirez says, smiling, putting his heavy hand on Savage's shoulder.

"It's more complicated than that, Mr. Ramirez. A lot more."

"It's not that complicated, Mr. Savage. I want that yard."

"You won't get it."

A woman at the table next to them looks up, sensing the tension.

Ramirez moves closer to Savage, leaning in close to his face. Savage smells his coffee breath. "This could turn out badly, Mr. Savage."

"I hope not," Savage says.

"This is my town, Mr. Savage. I know a lot of people."

The woman turns away and leans towards the man sitting with her. She mutters something.

Ramirez's eyes flit from side to side. The server watches. The kitchen door opens.

Paulo waits.

"It's not about who you know, Ramirez."

Savage's eyes are sharp, piercing. Ramirez takes a step back. Savage smiles at the woman at the table. She can't believe his eyes. She almost swoons. The moment freezes then gains its fluidity again. The man begins to saw at his steak.

"Good night, Ramirez. Great food, by the way. Great new server. Where's Maria?"

Ramirez's eyes grow hard and cold, and Savage notes the tendons tightening in his neck. Savage turns and walks over to the door where Paulo is waiting. He opens the door and ushers Paulo out.

"Man, you pissed him off," Paulo says. "I'm scared now."

"Maybe I did. Now walk. We need to get a few things straight."

Paulo walks.

"Tell me everything you know about Ramirez. And I'm serious. I mean everything." Savage squeezes Paulo's arm, hard. "You're going to tell me. If I give you up to Ramirez, he's going to kill you. Your choice."

"But what's he going to do if I do talk? He's still going to kill me. I can't win."

"I'm the better bet," Savage says. "When I'm done, Ramirez isn't going to be able to get to you."

"You planning to do what I think you're planning to do?"

"I've no idea what you think, Paulo. I don't need to know, and I don't care. Now listen. We're going to walk to Mallory Square, and you're going to talk. You don't, you're on your own."

"But Ramirez? He's not going to care. If he finds me, I'm dead."

"You tell me what I need to know, Paulo, I'll make sure you're okay. Now talk."

24

STOCK ISLAND

"THAT'S EVERYTHING?" Savage asks. The dawn adds a wash of color to the feathery low clouds on the horizon, spreading like tentative fingers.

Paulo nods, his face gaunt, his eyes tired and flat.

"Everything. Now you don't need me. And when Ramirez finds me, he'll kill me."

Savage rubs the bridge of his nose. He's tired, a deep, far-reaching exhaustion. But he has the strength, the stamina, to see this through.

"I'm a man of my word. We made a deal. I said I'd look after you. So I will. Is there someplace you can stay? Someplace quiet?"

Paulo shakes his head and looks at his feet.

The light begins to spill into the day. The yellow blooms and rich greens come to life.

"You want a job, Paulo?" Savage asks, after a long silence.

"A job? I'm not thinking about a job. I'm thinking about how to not get killed."

An old man is walking his Maltese. It stops and pees on a lamp post. The man waits patiently.

"Come work for me," Savage says.

"If I work for you, then I will definitely get killed." Paulo scratches his forearm and spits on the ground.

"No. That's how to not get killed. Trust me."

"Trust you? Ramirez told me to trust him, too. I don't trust no one no more."

"You don't have a choice. Like I said, I'm your best bet. You told me a lot. That's going to help me. I said I'd look after you."

"I know I can't trust Ramirez. That's all I know. Except I also know it's getting light and I don't want to be downtown in broad daylight, right under Ramirez's nose."

Savage says, "Follow me. We'll find a cab."

"Where we going?"

"Somewhere safe."

"Sure. Someplace I'll feel safe is gonna be a lot farther away than a cab ride from here."

Savage jogs across the road and hails a cab by the Shipwreck Museum. Paulo limps after him, and they climb into the back seat.

"Stock Island," Savage tells the driver.

"That's not safe," Paulo says under his breath.

The cab pulls away from the curb and into another sultry, hungover morning. Key West is unfolding in slow motion. The street cleaners are out. Breakfast places are opening up. The last of the revelers have only been in bed an hour or two.

Savage calls the boatyard. He hopes Maria answers, but the answering machine kicks in instead.

"It's me," Savage begins. There's a noise on the line, like someone picking up.

"Savage? Savage," Maria says. Her voice is urgent but muted. "There's a Mercedes parked outside the gate."

"I'll be right there. Don't let anyone in. Remember what I said," Savage lowers his voice. "Two hands. Safety off. Aim for the body. Keep watching."

The cab speeds up. The driver glances in the rearview, concern on his face. Savage's insistent blue eyes stare back.

He hangs up. "I'll give you an extra $50 to make it quick."

The cab turns onto Eaton, then Palm Avenue, then North Roosevelt, going fast, but not too fast. It's early and the traffic is light. They cross the bridge onto Stock Island, past the bushes where a couple of homeless men are waking up. The suburbs, Savage thinks, remembering Jake's words.

They turn right onto Maloney Avenue and finally weave south to Shrimp Road. Savage sees the Mercedes outside the gate, sitting with its engine idling. No one is visible through the tinted glass.

"Just drive real smooth. Take a left before the yard. Go down about fifty yards, then stop."

Savage evaluates the situation. Maria is in the main office, and Ramirez is probably outside. He may or may not realize that Savage is in the cab.

The cab stops, and Savage gives the driver the extra cash, pressing it into his palm.

"Now, drive straight. Nice and easy. Don't turn around. If you hear anything suspicious, don't call the cops, okay?

The driver looks at Savage, silent. Savage hands him another fifty.

"Got it," the driver says, folding the bills and slipping them into the visor.

Savage and Paulo get out. The cab pulls away nice and easy, just like Savage instructed.

Savage turns to Paulo. "You got a gun?"

"You took my gun. You got a gun?"

"Don't worry about me," Savage says. He scans the boatyard.

"You haven't got a gun?"

"You stay here. I'm going to sort this out."

Paulo looks towards Shrimp Road. Savage sets off at an easy lope. He has one hand in his jacket pocket, holding the switchblade. He hopes Ramirez will think it's a gun. He rounds the corner and walks up to the driver's side of the Mercedes.

The window slides down. Ramirez is at the wheel, with a broad, square-headed giant next to him in the passenger seat for protection.

"Maria?" Ramirez says.

"What about Maria?"

"So, you do know her, then?" Ramirez says. "Where is she, Mr. Savage?"

"A better place than she was," Savage says, staring at Ramirez, gauging his reaction.

The giant stares at Savage. His eyes are deep set. He begins what sounds like a growl, his lips parting. A very big man. Thick arms.

"Meaning what?"

"You know what I mean, Ramirez." Savage is alert, listening, knees bent, ready to move.

"Have you thought about what I said, Mr. Savage? I said name your price."

The giant is getting restless.

"I gave you my answer." Savage puts his hand in his pocket, and watches the giant do the same.

"Your brother. I saw him the other day." Ramirez taps the dashboard with his middle finger.

Savage is surprised, but tries not to show it.

"I know it was him. Dive boat?" Ramirez raises his eyebrows. "Things can happen at sea, Mr. Savage. It's dangerous out there."

Ramirez has tracked Jake down, Savage realizes. He says nothing.

"I was surprised to see your brother out so far. Anchored. No rods. Must have been looking for something."

"Vacation. He needs some time off." Savage's hand is still in his pocket. The giant is sweating.

"You're a stubborn man, Mr. Savage. First you won't tell me

about Maria, and now you won't tell me about your brother. Tell your brother to be careful. Diving is a dangerous business, particularly that far offshore. Anything can happen."

"Is that a threat, Ramirez?"

"You know what it is, Mr. Savage."

"I do know what it is. I just wondered whether you had the balls to spell it out," Savage says, leaning closer to the car window, almost putting his head inside.

Ramirez drums his fingers faster. "Is he looking for something? Or maybe he already found something?" Ramirez grimaces. "That wasn't a tourist boat. Let's say he found something."

Savage says nothing.

"Am I right, Mr. Savage?"

"Why are you here anyway, Ramirez? To make me an offer you know I'll refuse?"

Ramirez chuckles. "Just dropping in to see if anyone's home. Seems someone was."

A cold wave runs through Savage. Ramirez has been into the yard. He knows Maria's there. Savage stares at Ramirez.

The giant mutters something in rapid Spanish, through clenched teeth and quivering lips.

"I could have you killed right now, Mr. Savage. I'm a very angry man."

Savage eases his hand out of his pocket, the blade hidden.

"Pedro," Ramirez says.

Pedro puts his hand in his jacket. He's moving slowly. Savage is quick, though, and grabs Ramirez by the throat with his left hand and squeezes. At the same time, his right hand flashes forward and slices Pedro's nostril open. Blood instantly runs, gushing into his mouth and down his chin. Savage pulls his hand back, wipes the blade on Ramirez's shirt, folds it up, and then plucks the Beretta from Pedro's pocket. He points the barrel at Ramirez's temple.

Pedro's eyes are wild. He's spitting and thrashing in his seat.

"Well, you could have me killed," Savage says. "Or I could kill you." He unlocks the safety. "But don't worry. I'm not going to."

Pedro is trying to stop the bleeding. His nostril is flapping and there's blood everywhere.

Ramirez is staring straight ahead, fury and fear on his face. He curses in Spanish.

"It's just a flesh wound. Faces bleed. Take him to the emergency room, Ramirez. A few stitches will fix him right up. And don't threaten me again." Savage lets go of his grip on Ramirez's throat. Ramirez gasps for air.

"I don't want a blood bath, Mr. Ramirez. Let this go, okay?"

Ramirez is still coughing and gasping for air. Pedro swears in Spanish, blood covering his clothes and hands.

"Take him now, Ramirez. Now." Savage holds the gun steady, sweeping it from Ramirez to Pedro and back.

Ramirez mutters something unintelligible in Spanish and hits the gas. The back wheels spray gravel as the Mercedes fishtails onto Shrimp Road.

"Not how I planned that to go," Savage says, watching the sedan take a sharp left, then a right, heading towards Route 1. "Not at all."

"Jesus!" Paulo says. "What was that?"

"It was what it was," Savage says.

"Which was what?"

"A negotiation," Savage says. The Mercedes has gone. Shrimp Road is quiet, the sun high and hot.

"That was a negotiation? God, I'd hate to see a fight!"

Savage enters the security code and the gate opens. He walks inside, takes his phone from his pocket, and dials. Maria picks up.

"Are you okay, Savage?" Maria asks.

"I'm not dead, if that's what you mean." Paulo is behind him. A dog barks.

"I'll open the door."

"I've got Paulo here. Don't panic. He's on our side. But if he tries anything, kill him."

Savage smiles broadly at Paulo. They walk into the office trailer, where the air-conditioner is whirring.

"Paulo, you know Maria, right?"

Maria looks at Savage, her eyes wide. He sees fear.

"You know who he is?" Maria asks Savage.

"Yes. And now he's decided to work for me. Decided being alive is better than being dead."

"God, I hope so," Paulo says. "But I don't know—Ramirez, he's going to be pissed. Pedro's going to be pissed. They're all going to be pissed. Maybe being dead wouldn't be so bad."

"Paulo, you have an attitude problem. We're going to have to sort all this out quickly and efficiently. I'm not looking for a show-down. Methodical and precise is how it's going to go. I'm not going to blow this."

"Blow what? The only blow around here…".

"Paulo, shut up! Loose lips sink ships. You understand that, right?"

"Now, how come I can only understand half of what you say, Mr. Savage?"

"That's a good question, Paulo. I hadn't given it much thought. But now I do, perhaps it says something about you."

"You're the guy I can't understand. It's about you, not me."

"My point exactly."

"That's your point? But that isn't a point."

"It's like a koan, Paulo. You know what a koan is, right?"

Paulo frowns. His mouth opens, but nothing comes out.

Savage straightens up at the sound of tires on gravel. He goes over to the window and looks out across the white concrete. In the shimmering haze, he sees the Mercedes again. This time, four men get out.

Ramirez is a big man, but he's the smallest of the four.

"Oh, my God," Maria moans.

"Size isn't everything," Savage says. "Stay here. Maria, you have the Glock. Paulo, you take this." Savage hands him the Beretta.

"You giving this to me?" Paulo says, taking the Beretta and hefting it in his hand. "Nice piece."

"I'm lending it to you. It's Pedro's. Anything happens to me, you wait until they get to the door, then do what you have to do, okay?"

Paulo nods, adjusting his grip.

"I'm not looking for a fight. I'm going to talk. He's mad. It's an honor thing."

Savage opens the door and walks out, his hands to his side.

"Take the jacket off, Mr. Savage."

Savage pulls his jacket off his shoulders and lets it fall to the ground. He hears the knife hit the concrete.

The sun is high, and the sky clear and blue. The air shimmers. The four men wait for Savage to arrive.

"I'm very angry," Ramirez says.

Savage keeps walking forward, taking easy strides. "You told your heavy to kill me, Ramirez. I defended myself. Any man would."

"I'm still angry. And my throat still hurts, you bastard."

The three other men are gargantuan and tough. They have boxers' faces, battered and scarred. Savage sizes them up. He focuses on his breathing and empties his mind. Ramirez will go down first, then two more, then it would be fifty-fifty whether he could take out another one or not.

The men look big but past their prime. They exude testosterone and anger; never a good combination.

"I want to make a deal, Mr. Savage," Ramirez says.

"What kind of a deal?"

"You sell me the yard and I spare your brother. Sound fair?"

Savage's piercing blue eyes bore through Ramirez. He flexes his fingers and moves into kicking range.

"You have my brother?"

"No, but I know where he is. I can get him anytime I want." Ramirez steps back. The three other men shuffle, surprised at Savage's loose confidence. They're used to men crumbling and pleading. Not this.

Savage focuses on his own breathing and on letting go of his welling anger. Part of him wants to kill Ramirez, regardless of the outcome, whatever the three heavies would try to do to him.

Savage looks at the other men one at a time. One is scared already; he can see it in his eyes. Two are spoiling for a fight. Ramirez isn't thinking. He's just angry. Angry means out of control, unpredictable.

Savage thinks quickly. There is a way. One way that will work.

"I saw Juan," Savage says. "He's a beautiful little boy."

Ramirez starts, sweat beads on his head. His Adam's apple bobs up and down. Savage continues to stare right through him. He moves a step forward. Ramirez is losing his composure.

"In the park. With Angie. Really cute kid."

Ramirez is clenching his teeth. "Alexis!"

The biggest of the four steps forward and strides towards Savage. Savage can tell he's used to intimidating people with his size. But he's not a street fighter. Savage can sense there is no plan, just uncontrolled brute force. The other men watch as Ramirez barks in Spanish.

The haymaker is slow in coming—it's a sweeping arc. Savage darts forward with an elbow block. He's quick and balanced and keeps his center of gravity low. Alexis flails. His fist misses the back of Savage's head, but Savage's elbow hits him hard in the left eye socket. Savage gouges both Alexis's eyes with his left hand. He knees him hard in the groin, then delivers a lightning upper cut to his face before bringing Alexis's head down on his rising knee. It's all over.

Savage pulls a pistol from Alexis's pocket as he lies slumped on the ground, and places the gun against Alexis's temple.

"One move, Ramirez, and he's dead. Then you're dead. Your choice."

Ramirez is silent. Alexis is whimpering.

"I'm not looking for any trouble, Ramirez, but if you want it, you're going to get it. Anything happens to my brother... you don't want to know what's going to happen to you."

Ramirez stares at Savage. "And Juan?" Ramirez says.

"You've got a sick mind, Ramirez. I'd never hurt your son. You thought that because that's what you'd do, right? Now get out of here."

One of the other men puts his hand in his jacket. With phenomenal speed, Savage pulls Alexis to his feet and uses him as a giant shield. The pistol cracks, and the shot hits Alexis in the leg. Ramirez shouts, and Savage shoots the man in the knee. He yelps and drops on all fours. Savage sweeps the gun from man to man.

"Anyone else? No? Then get the hell out of here."

Savage's eyes are on Ramirez—wild, unblinking, and searing blue.

"No one's dead. You're just going to have to go back to the emergency room, Ramirez. It's not even noon. How many times does this make? It's like you never learn."

He lets go of Alexis, who staggers and hops towards Ramirez.

The men crawl and limp towards the Mercedes. There's blood on the concrete. The two wounded men are groaning, and Ramirez is ranting furiously in Spanish.

"Get in, Ramirez." Savage points the pistol at his head.

Ramirez gets behind the wheel. Savage aims the pistol into the back of the car and sweeps it over each of the men. They duck, hold up their hands, and shout.

"Go! *Vamos!*" Savage shouts.

The gravel sprays the gate to the boatyard for the second time as Ramirez heads back to the emergency room.

Savage watches the Mercedes make the same left, then right, tires squealing as it heads for Route 1.

Savage shakes his head slowly, then turns to face Paulo and Maria. Paulo's eyes are wide. Maria walks over to Savage and he hugs her.

"It's going to be okay, Maria." He squeezes her close.

"I hope so," she says.

Savage's thoughts soon turn to Jake. He needs to find him as soon as possible. It's going to be a long day, one that doesn't stop until the end.

"Shit," Paulo says, "I never seen Ramirez look like that. Guess I am better off with you."

"Not really a two-way street, is it?"

"You mean it's one-way? What does that mean? What street? I never know what you're talking about."

"Think about it," Savage says.

Maria relaxes in Savage's grip. She laughs, pressing her head against Savage's chest.

"What's so funny?" Paulo snaps.

"You. I don't know. Him. This."

"Me? Why am I so funny? I say I'm with him. Like being nice. And he's all one-way streets."

Savage releases his grip and stands tall. "Forget what I said about thinking about it, Paulo," he says. "Just do what I say. It'll be easier for all of us. Now give me back the Beretta."

"Beretta? What Beretta?" Paulo says.

"Look out!" Savage shouts, starting to duck as Paulo covers his head and falls to his knees.

Savage pulls the Beretta out of Paulo's pocket and kicks him hard in the side. He puts his foot on Paulo's neck.

"This Beretta. The one with the safety off. The one I'm holding at your thick skull. Remember?"

"Oh, yeah. That one. I forgot about it. The loaner, right?"

"Last chance, Paulo. First day, and I might have to fire you."

"Hey, look, I forgot, okay? Lot of pressure. I made a mistake. I work for you. I do what you say."

"You do. You do what I say. You do that and you might come out of this in one piece."

Savage looks over at Maria and rolls his eyes, shaking his head.

"You like pulled pork?" Savage asks.

"Yeah," Paulo says, "Yeah, I do." His face is still pressed against the floor.

"Not you, Paulo. Maria."

She nods her head.

"Well, let's go, then," Savage says. "Paulo, you stay here. Keep an eye on things. Okay?"

Paulo looks scared and dejected but nods his head.

Savage lifts his foot off Paulo's neck and pulls him to his feet. He squints at Paulo and taps the Beretta.

"You be good, Paulo. I know you're not going anywhere."

"No," Paulo says. He shakes his head and stares out of the window towards Shrimp Road.

"I ain't going nowhere, Mr. Savage. Nowhere at all."

25

SUGARLOAF

SAVAGE IS SITTING on the beach at Fort Zachary, watching a fishing boat work its way out to sea through the afternoon chop. The white hull slices the turquoise waves, sending spray into the air as the bow rises and falls in the swell. The tourists on board steady themselves for the impact, the captain at the wheel. It's another day in paradise for some.

He has just one text from Jake that says, "Watch Sugarloaf Key." Otherwise, there's been no response to his numerous calls, texts, or email. Savage doesn't know where Jake is, or what he's doing. He turns, hearing a helicopter flying fast and low overhead. The familiar thwack, thwack, thwack of the blades as they slice the air. To Savage, those blades sound like combat, jungles, obscure countries, tyrannical regimes, and the legacy of crumbling colonialism.

The fishing boat passes, the Coast Guard helicopter banks south and out to sea, continuing its trajectory, low and purposeful. Perhaps there's a boat in trouble, or smugglers. Maybe it's Jake.

Savage gets to his feet. Ramirez had said that things happen at sea. Jake is out there somewhere. He has to find him, before it's too late. Savage dials Nikki.

"Hey, it's me, Savage. Didn't think you'd pick up." Savage stops walking and steps into the shade of a tall palm tree.

"What are you doing?" Savage listens. Nikki sounds like she's been sleeping. Her voice has no energy.

"Nothing. It's Sunday. Day off. Don't feel like doing much."

"I need a ride. I'm at Fort Zachary Taylor."

"Call a cab."

"I have to talk to you, too, Nikki."

Savage hears movement in the background. Maybe Nikki is getting off the couch, or out of bed.

"I need to shower first."

"Come now. I'll take you as you are."

"I need a shower for me. Not for you."

Savage laughs. "I'll pick you up in twenty. End of Eaton Street."

He looks out to sea again. The fishing boat is smaller, the helicopter a speck in the distance. The sky is a broad blue dome. So pure. Savage rolls his shoulder. Simplicity, he thinks. Just simplicity.

Get this done. Then a vacation.

The air is sultry, prescient. He feels a bead of sweat begin to trickle down his back.

He picks up his phone and calls Jake. No answer. He calls Angie. No answer. He calls the boatyard. No answer. He starts to leave a message, "Hey, it's Savage. Listen ..."

The phone picks up.

"Savage? It's Paulo. You okay?

"I'm good. You?"

"Good. And Maria's good."

"Stay at the boatyard, okay? If you go anywhere, go together."

"When are you coming back?"

"When I can. Can't say. Tonight. Tomorrow. No more than a couple of days." Savage rubs the back of his neck. He can feel the knotted tension.

"Listen, Savage. That's cool. You can trust me."

Savage hangs up without replying. It's better to keep Paulo a little on edge. He calls the boatyard again. No answer. He starts to leave a message when the phone picks up.

"Savage?" It's Paulo again.

"Yeah. Listen, Paulo. I'll decide if I can trust you or not. Doesn't matter what you say. It's what you do. Got it?"

There's a pause on the line. "Got it," Paulo says, his voice flatter, the energy not quite there.

"Paulo, this is serious stuff. Life or death. You know that. You're going to look after Maria until I get back. You're responsible. Anything happens to her, it's your fault. Your watch. Okay?"

"Savage. Listen...".

"No. Just look after Maria. Make sure she has what she needs."

Savage hangs up. He needs Paulo to feel he has to prove his worth to him. He wants him to feel distrusted, vulnerable. He needs Paulo to earn his trust. Savage puts his phone in his pocket and starts walking back into town. Scooters, tourists, hotels, cyclists—another swirling day of color and sound.

A cruise ship is slowly moving out to sea like an apartment block with a bow. Savage shakes his head in disbelief.

The Mustang pulls alongside Savage, its top down and rap booming. "*Make a solution before I cause confusion.*" Nikki's hair is tied back and she's wearing Ray-Bans, a pink baseball cap, and a white tank top. On her wrists there are simple silver bangles. She kills the music.

"You look great. Is that for you or for me?"

"Funny. It's for me. Women dress to make themselves feel good. I thought you would have learned that by now."

"What makes them feel good?"

"Get in, Savage. Don't just stand there like some half-wit. And cut the humor. What is it about English guys, huh? Always got to be funny."

Savage laughs and gets in.

"Can I trust you?" he asks. "We really need to talk."

"You can trust me. But can I trust you? Can anyone trust anyone? Come on, Savage, what kind of dumbass question is that?" Nikki shakes her head.

Savage turns to face her. Nikki's jaw is set, no smile.

"You know you can," she says.

Nikki shifts gears.

Savage admires her profile. "I like your earrings."

"Thanks. Me, too. I bought them for myself in Mexico."

"You seem very comfortable in your own skin, Nikki."

"Is that a problem?"

"No. It's attractive. Could be uncomfortable for some men. You know—too comfortable can mean too independent."

"Where are we going?" Nikki asks, turning briefly to Savage, a hint of a smile forming.

Savage looks at Nikki, admiring her dark hair, high cheekbones, and dark olive skin.

"Sugarloaf Key."

"Any reason?"

"We have to find Jake."

"You think he's there?"

"I don't know." He sees an old man walking a little white Maltese and thinks he's seen him before. Not a bad life, Savage thinks. For some.

"I got a text. It said, *Watch Sugarloaf Key*. That was it. All I've heard." Savage drums his fingers on the dashboard.

"Okay ... then we'd better go look," Nikki raises her sunglasses. "You can trust me, Savage."

Savage knows he can. He doesn't know why he asked. You can tell. Sometimes.

"I think he's there. Or at least putting in to port there. Or someone else is there. I know he's been out diving. And here's something else."

"What?"

Savage goes quiet.

"Spit it out."

"I just hope Ramirez doesn't find him first. He's a hair's breadth from doing something bad. I think I drove him to that point. Kind of wish I hadn't."

"We'll find him," Nikki says. "I know we will."

They fall silent. The sidewalks are bustling with slow-moving tourists. A Harley comes down the street towards them, the engine rumbling noisily. The rider is big. He has a blue bandana and white, tattooed arms.

"Why did you think you couldn't trust me, Savage?"

"Just a feeling. You know. You're very independent. You look after yourself. Get what you want. I might be wrong; probably am. You know, some people are all about themselves."

"Jesus, Savage! And that means you can't trust me? Because I know what I want and how to get it? We're all selfish in the end. That doesn't mean you can't trust me."

"Then there's us. You know. The boyfriend thing."

"What about my boyfriend? He's not my husband. He's my boyfriend. You don't know what kind of relationship we have."

"You slept with me, but you're with him, right? Doesn't that say something?"

Savage feels a frisson in the air.

"About trust? No. It says I like you. You're attractive. I wanted you. My boyfriend has nothing to do with that. You slept with me, too. And you slept with Angie. And we're both Jake's friends. And Angie and I have both slept with him. And each other. None of that has to do with trust. I love Jake. I'd do anything for him. He would for me, too. *There's* trust. And a lot more than trust, too. Jesus, Savage. You almost sound like you're jealous of something."

Savage blinks and suppresses a grin. Small world, he thinks. Everything is related. Just connect the dots.

Nikki turns her head away from Savage and watches the road.

"Well, if you put it like that," Savage begins.

"Then what, Savage? I meet a lot of assholes in my business. You'd better not be another one. Your brother certainly isn't."

Savage straightens his back. "He isn't. And I don't want to be one. Sorry."

"Sorry," Nikki says, mocking Savage's accent. She turns and flashes a smile at him. Savage grins and squeezes her knee.

Nikki laughs, exposing her beautiful white teeth.

She turns from Bertha Street onto South Roosevelt, where there's less traffic. The sea shimmers, and Savage leans back in his seat, feeling the wind on his face. He closes his eyes and strokes Nikki's thigh.

"Sorry, Nikki."

"I'm not a demure Asian, Savage. I'm me. There's a lot of me. I know what I want and I'm pretty good at getting it. And you know what? Jake trusts me."

Nikki stomps the gas angrily and the Mustang responds. Savage opens his eyes and takes his hand off Nikki's thigh.

"Okay?" Nikki briefly looks at him; a flash of anger comes and goes. She eases her foot off the gas.

"Got it," Savage says, noting the sudden passion and anger in her voice.

They cross to Stock Island and then Boca Chica. Nikki changes lanes smoothly, shifting from second to third.

"God, I hope we find him," Savage says. "Alive. Soon."

Nikki changes gears again with a swift, deft movement. "You think we won't?"

"Ramirez was making threats. I don't know. He said, 'Things happen at sea'."

"Things happen at sea. They happen everywhere. Ramirez likes to act tough. He's got money with his restaurants and all. He wants to expand." Nikki pauses.

It's time to talk. Savage clears his throat and starts, staring at the road ahead.

"He's moving drugs. Drugs and people. He wants the boatyard because it would be the perfect coverup. Jake's storing Homeland Security boats there. Working on them. Ramirez wants the yard so he could keep the cover. He'd have someone else run the yard, and everyone would know that Homeland Security boats were there. No one's going to suspect that Ramirez would be storing stuff there, right? Drugs in. Drugs out. People in. People out."

"Guess not. Who else knows?"

Savage checks out Nikki's smooth, athletic legs. She changes gear, flexing her muscles.

"Question is," Nikki begins, "can *I* trust *you?*"

"You can trust me to do my best for Jake. For you, too."

"That's not what I mean." Nikki stretches her leg and depresses the clutch. Savage looks at the shape of her quads, at the smoothness of her skin.

"To not hit on you? I don't know. I'll respect what you say. I've been trained: no means no, right?"

Nikki smiles and laughs, shaking her head. "What happens if I say 'no' but I mean 'yes'?"

"Apparently 'no' always means 'no' in this country."

"Good answer. But not always."

"I can't take the risk."

They cross onto Sugarloaf Key.

"Where to now?" Nikki asks.

"Some bar where locals drink. Boat people. A place we can sit and listen. Maybe hear something useful."

Nikki turns right onto Sugarloaf Boulevard and drives slowly away from Route 1. There is a stillness; just the sound of a few seabirds and water lapping against the docks below the wharf. A fisherman is loading a cooler onto his boat.

She slows down and parks in the shade. They get out and Savage stretches, feeling the heat rising from the tarmac. Nikki's hair moves in the breeze.

"Let's walk a bit," Nikki says. "By the wharf—over there." She points towards the shimmering water and begins to walk. Savage follows, looking out at the mangroves.

There are no other people out, and no sign of a bar. Savage is thinking that perhaps this wasn't such a good idea. But Jake had texted, *Watch Sugarloaf Key*.

An old, weathered fishing boat is coming in slowly. A bowman is preparing a line, ready to jump onto the wharf and tie her off.

"Jesus!" Savage mutters, adrenaline coursing through him before he can begin thinking.

"What?" Nikki says.

"Quick," Savage says. "Don't let them see you."

"Why not? Hey, let go!" Nikki says as Savage spins her around and brings her back to the car.

"Get in. Put the top up. Quick. I've seen those guys before."

"Where?"

"Cuba. They're connected to Ramirez. I recognize them from Trinidad. They came after us there."

The boat turns to level up with the dock, directly behind the Mustang.

Nikki moves quickly and easily, no questions asked. She's miraculously calm and in control.

"I want to see what they do. Get in the car, Nikki. Now."

They get into the car, and Savage watches the boat in the Mustang's side mirror. It has nearly reached the dock. The bowman is ready. He jumps onto the wharf and ties the boat off, then runs to the stern. He ties her off there, too. The boat is around thirty-five feet with a small wheelhouse.

Nikki watches in the rearview and shakes her head.

"You're not scared of Ramirez's men, are you?" Nikki says.

Savage looks at Nikki. "No. I just don't want to waste any opportunities."

Nikki opens the door and gets out.

"Hey, wait!" Savage calls after her. She walks down the companionway to the dock slowly and easily. The men are in the wheelhouse with the engine still running, and they don't notice Nikki. Savage gets out of the car, clicking the door closed quietly. He walks to the companionway and watches.

The boat is fifty feet away. Savage could get there in seconds, but that would start something.

Not a plan, he thinks. Not a plan. He moves behind a green dumpster that smells of fish, fetid and rotten.

Nikki is inching towards the boat on her own. Savage waits. She's almost to the boat when she startles, takes a step back, raises her hand to her mouth, stumbles, turns towards Savage, and starts to run.

She's seen something.

A man comes out of the wheelhouse, shouting something in Spanish. Savage can't understand, but he sees the man jump onto the dock and run after Nikki. She sprints to the companionway and runs straight up it past Savage to the car.

The man lumbers up the companionway, focused on Nikki, determined despite limping as he runs. Savage waits, counts the seconds, then springs out from behind the dumpster, bending and hooking the man's right leg behind his left so he stumbles and fall to his knees, cursing in Spanish. He turns, confused and angry, about to struggle to his feet, when Savage's clenched fist smashes into his nose.

Savage feels it break, and the man goes down limp and still.

Nikki has started the Mustang. She's watching through the window.

Savage is breathing hard. His inner animal is awakened—fight or flight. He feels the fight rage within him.

The second man runs up the companionway, a younger, stronger man, moving fast and coming for Savage.

Nikki opens the door to the Mustang.

The man is cursing in Spanish. He pulls a fish knife from his belt, the blade thin and curved. It glints as the man begins to slash at the air as he bears down on Savage.

Nikki is running back towards them shouting, not scared but wild.

Savage is crouched, legs apart, all his senses tuned towards his attacker. The man is coming straight at him. He's played his hand and charges, teeth gritted.

He raises his hand for the attack and lets out a roar.

He doesn't feel the pain when Savage's foot breaks his knee nor understand why he can't bring the knife down until he feels his arm pop from the shoulder socket.

The knife falls to the ground and Savage spins, punching the man on the back of the head and sending him crashing to the ground. Unconscious.

Savage is breathing hard. He scans the sleepy wharf. Nikki arrives, and the air is still again.

Nikki runs straight past Savage to the boat, and he follows. She's heading down the companionway to the dock, and when she reaches the fishing boat, jumps on board.

Savage is right behind her. She's crouching over a blood-soaked body.

"Jake," Nikki shouts, "speak to me, Jake!"

The body moves. Savage is there, his chest heaving. He puts two fingers on Jake's carotid artery and feels the pulse. He lifts the blood-soaked t-shirt.

There's a flesh wound. Nothing deep.

Savage checks Jake's face, noticing his eye is swollen and that he has a bloody nose. A brutal beating, but he's alive.

Jake groans. "Bastards," he says.

"Got to get him cleaned up," Savage says.

Jake winces, opens one eye, and sees Nikki. "Vodka and tonic please, girl," he says.

Nikki puts her hand in his curly thick hair and strokes his head. "You okay, Jake?"

Jake sits up, rubs his head, and nods. "Fuckers," he says.

Savage stands and looks down at Jake. "We'll get you sorted, brother. Just a minute." He scans the boat, listens, and hears a noise, and turns.

The older man is at the top of the companionway holding a Glock, his face livid. He shouts in Spanish, holding the railing with one hand, aiming with other.

"Christ," Jake mutters.

Nikki crouches down to try and get below the gunnel.

Savage sees a 12-gauge Orion flare gun mounted in the wheelhouse. He darts for it, grabs it, breaks the barrel, and pops in a flare from the rack.

The man is twenty feet from the boat when Savage turns and pulls the trigger. The flare tears into the man's belly, a short trail of smoke behind it. The explosion is muted by his crumpling, falling body. He trips and goes over the side of the companionway into the water, thrashing and twitching.

The air smells of smoke. A gull flies overheard. The water laps the hull. The man is trying to swim to the dock.

Jake is on his feet now, although not fully upright.

"Let's get the hell out of here," Nikki says.

Jake moves towards the companionway, limping but mobile.

"Nikki," Savage says. "You take Jake back to Key West."

"You're not coming?" Nikki says, looking down from the companionway.

Savage shakes his head and looks at the man in the water. "Going to clear things up a bit," he says. "I'll find you in Key West."

Jake looks down at the man in the water.

The man is at the dock, his face contorted in pain, one hand steadying himself. He looks up and sees Jake; sees Jake's finger pointing at him. Then the face with the swollen eye and split lip. The curly hair. Then his voice.

"I told you it wouldn't end well."

26

THE END OF KILLING

JAKE LOWERS himself into the wicker recliner, which creaks under his weight. He leans back slowly, groaning. "Bastards," he murmurs, leisurely, in the way the English do, the first vowel having a round 'ah' quality to it.

Nikki leans forward and kisses his forehead, lays a damp cloth on it, and runs a hand through his curly dark hair. Jake takes her hand and squeezes it, and then kisses it.

"Savage will look after you. I've got to run. I was worried, Jake, really worried. That was scary," Nikki says.

"It looks worse than it is, love. Blood always makes things look bad." Jake smiles. His eyes linger on Nikki's. Savage sees the love, friendship, and history. Jake's eyes are tired and vulnerable.

They're in Jake's cottage at the guesthouse compound. Savage is in black surf shorts, a tank top, and a straw hat. He's turned darker after his time in Key West. He looks at his brother. He's shaved his head, and his body is lean and toned.

"I guess we've got some thinking to do," Jake says, putting his fingers to his temples and closing his eyes.

Nikki stands. "I've gotta go. I'll come back after work, around three. Okay?"

Jake nods and Nikki leaves. The fan turns slowly overhead and the sound of cicadas wafts in from the gardens. A couple sits in the pool, talking in the moonlight.

"I've got an idea," Savage says.

Jake opens his eyes. He looks tired. His black eye is swollen and his lower lip split. He looks over at Savage slowly and nods. A faint smile causes him to wince.

"Go on."

"Ramirez tried to get me knocked off. Twice. Once downtown, once at your place. Same guy. Paulo."

"Paulo? I know Paulo. No wonder you're still alive. He sent the wrong guy."

"He's not a bad guy. He's at the boatyard. Security. Maria's with him."

"Maria? Ramirez's Maria? What's going on there?" Jake straightens himself up.

"The webs we weave, right?" Savage says. "It's a long story."

"Get me a drink and give me the short version. And just soda water. Put in a bit of lime juice. Times have changed."

Savage goes into the kitchenette and returns with the drinks.

"Okay. Short version. I'd seen Maria in the little park near your place. Angie was playing with Juan. You know. Ramirez was watching. They didn't see me, but later, I was talking to Ramirez and he starts getting heavy, so I mention Juan. I knew that would piss him off. Guess it did, because after that he sends Paulo. Paulo jumps me downtown, but it doesn't go so well for him, so I drag him to Ramirez's restaurant."

Jake runs his hand through his curly hair, listening.

"Santiago's? What for?"

"He could give Ramirez back the $500 he'd paid Paulo to roll me."

Savage watches a gecko on the white wall. It darts up a few inches then stops.

"Sweet."

"Pissed him off even more. Maria's there. In the restaurant, I mean. I had no idea she worked there. No idea about anything, really. I tell her I've seen her, though, because I have. I kind of wanted her to know I was a good guy. She doesn't see this, of course. She's all jumpy and jittery. Really scared."

Jake leans back in his chair. He's watching the same gecko. The fan sweeps overhead. Outside the moon is a silver sliver in the black blue sky.

"Next, she gives me her number. I call her. She's pleading to be saved from Ramirez. We meet by the laundromat next to your place I take her inside. We go to your place. Paulo's been following Maria. While we're in your place, Paulo jimmies the door, so I jump him. And to make a long story short..."

Jake takes a tin from his pants pocket and begins to roll himself a cigarette. Big fingers, meticulous movements. It's a ritual. He places the tobacco in the paper, rolls it, licks the paper, and looks at his work but doesn't light it.

"Too late," Jake laughs.

Savage sees Jake's lighter on the counter, stands up, and gets it for him. He slides it across the table and sits down.

Savage continues. "Anyway, I take him back to Santiago's and let him sweat it out. He thinks I'm going to hand him over to Ramirez. I don't. Instead I offer him a deal, and he comes with me. So now Paulo's at the boatyard, looking after Maria."

Jake sips his drink, pushes his chest forward, and winces. "What about those guys on the boat?" he asks.

"Oh, yeah. They're okay."

"They're okay? Bastards tried to kill me."

The gecko darts across the wall, fast and focused. Savage can hear gentle movement from the small pool outside—soft voices beneath the moon.

"I forced them to drink a bottle of rum, then took the boat in to Key West Coast Guard station. They were both unconscious. I put the boat on auto, going real slow, right into the

Coast Guard dock. I took their skiff and rowed ashore. Last thing I saw, she was stuck between a Coast Guard frigate and the wharf. There was a lot of shouting, a Zodiac buzzing around... They'll have some explaining to do. I left the knife and gun on deck."

Jake smiles, "At least you didn't off them. Bastards."

"No. I'm mellowing in my old age. I've seen enough death for one lifetime." Savage sips from his glass and looks at his brother, the dark curly hair, the wrinkles, and the weathered skin. He's a strong, complicated man. Like himself, but good.

"What're you thinking?" Jake asks.

"Life. You know. You just never know." Savage shrugs.

"That's not life, that's people," Jake says. "Life's worse. So, what about the plan?"

"Why not set Ramirez up? Lease him the boatyard. Get set up. Watch him. Wait. Then..."

Savage watches Jake process the idea. He picks up the lighter and puts the roll up to his mouth. The flame touches the end of the paper, and Jake draws in slowly before letting the smoke out. The tobacco has a sweet smell.

"Turn him in?" Jake says, nodding, a glimmer in his eye.

"Or start putting on the pressure."

Jake nods. "My life would be a lot more pleasant if Ramirez wasn't around," he admits.

"I'm done killing, Jake. Done." Savage shakes his head. "After those two guys in the boat."

"They told you they'd killed me. It wasn't your fault. And they would have killed you, right?"

"Maybe. I still can't square it away, though. I didn't have to do that."

"Let it go, Griff. There's nothing you can do now."

Jake leans forward, draws on the cigarette, and tips the ash into the small yellow flowerpot on the table.

"Guess I want to make amends somehow, Jake. I don't know

how, though." Savage says. He reveals himself in a way he only fully does with his brother.

"Let's get Ramirez put away first. It's a good plan. Let's make sure he's got a lot of product in storage. A lot."

Savage shakes his head. "I've been here, what, a month? When I came here, I thought you were dead. I was going to figure out what had happened and settle the score. Guess I jumped the gun."

"I want to settle the score, too, Savage. Ramirez is a scumbag. He makes a lot of people unhappy—a lot of people I care about. He's messed with Nikki and Angie. Now Maria. He needs to go down. Hard."

Jake draws on his cigarette. The gecko moves again. They hear a man's laugh from the pool. It's late.

Savage nods and both men sit.

"What happened on the boat?"

Jake closes his eyes.

"Their boat, right?" Savage asks, not waiting for an answer. "Where's your boat? I'm assuming you were on your own boat."

"We were on my boat. I was out with this friend of Franky's— Cuban guy, Diego. He'd been diving with me on Franky's wreck. We'd got all the coins from the wreck, and Diego said he knew another one, but he wasn't exactly sure if he remembered the coordinates. So we were on an exploratory dive. I was on the bottom, looking around. We'd taken turns. We were on our last tank, and it was the end of the day. They must have come out of nowhere because when I got to the surface, they'd got Diego. They wanted to know where the wreck was."

Savage is stretching his fingers and flexing his fist, listening, his anger rising.

"I tell them I don't know, but we thought it was right here, right beneath the boat. They ask why I haven't brought anything up. I tell them I haven't because I can't find anything. They want me to go down again, but I tell them we're out of air, which we are, of course. They're pissed off."

Jake swallows, lowers his cigarette, and looks at the gecko.

"Ramirez had seen a coin, one with the Pillars of Hercules, but he didn't know where it was from. But he knew that I knew. That's why he'd sent his men after me. Anyway, I make a deal. I tell them to keep me, but to let Diego go. And they did. He takes our boat, and there I am on their boat trying to figure out what to do.

"I tell them I know a couple of wrecks, but I'm not going to tell them where they're located when we're out at sea. I know what they'd do after they found out. Who'd need me then, right? Maybe Diego would tell the cops when I didn't show up, or maybe he wouldn't.

"So I tried to make a deal. I told them I'd tell them when we got into port, when I could walk away. They didn't like that either, and they started smacking me around. I still had my tank and fins on, and couldn't do anything, so down I went, hard. Bastards."

There's a splash from the pool outside and then laughter. Savage gets up to get another drink, and Jake leans back in his chair.

"Then we came back into Sugarloaf Key. And there you were," Jake says. "And we all lived happily ever after, right?"

Savage snorts, sips his drink, and puts it on the table. "And we each get a princess," he adds, shaking his head, drumming his fingers on the bamboo armrests of the chair.

"Lucky, I guess," he continues. "All I had was that text from you to watch Sugarloaf Key."

"I managed to send that just as we went out. I had a hunch." Jake looks over at Savage. "What do you make of all this?"

"All what? Key West? This?" Savage asks.

"All of it. Everything. The yard. The tourist train. The perfect weather. The scooters. Paradise. We haven't even had time to talk, really. You come here to bury a brother and then suddenly it's one thing after another. And now, here we are."

"I kind of like it," Savage says.

"Like what? Living like this?" Jake laughs, surprised.

"No. Key West. There's this weird, funky feeling, especially if you're not here on vacation. It's just that I'm not. I see the potential, though."

Jake begins to smile. He touches his split lip. "You're not here on vacation?" he asks, laughing. "Really?"

He coughs and his large body convulses, causing the chair to creak. Savage wonders how much he smokes and drinks.

"Really. No, seriously, I like the pace of life, here, the climate. I think I could live here."

"You should, after all this has gone away." Jake sighs wearily, stubs the cigarette out in the flowerpot, and drums his fingers on his roll-up tin.

Savage picks his drink up, puts it down, watches Jake, and clears his throat. "What about all the other coins? From the first wreck."

"Right. Well, that's one of the wonderful things about Key West. You meet a lot of people, and in the boat business you meet a lot of very rich people. And rich people know a lot of people who know how to get things done."

Jake moves in his chair and it creaks. Savage stands up. He's restless and tired. There's another gecko on the wall. Two of them. The fan sweeps round and round.

"There's this one guy, Liam. Made his millions in the dot-com days. He's super rich, but his big thing was collecting--paintings, sculptures, you name it. I showed him three of the coins, and he asked me how many I'd found. I asked him how many he needed. He said he didn't need any of them, but he wanted to buy everything I had at fair market value, without a middleman or questions. It was a pleasing symmetry. So, I sold nearly all of them. I kept a few, along with a few other artifacts for myself."

Jake coughs, touches his chest, and closes his eyes.

"I hope you got a good deal." Savage cracks his knuckles and rubs the back of his neck.

"A very good deal."

"That's good," Savage says. He looks over at his brother and says, "You deserve a break."

"I'm talking many, many millions of dollars, Griff."

"Tens?"

"How about over a hundred and fifty million?"

Savage whistles. He puts his hand in his pocket and pulls out a roll of hundreds. He counts them off. "Five hundred. And I thought I was in the money."

"You will be, when we're done."

"Done?"

"Yes. After we clean up this town a bit and get rid of flaming Ramirez. He's beginning to get on my nerves. You know? Spoiling my party."

"You want me to meet with him? To talk about leasing."

Their eyes meet, dwelling on each other for a moment. They're in this together, bound by the bonds of brotherhood.

"Yes. Make him think it's a good idea. See if you can make him offer the idea first. That would be even better. Much better."

"Okay. I'll talk to him," Savage says.

"Good." Jake pauses and looks over at his brother. "We really haven't spent much time together, you know, over the years. We need to go tarpon fishing. You've been here, what? Four or five times?"

"Four, not counting this one. I guess this is business."

"Not a vacation?" Jake laughs. "It could end with a vacation. That would be good."

"If we get to the end in one piece, I mean," Savage says.

"Anything you want to tell me?" Jake asks, "I sense something. You've got that quiet look going. Like you broke something, but you don't want to tell me."

"You want me to confess?" Savage laughs, then swallows, then looks at his brother. "Actually, I do want to confess."

"You don't have to. I already know," Jake says, opening the tin and pulling out the papers.

"About Angie?" Savage asks.

"About Angie and Nikki. Is there something else I don't know that I should? Like Maria?" Jake looks over. "I hadn't thought of that."

"Not Maria," Savage shakes his head.

"Not yet," Jake says, a smile growing across his face. "Some things never change."

"Should I feel bad? I thought you were all just friends, not..."

"Lovers?"

Savage shrugs his shoulders, unsure what to say. Vulnerable. Waiting for his brother to speak.

"Savage, there were some crazy years here. Believe me. I was in love with Nikki for years. She kept dating all these guys who were unbelievable. Twits, the lot of them. Never understood it. They were all rich and successful, but she was always in control. We had a great friendship. We were very close, but talking about the guys, that was off limits."

"So, what happened?" Savage asks.

"Well, during one of her messy break-up times, we slept together."

Jake takes out the tobacco and neatly works it into the paper, slowly and carefully.

"She plays a close hand. She got scared of something inside herself. I think she was falling in love with me, so she broke it off. A lot of people here have pasts they're running away from—pain, hurt, the usual."

"I'm learning that. Half the people here are running away. The other half is on vacation."

They both laugh. Jake lights his cigarette, draws in, leans back, and lets the smoke rise towards the fan.

"I didn't see her for about a year, and then we got to be friends again, through Angie. Angie was subletting from me and met Nikki. Nikki was confused and feeling better with women than men, and they hit it off. Then that ended, and I was with Angie for a bit, but then that fell apart because she was still doing drugs. I got her off that. Then it was Ramirez. That's the short version."

"It's all about the ladies," Savage says.

Jake shrugs his shoulders. "Great ladies, and mostly good friends now, though sometimes Angie can be a little catty and Nikki can be a little hard and cold. An ice cube." He pauses. "So that's that. Love them both."

Savage frowns and feels guilty. He'd encroached.

Jake watches the smoke being swept by the fan.

"I guess I got a little carried away," Savage says. "Been awhile."

Jake touches his black eye. The other is heavy and tired.

"They like you—the Savage thing. He can't be tamed. He roams free. They say you have this quality. They want you, but they can't get you."

"Don't you start. I've heard it all."

Jake coughs. "I believe them, though. Something that can't be explained. I think we both have it. But you have more."

The geckos move together, darting across the wall. Savage watches them in their green perfection, stuck lightly on the wall.

"I don't know, Jake. Makes me uncomfortable."

"Apparently, it made them pretty comfortable," Jake laughs. "Both of them."

"One big happy family," Savage says.

"Not yet," Jake says. "Soon. So, you think you're up for sorting things out with Ramirez?"

"You think I'm not?"

"Just checking," Jake winks.

Savage begins to imagine talking to Ramirez. He's up for it.

"We need to be careful, though. Let's not piss him off too much. He's right on the edge already. We don't need any more deaths. And I don't want him dead; I just want him put away for a long, long time. I want him to hear what happens on the outside when he's on the inside. And I want some justice. Rough justice."

No killing, Savage thinks. He begins to pace.

Jake draws on his cigarette before continuing. "Some justice for Angie and for Nikki. Maria, too. I want Juan to be okay as well. This is important for a lot of people, you know. They're all good people. And remember, Ramirez's brother would have killed you rather than look at you. Don't be hard on yourself. This can be your atonement."

Savage wonders if it will.

"This is it, Griff. The finale."

"I'll give it a shot. The best one I've got."

Jake takes a key from the table and throws it to Savage. "It's for the Triumph outside. The Bonneville. Take it. I won't be riding for a while."

Savage looks at the key, then back at his brother. "We should get a couple of Harleys after this is done."

Jake coughs and shakes his head. "You've got to be kidding. Triumphs. With sidecars for the girls."

"Yes," Savage says. He imagines them tearing up the Keys beneath the endless blue. "Let's do that," he adds, promising himself to tie things up and make sure Ramirez goes down.

Jake smiles. There's a light in his eye. He nods.

"Guess I'll get back up to the boatyard, and tomorrow I'll be paying Mr. Ramirez a visit," Savage says.

He stands, opens the door, and walks out. He strides through the garden past the pool and the couple lying in it, who are now kissing.

Whatever, Savage thinks. Guys kissing. Girls kissing. Kissing is always good.

He opens the gate. Beneath the silver moon, he straddles the Bonneville, inserts the key and turns it, kicking the engine to life.

27

ROAD RAGE

SAVAGE IS three miles east of Shark Key when he spies a black Mercedes with tinted windows ahead. He twists the throttle and feels the pull on his body as the Bonneville surges forward. He pulls closer and sees the license plate—RAM 2—Ramirez. He feels a rush of adrenaline. It's just an evening ride. He isn't out to meet Ramirez; but here he is, right in front of him. Savage sits on his tail, just far enough back not to be intrusive, but close enough to be noticed. At sixty miles per hour the bike is purring, but it still has plenty of power left to play with.

He twists the throttle again, hears the engine open up, and pulls into the left lane to pass. A truck ahead comes towards Savage, but he takes his time and accelerates, feeling the wind against his chest as the engine roars as they approach the bridge ahead. The Mercedes accelerates at the same rate as the Bonneville, leaving Savage stuck in the left lane with an eighteen-wheeler barreling towards him. There's a narrow shoulder to the left, then a guardrail, and then a forty-foot drop to the ocean.

Savage speeds up, and the Mercedes does, too. Savage cannot get in front and there's no room to drop back. It's a split-second decision. The semi blares its horn, and Savage weaves left onto the shoulder. There are mere inches between his left knee and the guardrail as the truck roars past.

Savage's heart thunders like a drum in his chest. He twists the throttle again, winds the bike up to a hundred and twenty miles per hour, and passes the Mercedes. Ahead is a traffic light, changing from green to red. Savage works his way down through the gears, keeping the bike in the middle of the lane. He's jittery with fear, excitement, adrenaline, and anger. He revs the engine, then eases forward and loops around until he pulls up to the driver's window of the Mercedes. Savage taps on the glass, and the window slides down.

It's not Ramirez. There's a large man at the wheel, his left arm in a blue cast: the man from the fishing boat. Savage can tell that with his bandana and shades, but the man doesn't recognize him with his own shades and bandana.

"What you want?" the big man asks, hissing.

"You nearly got me killed back there," Savage says. He restrains himself, but his anger is surging inside, his heart sill racing like an Olympic sprinter.

"You were on my ass," the big man says. "Asshole."

Savage leans towards the open window. "You nearly put me on the grill of the eighteen-wheeler. I think you thought you did."

"What?"

"You heard. You tried to kill me. I don't like that."

The big man looks more closely at Savage. His lips begin to move. There's a glimmer of recognition, and then his eyes widen as fear takes over.

The light turns green, but the Mercedes doesn't move. The fat man is in a daze as if time is suspended. Savage stares.

There's a red Corvette behind the Mercedes with its top down, driven by an older couple dressed in white. The man driving honks the horn and takes his hands off the wheel.

"It's green! Come on! Let's go. You can lie around on the beach. Not at the light."

The woman laughs. The man grins.

It's another perfect day in paradise.

"What the hell!" the big man shouts, glancing in his mirror. "That ugly ass gringo can wait."

Savage is loose and calm, his anger gone. He has the edge, and the edge always wins. The man is all tension and anger, with sweat on his brow.

Savage removes his sunglasses and looks straight at the Mercedes driver.

"Remember me?"

Recognition.

The Corvette honks again. Twice.

"Hey, come on," the woman in the passenger seat shouts. "Not the right shade of green for you?"

Savage turns and raises his hand, waves at the woman and smiles.

"One second! I think he's having a medical emergency," Savage says, nodding towards the open window of the Mercedes.

The big man is starting to open his mouth. His hands twitch on the wheel—fight or flight.

Savage waits.

"Go on then," Savage says, "make your move."

The light turns red again, but the big man hasn't noticed. He's staring at Savage. Savage can feel the pent-up tension, the impotent fury. He looks at the man's cast and smiles.

"What you got, big boy?" Savage spits through clenched teeth.

"Bite me!" the fat man roars as he punches the gas. The tires squeal as the Mercedes takes off. Then there's a metallic crunch as it slams into a truck that was pulling out in front of him. The hood is wedged under the side of the trailer. The windshield shatters, and the truck screeches to a halt. There's a hiss of compressed air from the brakes.

"Jesus H. Christ," the woman in the Corvette roars. "Did you see that?"

The truck driver's door swings open. The big man slowly extricates himself from the Mercedes, shouting in Spanish and looking at the crumpled hood of the car. He looks at the truck driver, then at Savage. He puts his hand on his forehead.

"Ramirez isn't going to like that, is he?" Savage says.

"Your light was red," the truck driver says. "Red. You trying to kill yourself? I'm calling the cops."

The big man is panicked, at a loss, angry, and confused. Cars are backing up behind the Corvette. The truck driver is on his phone.

"Tell Ramirez I need to see him, okay?" Savage says. "Boat-yard. Tonight."

Savage revs the Bonneville and weaves around the front of the disabled semi to the road back to Key West.

Five minutes later, a fleet of emergency vehicles approaches in the other lane, sirens blaring.

Show time, Savage thinks, twisting the throttle and feeling the wind against his face. Key West ahead in the distance.

He knows Ramirez will come.

————

Savage is alone in the office at the boatyard sitting at the desk, drumming his fingers, and waiting.

Even though it's humid and hot outside, Savage turns off the air-conditioning and opens the window. He wants to hear every sound. He needs to be ready.

The office is lit by a single desk lamp that illuminates the lease agreement Savage has prepared.

He cocks his head, hearing tires on gravel. A vehicle moves slowly towards the gate. Savage's mind is clear; he feels ready. He steps towards the window and sees the silhouette of a low vehicle coming into view. It pulls to a stop outside the gate, the engine idling. The windows are up, and no one gets out.

Savage opens the door and steps into the night. He walks towards the car. Ramirez cuts the engine and gets out. Savage opens the gate.

"Ramirez."

"Mr. Savage."

There is no one else—just Ramirez and Savage. Moths flit around the streetlight. The cicadas are incessant. Ramirez's brow is furrowed. The arrogant confidence is not there.

"Come in," Savage says, waving Ramirez through the gate. They walk together towards the office.

"I said we could do business, Mr. Savage."

Savage turns. "We'll see."

He opens the office door, and signals to Ramirez to go in ahead of him. Savage can smell his breath, a mixture of garlic and sweat.

Fear.

"Drink?" Savage asks.

Ramirez shakes his head.

Savage closes the window and turns on the air conditioning.

"Business, then." Savage points at the plastic office chair in front of the desk. "Sit down," he says, "and read this."

Ramirez lowers himself into the chair. It's too small for him. It moves on its plastic wheels.

He takes the two sheets of paper. "What's this?"

"Read it," Savage says. "Carefully. It's very clear."

Ramirez begins to read, skimming the paragraphs impatiently. Beads of sweat form on his head. His eyes are darting across the page, scanning.

Savage watches.

Ramirez finishes the first page and puts it behind the second noisily.

Savage smells the garlicky breath again. And the sweat.

Ramirez finishes reading and snorts defiantly, straightening his back. The chair wheels squeak. Ramirez draws his feet towards himself, preparing to stand.

"A lease? I was talking about buying. Not leasing," Ramirez says, handing the contract back to Savage.

"Read it again," Savage says. He refuses the papers.

Savage watches. Ramirez reads slowly and carefully this time. He mouths some of the words.

"Take your time," Savage says. Ramirez says nothing, and keeps reading.

A vehicle drives by on Shrimp Road, slowing at the gate. It catches the attention of both men.

"Your people?" Savage asks.

Ramirez shrugs and continues reading. He turns a page, smooths the document, and keeps reading.

Savage listens to the sounds outside. He stands and goes to the window, watching the headlights. The vehicle stops and turns around.

Savage opens the door and looks back at Ramirez.

Ramirez finishes reading. He leans forward, leaves the document on the table, draws in a long breath, and leans back in the chair.

"I don't understand."

"What don't you understand?" Savage asks. "It's really very straightforward."

"We never talked about Santiago's or the Whistle."

"Change of plans."

"If I bought the boatyard, you could retire. In fact, both you and your brother could." Ramirez leans forward and scratches his belly. The dance has begun.

Savage listens for noises outside. "We're not done yet. I like it here."

"And you want me to pay you $5,000 a month." Ramirez shakes his head.

"Living expenses. We'll run Santiago's and the Whistle. We'll take care of the businesses. A two-year lease."

"And if I default, you get the deeds to both?" Ramirez says. "You're kidding, right?."

Savage can see Ramirez's chest begin to heave. Anxiety.

"I'm not kidding. You get what you want. Just don't default."

"Oh, I won't default, Mr. Savage. Believe me," Ramirez says. "But why would you want to get into the restaurant business? You're brother's a boat builder, and you... I don't even know what you are. What are you?"

Savage doesn't reply.

"Let me think about this for a couple of days. There's something I'm not getting here."

"No, that's not how it works. You get one shot. Tonight. Read it again. Sign it or don't sign it. But you decide today."

Anger washes across Ramirez's face. There's a sudden pulsing in his neck and fury in his eyes. Ramirez clenches and unclenches his right hand. Savage hears a vehicle stop outside the gates. He walks over to the window, and sees two men get out of a pickup.

The air conditioner whirs on the wall. A moth flies around the bare lightbulb.

Savage looks out the window again. "They waiting for you or for me, Ramirez?"

Ramirez doesn't reply. "A two-year lease, and I get the boatyard. You get to run Santiago's and the Whistle. I pay you."

"That's the deal," Savage says.

"Unless I default. Which I wouldn't. So, what's the trick?" Ramirez turns to face Savage.

"No trick," Savage says. "What you see is what you get."

"But if I do default, I lose the boatyard, Santiago's, and the Whistle?"

Savage nods.

"You have an interest in me defaulting, don't you?" Ramirez asks.

"Just business, Mr. Ramirez."

"You can't lose," Ramirez says.

"You're the one who wants the boatyard, Ramirez. We don't have to do this. Walk away."

"I don't know if you're really smart or really stupid."

"That's for you to decide, Ramirez." Savage is standing by the window. The two men are outside their truck, standing.

"They're waiting for me," Ramirez says.

"Not me?" Savage asks, turning back to Ramirez.

Savage moves towards the desk and opens the drawer. The Glock is sitting where he left it.

"You're a difficult man to do business with."

"Maybe. Maybe not. I don't know, Ramirez."

"Oh, you know, Mr. Savage."

Savage moves closer to the drawer. He can see the lights from the pick up outside.

"Your call. Those are the terms. Take it or leave it."

"Something's telling me not to sign."

Savage moves, turns the air-conditioner off, and takes a step back to the desk. "Then don't. I'm not twisting your arm."

He hears the men talking.

"But I need that boatyard." Ramirez's breathing is getting heavier. He leans forward in his chair, rocking.

"Guess it depends on how much you need it," Savage says.

"Then I think of you and your brother in business in this town. My town." Ramirez shakes his head.

"Your town?"

One of the men outside coughs. Savage can hear the engine idling.

"I'm a powerful man, Mr. Savage. You don't know that?"

Savage cocks his head. "I know some people are scared of you. I don't know if that's the same as being powerful."

"Are you scared of me?"

"No, Ramirez, I'm not scared of you."

"That worries me. You have good reason to be afraid of me."

"Are you afraid of me?

Ramirez looks surprised. Savage's icy, sharp blue eyes bore through him.

"You expect me to say yes?" Ramirez says, beginning to sit upright.

"I don't expect you to say anything. It doesn't make any difference." Savage moves his feet, loosens his shoulders, and flexes his fingers.

"I'm not afraid of you, but you make me uneasy. I don't know what drives you."

"It doesn't matter what drives me," Savage says.

"But it does. If you were driven by money or women, then I could understand you. If it were fear or anger, then I could understand you. But it's none of those things."

Ramirez scoots himself forward towards the desk. He picks up the pen on the desk and twirls it. He looks at the agreement.

Savage turns away, and hears the scribble of the pen on paper. "There are two copies," Savage says. He doesn't look at Ramirez. "Sign them both."

He hears pen on paper again.

"I won't default, you know. I guarantee that." Ramirez lays the pen on the desk firmly. He straightens his back and stares at Savage, then heaves himself to his feet.

He's a big, heavy man.

Savage is the younger lion.

Ramirez knows.

"I don't know why you want to get into the restaurant and bar business. But you're assuming the risk. Any loss, you pay me, right?"

"That's what the agreement says."

Ramirez looks Savage up and down. "You know how to judge a man, Mr. Savage?"

"By his shoes?" Savage says.

Ramirez stares at Savage's shoes. He's wearing desert boots with crepe soles.

Savage thinks about the Glock in the drawer.

"No. My father said that, but times were different then. No, not his shoes."

"What, then?"

"You judge a man by the reputation of his enemies." Ramirez sneers as a bead of sweat runs down his brow.

Savage smiles.

"Guess I'm in trouble then."

28

SHOWDOWN

JAKE IS asleep on the couch at the guesthouse. Savage is watching him. He rubs the bristle of his short black hair, listening to Jake's steady breath. It's late. The fan turns slowly overhead. Maria is sleeping in the loft, and Paulo is sleeping in a wicker chair. It's been a long day. Savage stands up, stretches, and draws in a deep breath and lets it out slowly.

"Show time," he whispers, taking a final look at his brother.

He opens the door and walks into the warm night. A half-moon hangs over Key West, silver and bright. Outside the compound is bathed in an eerie light.

The Bonneville springs to life. Savage kicks up the stand and steers the bike down the narrow alley next to the guesthouse, heading east towards Stock Island. Savage hasn't been back to the boatyard since Ramirez took over. He hasn't seen him either, or run into any of his people. It's time to check in.

A police cruiser pulls onto Roosevelt and follows Savage for a mile then turns onto a side street. Savage opens the throttle a little and feels the power of the engine. He wishes he could open it up and drive up the Keys, fast. He crosses the bridge to Stock Island and works his way to the boatyard.

Savage brings the bike to a halt outside the gate. The yard is still. There's no movement, no lights.

Savage had installed the security system the previous month. The lights are programmed to come on automatically at dusk. He hears a boat motoring slowly in from the channel, approaching the dock behind the storage shed.

He clicks the bike's lights off and puts it into gear. He turns and drives by the side of the yard so he can see the boat come in. It has no running lights. Its engine throttles back, and it glides to the dock. There are two men on board that he can see. One jumps onto the dock and ties off the boat.

Savage parks the bike and walks along the fence to get a better view. Another man comes on deck and begins passing up boxes to the dock from the boat. The other two are taking them and making their way to one of the smaller storage trailers next to the office. They are working fast and silently in the way men do when they are familiar with a task. Savage watches the operation for twenty minutes.

The men lock the trailer and head to the main office. They enter and close the door, and the yard falls still again. A light comes on in the main office, and then the door opens. A big man comes out. Savage recognizes him. The man looks around the yard, then walks towards the boat. Then he turns and looks over towards Savage. Savage freezes. He can't tell if the man has seen him or not. The man takes a step towards Savage.

The door to the main office opens again, and another man steps out and waves the big man over. The big man is still looking towards Savage, but he turns and walks back toward the main office. The two men talk, and the big man turns in Savage's direction and points. Savage still doesn't know if they've seen him or if maybe the big man heard something. He remains still and watches.

The big man stands just outside the door, squinting into the darkness, the other returns to the office and comes out with a gun in his hand. They walk towards Savage, but they're still out of range. Savage quietly walks back to the bike, swings his leg over, starts the engine, and heads back to Shrimp Road, looking over his shoulder at the yard.

"Game on," Savage says quietly, glancing in his mirror.

The men are running towards the fence. He hears the crack of a single shot as he opens the throttle. Instead of taking a left at the end of Shrimp Road, he zigzags through the neighborhood, zipping by a Cuban barbecue shack. He turns into a dark, narrow alley next to a bicycle rental shop. Finally, Savage turns off the engine, gets off the bike, and walks back down the alley. He stops and looks back towards Shrimp Road. A Camaro drives by fast, heading towards Key West.

Savage could go back to the boatyard for a closer look. The yard is still. Savage listens; nothing. The Camaro was after him.

"Good," Savage says. Angry men make bad decisions.

Savage returns to his bike and wheels it out of the alley, turns it around, and takes off after the Camaro,

Up ahead, the Camaro's brake lights come on, and it turns into the parking lot by the Hogfish Bar and Grill. It's three in the morning and nothing is open. There's only one reason these men would pull into the restaurant: Angie.

Savage shakes his head. Angie doesn't even know where he is.

Trouble. His heart begins to race, all his senses honed.

Savage reaches the parking lot, and only the Camaro is there. The men are nowhere to be seen. Savage moves quickly. His desert boots are quiet on the wooden dock. He runs past the moored boats taking long, quick strides. He feels the sweat on his back. He slows at the corner of Angie's dock and arrives just in time to see the men enter the houseboat. One of them pushes Angie inside.

She must have heard them, Savage thinks.

He creeps along the dock in a low crouch. He can hear one of the men shouting, and then Angie yells back. Savage leaps silently onto the deck of the houseboat. The lights are on, allowing him to see inside.

The men are standing in front of Angie with their backs to him. Angie looks from man to man.

"I don't know where he is, and even if I did, I wouldn't tell you," she spits, venom in her voice.

"You know," the smaller of the two men says, his voice heavily accented. "And you're going to tell us. I have to settle some business. Got it?"

"Settle what business? Some pathetic little man business? You ended up looking like an idiot, and the only thing you know is violence, right?"

"That bastard broke my arm. Now he's snooping around at the boatyard. We just saw him. And I want him. Where is he? He must have come here."

Angie is furious, eyes blazing. She looks from man to man and then straight ahead, directly at Savage. Savage can tell she is trying not to react, but her face gives her away. Savage ducks and moves along the side of the houseboat, out of sight.

The door opens, and a man walks out onto the deck. Savage presses himself flat against the side of the houseboat.

"Okay," Angie shouts from inside. "I'll tell you."

The man walks back in. "Talk," Savage hears him say.

"You won't find him. But I'll tell you one thing—if *he* wants to find *you*, he will, and when he does, you're going to wish you were somewhere else."

Savage slides along the side of the houseboat until he's by the door again. He can see through the window.

The big man slaps Angie. "What the hell!" he says. "Where is he?"

"That hurt, you idiot. I told you," Angie rubs her face.

Savage steadies his breathing and readies himself.

"You want me to hit you again, or are you going to tell me?"

Angie darts forward and slaps the man, hard. He swings at her and catches her in the eye. She reels and staggers, holding her eye.

"You bastard!" Angie shouts.

"Jesus!" the big man says. The flesh around Angie's eye swells and begins to color. Angie is breathing heavily and leaning forward to steady herself.

She looks at the two men. Her eyes meet Savage's outside the window, and he sees the fear and sudden desperation, the anger gone. The big man reaches out to grab her while the other man begins to turn to see what Angie is looking at.

Savage blasts his way into the cabin. The big man turns to face Savage just as Savage's fist crashes into his jaw. He sags to the ground. Savage rushes past him and grabs the other man's hand and pulls it back then twists it counter-clockwise. He puts the man in an arm lock and a chokehold.

Savage is strong. The man kicks at him, flailing with his free arm as he feels Savage's forearm beginning to stop the flow of blood to his head.

"Never hit a woman. Didn't your mother teach you anything?"

The man on the floor is out cold.

The man in his hold struggles for breath, kicking his feet as Savage drags him across the floor. Angie steps forward and slaps him hard twice, and then kicks him hard in the groin.

The man buckles but Savage holds him upright, his mouth close to his ear.

"Did Ramirez tell you to come after me?" Savage asks.

The man shakes his head.

"That a 'no'?"

The man nods.

"You okay, Angie?"

"Sure am," she says, the anger and feistiness returning.

The man on the floor isn't moving.

"Search his pockets. See what he's got," Savage says.

Angie pats the big man down and pulls out a wallet, keys, and a nine-millimeter Glock. Angie clicks off the safety and points the gun at the man's head.

"I'd like to," Angie says, "but it would make too much mess. And you wouldn't be around to clean it up."

Savage twists the man's arm another quarter turn, and shoes him towards the couch.

"You're going to sit down and listen to me. You're not going to say anything unless I ask, and you're not going to try anything. Got it?"

The man nods. Savage twists the man's arm further.

"Ramirez didn't send you. You're all on your own. Is that right?"

Savage pushes the man onto the couch. The man rubs his throat and coughs. He holds his wrist and winces. The fight has gone from him.

"Talk!" Savage commands.

"Ramirez. He told me to leave you alone."

"Why?" Savage asks.

"He said it was business. That he'd deal with you later. But not now."

"Later? He said later?"

The man nods and looks up. His eyes dart from side to side. He places both hands on the couch and flexes his legs.

Savage lifts his arms, his palms facing the man, his ice-blue eyes watching every move.

The man lunges forward, reaching for Savage's body, but Savage is too fast. He steps to one side and forces the man's head down as he stumbles forward. Savage knees him hard in the rib cage, and the man falls to the ground where he rolls and tries to stand. But Savage kicks him hard just above the knee, then in the groin.

The man collapses to the ground. Savage manages to stop himself from driving his fist into the back of the man's skull.

He is seething with anger and adrenaline. "Got any rope?" he asks.

"Even better," Angie says. "I've got handcuffs."

"Handcuffs? I'm not even going to ask. Get them."

Angie goes into the bedroom and returns with two pairs of handcuffs. Savage takes them and cuffs both men, hands behind their backs.

He picks up the Glock from the table and points it at the big man.

Both men are groaning, trying to move.

"What's your name?"

"Rudy."

"His name?" Savage nods towards the man on the floor.

"Simon."

"Okay, listen, Stefano. I'm going to give you a choice. I can put you back in the Camaro, take you back to the boatyard, and then you're going to have to explain to Ramirez what happened. You want to do that?"

"No. Am I stupid?"

"Then you can do something for me, and I'll let you go."

"What? Do what for you? I ain't doing nothing for you."

"I need you to rat on Ramirez. I need him put away for a long, long time."

Stefano is sweating. "I can't do that. No." He shakes his head and struggles to stand but can't. His body falls forward.

"Why not? He's a bad guy. People get killed because of him."

"Like me. He'll have someone kill me. That's how it works."

The big man turns his head and tries to get his bearings from the floor.

"He's won't know it's you. Ramirez is a big deal. Get him put away and you'll be scot free. A new life."

"Scot free? What's that? Scot what? I'm not ratting. No." The man spits on the floor, grunts, and gets himself into a kneeling position.

"Completely free. Start over. Do your own thing. Begin a new life—somewhere else."

"You can take me back to the boatyard. But I can't rat on him. He'll kill me."

"Your choice," Savage says. "Wrong choice, but your choice."

Savage takes the keys from the table, drags Stefano to his feet, and frog marches him out the door.

"Stay with Simon, Angie," Savage says. She has a harpoon gun trained on him.

"You sure about this? It would be easy. I'll tell you what to do. You want me on your side. Trust me," Savage says. He steps from the houseboat to the dock, keeping Stefano close.

"I don't know," Stefano says, "I don't know."

Savage drags Stefano along the dock, then down the wharf to the car. He opens the door and shoves Stefano into the back seat. It's a tight squeeze. The man gasps for air, fear in his eyes.

"Stay there. You get out of the car and you won't get far."

Savage stares hard at Stefano. Stefano cowers. Savage's eyes pierce him to the core.

"You're making a big mistake. You're going to go down, too. Now you're part of this thing."

"How am I going to go down?"

"Someone's going to let on what you've started bringing through the boatyard. What's in those boxes. You know—the ones I saw you unloading. The stuff that people come and pick up and take up to Miami."

"How do you know about that?" Stefano asks, his eyes widening.

Savage doesn't know for sure. He's partly guessing. He's had Paulo watch the boatyard to take some pictures and note license plates.

"People talk," Savage says. "Word gets out. Word on the street is that Ramirez is bringing a lot of product in. A lot. You know the story. The boatyard is storing Homeland Security vessels.

Who'd ever guess what was in there? And Ramirez is leasing the yard. Jake owns it. Jake's a boat builder. Who'd know?"

"Jesus," Stefano says, "Jesus. I gotta think. Lemme think."

"Good luck with that," Savage says. He closes the door before heading back to the houseboat. The man begins to struggle, but he's crammed in too tight, hands cuffed behind him. He begins to curse.

Savage jogs back to the houseboat. The sooner the better, then. He had wanted to wait, but now is as good a time as ever. There's product at the yard, enough for sure to put Ramirez away for a long, long time. Then it would be time to get everything else straightened out—put all this behind them and move on. Take a vacation.

Dawn breaks with a soft pink glow.

Savage steps onto the houseboat and walks in. Angie still has the harpoon gun trained on Simon.

"My jaw's broken," Simon says. "I can feel it."

"You're alive. Stop complaining."

Simon's jaw trembles as he looks from Savage to Angie. "What are you going to do?" he asks.

"I'm taking you both back to Ramirez. Going to leave you at the boatyard and let him find you. Then you guys can figure something out."

"Figure something out? We don't have to figure something out. He'll kill us," Simon says. "He told Stefano to leave you alone. But Stefano wants you bad. And now look at us." Simon's voice cracks with despair.

"Why does Ramirez want you to leave me alone?" Savage looks at Simon. He's wincing in pain. Savage leans closer to Simon and grabs him by the elbow.

"Why?" Savage hisses. "Why?"

"Because he wants to take care of you himself."

Savage nods, thinking that it has to be now. Ramirez has to go down.

"He does, does he?" Savage says.

"Now what?" Angie asks.

"How are you on a motorcycle?" Savage asks.

"Harley girl."

"Disappointing. Try a real bike." Savage gives the key to Angie. "Follow me to the boatyard."

Savage pulls Simon to his feet. He stands, hands cuffed behind him.

"I don't want to die," Simon says. "I don't want to die."

"Move," Savage says, pushing him towards the door.

Angie follows them along the dock, then down the wharf to the car. Savage opens the passenger door, pushes Simon in, and looks at Angie.

"Today then," Savage says. "Today's the day. Follow me close."

Angie nods and turns to get on the bike. Savage gets in the car and adjusts the rearview so he can see Stefano.

"I'm giving you back to Ramirez; you understand that?"

Both men stare at him. Neither of them speaks. Savage adjusts the rearview mirror. He sees Angie on the Bonneville, and then another vehicle appears behind Angie—a black Mercedes.

Ramirez.

29

THE RULE OF RAMIREZ

SAVAGE SEES Stefano and Simon slumped in the back seat of the Camaro, and his senses come alive. The adrenaline begins to flow.

He takes a right off Route 1. He can see that Angie is following him on the Bonneville, but there's no sign of Ramirez. Savage slows down and takes a right onto Fifth Street, then a left onto Fifth Avenue, and finally a right onto Shrimp Road. Angie is still there, but no Ramirez yet.

In the soft dawn light, Savage can just make out the boatyard sheds. And there he is. Ramirez. Opening the gate as the Mercedes idles just outside. He's moving with purpose. Savage watches as Ramirez gets back into the Mercedes and drives into the boatyard, leaving the gate open. Savage eases into the yard and turns off the engine. Angie pulls up alongside and Savage opens the driver's window.

The Mercedes is running fifty feet ahead, its trunk open. Savage watches Ramirez unlock the storage shed and enter.

"What's going on?" Angie asks.

"Looks like Ramirez is loading up. He's in a hurry. I don't think he knows I'm driving the Camaro. Wonder if he knows it was you on the bike?"

Angie shrugs.

"Quick," Savage says. "Get the bike out of here. He hasn't seen you. Stay outside. Keep an eye out."

Angie turns the bike and drives smoothly out through the gate. She parks behind the shrubs outside the boatyard fence.

Ramirez comes out of the storage shed holding a box the size of suitcase. He glances over at the Camaro and puts the box in the trunk of the Mercedes. He's breathing heavily as he turns back to face the Camaro.

"*Stefano, ven aquí,*" Ramirez shouts. He goes back into the storage shed and comes out with another box.

"*Ahora!*"

Stefano begins to groan in the back seat.

"Quiet!" Savage hisses, glancing in the rearview mirror.

He opens the door and gets out of the car. He leans back in and moves the driver's seat forward, grabs Stefano, and pulls him out of the vehicle. Stefano is standing next to the Camaro, his hands cuffed behind him. Savage gets back in the Camaro, closes the door, and waits.

Ramirez comes out with another box, puts it in the trunk then looks over at Stefano. He pauses. His white shirt is sweaty, sticking to his potbelly, and his chest is rising and falling with the effort of carrying the boxes.

"Stefano?" Ramirez straightens, pulls a pistol out of his pocket, and points it at Stefano.

"Drop whatever you've got behind you, Stefano."

"I don't got nothing behind me," Stefano says, turning around to show his handcuffed hands.

"What the...? How'd you drive the car like that?" Ramirez starts, as a look of understanding begins to cross his face. Ramirez squints at the Camaro. Savage opens the door and gets out.

"What's going on?" Ramirez shouts, panic in his voice. He points the gun at Savage, then back at Stefano, then back to

Savage. His movements are jerky, his breathing heavier. Fear glows in his eyes.

"Nobody needs to get hurt, Ramirez. I brought Stefano and his pal back."

Savage is thirty feet away; it's a tricky shot. His weight is on the balls of his feet, legs bent.

"Back? What you talking about? Where from? He's hand-cuffed. Simon's in there?"

"Yeah. Stefano came to see me," Savage says.

Light is spilling into the day. The softness of dawn has left.

"Don't do anything," Ramirez shouts. He puts the pistol back in his jacket pocket, goes back into the storage shed, comes out with another box, puts it in the Mercedes, and closes the trunk.

"Listen, Mr. Savage. I gotta go to Miami right now. I mean right now. I don't need this. Okay?"

He looks from Savage to Stefano.

"What's going on? Stefano? Talk."

Stefano is silent. Ramirez takes a step forward, reaches into his jacket.

"Mr. Savage? You going to tell me?"

"Stefano was looking for me. Like I said." Savage clenches and unclenches his fists.

Ramirez takes his hand out of his jacket pocket. No gun.

"What for? What was he coming to see you for?" Ramirez demands, then turns to Stefano. "I told you to leave him alone. Right?"

"He broke my arm," Stefano says. "I wanted to scare him."

"Didn't I tell you to leave him alone?" There's anger in his voice, a tremble.

Simon begins to struggle to get out of the back seat of the car. He's gasping.

"Simon?" Ramirez spits. "Two of you. Useless." Ramirez raises both his hands and looks upwards, shaking his head.

"Simon," Savage says, turning towards the car. "Stay where you are."

"I've had enough of this, Mr. Savage. I have work to do. People to see in Miami. And you," he shouts, pointing at Stefano. "I'm not done with you."

He shakes his head, sweat dripping from his brow. "I told you to leave him alone. You didn't, and now look. What do you want, Mr. Savage? What do you really want?"

Savage steps forward. Ramirez moves his hand towards his jacket pocket.

Twenty feet.

Stefano's feet shuffle on the gravel.

"What are you going to Miami for, Ramirez?" Savage asks.

"Business."

"What's in the boxes?" Savage asks.

"My business. Not yours."

Savage hears footsteps behind him, and Angie walks into the yard, approaching the Camaro.

"Angie? What are you doing here?" Ramirez says. "And what happened to your eye? Did Mr. Savage do that? Did he?" Ramirez takes the pistol from his pocket and points it at Savage and starts to walk towards him. "Did he, Angie?"

Angie shakes her head, turns and stares at Stefano.

Savage's eyes are on the pistol. He can hear Ramirez's labored breathing.

"No, he didn't," Angie says. "In fact, he saved me from this animal. From your ape." She points at Stefano, her right eye swollen and blackened, the other full of anger.

"You did that, Stefano? She's the mother of my child. You beat her?"

"It was an accident," Stefano says, looking over his shoulder towards the open gate.

"Don't even think of running," Savage says.

"An accident? That eye? An accident! You hit her. What for?" Ramirez points the pistol at Stefano. "Get on your knees. Now!"

Stefano lowers himself to the ground, unsteadily, his shoulders shaking. He begins to whimper. Ramirez points the pistol at Stefano's head.

Ten feet. Savage flexes his knees and feels his weight on the balls of his feet.

"I should put a bullet in your head right now, Stefano."

"Don't kill me. I'm sorry. It was a mistake. I just wanted to scare him."

Stefano shakes his head and lets out a single sob.

Ramirez swallows.

Savage inches forward.

Ramirez turns the gun on Savage, then back to Stefano. "No, Mr. Savage. Don't move."

Angie pulls her phone from her pocket.

Ramirez takes a step back. He points the gun at Savage again, then Stefano. He walks backwards towards the Mercedes and closes the trunk.

Angie dials.

"No," Ramirez says. "Put it down, Angie."

She's thirty feet away, talking into the phone, her voice hushed.

Ramirez opens the back door of the Mercedes. His chest begins to rise and fall. "Stefano, get over here. You're coming with me. Now!"

Ramirez walks back towards Stefano, his arm outstretched, pointing the gun alternately at Savage and Stefano. "Get in the car!"

Ramirez is breathing rapidly, his eyes flitting from side to side. "I gotta go to Miami. Now. Stefano you're coming, too. And Simon. I'm not leaving you here. Get Simon out of there. Mr. Savage, get him out of the car, now."

Savage moves towards the car. Simon is gasping in the back,

drenched in sweat. He looks up, eyes wide. Savage pulls Simon towards him. His jaw is swollen and bruised, and he's trembling. There's dry blood on his swollen lip.

"No," Simon says. "Leave me here." His voice is weak and desperate. Savage pulls him from the car, his grip firm on Simon's arm.

"And get those cuffs off," Ramirez says. "Both of them."

Savage moves Simon towards Ramirez, holding him close, eyes on Ramirez.

"Stop!" Ramirez shouts.

Ten feet. Savage has a strong grip on Simon's arm. His own is bent. He feels the power. He could hurl Simon forward and into Ramirez.

Ramirez's hand begins to shake. Savage is too close.

"The keys," Angie says, touching her swollen eye. "They're at my place."

"At your place? What the hell?" Ramirez shouts.

"I hadn't planned on taking them off," Angie says, a smile erupting on her face.

Savage looks at Angie and nods his head towards the gate in the direction of the bike.

"So, Ramirez," Savage says, moving behind Simon, gripping him firmly. "Looks like you've got a problem," he continues.

"I've got a gun. You've got the problem," Ramirez shouts. "You've all got a big problem."

Savage amends his grip on Simon's arms, adjusts his feet, and begins to rock Simon back and forth, preparing to hurl him forward and into Ramirez.

Ramirez points the gun at Savage's head, then at Stefano, then back to Savage.

"Are you going to shoot, Mr. Ramirez, or what?" Savage moves closer, his body behind Simon's.

"No," Simon says, imploring, as Ramirez levels the pistol at his chest.

"Go, Angie!" Savage barks. "Now. The bike."

Time slows then speeds up. Savage launches Simon towards Ramirez and dives to one side, rolls, and then springs to his feet. The pistol cracks three times before Simon's body flattens Ramirez like a bowling pin.

Simon cries in pain, lying on top of Ramirez, who is thrashing to get up. The pistol has fallen from his hand.

Savage turns and runs towards the gate, sprinting hard. He hears the pistol crack again behind him and Ramirez shouting in range.

Angie is on the bike. It's fired up. She eases it off the stand and Savage jumps on behind her. Angie turns the bike and heads down Shrimp Road and past the gate, not towards the main road and Key West but towards the boat storage yard at the end of the road.

"Go, Angie, go!" Savage hisses.

A siren is blaring, coming from Key West.

"I called the cops," Angie shouts, leaning forward, working through the gears as the Bonneville hurtles down Shrimp Road.

"This is a dead end, right?" Savage screams as Angie opens up the throttle.

The sirens are getting closer.

"I hope you know where you're going," Savage shouts. Angie looks over her shoulder and nods decisively.

They accelerate to sixty miles an hour, and then Angie starts to work her way down through the gears and slows to a near standstill at a break between the fence and brush to the right. There's a path wide enough for the bike. Angie turns the bike onto the path and eases it slowly through the undergrowth until it opened up on Fifth Street.

The sirens have stopped. Angie drives slowly towards Route 1.

"You think the cops saw us?" Angie asks.

"No. They weren't even on Shrimp Road when we took off."

"Let's go back," Angie says. "See what happened."

Angie turns off Fifth Street to Fifth Avenue. A police cruiser has blocked off Shrimp Road, lights flashing but no siren. Angie slows down. An officer is standing by the cruiser.

"What's going on?" Angie asks.

"You'll have to move along, please, ma'am. It's an ongoing situation. We've got a team coming in. Move along, please."

Angie nods, lets out the clutch, and the bike moves forward.

"Let's go back to your place," Savage says.

"No. There's another way." Angie continues down Fifth Avenue then turns into a parking lot at a condominium development. She drives to the end of the narrow street and stops. Savage dismounts, Angie parks, and together they run across the grass to the fence that connects the small road next to the boatyard. Angie scales the fence and then lopes up the road with Savage following her.

The sky is bright blue. The day is heating up. Savage is sweating and squinting into the sun. Angie squeezes through a break in the boatyard fence, and Savage follows her. They run towards a boat that's chocked up in the yard. The keel, which is just six inches off the ground, conceals their view of the storage shed and the main office. Angie and Savage peer underneath.

"Jesus," Angie says. "He's shot Stefano and Simon."

The two bodies are lying on the ground in front of a police cruiser. The front doors are open, and an officer is crouching behind each door. One is holding a pistol, the other a pump-action shotgun. Ramirez has ducked down behind the Mercedes, its engine still running.

"What's he doing?" Angie asks.

"I don't know," Savage says. "He's going to have to make a run for it, but there's nowhere to go. The gate's blocked."

Savage looks over at Ramirez. He's still by the Mercedes, but he's opening the door.

"He's going for it," Savage says.

"But there's nowhere to go," Angie says.

"He'll have to drive right by us and break through the fence."

"He'll never make it," Angie says.

"Not much choice. It's that or spend the rest of his life in prison," Savage says.

Ramirez springs to his feet, leaps into the Mercedes, and takes off. The officers both fire on the car, taking out the rear window, but the Mercedes doesn't slow.

The officers get into their cruiser and reverse onto Shrimp Road. Tires squeal, and the Mercedes heads straight for Angie and Savage. Then it takes a hard left towards the fence.

Ramirez is swerving but maintaining control as he crashes into the fence. But it remains mostly intact. He flings open the door, gets out, clambers through the broken fence, then scales another fence to the condominium complex.

The police cruiser skids to a halt as Ramirez starts to run across the grass towards the building.

Savage looks up as he hears the blades of a helicopter slicing the thick air. It's low and loud. Familiar. It passes overhead, and a shiver runs down Savage's back. He starts to sweat.

Ramirez is fifty yards away, running. He's limping, arms flailing like a frightened animal.

"Guess it's over," Angie says. "You think he's going to try and get himself killed?" She looks at Savage, eyes wide, frightened and sad.

Savage reaches out and strokes her hair. "No. He's just desperate. Angry. Panicked."

Savage gets up and pulls Angie to her feet and holds her against his chest. She begins to cry. He kisses the top of her head, feels her body against him, and closes his eyes. They listen to the sirens and the helicopter until Savage shakes his head.

"Let's get the bike," he says, "and get out of here."

They cross the yard, walk through the broken fence, scale the condominium fence, and walk across the grass to the bike. The helicopter has gone. There are no sirens, just a hot empty stillness beneath the blue.

Angie takes the key from her pocket and gives it to Savage. "I'm too fried to drive," she says.

Savage takes the keys, straddles the bike, and starts up the engine. Angie gets on behind Savage, puts her arms around him, and leans against his body. Savage kicks up the stand and the bike moves off.

He takes a right, then a left, working his way towards Route 1. Ahead, he sees three police cruisers on the right, one blocking the road. The other two are facing Ramirez, who is handcuffed, an officer on each side of him. Savage indicates left, but before he drives off he looks at Ramirez.

"They got him," Savage mutters. "Bastard."

Ramirez looks at Savage, then at Angie. His fight has gone. There's nothing left. He mouths a single word.

"Juan," Angie says. "He said 'Juan'."

"He wants you to take Juan," Savage says. "Maybe he's not all bad."

Savage can feel Angie sobbing on his back. He squeezes her leg, and she grabs his hand.

"He's bad enough," she says.

30

THE PLAN

SAVAGE SITS at the bar at the Whistle, watching Nikki's reflection in the mirror as she mixes a martini. She catches his eye, flashes a smile, turns, puts the the drink on a coaster, and slides it across the bar to the woman sitting next to Savage. Nikki shakes her head and rolls her eyes towards the girl. Savage purses his lips, raises his eyebrows, and holds his palms up innocently.

"You never know," Nikki says, pausing. "Especially with you."

"Lot of cops out tonight," Savage says, ignoring the comment. "Hear anything?"

"Nope," Nikki says. "I thought things would be a bit quieter, you know, but it isn't.

Savage drums his fingers on the bar. The woman next to him tries to catch his eye.

"It isn't quieter," Savage says. "Something feels off. I don't know what it is."

"Savage doesn't know what it is?" Nikki's intonation rises. Teasing. "That's not good."

"Hey, Nikki, come here," Savage beckons to her. She steps over, and Savage leans towards her, speaking softly. "You mad at me?"

"Yes," Nikki says. "I am mad at you." She steps away from him.

"But I haven't done anything."

The woman next to Savage picks up her glass, looks in the mirror behind the bar, sees Savage's ice-blue eyes, and lets out a little sigh.

"That's the point. You haven't done anything," Nikki says, wiping the bar and taking some dirty glasses to the sink before coming back.

"You mean about us?" Savage chuckles. Nikki ignores him.

She turns to serve another customer, all eyes and smiles, then passes close to Savage.

"We'll talk when I have time. Come back later. Closing time," she says, running a nail across the back of his hand. He feels a chill. He looks in the mirror behind the bar and sees the woman smile optimistically.

His phone vibrates. He turns it over and sees a text from Jake: *He's out of jail.*

Savage freezes. His body goes on high alert. The adrenaline is back. He types *WTF* and hits send. He leaves a twenty-dollar bill under his untouched tonic water, waves to Nikki, and leaves. He goes down the stairs onto Duval and then back towards the guesthouse. He is walking purposefully, but not too fast. It's seven o'clock.

Out of jail, Savage wonders. How could Ramirez be out already? And if he's out, what is he going to do? Where is he? Savage's mind is churning. He walks faster, weaving between a strolling couple who are both wearing beads around their necks. He bumps the lady's shoulder as he passes.

"I'm sorry," he says, turning and smiling.

The woman nods and smiles. "That's okay, dear," she says.

Savage begins to jog in the street; the sidewalk is too crowded. A steady, easy jog. Ramirez shot two men. He couldn't be out.

He enters the code for the guesthouse gate and hears the

click as it unlocks. His heart is thudding powerfully in his chest. His t-shirt is damp with sweat. Only the sounds of the small fountain and the ambient sounds from the town fill the humid air.

He knocks on the guesthouse door.

"Jake, it's me." He tries the handle, but finds it's locked. There are footsteps on the other side of the door, flip flops slapping on the tiles. The lock turns and the door opens.

Jake's dark face is serious, his curly hair unbrushed, three days growth of stubble on his face.

"Come in. Want a drink?" Jake turns and walks towards the kitchen.

"Sure—tonic. Ice and lemon. What happened?" Savage sits on the wicker couch.

"Who knows? Sounds like an inside job. He was in the detention center on Stock Island, locked up for the night. And then this morning, gone."

Savage remembers Ramírez mouthing the word 'Juan', the defeat in his eyes, the acceptance.

"I thought that chapter was over," Savage says. "I was looking forward to cleaning things up and having a bit of down time and vacation."

Jake walks over and hands Savage his tonic. "To better days," he says, raising his own glass of vodka and tonic.

"Amen to that," Savage says, raising his glass and then taking a drink. He feels the tight, cold bubbles tickle his throat.

"What would you do if you were Ramirez?" Savage asks.

"I'd get out of Key West, maybe out of the country. Take the money and run. But Ramirez, I don't know if that's what he'll do. He's hard to read."

The fan turns overhead. The gecko is back, stationary on the white wall.

"Someone's going to find him," Savage says. "Sooner or later."

"Maybe he doesn't care. Nothing more dangerous than a man

who doesn't care," Jake says. "They've got nothing to lose, so nothing matters."

Savage looks up, "You think he's going to try and kill me?"

"Maybe. Or kill me. Or get his son. Who knows?"

Jake rubs his belly again and sips his drink. Another gecko appears. Savage smiles.

"When a man doesn't care if he lives or dies, things can get bad. Believe me. I've seen desperate men before," Savage says.

"Like I said, nothing to lose. Right?"

"Right," Savage says, letting out a sigh. "I think I know what he's going to do. What he's going to try to do."

"You do? I don't," Jake says, walking to the fridge and taking a bottle of vodka out of the freezer.

"I think he's going to try and kill you. Not me."

Jake tops of his glass and puts the vodka back in the freezer. He's frowning. "Me? Why not you?"

One of the geckos darts up the wall. The other follows.

"I killed his brother. Now he wants to kill my brother. An eye for an eye, and all that. That first; then he'll try to kill me. Revenge."

"Well," Jake says, "that does make sense."

Savage stands and begins to pace. He rotates his right shoulder. "Paulo will know," he says, thinking aloud.

"Know what?"

"What Ramirez will do. Paulo may not be that bright, but he knows Ramirez inside out."

Jake puts his glass down and leans against the counter.

"I need to talk to him," Savage says, his mind clearing. "Find out where he thinks Ramirez would go, where he could hide. His access to boats, planes, anything. We need to track him down fast."

Savage stops and rubs the back of his neck. His eyes are distant, no longer noticing the geckos.

"Griff?" Jake says. "What are you thinking?"

Savage blinks and clears his throat. "I can't stop thinking about killing his brother. I did it because I thought he'd killed you."

"We've been through this, Savage. You can't change that. You have to let go of it. We're here now. And Ramirez is out there."

"Call Paulo, get him to come over. I'll talk to Angie," Savage says, putting his glass down. "I'll see you later," he adds, walking to the door and putting his hand on the handle. Pausing before turning it, he lets out a sigh.

"Be careful, Griff," Jake says.

"You, too, brother," Savage says. He opens the door and feels the warmth of the night flood in. He hears the cicadas, a couple talking on their veranda, a door opening and closing, and water burbling in the fountain.

"Wait," Jake says. He fishes a key from his pocket and throws it to Savage. "Take this. It's for the scooter—it's next to the Bonneville. Take that instead. Too many people know the bike."

"Good thinking." He takes the key and walks back into the night.

He texts Angie and then Nikki, hops on the scooter, and rides down the alley to the street, then east towards Stock Island. A big man on a pink scooter.

When he arrives at the houseboat, Angie is already outside. Her long hair is down about her shoulders. She's wearing a tank top and surf shorts. Her eye is looking less swollen.

"You heard, right? About Ramirez?" Savage says, running his hand over the black stubble on his head.

Angie nods and gestures for Savage to go inside. She follows close behind him, closes the door, and locks it.

"You know him as well as anybody. What's he going to do? Is he just going to make a break from it? Try to get out of the country? Any ideas?"

Angie raises her eyebrows and runs a hand through her hair. "I don't know. He's not an idiot. He seems like it sometimes, but he's not. He has his passion and his anger. And his sense of family."

She runs her hand along the counter top back and forth. "He'll want to settle the score," she says, looking down at her hand.

Savage sits down on the love seat, then stands and begins to pace. "But he can't just walk the streets looking for me. He can't just wait for the Bonneville to turn up at the boatyard, can he?"

"It doesn't have to be him. Maybe someone else," Angie points out. "He's got a lot of money. He can get anyone to do anything."

"Yes," Savage says. He stops pacing and rubs his head again. "That makes sense. And it makes sense for him to get away. If they catch him, he'll be inside for the rest of his life. Unless he doesn't care if he lives or dies, I mean. Right?"

Savage makes his right hand into a fist and rubs it into his left palm, pressing hard. "He really didn't want Juan to know about his life. He wanted Juan to love him, and he does, but he wants him to respect him, too. And he sees a future where that won't ever happen. Eventually, Juan will find out about his father's life, and Ramirez doesn't want that. That's his pain. He has a weird sense of honor. He'd die for that."

"You mean you think he'd rather be killed than have to live to see his son not respect him?"

The sound of laughter comes from a boat moored further down the wharf.

"Yes. And I know he wouldn't want to have to watch his son grow from inside prison. It's sad."

"It's going to be a showdown, then. The grand finale." Savage rolls his shoulder again and winces.

"Maybe," Angie says. "It's Juan's birthday the day after tomorrow."

"Ramirez will want to see him," Savage says.

Angie begins to sweep her hand across the counter again.

"I think he's going to try and kill Jake. Then me after he's seen me suffer."

"Who knows?" Angie says, pulling at her ring finger.

"He's predictable and unpredictable. When you put anger and passion together, you never know. But he will know. He'll have a plan."

"Juan's birthday," Savage says to himself.

He sees a look of fear in Angie's eyes. He presses his fingers against his forehead.

"What?" Angie asks.

"It was all going so well." He opens his eyes and lowers his hands. "Relatively well, anyway. Now this."

"You call all this 'well'?"

"You know what I mean. With Ramirez put away, we could start to get everything sorted, so everyone would end up where they should be."

"And where would that be?" Angie asks, raising her eyebrows, a look of anger flashing across her face.

"You know what I mean, Angie." Savage stretches out his hand and strokes her shoulder, squeezing it lightly.

"Do you want to stay?" Angie says.

Savage feels a flutter in his belly. "No," he says.

He sees her searching for her answer in his eyes. "So, you do care," Angie says.

Savage is silent, the flutter still lingering, the cold excitement.

"I want you to stay," Angie says.

Savage feels the stirring again. "I'm going to go," he says.

"And do what?" Angie asks.

He could say, "Talk to Nikki," which would be true, but not the whole story. Or, "Talk with Jake," which could also be true, but not the whole story. Or, he could say, "Sleep with Nikki, because I care about you too much to sleep with you." He could say any of those things, but he doesn't.

Instead, he says, "Do what needs to be done."

"And who decides what needs to be done?"

"I do," Savage says. "At least I'll know when it's time to do it. What has to be done, I mean."

Angie laughs. "I hope you realize how funny that sounds."

He does and he doesn't. He doesn't feel like laughing.

"Silly boy," Angie says.

"Silly? I've been called a lot of things in my times. But not that."

"Well, maybe not silly, but definitely 'damaged goods'."

"And you're not?"

"We all are. The problem is getting undamaged. I'm ready. You're not." Angie steps back from Savage, the chemistry of possibility having dissipated. It's time to go.

"Be careful," Savage says, as he turns to leave.

"Savage?"

Savage turns back. "What?"

"I just wanted to look at your eyes."

"Why?"

"They say a lot more than you ever do."

Savage turns and walks out the door, closes it, and feels the warm night envelop him.

———

He parks the scooter at the guesthouse and walks to the Whistle. It's late—nearly closing time. The bars are emptying, and people walk down the sidewalk swaying, holding hands, and putting their arms around each other. A man staggers and a woman holds him up, grabbing his sleeve and laughing.

Savage runs up the outside stairs to the Whistle. As he walks through the door, he catches Nikki's eye, and she smiles. He walks over to the bar. Nikki holds out some keys.

"What's this? Everyone's giving me keys tonight. What's up?"

"There's a black jeep around the back. Go get it. I'll be at the bottom of the steps in five minutes."

Savage takes the keys. Nikki yells out that the bar is closing.

Savage jogs downstairs, finds the jeep, and brings it around to the steps. He watches Nikki come down. She's tall for a Japanese woman. She's wearing black jeans and a black t-shirt. Savage admires her athletic figure.

"New ride?" he asks.

"It belongs to a friend. I'm housesitting, and the car comes with it."

"Where are we going?" Savage asks.

"The house where I'm sitting."

"You know Ramirez is out of jail?"

"I know. Jake told me. You'll be safe with me," Nikki says. "Go left, then two blocks and take a right."

Savage puts the jeep into gear. They drive for ten minutes, Savage following directions. Three scooters tear past, one weaving through traffic.

"Crazy," Savage says, shaking his head.

"There," Nikki says, "just before that yellow house. Park there." She points to a neat driveway, nestled in a well-manicured garden.

"Nice," Savage says. He exits the jeep and admires the house.

"It's been completely remodeled. Six million, or so I read on Zillow."

"Your friend's?" Savage asks.

Nikki doesn't reply.

"What's Ramirez going to do?" Savage says.

"Kill Jake. Then kill you," she says.

Savage follows her to the front door. "That's what I like about you. You tell it like it is."

"Did you speak with Angie?" Nikki says, her voice clipped.

"Yes, earlier tonight."

"Did you sleep with her?"

"No."

"Did she ask you to?" Nikki unlocks the door.

"She asked me to stay," Savage says.

"Do you want a drink?" Nikki asks.

Savage shakes his head. He can smell Nikki's perfume, her hair. He feels the flutter.

"Come with me," Nikki says. She takes Savage upstairs, guides him to a bedroom, and pushes him into the room.

"Stay here. I'll be right back."

Savage's thoughts are jumping. His heart begins to race.

Nikki returns. She's wearing black panties and a black bra. Her body is taut and lean. She walks over to him, comfortable in her own skin. She puts her arms around his neck and kisses him.

"Bathroom's over there. There's a new toothbrush for you. Take a shower. Use the green towel."

Savage smiles. *Women*, he thinks. All different and all the same. He goes to the bathroom, takes a shower, and brushes his teeth. When he returns, Nikki's hardness has gone. She runs her hand across his chest and then down to his belly.

"No talking. Nothing, okay?" she says, pressing her body against his.

Savage nods, trembling.

They're on the bed, skin touching, bodies pressing together. They both draw each other closer, kissing and biting. They breathe in each other's breath.

Sometimes, Savage thinks, it's just better to let go and not think. He takes in Nikki's smell, her softness, her lean perfection.

She moans and nibbles Savage's ear. He slides down her body, kissing her belly.

Ramirez can wait, Savage thinks. *Right now, I'm right here.*

31

THE CHASE

"I CAN LOOK for him or wait for him," Savage says. He and Jake are sitting by the pool at the guesthouse. It's eleven in the morning, and the day is heating up. A humming bird darts by Savage's line of vision, merely a blur of green.

"Wait for him to do what? Find me, or you, or both of us, or what?" Jake says. He stretches and scratches a bite on his arm.

Jake's face is tired. He's staring at the granite tiles, his eyes wide. He puts a hand in his thick black hair and scratches his scalp, thinking. Savage can tell he's had enough.

"Jake?" Savage says. Jake looks over, his eyes heavy and slow. "It's us or him, now. Simple as that. Either we find him or he finds us, and then it'll be over."

"Shootout at the OK Corral?" Jake says. He takes a maritime chart from the small round table next to him. He opens it and spreads it on his knees.

The hummingbird darts in front of Savage again, pauses, and then it's off, wings a blur.

"No. We've got to think. Carefully. Whatever the mistake is, he has to make it. Not us."

Savage drums his fingers on the armrest of his chair.

"How are we going to know if *we're* making a mistake?" Jake says, rubbing his forehead with his thumb and index finger, before looking down at the chart.

"We don't do anything," Savage says.

"That might be the mistake," Jake says. He peers closely at one section of the chart.

"We don't do anything yet. We plan our movements. We change our routines. No one knows we're here in the guesthouse, do they?"

Savage waits for Jake to answer. He watches his brother's tired face poised over the chart.

"Who knows?" Jake says. He taps the chart and nods.

"Wait!" Savage says, leaning forward, then straightening up, his eyes bright.

"What?" Jake asks.

"Something Angie said. I was only half listening. The day after tomorrow is Juan's birthday." Savage looks at Jake. He doesn't have to explain. Energy returns to Jake's face.

"Okay," Jake says.

"Right," Savage says. "We know where someone's going to want to be."

"What are you thinking?" Jake asks. "We don't want a shootout at a kid's birthday party. At least I don't."

"No. But we do know that Ramirez is going to want to see Juan on his birthday, right? It might be the last time. He's a wanted man."

Savage is talking softly, in a near whisper. A door opens to one of the cottages, and a young man steps out. His skin has not seen the sun in a long time. He raises a hand and smiles at Jake and Savage then goes back in the cottage.

Jake raises a hand.

"We find out where Juan is going to be on his birthday, right?" Jake says.

The brothers fall silent, both thinking. Jake looks back at the chart.

"And we go there, to wherever it is," Savage says. "And Ramirez shows up."

"And?" Jake says.

"And Ramirez is going to blow it. Do something he shouldn't."

"How do you know?" Jake asks, a note of surprise in in his voice. "You were like that when we were kids."

"I just do," Savage says. "Sometimes you know. This is one of those times. I feel it, right here." Savage taps on his chest, above his heart.

"You always looked on the bright side. Glass half-full," Jake says, a smile growing on his face.

"Not exactly the bright side, but yeah. I was worse, though. I used to think that things worked out in the way they were supposed to. That there was some sort of Karmic justice principle at work."

Jake shakes his head. "Doesn't work like that."

"I know. So we've got to engineer something."

"Like what? You have any bright ideas?"

Savage pauses and scratches the back of his freshly-shaven head, the skin brown and smooth.

The young man comes out of the cottage again, wearing white pants, a white shirt, and a straw hat. He waves again. Jake raises his hand and smiles. Savage nods. The young man walks towards the gate.

"His first day," Jake says. "You can tell."

They watch him open the gate and disappear into the alley behind the wall of the compound.

Savage drums his fingers again. "First we need to know where he is. That would be a start. Then we keep an eye on him. Otherwise, what? He or one of his people will turn up, and then it won't be good."

"There's nothing in the paper about Ramirez," Jake says.

"Think that's odd?" Savage asks.

"Well, not really. It's a tourist town. Things like this are bad for business. It would scare the tourists off. Like that guy who just walked down the alley. Ready to spend. All the money would stop coming. This is a town that likes good news, and Ramirez isn't good news. People pay to keep the news good."

The sun is moving higher. The full heat of the day is beginning. Jake folds the chart, gets up, and moves the parasol so they're in the shade.

"Ramirez is a wanted man," Savage says. "He's going to want to see his son on his birthday, and after that, who knows. He might not even care anymore."

"Are you going to kill him, Griff?" Jake says, his voice barely a whisper.

Savage's eyes are unfocused. His breathing is measured, slow and deep. "I don't want to. But I will if I have to." He clenches and unclenches his fists.

Jake's phone rings. He picks it up from the table and sits upright.

"Hey. Yeah. Fine," he says. He mouths the name *Angie* to Savage. "This week. Okay," Jake continues. "Tomorrow? Okay. Party's the day after tomorrow. Got it. Right. Uh huh. Bye."

Jake puts the phone down, and Savage waits for him to speak.

"You probably heard–the party's the day after tomorrow. Ramirez will see him tomorrow. He'll pick him up at the grandmother's place. They'll spend the day together, a kind of private pre-birthday. Sounds like Ramirez thinks the party would be too risky."

"We could just turn him over to the cops, right? An anonymous call." Savage waits for Jake to react.

Jake rubs the muscular bicep of his left arm, flexing it. Then he shakes his head. "No. That wouldn't work. There's something going on in the Police Department. Ramirez must own someone there, someone who has an interest in Ramirez not going down."

"Something has to happen in the next twenty-four hours, then," Savage starts drumming his fingers on the armrest, thinking.

Jake opens the chart again. "Looks like it, Savage. You thinking of doing something?"

"Maybe," Savage says, getting to his feet.

"Where are you going?" Jake asks.

"Got to check on a few things. I'll be back later. I'm taking the bike."

"Not the scooter?"

"No. I'm not hiding anymore. If he wants me, he'll be able to find me."

"A bit vulnerable," Jake says. "On the bike in the open."

Savage's face is impassive. He knows. "Maybe," he says. "Maybe. We'll see. We're nearly there. I think I've got this."

Jake watches Savage as he cracks his neck, and then his knuckles. He stretches his left arm and then the right and shakes his arms out, bouncing on the balls of his feet, light and limber.

"Don't do anything stupid," Jake says. "We've got this far in one piece. Let's keep it like that."

"Can't guarantee anything. Not this time. But I'll do what I can."

Savage walks back into the cottage and emerges a few minutes later with a backpack and the keys to the bike. He nods at Jake, walks to the gate, opens it, and quickly slips into the alley. He hops on the bike, and the Bonneville springs to life. Savage engages first gear and releases the clutch. It feels good to be on the bike again.

Jake sits alone in the guesthouse. Another hummingbird appears, a different one.

———

Angie and Savage are sitting in the shade at Fort Zachary. Angie is gazing out over the water, watching tourists fish for tarpon in the channel.

"I just want Juan to be safe, Savage," Angie says. "He's a little boy. He needs to see his father and he needs a birthday. He's just a baby."

Savage puts his arm around Angie. "I can't promise anything. I need to know what Ramirez is up to—where he's going to be and when. I know he needs to see Juan, but I think he also wants me and Jake. You know? You pretty much told me that."

Angie nods and says, "I know."

"Tell me their plan."

"Someone's going to pick Juan up after breakfast with his grandmother. They'll take him to Ramirez. He'll call every hour on the hour so I can talk to him. And he'll bring him back at six sharp. If he doesn't call on the hour, I'll call the police and say he's been kidnapped. And I'll call every TV station and radio station, too."

"He agreed to that?"

"No. I just told him that's what I'd do."

"What do you think? Think he'll keep his end of the bargain?"

"He has to, right?" Angie pauses. "Right, Savage?"

Savage shrugs. "Who knows," he says. "He's getting to the end of his tether, though. He's on borrowed time right now. Pressure's on."

"Listen, Savage, all I know is that we made an arrangement. I don't believe he'll hurt Juan."

"Okay. But what happens if, say, he doesn't bring Juan back at six? What happens then?"

"I told you. I'll call the police. I'll call everyone."

"What happens when they can't find him or Juan?"

Savage's phone vibrates in his pocket. He takes the phone out of his pocket and checks the caller I.D.

"Stay here. I need to take this." He walks a few paces away

from the beach into the shade of the tall palm trees, out of earshot.

"Paulo? Okay, yeah. Go on. Sugarloaf Key? You sure? Okay. We're going to keep quiet about this. Just you and me. That's right. Keep your phone on."

Savage walks back to Angie and sits down. He feels the adrenaline begin to flow. His energy is high.

"Now I'm worried. I don't know what to think. You unsettled me, Savage. Are you saying you don't think he'll bring Juan back?"

"No, I'm just saying I don't know. Nobody knows."

Angie reaches out and strokes his hand. Their eyes meet.

"Who were you talking to?"

"Paulo," Savage says. "Just Paulo reporting in. No big deal."

Angie raises her eyebrows and takes her hand off Savage's fingers.

Savage starts to rock on the sand. He's watching a tarpon fishing boat. "I want to do that," he says. "Be out on a boat with Jake fishing." He shakes his head.

Angie strokes his arm. He smiles, but continues staring out at the blue-green sea.

"You will," Angie says. "I know. I can tell."

Savage turns. "You can?"

Angie nods and laughs. They both laugh. Savage feels a stirring inside him.

"First, though, Juan has to see his dad and get home safely."

"Nothing can happen to Juan," Angie says. "Nothing."

"Tomorrow, you call me every hour, right after Ramirez calls and you talk to Juan. You tell me everything he says. Got it?"

Angie whispers, "I'm scared."

Savage pulls his wallet from his pocket and takes four hundred dollars out in fifties, giving it to Angie.

She takes it.

"I can't take you home. I don't want you on the bike if

anyone's coming after me. I'll give you a ride up to Eaton Street. Get a cab from there. Okay?"

"God, I can't wait until this is over."

"It'll be over soon," Savage says, staring out to sea. Angie smiles, a sad smile. She doesn't say anything. They get to their feet and walk to the Bonneville. Savage puts his arm around Angie, and she leans into him and presses her cheek against his chest.

They could be a happy couple. But they aren't.

———

At 9:05 a.m. the following day, Savage's phone rings. He's at the boatyard with Jake and Paulo.

"Angie? Good. Keep me posted." Savage turns to Jake. "Someone came for Juan. He's going to spend the day with Ramirez."

A sailboat moves away from the wharf, crawling towards the channel that leads out to sea. Savage watches as he listens.

"How does Angie sound?" Jake asks, concern in his voice, scratching his arm.

"Tense. Can't blame her. Her son is with a desperate man."

"Why don't we just go get Ramirez?" Paulo says. "Get this over with. I can't relax knowing he's out there." He begins to pace.

"We don't know where he is."

"We should have followed the guy who took Juan to him."

"Ramirez has people watching for that."

"Jesus. I don't like this," Paulo says. "Something's putting me on edge."

He clears his throat and his eyes flit back and forth. A cloud drifts overhead, blocking the sun temporarily. Paulo looks up and crosses himself.

"It's a cloud, Paulo," Savage says. "Not a sign." Paulo looks away.

It's heating up. Jake leads them to the office. The air-conditioner whirrs.

They wait. Shortly after every hour, Angie calls. Time moves slowly. She calls again after two and tells Savage everything is fine. She says that Juan sounds happy, says she could hear Ramirez laughing. Savage notes that she's more at ease.

She calls at three and tells Savage that Ramirez will bring Juan home at six.

Savage, Jake, and Paulo sit in the office at the boatyard with the air-conditioner droning on. Then, at 3:30, Angie calls.

"What?" Savage says, standing up. "Slow down. Tell me again." He paces back and forth across by the window, scanning the boat yard as Angie continues to talk. "Okay. I'll call right back."

"Seems Ramirez butt-dialed Angie," Savage begins. "She said she could hear Juan saying that he wanted his mama, that he didn't want to go in a plane. He wanted to go home."

The waiting is over. Savage rubs the back of his neck and flexes his fingers. There's a tension in the air.

"Sugarloaf Key," Paulo says. "He's got two planes out there. That's where he's headed. I told you, right? I did. I remember. I said he had planes out at Sugarloaf Key."

Savage shoots Paulo an impatient look, and then turns to his brother.

"Jake," Savage says. "I think he's right. He's making a break now. His son means more to him than killing us. He's not coming back."

"We could just let him go," Jake says. "Let him take Juan and go. He won't come back, and he won't hurt his own son. We could figure everything else out later."

"No!" Savage shouts. "Juan is Angie's kid, too. Paulo, go get Angie. She's at the houseboat. I'm going out to Sugarloaf Key. Jake?"

"I'll come with you on the back of my own bike."

Savage goes over to the cupboard by the desk, unlocks it, and takes out a black Pelican gun case.

"What's that?" Jake asks.

"A Paratus 16 folding sniper's rifle. Just in case."

Jake puts his right hand on this forehead and closes his eyes. "I guess it's party time," he adds.

"He's not going to take Juan, Jake. The deal was he'd bring him back at six. This is Angie's kid we're talking about here."

"You sure this isn't something personal?" Jake asks.

"Of course it's something personal. Very personal. Now come on."

Savage takes the case, strides to the door, opens it, and lopes over to the Bonneville. Jake is close behind. Savage puts the case in one of the panniers and jumps on the bike and starts it while Jake gets on behind him.

"Let's not get stopped for speeding. Wait until we're out of town, then open her up."

Paulo is ahead of them in a red F-150 pickup. At the end of Shrimp Road, he takes a left, while Savage goes right. The traffic is light heading out of town. Savage checks the mirrors, passes a couple of vehicles with smooth sweeps. He opens up on the Overseas Highway and hits 100 mph as he passes Shark Key.

The warm air rushes past them. The sky is blue, the sun merciless.

"Take a left on Bat Tower Road," Jake shouts over the roar of the engine and the wind. Savage throttles back, changes down, makes the turn between two oncoming cars, and heads down Bat Tower Rd. right to the end to where the rough runway heads north and out to sea.

A single engine Cessna Skycatcher is near the end of the runway. It's stationary, its engine humming. Savage stops the bike. They watch the plane.

Savage squints. "They're getting ready to take off," he says, shielding his eyes from the sun with his hand.

"You sure it's him?" Jake asks.

"I know it's him," Savage says. "It has to be."

Jake doesn't bother responding. He watches the plane making its way to the end of the runway. The engine pitch is getting higher.

Savage gets off the bike, takes the Pelican case out of the right pannier, lays it on the ground, and opens it. He quickly assembles the Paratus 16, putting on the scope and silencer. He raises the rifle and looks at the plane. Through the crosshairs, he can see Ramirez trying to comfort Juan, who is struggling in his father's arms.

"Jesus, Savage! Don't shoot him."

"I'm not going to shoot him. I'm just confirming that it's him."

"It better be him," Jake says, shading his eyes with the palm of his right hand.

"It is," Savage says. He lowers the gun, his eyes still on the plane.

The red F-150 appears from behind them, driving fast. Paulo is at the wheel, focused on the Cessna, Angie alongside him. It heads straight past Savage and on towards the Cessna that has now started taxiing down the runway in order to turn and take off into the wind. Savage takes the Paratus 16, opens the tripod, and lies down on the ground. He spreads his legs and adjust the sights.

"What you doing?" Jake says.

It's a rhetorical question. Savage is in the zone, steadying his breathing and watching.

He steadies himself on his elbows and finds his focus. It will be a difficult shot—a moving target, close to the ground. He waits for the aircraft to turn and come towards him.

The truck is gaining on the Cessna, which is not quite at the runway. Paulo arrives just as the Cessna is about to turn north for take off. He skids to a halt twenty feet in front of the plane, tires squealing. The Cessna engine throttles back, the tone suddenly dropping as the plane comes to a stop inches from the pickup.

"Change of plans, Jake."

Savage springs to his feet, crouches down, disassembles the rifle, puts it in the case, puts the case in the pannier, and gets back on the bike, Jake behind him again.

Savage kicks up the stand and he and Jake speed off. Savage twists the throttle and works his way through the gears with efficient precision. The Bonneville arrives in seconds. Savage works back down through the gears and comes to a halt next to the F-150.

Ramirez is standing next to the plane, holding Juan's hand. Juan is crying, reaching for his mother. Paulo is standing next to the driver's side door.

"Don't scare him," Angie says softly but urgently, staring at Juan's frightened eyes. "Let him come to his mama. Let him go." Angie crouches down and holds out her arms.

Ramirez looks from Savage to Angie, his eyes bristling with anger and frustration. He swallows, unable to say anything, knowing his son will remember this.

"It's his birthday, Ramirez. He wants to see his mama. Let him see her." Savage's voice is slow, measured, and deep. There's no anger in it.

Juan looks at Savage, then his mother, then up at Ramirez.

Ramirez lets go of his son's hand, and Juan runs to his mother, his arms reaching out in front of him. Angie swoops him into her arms, kissing him and comforting him. Holding him close.

"Go. Paulo," Savage says, urgently. "Take Angie and Juan. Now."

Ramirez looks from Savage to Jake. He has begun to breathe more heavily as he summons energy. Paulo looks at Savage. Savage nods. Angie and Juan climb into the cab with Paulo and they head back to Bat Tower Road.

Ramirez is standing next to the Cessna. Savage and Jake are standing next to the bike at the end of the deserted runway.

A breeze picks up, warm and steady.

"The Savages. Here we are. And now what?"

Savage takes a Glock 9mm pistol from his pocket and passes it to Jake. Ramirez brings a pistol out of his pocket, a Sig Sauer P226.

"You gave your weapon to your brother, Mr. Savage. So, what do you have?"

Savage reaches behind him and pulls a throwing knife out of a sheath on his belt.

"Say I shoot your brother. Then the question is, can you throw that knife before I shoot you?"

"Or can you shoot my brother before I throw the knife? Look at me."

Jake clicks off the safety and aims at Ramirez, squinting in the sun.

"How fast are you, Mr. Savage?"

"I don't know, Ramirez. There's really only one way to find out?"

Ramirez swallows. He is sweating heavily. His eyes don't leave Savage.

Jake is holding the pistol with two hands. His grip is firm, solid, and relaxed. He doesn't want to shoot, but he will if he has to.

"We could make a deal," Ramirez says.

"Are you in a position to make a deal?"

Savage brings his arm up, holding the knife. His feet are parted for perfect balance, his other hand out. He's taking aim. Ramirez raises his pistol.

"Drop your weapon, Ramirez, and get in the plane. Go and don't come back. Do you hear me? It will be better for everyone. Especially your son. Think. What do you want him to remember about you?"

Sweat drips from Ramirez's brow. He is fraught, frowning.

Jake looks over questioningly, then back at Ramirez

Ramirez stares at Savage, his eyes angry and scared. "If I didn't have a son, you would be dead. I would kill you."

Savage moves his feet, adjusting his weight.

"Go! Now!" Savage shouts.

Ramirez lips start to tremble with anger. He mutters something in Spanish under his breath and spits on the runway.

He drops his weapon, turns, and climbs into the Cessna, heaving his large body into the cockpit. He starts the engine, eases the plane onto the runway, pauses for a second and then it begins to move, quickly accelerating down the runway. The engine whines higher and higher until the plane is airborne, heading due north.

"I didn't expect that," Jake says, watching the plane climb and then bank to the east.

"Neither did I," Savage says.

"So that's it? He's gone? We never see him again. It's almost too good to be true," Jake adds.

Savage listens to the drone of the Cessna. He watches and wonders as he rolls his shoulder and flexes his hands.

"Yes," he says. "Too good to be true."

The brothers turn, get back on the bike, and head back towards the Overseas Highway to Key West.

There is no rush. The tension, like Ramirez, has gone. But not quite. Savage still feels unsettled and tense.

"Where do you think he's going?" Jake shouts, the wind ruffling his curly black hair.

"No idea. And I don't care," Savage says, "I just want a vacation."

But he does care. And something inside him tells him it's not time for a vacation. Not quite yet.

Jake pats him on the back and lets out a whoop.

Savage keeps his eyes on the road. He listens and checks his peripheral vision and the wing mirrors. He's remembering the anger in Ramirez's eyes, the disdain with which he dropped his gun. The final look, the desperate glare.

The light is beginning to change in the early evening. The sun slips lower towards the western horizon, a huge orange orb. Savage squints and adjusts his sunglasses.

He remembers being on patrol in the Congo, knowing that sooner or later the ambush would come.

And men would die.

It feels like that.

The sun is pulling him on, drawing him in. The engine drone is mesmerizing. Perhaps, he thinks, Ramirez has gone. Perhaps the page has turned.

Perhaps.

His mind commences to empty and he begins, for the first time in a long while, to feel the tension he has been carrying leave his body.

He sighs and eases off the throttle just a bit, enough to become aware. He senses something, hearing a sound above the sound of the Bonneville, an engine sound from above.

"Shit," Savage spits through his teeth, adrenaline coursing through his veins.

"Savage!" Jake shouts, "There! Up ahead."

Out of nowhere, the Cessna appears, coming out of the sun, approaching the bike at full speed.

Time changes. It slows and speeds up. The air is filled with the roar of the Cessna's engine.

They are on the bridge. It stretches out ahead above the shimmering waters. There is only one thing to do: keep going. Savage twists the throttle and feels the Bonneville surge forward.

He instinctively ducks and feels Jake pressing into his back as he does the same. The plane misses by mere feet, roaring past, the slipstream causing the bike to wobble. Savage deftly regains control, his eyes on the road ahead.

"Ramirez! What's he doing?" Jake shouts.

"Buzzing us. Where is he?"

Savage estimates the bridge is three miles long, perhaps more. He twists the throttle.

On the second sweep, Ramirez comes from behind.

Savage can hear the Cessna's engine as the plane gains on them, the propeller thrashing the air. Savage leans forward, and Jake presses himself into Savage's back. There's nothing to do but hold on and keep the bike straight.

Savage clenches his teeth as the engine roars from behind him. He waits for the impact and winces.

"Hold on!" Savage shouts and feels Jake's arms squeeze him tight.

Savage doesn't want it to end like this, with his brother on a bridge.

The roar is deafening as the plane soars directly above them. They're in shadow, one of the wheels a foot above Savage's head. Then the plane is ahead and the slipstream creates a twisting turmoil of air.

Savage weaves across the road as the bike wobbles and leans before Savage regains control, blood pounding in his ears. A mile to go.

The Cessna sweeps around, banking steeply, turning for another run, this time at a right angle.

"Just stop, Griff!" Jake shouts. "We can just get off the bike. What's he going to do?"

Savage knows what Ramirez will do. He keeps going. When a man doesn't value his own life, there is no knowing what he will do.

"No," Savage shouts. "We'd be sitting ducks."

He hears the whining of the Cessna's engine coming from his right, and catches sight of it out of the corner of his eye, just above the height of the guardrails.

Savage eases off the throttle, changes gear, and sees the

Cessna wobble as Ramirez adjusts his angle. The wings tilt, almost hit the guardrail, and then straighten out.

The wing tip was just in front of Savage's face; he could have touched it.

"Jesus," Jake says. "That was close."

They both turn and watch the plane climb and bank to the southwest.

"You think that's it?" Jake says.

"No," Savage says. "Definitely not."

The plane banks to the north, tilting as it begins a slow arc high in the sky.

"He's coming around again," Jake says.

"Keep your eye on him," Savage shouts. He checks the mirrors. There's a big eighteen-wheeler a few hundred yards behind them.

Ahead, at the end of the bridge, Savage sees an intersection. Traffic lights. The Cessna is leveling out, directly in front of the bike, coming in fast and low.

Savage checks the mirrors again and eases back on the throttle. The bike slows down. The eighteen-wheeler starts to gain on him as they approach the intersection.

"What are you doing, Savage?" Jake shouts. "He's coming right at us."

Ahead, the Cessna is leveling out, coming in low, flying directly at the Bonneville. It's twenty feet off the ground two hundred yards ahead, but Savage knows Ramirez will come lower. The semi is gaining.

Savage glances in the mirror and looks ahead.

"Hold on, Jake! Hold on!"

The Cessna begins to drop fifteen feet, ten, aiming directly at the bike, one hundred yards ahead. Savage accelerates, working through the gears, gaining rapidly on the incoming plane.

He can see Ramirez at the controls, staring at him, confused by the sudden acceleration of the bike.

The engine roars closer. The semi blasts its horn, renting the air. The driver uses the gears to slow down. There is a tremendous roar as the engine is forced to slow. Two blasts of black smoke leave the stacks as the driver pumps the airbrakes.

Savage decelerates and brakes, banking the bike into a tight right turn at the intersection, before straightening up and accelerating down the road, then slowing down and stopping.

The horn is still blaring, but the semi is no longer braking; it's pulling away.

Savage brings the bike to a halt, and the brothers turn back towards the bridge. The Cessna's engine pitch is getting higher and higher. Trying to avoid the semi, Ramirez begins a steep and desperate climb.

"He's not going to make it," Jake says.

The Cessna climbs erratically and suddenly stalls. It comes to a halt midair, and the engine cuts out.

For a moment, the plane is suspended, weightless in the perfect sky. Then it begins to fall, slowly at first, and then twists to one side, spiraling into an uncontrolled dive. It drops two hundred feet to the highway, hitting the guardrail hard with a metallic grating crash.

A wing is torn off, and the plane temporarily pauses before exploding then rolling off the bridge into the water below.

"Holy cow!" Jake says. "That was…"

There is a sudden, brief silence.

"Should we…" Jake begins.

"No," Savage says. "There's no point. No one could have survived that."

Everything seemed to have happened in slow motion. The plane is out of sight. A few vehicles have stopped on the bridge.

"No one could have survived that," Jake echoes.

"No," Savage says. "No one."

Time begins again.

"Come on," Savage says. "We don't need to be around here anymore."

They get back on the Bonneville. Savage starts the engine, puts it into gear, and heads back to the highway. He turns right at the intersection, pulling away from the bridge and whatever is left of Ramirez.

And then the sirens come, blaring into the pristine sky of paradise.

32

HAPPY HOUR

IT'S early morning and the streets of Key West are deserted. Two police cruisers are parked outside the diner near Jake's apartment. Savage opens the door and lets his gaze sweep the room. It's a military habit he can't break. He checks for threats and the closest exits. Four officers are sitting at the table eating breakfast. One of them looks over at Savage, and Savage nods. The officer keeps looking at Savage, as if he thinks he knows him but can't quite remember where from. Savage smiles. The officer keeps staring, expressionless. Savage walks to the counter and sits down.

"I wasn't sure I'd see you again," the server says, coming up behind him. "Been a while, huh?" She places a menu in front of him.

"Yes," Savage says, turning and smiling at her. "I suppose it has."

She looks over at the officers. "Full circle," she says, taking out her notepad.

"Except it's not raining," he says, stretching his fingers on the bar, tapping the countertop.

"The usual?" the server asks in her southern drawl, drumming her pencil on her notebook.

Savage catches her eye. There's that sparkle again.

"I think I'll check the menu," Savage says. "And I'm paying this time."

He stops drumming his fingers, noticing the curious look on her face.

The police officers are chatting, laughing, and eating.

"Let's just say things worked. Jake's okay. Long story. Another time, maybe."

Savage wonders whether there will be another time.

"Good," she says. "About Jake. The 'another time' bit... I've heard that one before, hon."

She turns and walks over to the officers. They chat, laugh, and enjoy her company.

Savage listens and feels the stiffness in his shoulder, remembering the sound of the Cessna roaring towards him and the way the Bonneville swerved as it got caught in the slipstream.

The server comes back with a carafe of coffee and a mug.

"Sorry if I was a bit snippy," she says, pouring the coffee into the mug.

Savage can smell the strong, black aroma. "Thanks," he says.

"You really are kind of different, aren't you? That English accent, those eyes. A girl could... I don't know," she pauses. "Actually, I really don't know."

"Sometimes it's better not to know," Savage says.

"No," she says. "I used to think that, but believe me, it's better to know."

Savage thinks about this.

"So, how's business?" she asks, her voice brightening.

"Vacation," Savage says. "I'm on vacation."

"You are? Well, isn't that nice. I could use a vacation. Going to do some fishing?"

Savage chuckles.

The four officers begin to get to their feet, their chairs

scraping the linoleum. Their plates are all empty. They saunter towards the door.

"Thanks, guys," she says. Savage doesn't watch them leave. He hears the door close.

She comes back with the coffee carafe and tops off his mug.

"Thanks," Savage says. She's looking at him again.

"What?" Savage says. "You're making me feel I've been naughty."

"Naughty," she says imitating Savage's accent. "That wouldn't surprise me, but no, it's not that. I thought you might have a story. That's all," she says.

"I've got plenty of stories," Savage says. He opens the menu. "I'll have the cheese and avocado omelet with hash browns and rye bread, please."

"Sure," she says. She turns and walks towards the kitchen, but then stops and turns around.

"I remember you so clearly—that rainy day, same cops. I would have remembered you even if you weren't Jake's brother. I told you, right? Some people, they're just different."

Savage nods. "It was coming down. Great tubs of rain. I was soaked. I'd just arrived. I remember those officers."

"They're here just about every day."

"That was just the beginning," Savage says, shaking his head. "Just the beginning. But you know what, it all worked out in the end."

Savage thinks of Jake on the back of the Bonneville as they headed back to Key West after Ramirez's plane crashed. He wonders if they'll fish for tarpon.

"You mean you got the girl?" she asks.

"No. It wasn't about a girl."

"It's always about a girl. Doesn't matter what it is."

"Well, let's just say the girls are all fine."

"There's more than one?" she says. "My, then it *is* a story. They got what they wanted and you didn't get anything?"

"I didn't say that," Savage says, drumming his fingers. He's beginning to feel hungry and restless. He's not sure if he wants a vacation. He's not sure if a vacation is possible.

"I don't think I need to know," she says. "I'm sure you could get whatever you want." She waits for a response, and then touches Savage's shoulder. "Just kidding, hon. Really, about the girls. But you could get whatever you want."

Savage turns to face her. There are years in her eyes, but also a youthful sparkle.

"You know about Jake," Savage begins. "That he's okay, I mean. Mistaken identity, you know."

"I heard. Word gets out. People talk. That was such a relief," she says. "Seriously. That day when I saw you, you looked devastated, like a drained man."

The door opens and a bell jingles. Jake walks over to the bar and hugs the server. He takes the stool next to Savage.

"I'll have what he's having," Jakes says. She winks at him. "And don't say anything."

"Me? I wouldn't dream of such a thing," she says.

"So here we are," Jake says.

"Still in one piece," Savage says.

"Just," Jake says, looking at his brother. "I mean we could both be in a lot of pieces."

"That's right," Savage says pausing, "So, what are you going to do now? I mean, you could do anything you want, right?"

Jake nods, "I could. That's true. I've been over those charts again. I have some ideas. There's a pattern with the wrecks."

Savage listens, nods, and thinks. "I mean, those coins. I don't know how much you got for those."

Jake lifts his finger to his lips as she returns with food. "We don't have to worry about that."

"We?"

"I'll tell you later. Small town. It's better to keep things quiet."

The server puts Jake and Savage's orders in front of them.

Savage's stomach rumbles. He can smell the cheese and the hash browns.

The door opens and the bell rings again. An older couple comes in, untanned. They must be new.

"I think this is the place," the white-haired woman says to her potbellied husband.

"It absolutely is the place," the server says. "Come right on in and let me sit you down. First time in Key West?"

She leads the couple to a table in the corner, putting them at ease, laughing and working.

"But you'll be staying here?" Savage asks.

"Key West? Hell, yeah. Why would I leave?"

"Well, given what's happened, I could understand if you decided to leave."

"It'll be fine with Ramirez gone. Things will calm down. There's going to be a shake up in the police department. It's home. Can't imagine being anywhere else. And then there's Angie and Nikki."

"You don't think about going back to England?" Savage asks, surprising himself with the question. They'd left as young men and never gone back.

Jake shakes his head. "I think about England, but not about going back—the gray, the rain. Here in Key West, a cold day just means you turn your air conditioner off. It would be hard to go back. What about you?"

Savage doesn't answer for a minute. He drums his fingers, picks up his fork, and prods the hash browns.

"I don't know. I think I need a road trip to clear my head."

"Take the Bonneville."

"Thanks."

"I mean keep it, Griff. It's yours." Jake begins to eat. He leans forward, shovels in some hash browns.

"You don't have to."

"I know I don't have to. That's why I'm doing it."

"Thanks." Savage cuts his omelet, watches the steam rise, and takes a bite, tasting the gooey cheddar. He thinks about England.

Jake waves his hand in dismissal. The brothers fall silent as they eat and sip their coffee.

"I'll go away for a while," Savage says. "But I'll come back." He turns to look at Jake. "And you know what? I think I could live here."

"You should think about it. We could set something up, like fishing charters."

"We'd be good at that. A couple of English rakes charming the Midwestern tourists."

"Something like that."

Savage puts some cream cheese and strawberry jam on his toast.

Jake stares at the counter and draws in a breath. "You saved me, bro. I owe you. I'm cutting you in." He looks over at his brother. "Don't say anything. Take the Bonneville. Go as far as you like. Clear your head. Then come back."

Savage swallows and thinks as he rubs the back of his neck. Perhaps it's time.

"You know what, Jake? I think I'll do that. I will. I'll say my goodbyes, then head on up the Keys. Then who knows where."

"Born to be wild," Jake says.

"Something like that."

Savage stands and takes some cash out of his wallet and tosses it on the counter. He puts his arm around Jake's shoulder.

"Thanks, brother," Savage says.

"Just like that?" Jake says. "You're off."

"Just like that. Same as always. Best way."

———

Savage parks the Bonneville outside the Hogfish Bar and Grill. It's happy hour. The place is alive with voices and laughter, the comings and goings of wait staff, and the bustle of the cooks at the outdoor grill.

He walks along the wharf to the dock. As he turns the corner to the dock where the houseboat is moored, he sees Angie and Juan sitting in the shade of the awning. Juan is nestled between Angie's legs as she reads to him.

Savage stops and takes a slow step backwards. He doesn't want to interrupt the moment. He doesn't need to be there. He stands for a moment, thinking. Does he need to be in Angie's life, in Juan's life, at all? He thinks about all the killing. He killed Juan's father. How could he raise this child? How could Angie want him to?

He walks back along the dock to the wharf and then to his bike. He starts the engine, kicks the stand up, and rides out of the parking lot, heading downtown.

The sea sparkles in the late afternoon sun. He sees a sail out to sea and a fleet of jet skis tearing along close to shore. A Hobie Cat skims over the light chop, and a plane banks as it turns to land. Savage feels the warm wind rush by him. He wonders where he'll go and when he'll come back. Or if he'll come back. There's always the chance he'll keep on going.

He parks off Duval and goes up the side stairs to the Whistle. He pauses at the door. Nikki is behind the bar mixing drinks, chatting with customers. He walks in and takes a seat at the bar.

Nikki carries on serving customers, ignoring him. He wonders why he bothers to stay, to say goodbye, to try to sleep with her one last time. He's been in this place before. It never ends well.

He thinks about the bike, and the Overseas Highway beckons. Ten more minutes pass, and Nikki doesn't acknowledge him. He stands and walks out of the Whistle. He doesn't look back.

Savage walks down the steps and back to the bike. He starts the engine and drives up South Roosevelt, across the bridge to Stock Island. When he reaches Shark Key, he opens up the throttle. In his mirror, the orange sun is sinking behind him. Savage twists the throttle, and the bike passes 100 mph.

When he gets to Marathon, he slows to a stop and gets off the bike. He stands by the side of the road, and a weight lifts from his shoulders. He looks out to sea, the waves shimmering in the light breeze.

He gets back on the bike, starts the engine, and drives east, mile after mile after mile until Key West fades into the distance.

———

———

T

ABOUT THE AUTHOR

Chris Mares is a teacher, teacher trainer, and writer. Currently working at the University of Maine, he has lived and worked in England, Japan, France, and Israel. Chris is an avid reader, cook, and outdoorsman who likes nothing better than a long walk in the woods of Maine with his dogs.

DON'T MISS THE NEXT EXCITING INSTALLMENT!

The next book in the series is ***Savage Strike***. Travel with Griff Savage to the jungles of Thailand for more adventure and intrigue.

———

- *Savage Pursuit* (#1)
- *Savage Strike* (#2)
- *Savage Storm* (#3)
- *Savage Judgment* (#4)
- *Savage Vengeance* (#5)

———

To be notified about the release of new titles, including the Griff Savage series, and special contests, events, and sales from Wayzgoose Press, please sign up for our mailing list at

http://eepurl.com/bSGudb

We send email infrequently, and you can unsubscribe at any time.